Queen of Martyrs

The Story of Mary I

Book III of the Plantagenet Embers Trilogy

Other books by Samantha Wilcoxson

The Plantagenet Embers Trilogy

Plantagenet Princess, Tudor Queen: The Story of Elizabeth of York
Faithful Traitor: The Story of Margaret Pole

Middle Grade Historical Fiction

Over the Deep: A Titanic Adventure

Middle Grade Inspirational Fiction

No Such Thing as Perfect

Queen of Martyrs

The Story of Mary I

Samantha Wilcoxson

Queen of Martyrs

The Story of Mary I

Samantha Wilcoxson

ISBN10: 1542639360
ISBN13: 978-1542639361
Printed in the United States of America

Family Tree of Mary Tudor

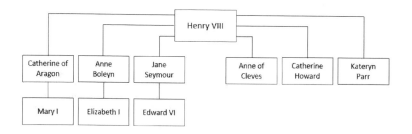

She is singular and without an equal, for not only is she brave and valiant, unlike other timid and spiritless women, but she is courageous and resolute that neither in adversity nor peril did she ever even display or commit any act of cowardice or pusillanimity, maintaining always, on the contrary, a wonderful grandeur and dignity, knowing what became the dignity of a sovereign as well as any of the most consummate statesmen in her service; so that from her way of proceeding and from the method observed by her (and in which she still perseveres), it cannot be denied that she shows herself to have been born of truly royal lineage.

Giovanni Michieli
Venetian Ambassador
1557

June 1541

"Bless me Father, for I have sinned against God and his Holy Church."

Mary knelt upon a silk cushion, hands folded and eyes closed. Her auburn hair was tightly pulled back and hidden beneath a stiff, gem-studded hood. Luxurious silk skirts were carefully arranged about her to avoid wrinkles. It had been done subconsciously, for her dress was the last thing on her mind this day. Even as she reflected upon her sins, she silently prayed that her worst fears had not come to pass.

"What confession would you make?" her chaplain asked in a carefree tone. He was used to the venial sins of the Lady Mary and expected her to reveal nothing of import.

"Father, I confess before you and before my God that I am guilty of the sin of wrath against another of God's children. In this, I am also convicted of thoughts against the fourth of God's commandments, for it is my earthly father that I find my unrestrained anger directed toward."

Mary waited. What penance would she be given? What could absolve her of such a sin? The chaplain remained silent, so she added, "I am fervently sorry for these sins that I have committed and ask God to help me live according to his will."

Surprised by the need to enforce more than Mary's typical light penance, the priest bought himself time to consider by clearing his throat and smoothing his robes. "What has caused this anger to blacken your heart, my child?"

Mary took a slow, deep breath without opening her eyes or shifting her position. In her mind's eye, she pictured a woman who was tall and proud with auburn hair to match her own. She could not imagine the image drenched in blood. The chaplain gave a little cough to urge her on.

"It is the execution of my second mother, when he has already taken from me my first," she said in a rush. Though she attempted to remain steady, she could hear the hurt and fury enliven her words. "She was an innocent," Mary added. "More than that, she was family."

Mary was surprised to realize that this outpouring was not helping as confession typically did. Instead of feeling freed of her burden, saying the words aloud caused pain to build in Mary's gut. She had hoped for peace and forgiveness, but the unjustness of what was happening tore at her soul. Tears threatened to squeeze between her closed lids.

"Please, Father, help me," she begged.

He reached out and made the sign of the cross upon her brow, saying, "I absolve you of your sin, my daughter. Remember that your father is God's anointed king. Your anger toward him is just as squarely directed at your Heavenly Father. That is not what you desire, is it?"

Mary shook her head in a movement that was almost a shiver. "No, Father."

"You must say a dozen Hail Marys as well as give alms to the poor. It will also help clear your soul of sin to fast until vespers of the morrow."

"Yes, Father. Thank you, Father." Gratitude filled Mary's voice, but in the back of her mind the feeling that she could never forgive her father still nagged. She would gladly serve her penance and hope that it quieted the voice of the devil within her.

The chaplain touched her elbow to help her rise, though she did not feel ready to leave. The peace she had hoped for continued to elude her, and she was uncertain how to rediscover it. With one last silent prayer that was more like a sigh, she gave up.

Mary opened her eyes and squinted upward in order to bring the chaplain's face into focus. The lines drawn across his brow told her that he was in no mood for further conversation on the matter. As she rose, she automatically fluffed her skirts and ran her hands over headdress and necklaces, ensuring that all was in place.

"God's peace be with you, daughter," the priest said absentmindedly.

"And also with you," she sadly replied. He had not given her peace this day.

"Go forth and give glory to God with your life," he said and turned away without giving her an opportunity to respond.

Mary watched him leave the small chapel before she fell to her knees once again. Caressing the beads of her rosary in her hands, she began, "Ave Maria, gratia plena. Dominus tecum. Benedicta tu in mulieribus...."

~ ~ ~ ~

When Mary returned to her rooms, she was surprised by the sight of a woman dressed in shabby clothing with her head hung low and turned away from the entrance. Whether it was in shame or to hide her identity, Mary could not ascertain. A note was tightly grasped in the woman's hand, and Mary felt her heart fill with dread once more. This was the confirmation that she had been both waiting for and hoping would never arrive.

"Is that you, Katherine?" she asked in a voice that was scarcely more than a whisper.

The woman turned more quickly and gracefully than her previous posture had indicated was possible. She had crept through darkness and unfamiliar sidestreets to bring this note to the woman whom she was no longer allowed to address as Princess

Mary.

Katherine Hastings curtseyed low before Mary, swallowing hard and trying to force forth the words she had been preparing these last few days.

"I beg you to forgive me for the news that I am about to impart," she whispered in a voice hoarse from disuse. She had not wished to draw any attention to herself as she made her way from the Tower to Mary's lodgings. Each time her eyes had met those of another person, Katherine had cringed and pulled her hood down to hide her face in a way that her proud grandmother would have found extremely unfitting for one of her rank. None were likely to recognize her, but her heart had beat faster all the same each time she felt a stranger's eyes upon her.

"It is news that has pierced your heart even more deeply than my own," Mary replied, her voice thick with emotion as she pulled Katherine up and into her arms.

Finally, Katherine broke as she had not had the freedom to do before this moment. Tears streamed down her face and sobs shook her narrow shoulders. Any other day, she would have been horrified to cry on the shoulder of England's princess. However, today, she could feel Mary quake as well as their tears mingled. Still, she was the first to pull away, not able to prolong the impropriety or continue being the sole bearer of her grandmother's final message any longer.

The note in her hand had become creased and grimy in her sweaty grip. Her brow furrowed and mouth downturned at the sight. This was the last testament of the esteemed Countess of Salisbury, and she had hoped to keep it unmarred. She had already unfolded it many times, not willing to wait to learn what message Margaret had been eager to convey before she died.

The note had given her strength as she crept through

London's alleys and narrow streets. She was no criminal, but she understood that carrying the note could be construed as treason. What could not be considered treason in Henry's England?

Once she had taken a hidden passageway into Mary's grand manor, Katherine had finally felt free to lower her hood and rub dirt from her face. Princess Mary would expect to find her in peasant's garb but was unfamiliar with the smells and filth that often went along with it.

She had just read the last word of the message for the hundredth time when Mary strode into the room. As she put space between them and each took a moment to wipe away tears, Katherine took in the sight of the woman she was certain was her future queen. Mary's gown was crimson where it was not crusted with jewels and must have been unseasonably warm. The princess seemed not to notice nor be weighed down by the yards of fabric and trim. She carried herself confidently and easily, as if the heavy gown were a linen shift.

"Katherine, my dear," Mary said, breaking the silence. "Has the sentence been carried out?"

Any hope that she had held on to had been squashed by Katherine's countenance, but she needed to hear the words.

"I regret to say that it has, your grace, and most horridly done it was," Katherine said with passion fueled by watching her elderly grandmother kneel before an unskilled executioner and give up her life with not half the dignity with which she had lived it. She felt some guilt for breaking the news so harshly to Mary, but the young woman was accustomed to the bleakness of this life and could cope with it better than most.

Mary's lips pressed tightly together as she fought for control of her emotions. Margaret Pole had been her governess and had served her more loyally than any other in her life after the death of Mary's mother. Now her father, the king, had taken them both from her.

After a moment to calm her inner turmoil, she calmly asked, "Was she able to speak to you?"

"No," Katherine said and then felt cruel for her sharpness and the way it made Mary's face fall. She continued, "She did manage to pass a note." She almost smiled at the brightening in Mary's countenance but could not quite lift the corners of her mouth. "It is here, your grace." Katherine bowed her head as she offered the precious missive.

For a moment, Mary simply held it as though it could infuse her with a portion of the spirit of its writer. She liked to remember that Lady Pole had been her grandmother's cousin, so that same steadfastness of spirit ran through her own veins. Somehow, she knew that her life would continue to give her cause to call upon that strength. Moving to a window, which allowed in a fair amount of light, Mary finally unfolded the paper. She was forced to hold it close to her face in order to make out the words, written with great haste and purpose.

Mary felt her eyes once again fill with tears at Margaret's last words, though an avalanche of emotions kept her from noticing the satisfied yet grim look upon Katherine's face. Mary would see that she fulfilled the mission given her by the woman who had been so much more than a governess to her.

"She repeats her surety that I will be queen," Mary whispered, a little in awe that Margaret had been thinking of her in her final moments.

"She does," Katherine stated flatly, waiting to see if Mary would prove worthy of her grandmother's faith.

"I would not ask your family to do anything more that could endanger anyone," Mary said. She could tell that Katherine, too, fought with her emotions, both relief and anger struggling for supremacy upon her stress-lined brow.

"I would not belittle your dear grandmother's sacrifice," Mary continued, "but we must move forward with caution and patience."

She had moved close enough to study Katherine's face and take up her hands. Katherine tried to pull away, mumbling something about not being clean enough for the princess to touch, but Mary held her firmly.

"Too many have died in the attempt to wrest power from my father. Though it is a trial, I can see now that God intends it for good and will refine us for the future."

Katherine nodded half-heartedly. She could see the sense in it, but it somehow seemed a betrayal of Margaret's sacrifice and that of her father. Not only Margaret had died at the hands of the jealous and suspicious king. Katherine's father, Lord Montague, had gone to the scaffold two years earlier as part of Henry VIII's tyrannous decimation of the York remnant. Her younger brother, Henry, remained in the Tower. She did not wish to join them but also could not in good conscience give up their fight.

Again, Mary spoke, seeing that Katherine remained unconvinced. "We must use the examples we have been given and discern when best to emulate them. My mother was bold and outspoken when it earned her exile and loneliness. Your father served mine as best he could until the actions of others were his undoing. We must move forward with prudence, as Lord Montague would advise."

At the mention of her father, Katherine gave in. He had been to her the ideal example of what a nobleman should be, yet it had not been enough for the king. Her shoulders sagged and a frown created lines in her face that would soon become permanent. She could only nod her acquiescence.

Mary placed a small, soft hand on Katherine's chin, forcing her to gaze into her eyes. Katherine was surprised to see that they were no shade of blue like many in their shared family, but a kaleidoscope of browns and greens that must have been inherited from her Spanish mother.

"I will honor Margaret's memory by seeing her wish for me come true." For a moment, Mary faltered and her gaze lowered to the glittering jewels on her bosom. "I do not yet know how, but I shall achieve the dream that she and my mother shared for me."

June 1541

Mary's head throbbed, and she knew before opening her eyes that she would be forced to relinquish her duties for the day. The anger that threatened to bubble within her only made the pain pulse with greater vigor, so she forced herself to take a slow deep breath and pray to God for strength.

When the weak morning sunlight struck her pupils, it felt like a pair of daggers thrust into her skull. Mary clamped her eyes shut and called for Katherine before remembering that she would not be there and was not supposed to be. Margaret's granddaughter had left as unnoticed as she had arrived and was hopefully comfortably in her own bed by now. Mary did not know when she would ever see her again.

Thankfully, the name was common enough and one of Mary's ladies was promptly at her side, though this Katherine would puzzle over why she had been singled out for several days.

"Please send word to my chamberlain that I will be unable to discuss household matters today." Mary paused, waiting for a wave of nausea to pass. "Also, arrange for mass to be said in my rooms after a piece of bread to break my fast." And hopefully settle my stomach, Mary thought to herself.

She rolled over, not hearing the girl's, "Yes, my lady," that was quickly mumbled before rushing to do Mary's bidding.

Mary silently pleaded with God. Why now? She had been determined to renew her ambition to reach her destiny. What path could lead her to the dream so many others had held for her? They were no longer there to help her achieve it, and she felt lost. It seemed that God's plans were never what Mary thought they were.

Addressing nobody in particular, she requested her rosary. It was quickly placed in her hand, and she did not attempt to discern the voice of the woman who brought it. Instead, she immediately gained comfort from the feeling of the beads as they slid through her fingers. Her silent prayers served to begin the calming of her mind.

Grief over the execution of Margaret Pole had brought on this illness, she knew. Stressful situations always seemed to unbalance her delicate humors, and she could think of few events more horrifying than the inexperienced axe-man hacking away at the neck and shoulders of her aged governess. Mary wondered if those who whispered these details where she was sure to hear them thought they were doing her a kindness in providing information she would not have through any legitimate channel or if they enjoyed seeing her squirm.

Mary tried to imagine the thoughts that would fill her own mind were she in Margaret's position, but she simply could not. The gore was too much and left her wondering if God had not immediately taken Margaret into his arms to shield her from the horror that would be done to her body. Mary hoped so.

Nausea swept through her again, and she stiffened to keep the muscles in her abdomen from spasms. When she thought it safe, she let out the breath she had been holding and forced her mind to focus on things that gave her joy, of which there were far too few.

Her young brother came to mind. Thoughts of Edward could always draw her from melancholy moods, so she called again for letters from his governess to be read aloud to her. Mary leaned back into her pillows to listen, her headache already fading.

Edward might be the sole person on earth who loved Mary unconditionally. Of course, this was greatly due to his youth. He looked up to Mary more as a mother figure than a sister, which was acceptable to Mary since children of her own remained out of reach. His childish greetings included in the missives gave her simple joy, but part of her wondered what Margaret had meant by ensuring Mary of her future when she now had a brother to supersede her.

Perhaps, the hastily scribbled missive had only meant to encourage Mary in her hopes for a marriage that would make her queen consort to one of Europe's kings, but Mary did not think so. However, there seemed less chance than ever that she would serve as queen of England. Her brother might become king at a young age and require her guidance, but Mary could not envision a crown upon her own head. It was too much for her hazy mind to consider at the moment, so she released her worries and let the soft voice and Edward's words lull her to sleep like a lullaby.

February 1542

Mary could not rejoice at the fate of her fourth stepmother, however eagerly she would take the open place at her father's side. Catherine Howard had been a silly girl, and Mary would admit only in her private heart that her father had been equally silly to marry her. It had been humiliating to witness her father making a fool of himself over a woman younger than his own daughter.

It was difficult to imagine that lovely face never dimpling in a flirtatious smile again. Mary could not respect Catherine, but she could feel sympathy for a life ended too soon. What else could her father have done though? Adultery, when committed by a queen, was undoubtedly treason. It was far more reason than he had for punishing others, certainly more than he had against Margaret.

Mary turned over her mixed feelings to her confessor and to God, knowing that he would be the final judge of the late queen's actions. Her duty now was to ensure that her father avoided any more catastrophic marriage decisions. At twenty-six, Mary was more than capable of serving in the role of queen at her father's side. What need had he of anyone else?

Though she had not spent much time at her father's court, Mary had been trained from the time she could walk to serve at a king's side. She tried not to think about the fact that she should be married to a king, not clinging to her father, but that was a worry for another day. God had a plan for her.

Several years ago, Lord Montague had assured her that it was her destiny to be queen. He was gone now, another victim of her father's wrath, but Mary clung to his promise, even as it seemed further from her reach than ever before.

Despite the cruel actions of her father toward many she loved most, Mary could not help but crave his affection and approval. He would have no reason to be displeased with her as she brilliantly filled the public role of his consort.

Her purple gown was gloriously arrayed about her, and diamonds glittered at her fingers and throat. Her posture would not reveal the pain that stabbed through her lower abdomen, and she forced herself not to squint at the blurry figures that she knew to be the closest men of her father's household.

"Daughter, what think you of your brother's progress in his studies?"

A genuine smile lit Mary's features as she considered her father's inquiry. Could he be thinking of bringing Edward to court as well? How lovely it would be to have a feeling of family once again.

Mary bowed her head slightly toward the king and responded respectfully, "Both he and my sister are accomplished and demonstrate skill in any task they put their hand and mind to. It is a great testament to your own great wisdom that your children are the most learned in the kingdom."

"Very good!" Henry exclaimed, rubbing his hands together as though he was already thinking of something else. Though injuries and weight kept him from formerly favorite activities, he still was a man that observers could perceive was full of energy and ambition.

But Mary wished to know more. "Do you think to bring Edward and Elizabeth to court as well, your grace? It may be a great consolation to you to have all of your children surrounding you."

The king's face scrunched up in a thoughtful frown. As he considered her words, Mary waved away the servant who approached with a tray of sweetmeats. She was worried for her father's health, and he continued to eat as though he were an athletic young man. Mary could tell that he hesitated to bring the children together, but she could not guess why. His mind simply worked differently than hers, for she could see no disadvantage.

"Let us be together for Christmas this year!" Henry announced as if imparting a generous gift.

Christmas was months away, the celebration of the last one not long past. However, Mary accepted it with the graciousness that she knew her father expected. She had given in to his wishes when she signed away her inheritance and gave up all that her mother had fought for. For as long as he reigned, she must practice humility and patience.

"In the meantime," Henry added, "I shall be considering potential suitors for you, my dear Mary."

He said it casually before turning back to Charles Brandon, who never seemed far from his side, with no awareness of the shock that he had given his oldest daughter.

Rather skilled in the art of keeping her feelings hidden, Mary gave him no reason to understand the inner turmoil that exacerbated her stomach pain. Past betrothals, made and broken, flashed through her mind, but the match that she thought of now was one her father would never make. Henry had been made aware of his first wife's desire for Mary. It would have been a joining of York and Tudor bloodlines. In addition, the groom's mother was one of Queen Catherine's closest friends. Mary wondered, not for the first time, if she would ever become the wife of Cardinal Reginald Pole.

Her distant cousin was in the unique position of becoming a cardinal without taking orders. Therefore, it was still possible for him to return to the secular world and take a wife. Mary knew that it had been the wish of their mothers but wondered if it had ever been Reginald's. Did he think of her and their possible future or was his focus completely on the work of the church?

As chatter quieted for the evening's entertainment to begin,

Mary's mind was on a man very far away whom she may never again lay eyes upon.

Reginald had been in Europe for several years, completing his studies and avoiding the wrath of the king visited upon his family. Mary did not know him well but held on to her image of him as the ideal husband that the two women she loved most had desired for her. She knew that he was as handsome as his brother, Lord Montague, and that he had inherited the inner strength and piety of his mother. There were no stains of character upon her limited vision of Cardinal Pole.

Her father let out a burst of laughter that jolted Mary from her wandering thoughts. She smiled at him as if she shared in his amusement, though she had not a clue what was going on around her, so lost had she been in her own dreams. It was sufficient for Henry, who turned to nudge Brandon instead. Mary forced her mind back to the present, allowing her father's joviality to lift her spirits as the performers made their best efforts to impress their king.

When the sun woke her the next morning, Mary took her head in her hands and screwed her eyes tightly shut. Never one to imbibe upon the wine that was plentiful at her father's table, she knew that the headache was a result of fretfully worrying over her future late into the night.

The entertainment had been only a momentary distraction. Once alone in her own bed, Mary had not been able to halt the concerns that presented themselves one by one. Her sleep had been elusive and restless.

She curled her body into a ball as her womb cramped and flared in pain as well. God cursed her for her anger against her father, she thought, even as the king had likely already forgotten that he had even mentioned the possibility of finding Mary a husband.

Hearing movement in her room, Mary moaned, "Susan, please make my excuses. I am feeling far too poorly to do more than hear mass."

"Shall I have your chaplain come to your rooms, my lady?" Susan asked in a low voice, accustomed as she was to her lady's ailments.

Mary could only groan, not able to think about the simplest decision.

"Do not try to get up, my lady," Susan quickly amended. "I will send the message and then help you prepare to receive him here."

Mary wondered how each segment of her thin form could feel so heavy. She could not lift her head from the pillow let alone raise her body to stand. Mass was something she rarely missed and she hated to do so now, but she would have to content herself with hearing it privately. Tears threatened to form when she remembered that she would not be able to preside with her father over the court.

She pressed her lips together into a disappearing line. All the years she had waited in hope that he would restore her to a position worthy of her birth and now she would miss her moment because of the poor health that had plagued her since the first whispers of her parents' difficulties.

Closing her eyes, she began to murmur prayers for strength, patience, and healing. God had brought her through her trials thus far. He would not abandon her today.

She grasped her rosary and began whispering her prayers that did not cease until Susan returned with Mary's chaplain at her side. The sonorous tones of his voice were surprisingly soothing. Though his words filled the room, it was a deep, calming sound that lulled Mary to sleep. Her worries finally scattered in the face of the Word of God, and Mary fell into a deep, peaceful slumber.

May 1542

What Mary had hoped would be a week in bed due to her courses, which always troubled her more than they seemed to other women, had become two months of headaches and fatigue that left her unable to serve at her father's side.

As the sun gave hints of the warm summer quickly approaching, Mary gave thanks to God that she was feeling better. She would not waste more time feeling sorry for herself over what had been missed but would throw herself wholeheartedly into whatever her father required of her.

She had a fleeting thought that those duties may still include a betrothal but was determined not to concern herself over that until she received information that warranted it.

Her dress hung loosely. However, she did not wish to have it taken in to emphasize her increased thinness. Now that she could tolerate it, she would strive to eat enough to fill her gowns again.

Lost in her own thoughts, she almost did not catch the words of her gossiping ladies as they prepared to join the king for supper.

"Susan," Mary said more harshly than intended, "who are you speaking of?"

Susan Clarencieux was more than a lady-in-waiting to Mary. She was a dear friend, but this status made her loose in her manners at times. With a sideways glance at her companions, Susan left them and glided to Mary's side.

"It is nothing of concern, Lady Mary," she soothed.

She should have known that few things aggravated Mary more than being referred to as 'lady' rather than 'princess.' It reminded her of too much, including the fact that she had signed the Act legally making it the correct form of address for Susan to use.

"Tell me," Mary demanded, her already low voice made gruff by weeks of disuse.

Susan sighed but acquiesced. "It is simply speculations regarding your father's intentions toward taking another wife," she said as if the news was of no consequence.

"A sixth wife?" Mary exclaimed, her eyes widening in horror. "Surely, he can be content with me to assist him with royal duties."

An unladylike smirk marred Susan's lovely features. "To be sure, my lady, but there are certain duties that you cannot attend to for the king."

"Like what?" Mary asked, not understanding why the question sent ladies giggling as Susan looked to them with her brows raised.

Mary waved her away. She hated feeling like the only one in a room who did not understand what was going on, but she would not involve herself in tawdry talk. Except, she must know.

"Who is it?" she asked Susan's retreating back.

Susan turned gracefully, her skirts billowing out around her as if by chance rather than skill. "A woman I believe you know," Susan replied as she watched Mary's face for her reaction. "Kateryn Parr."

Mary's lips pursed into a frown that made her appear much older than her true years. "Kateryn Parr has a husband," she stated in a matter-of-fact tone, hiding her true disgust that her father would not only be considering another wife but be willing to take one already claimed.

Susan tipped her blonde head to Mary, saying lightly, "As I said, only rumors and gossip, my lady."

With a masterful sway to her hips, Susan strolled back to

her audience and left Mary wondering why a cloud always seemed to immediately darken her sunshine.

December 1542

The summer and autumn had passed in a whirlwind for Mary, and the Christmas season was upon her before she could think again about her ladies' chatter regarding her father taking another wife. He had given her no indication of it as she proudly demonstrated to him that she was more than capable of the responsibilities of queenship.

She could almost forgive him for the injuries of the past. Almost. Mary found that it was best if she did not allow herself to dwell upon what he had done to her mother or the fact that she herself was still legally a bastard, known only as 'the king's daughter' rather than 'princess'.

On this day, she would be at his side as they welcomed all who had been invited to join them for Christmas. Mary was cozy in her layers of green velvet, which she thought suited the occasion very well. Diamonds, rubies, and emeralds glittered as she moved, and she was certain that she was the very vision of a queen.

The wet summer and poor harvest may have left some of the country's residents with an unsubstantial Christmas dinner, but that did not impact the king's stunning display. The fragrance of roasted meat filled Mary's nostrils long before she entered the great hall. Her mouth watered, and she was pleased to find that her appetite had been restored.

Sounds filled up the room to the soaring hammerbeam ceiling and leaked out windows and doorways. Women in a rainbow of gowns flirted and danced their way around men who were less at ease in their finest doublets and hose. At the center of it all was her father.

King Henry VIII sat upon a gaudily decorated throne where once he would have been chief among the dancers. Mary had only fond memories of him as an athletic younger man, and she was saddened by the great girth he had obtained. It made many of his previously favored activities painful when combined with old injuries, so he sat them out and added more to his ever widening middle. The vicious circle often left him in a poor temper. Therefore, it was best to let it alone rather than suggest that he take smaller portions of each dish.

He was clothed in swathes of red velvet and cloth of gold, which only added to his enormity. Since his hair was thinning and, even worse, going grey, he had begun wearing hats even when they made him sweat, as Mary could see he was doing profusely. She ordered the fires reduced to decrease the heat of the room, which was largely maintained by body heat by this time, before turning again to join her father.

She saw that he was jovially entertaining Lady Latimer, Kateryn Parr.

Mary stopped in her tracks, the words from all those months ago rushing back to her. She had not endured four step-mothers without understanding the look upon her father's features. Kateryn, for her own part, appeared polite but did not seem to be encouraging the king's attention.

Smart woman. Mary loved her father, when she was not despising him, but she would not wish marriage to him upon anyone. And she rather liked Kateryn Parr. They were of an age and similar temperament. Mary's mother had been a dear friend of Kateryn's mother who had proudly served as the princess' godmother.

Kateryn was also already married to a much older man. Word was that his health was failing. If that were true, the last thing Kateryn needed was the attention of another aging suitor.

Mary knew that it was treason, not to mention evil on the part of a daughter, to consider the death of the king. However, she could not help but see that his habits would not lengthen his life. Her younger brother would wear his crown, but, surely, at more than twenty years his senior, Mary would guide and assist him.

Pulling herself reluctantly from her inner turmoil, Mary forced herself to regally make her way to the place next to her father's, carefully clearing any sign of her wandering thoughts from her countenance.

"Daughter," Henry boomed as Mary took her place, "you remember the lovely Lady Latimer."

Mary tipped her head to Kateryn. "Indeed, I do and count her as a friend," she said. "And you do look lovely. I especially adore your pearls," Mary added in Kateryn's direction. The two shared a love of jewels and fine clothing that had often provided them with time spent in pleasant conversation.

"My thanks to you, Lady Mary," Kateryn said gracefully curtsying to Mary though she need not do so. "Your own jewels are most festive, and your presence has brightened the room."

Henry beamed at the young women, happy to see a connection already formed between them. Then his daughter's words caused him to frown.

"How is your husband?" Mary asked, taking Kateryn's hand in her own. "I have lifted Lord Latimer up in prayer. Do let me know if I can be of any help to you."

"You are most gracious, Lady Mary," Kateryn said with her head bowed slightly. Both women pretended they did not notice the darkening of Henry's mood. "He has been poorly since the last Scottish campaign, yet is comforted by placing his life in God's hands."

"Amen," Mary solemnly replied.

"I will send my own physician to attend to him," Henry interjected by way of bringing attention back to himself.

"That is most generous of you, your grace," Kateryn demurely replied.

"Nonsense," Henry said. "Latimer has done great service for me in keeping the Scots at bay. With James' death last month, a great opportunity has arisen. I shall see to it that the crowns of Scotland and England are truly united under a single monarch."

At this, Mary turned quizzically to her father, a single eyebrow raised, but Kateryn allowed no emotion of her own to be displayed.

"It is quite simple," Henry continued, seemingly unsurprised at needing to explain his strategy to women. "The young Scottish princess," he carefully did not refer to her as Princess Mary, "will need a husband, as our Edward needs a wife."

Mary gazed toward the rafters as she considered this. "You are right, your grace. It is a match that would rid both countries of the ongoing border disputes and unite us in one purpose."

"Precisely," Henry agreed, grinning widely at his own genius as he signaled for more wine. Kateryn quietly refused to have her own goblet refilled.

Mary smiled at her friend. Maybe her father had met his match after all. Kateryn continued to give Henry politely correct responses without a hint of encouragement toward anything more.

Mary believed her father's plan to negotiate a match between his son and his sister's granddaughter was a fine one, even as it pushed Mary's own dreams of being queen further from the realm of possibility. She was beginning to believe that her role would always be to support England's king, whether it be her father or brother, rather than serve as queen. If that was God's plan for her, she would embrace it and serve to the best of her abilities.

March 1543

"My most heartfelt condolences to you, Kateryn," Mary said to the young, twice widowed woman. Kateryn Parr was wrapped in warm layers of black fabric yet still appeared chilled. Mary wished to pull her into an embrace but thought Kateryn may find it shocking. Instead, she added, "Please know that there is a place for you in my household, if you desire it."

Kateryn did perk up at this and almost smiled. "I would like that very much, especially if I may bring my stepdaughter, Margaret."

"Of course," Mary gushed, unable to contain her pleasure at providing Kateryn with some hope for the future without her husband. "She is quite welcome. What arrangements have been made for your stepson?"

Kateryn seemed not as concerned for the older boy. Waving the question away, she explained, "John is of an age to accept the responsibilities that come with his father's title and estates, and he will have the assistance of my brother as needed."

Mary fought back a blush at the mention of Will Parr who had been scandalously divorced from his wife after she ran away with a lowborn lover. Kateryn seemed unaffected by the situation.

"Praise God he is well provided for," Mary mumbled in response.

"He is," Kateryn agreed amiably, "and now, so am I. You have my thanks."

The women smiled at each other, pleased that the situation suited them both quite well.

~ ~ ~ ~

Mary was happy to see Kateryn unpacking her things and settling into her household. It would do her good to again be in the company of women after months of caring for her dying husband. Mary knew that Kateryn loved music and dancing as much as she did, so she looked forward to bringing some simple joy into her friend's life. It was something that she needed more of as well. Husbands would likely be found for each of them before too many months passed. Therefore, Mary was determined to enjoy this time to the fullest.

They did.

Mary and Kateryn rose each dawn to attend lauds before filling their morning with books and discussion of a deeper sort than Mary was able to enjoy with her other attendant ladies. They especially shared a passion for religious texts and languages, which led to them working translations together. After midday mass, they would practice music, composing their own simple songs and sharing their favorite works as the other ladies danced. This was the time of day when Mary's father often chose to visit his daughter's chambers.

The women did not discuss the king's intentions. They seemed to silently agree that it could achieve nothing. Anything that happened would be solely at the discretion of the king, so gossiping over it or wishing something may happen differently was a waste of precious time and freedom.

While Mary felt that Kateryn may be the first stepmother whom she could welcome wholeheartedly to the family, she also felt that Kateryn deserved her own choice for a third husband. Henry, king or not, was clearly not the one she would choose.

It was not difficult to discern who had won Kateryn's heart. Thomas Seymour had also begun visiting, and his social calls were much more enthusiastically greeted than Henry's. Mary could not see what her friend found so appealing about the man. Of course, he was handsome and charming, but it seemed like a veneer. Mary believed his qualities to be shallow and used to cover something less attractive. She said nothing of her feelings to Kateryn, knowing that her opinion was irrelevant. A few moments of happiness could be stolen before more powerful forces determined Kateryn's future.

Where Kateryn was the embodiment of discretion, Seymour was bold and daring. This seemed to draw Kateryn to him rather than repulse her. Mary shook her head as she observed them from across the room, stunned and disappointed that one so recently widowed would carry on so with a man who could only be described as a rake.

Thomas casually brushed aside a few golden locks that had escaped Kateryn's hood, and the look she gave him in return made Mary feel that she was eavesdropping on something far more intimate than it appeared to be. She sighed and stood. This could only lead to embarrassment and heartache, better to put a stopper in it now.

Before she had a chance to speak, Seymour was bowing gracefully before her, Kateryn curtsying by his side. Mary had to admit that the happy flush made her friend radiant in her red gown with intricate gold trimming. The man also preempted anything she may have said.

"I was just telling Lady Parr that I am on my way to do the king's bidding," he began. "Alas, it would be much more agreeable to remain in the presence of such beauty and pleasant conversation."

His eyes boldly pierced into Mary's, a twinkle of amusement glittering there, while Kateryn subtly averted her own gaze. Not skilled in the art of courtly love, Mary lost the words she intended to say as she struggled with the intensity of his eyes unashamedly taking in her features. She noted that his dark hair fell across his brow in an unfashionable way that entirely suited him. Her hand twitched with the urge to smooth it back, and Thomas smirked as though he could read her mind.

"Until I am free to come again," he said with a bow that made Mary wonder if the previous moments had been imagined, "Lady Parr. Lady Mary." He tipped his head to each in turn and was gone.

When Mary turned to Kateryn, she was once again cut off before she could begin.

"Oh Mary, I know what you would say, but you need not."

Kateryn's hands went to her face as though she would feel the joy that had just been there before it flitted away.

"Dear Kateryn," Mary began, but she was uncertain of the words that a few moments ago seemed to need saying.

"Truly," Kateryn said, laying a hand on Mary's arm. "It is a passing moment of innocent pleasure. A vapor already gone." It was. Kateryn's face had regained its almost cold composure. "I shall do my duty as God calls me to it," she added.

Mary clamped her lips on anything else she might have said. "That is all any of us can do," she agreed.

July 1543

As Mary stood in the Queen's Closet of Hampton Court, absentmindedly fingering her rosary beads, she wondered if ever before there had been a marriage between a woman taking her third husband and a man taking his sixth wife. Was such a thing God's will? The words of Bishop Gardiner could scarcely break through her veil of private thoughts as he declared Kateryn the well-beloved wife of King Henry VIII.

It was almost surreal to look upon her fifth stepmother who was just a few years older than herself. The image of her father's last unfortunate wife sprang to mind, and Mary's attitude quickly transformed from incredulity to thankfulness. She had a great love for Kateryn and knew of none other who had the steadfastness of spirit to be a pleasing wife to the tempestuous king. Mary's prayers for her would be unceasing.

Mary gazed up, hoping that gave her prayers a more direct path to God. She could not help but wonder at the artistry on display in the jeweled and gilded work that her father had ordered for the ceiling of the room that was often used as a private chapel. Vibrant azure was highlighted with work of pure gold upon textured carvings that made one feel as though they were standing below the roof of heaven. For a moment, Mary could forget her many concerns regarding the day.

As she lowered her eyes to take in those gathered for the wedding ceremony, she was immediately reminded of a few of those concerns. Prince Edward, only five years old, managed to remain still and quiet throughout the service. Mary watched Kateryn lean down as best she could in her voluminous white and gold gown to speak earnestly with the young boy.

He responded with a serious expression that gave no clue of their topic. One day soon, he would participate in his own much grander wedding when he and the little Mary of Scots were united. Henry had acted quickly upon his plan to unite the kingdoms and was insistent that the child would be his daughter-in-law.

Mary shifted her gaze to meet that of her half-sister, Elizabeth, and finally a genuine smile lit her face. With coppery hair, a sharp nose, and slender build, Elizabeth was almost a perfect duplicate of her sister. Though time promised to make the nine-year-old taller than her older sister, Mary could, at this point, still feel that she was the substitute mother in the relationship.

It had not always been so. Mary did not often allow herself to remember hearing the announcement of Elizabeth's birth, which was promptly followed by the dissolution of her own household so that she could serve her infant sister. Any anger that Mary had felt toward the younger girl had evaporated over the years as they both struggled with the fate of their mothers. Mary did not feel one iota of sympathy for Anne Boleyn, but she had softened toward her daughter.

With no children of her own, Mary doted upon Edward and Elizabeth in a way their father never would. She made her way now through the small, crowded room to her father's other bastardized princess.

Elizabeth performed a perfect curtsy for her sister before letting her guard drop and offering a smile.

"I pray you are well, sister," Elizabeth said with a sincerity of one unaware of the former bad feelings one has had toward them.

"My thanks to you and to God for seeing that I am indeed restored to health and able to see a good friend and my dear father united in marriage." As she said it, Mary was surprised to find that she meant it.

"I wish them great happiness," Elizabeth agreed without

emotion.

"You will find Kateryn to be a loving mother, and she may be a calming presence for our father," Mary encouraged her.

"Undoubtedly, you shall be proven correct."

Sometimes Elizabeth's habit of saying only what was expected could annoy, but Mary knew that she was simply doing her best to play her part to perfection. It was an effect of the quick succession of stepmothers and the gruesome connection between marriage and death that the young girl had witnessed.

Mary laid a hand on Elizabeth's arm and directed her gaze at their younger brother. Elizabeth did not pull away but neither did she reciprocate the familiar touch. Her smile at watching Edward behave so seriously in his miniature finery seemed cold, expected rather than felt. With a sigh, Mary wondered how she could encourage Elizabeth to feel a greater connection, at least with her siblings. One day they would be all that each other had left.

Elizabeth defined herself by her accomplishments rather than her personality or relationships. It was sad to see one so young afraid of friendships that should come naturally at that age. While Elizabeth would strive to perform any skill better than anyone else, she did not enjoy sharing these moments with anyone. Mary wished that she could crack her younger sister's shell and see inside her heart.

Edward was too young and pampered to consider hiding any of his feelings. He basked in his sister's embrace after composing himself long enough to be formally presented. Mary closed her eyes as she held the boy firmly until he began to wriggle. She smelled the lavender water used to bathe him, and his hair felt like silk against her cheek. Sometimes, when she held him like this, her heart ached to hold her own child, but on this day she was simply grateful to have her family together and happy.

Edward did not notice the difference between Mary's heartfelt embrace and Elizabeth's obligatory kisses. He adored his sisters with the unbridled enthusiasm of one who has been shown nothing but affection. It was one of the things that Mary loved about him most. She hoped that he never lost that quality as he grew intelligent enough to know that no one could have everyone's love at all times, not even a king.

His little cap was slightly tilted, so Mary straightened it, allowing her hands to linger over his soft cheeks before returning them to her side. She was just about to ask him what he thought of his father's new bride when the groom himself made himself heard above all others.

"My girls!" Henry boomed, pulling Mary and Elizabeth into his arms. Mary giggled at his uncharacteristic display but Elizabeth stiffened as a flush rose to her face. "You are both beautiful," he continued, taking no note of their reactions. "I am reminded of my mother, God rest her soul, when I look upon the beauty that you have each inherited from her."

"Thank goodness, they do not look like their father," a voice joked, and Mary did not have to look to know who would dare to say such a thing and earn nothing but laughter from her father.

Charles Brandon slapped the king on the back hard enough to make Mary wince, though her father seemed hardly to notice. The men roared with laughter as if Brandon has been brilliantly witty, and Mary silently thanked her late governess for training her to never roll her eyes. It was stunning how they could revert to the behavior of young adolescents when together, regardless of their ever increasing age.

"Have you found a husband for Lady Mary yet?" Brandon inquired, giving Mary a rather inappropriate gaze that made her wish she could run away. Yet she stood firm, because she would not be made to feel of lesser importance than Brandon and because she knew that he looked at all women that way. Most seemed to enjoy it, even as he neared his sixtieth year. There seemed to just be something about him, something Mary could not see.

Henry laughed and slapped Brandon on the back in return. "All in good time, my friend. All in good time."

They turned away as if Mary did not exist, so she was left standing with eyes wide. Her father would not truly consider marrying her to a man like Charles Brandon, would he? The very thought of it made her skin crawl. Thankfully, the man himself was securely married to Catherine Willoughby, who adored him despite his rough manners and the fact that he was more than thirty-five years her senior.

Mary gave her head a quick shake. Puzzling out other people's romantic feelings always left her baffled, so there was no purpose in wondering how young, beautiful Catherine was attracted to her husband. Mary observed the flirtations of the court but never felt a desire to participate in them. It seemed so demeaning. When God sent her a husband, she would love him and no one else.

"Praise God that our father is easily distracted from his thoughts," Elizabeth piped up.

She had almost forgotten that Elizabeth and Edward were there, so far had she escaped into her private thoughts. Mary cast a questioning gaze at her sister, her brow furrowed at the idea that she had missed some other subtle facet of the conversation.

"Surely, you do not wish for him to find a suitor for you?" Elizabeth snapped.

Mary stumbled over her words. "I am not sure. If it were the husband that God intends . . ." she faltered.

"Oh, bah," Elizabeth snorted with a dismissive wave. "Father cannot even select a spouse of his own, let alone yours."

Mary simply stared at her sister, wondering how anyone, especially such a young girl, could talk about their father in such a way. She felt her jaw drop and clamped it shut so tightly that the thin line of her lips disappeared.

"Elizabeth, has your governess not schooled you on giving our father proper respect? He is not only our father, deserving honor as our Lord instructs us, but he is also our king." She felt like yelling at the smug-faced girl, but kept her voice low and calm. As much as she had grown to love Elizabeth, the girl could ravage the nerves. And she seemed to enjoy it.

"Of course, she has," Elizabeth said repentantly with her head bowed demurely, "but I believed that I could speak freely with my beloved sister if with no one else in the world."

Mary sighed. "You may, but you must also remember that our father is God's anointed. His decisions are those that God would have him make for us."

Elizabeth appeared to be struggling to keep her emotions from her face, but Mary could see that she was dismissive of her instructions. Looking for another angle Mary grasped the arm of their brother.

"You, after all, are an example to Edward, who must know not only how to respect our father but understand that he, too, will command that respect one day when he is king."

Elizabeth smirked and asked, "Is it not treason to speak of the death of the king?"

Mary was losing patience with the girl, so she turned her attention to the boy. She squatted down as best she could in her heavy gown to look into his stormy blue eyes.

"Edward, did you speak to our new mother?"

He nodded solemnly, seeming to understand that his oldest sister was on edge. When Mary smiled, his face broke into a gap-toothed grin in return.

"Tell me what you think of her," Mary prompted.

"Lady Kate is rather pretty," he replied with only a slight lisp.

"Yes, she is," Mary agreed, ruffling her fingers through the hair that peeked from beneath his cap and then smoothing it down.

She stood and shot a look at Elizabeth that indicated Edward had proven it was not that difficult to be civil. But she said nothing.

Elizabeth shrugged, and they silently agreed to move on.

The strain between them was quickly forgotten, as it always was, so that by the time they were seated at the high table next to their father conversation flowed smoothly. Elizabeth enjoyed sharing her academic progress with Mary, and the older girl felt like a proud mother hearing of her achievements. Mary did not concern herself over the fact that there were some subjects that Elizabeth was certain to surpass her in. God gave them each strengths and weaknesses for a reason. Jealousy did not often plague Mary.

They were contentedly chatting when Henry leaned their way once again. "You should know," he said in a serious tone, "that my dear Kate has convinced me that you girls should be restored as my successors."

Mary could only gape at her father, wanting to search Kateryn's face for more information but unable to shift her eyes.

Elizabeth took the news as she would have the next passing dish. "Thank you, father," she murmured demurely.

Mary fell from her chair to her knees in front of the king. "Your majesty," she whispered, "this means a great deal to me."

She wanted to say that it would have meant much to her mother, but her voice caught in her throat. He would not have wished to hear it anyway. His hand caressed her hair before moving under her chin to direct her up.

"It warms my heart to see you a submissive and dutiful daughter, Mary," he praised, unaware that his words stabbed through her heart just as she was opening it to him.

She could not look away with her chin firmly in his grasp, so she whispered, "Thank you, your grace," as tears filled her eyes.

Before she knew it, his hand was away from her face and waving to the gathered crowd. "Now let us dance!" he exclaimed, his daughters already forgotten. Again.

May 1544

"Your father feels certain enough with the succession settled to attempt to relive past glories by invading France."

The words were said by Mary's stepmother, whom she preferred to think of as her friend. She had fewer friends than stepmothers, so Kateryn was well placed. They worked embroidery, often in silence, but Kateryn had broken that peace to broach the topic of King Henry's plan to leave England for the first time in many years.

His concerns for his lack of heir had made him cautious, but a king could not live in fear. If no baby was growing in Kateryn's belly, Edward would suffice. Of course, he never expected his daughters to reign, though restoring them to the succession enabled him to breathe a bit easier.

"Will he leave you as regent, as he did my mother?" Mary asked without pausing in her stitches.

"I believe so, and I am happy that I will have your support," Kateryn replied as though it were an everyday occurrence for a pair of women to rule England.

"You would have me help you?"

The look of hope, of wanting to be wanted, on Mary's face caused a softening in Kateryn's features in response. She set aside her cloth in order to lay a hand on Mary's arm. "Of course, Mary. You must be prepared for your future."

Mary felt her face scrunch in confusion. What could Kateryn mean? Coming from certain others, she knew that a future as queen was indicated, but Kateryn must expect to give the king sons.

Seeing her hesitation, Kateryn continued, "Your brother is very young. He will need you . . . when the time comes."

Mary could only nod, taking any step close to the edge of

treason caused a fist to tighten around her heart.

~ ~ ~ ~

By July, Henry had landed in Calais with his shiny new armor, specially made to protect his amazing girth. Kateryn took to her new duties with the same skill that she had used to order her previous husbands' houses. That this husband left her in charge of an entire kingdom seemed to challenge her not at all.

Mary felt happier at Kateryn's side than she remembered being since her mother was sent into exile. They had moved their council to Hampton Court where Edward and Elizabeth joined them. Elizabeth seemed in awe watching the older women govern a land that had never been ruled by a queen. Mary was happy to include her as much as her abilities allowed.

"You will be a great prize as a bride," Mary happily praised her sister. "How many men can say that their wife has assisted in the governance of a kingdom?"

Elizabeth's face was cold and still and did not express any pleasure at the words. Mary had thought Elizabeth was enjoying their work and wondered if she would ever truly understand what went on in Elizabeth's quick mind.

Instead of trying to think of the words that would please her complex younger sister, Mary cast her gaze around the room and sighed. She had never spent much time at Hampton Court, it having been a favorite of the stepmother that she would only refer to as the concubine. However, enough time had passed that she could enjoy the stunning surroundings without bad memories invading.

Mary's private rooms were sumptuous with a scattering of cushioned chairs, and fine tapestries hung on every wall. Her father had chosen peaceful religious scenes that he knew Mary would appreciate, and she could inspect them for hours, never tiring of noticing new little details and applications of color. Her favorite was an image of the Virgin Mother in a blue robe that was made to shimmer by pinpricks of silver. The Holy Child's halo appeared unearthly with its golden glow that made her reluctant to reach out and touch it.

"Shall we walk in the garden?" Elizabeth asked, rubbing her weary eyes and already standing as if she knew her sister would do her bidding.

Mary did not mind. In fact, she loved Hampton Court's elaborate gardens, which were in full summer bloom. "Let us fetch Edward and take him as well. All of us together," Mary said with warmth that was rewarded by a small, reluctant smile from her sister.

The girl was too cold and unemotional, Mary thought. She needed this time surrounded by family to thaw her. When she took Elizabeth's hand to pull her into the corridor toward Edward's rooms, she ignored the fact that the girl tried to pull away.

Mary knew that Elizabeth had been through much and that, from the younger girl's point of view, her mother had been no less a victim than Mary's. She tried to keep this in mind as she strove to demonstrate to Elizabeth that they would do better to support and trust one another.

When Edward joined their party, Mary was warmed, as she always was, that he had no trouble loving his sisters. He did not remember his mother, who had died giving birth to him. The least sensational yet most celebrated of Mary's stepmothers, Queen Jane had shared Mary's quieter qualities. If only God had given her more time to bring together Henry's scattered family.

Having made their way to the gardens, Mary was happy to

let go of the past and enjoy the simple pleasure of watching Edward scamper down the paths as she breathed in the sweet scents of early summer. Even Elizabeth allowed a genuine smile to brighten her features as the Tudor children basked in the glories of the beautiful day.

June 1545

"This is beautiful," Mary whispered as she gently turned the pages of the handwritten manuscript on the table before her. There was no jewel-colored illumination or other decoration. It was the words of the small volume that closed her throat with emotion.

Watching Kateryn and her stepdaughter, Margaret, Mary had felt that she had missed out on something vital in her life. That cozy comfort of snuggling up to someone with no doubt that they loved you – would Mary ever experience it? She had watched Margaret lay her head on Kateryn's shoulder as she dozed and longed for one to experience that closeness with.

Within weeks of that moment, Mary had been given cause to feel convicted for her thoughts. Margaret Neville had slowly faded away over the spring months, until summer blooms attempted to brighten a world without her. Kateryn had mourned in her own quiet way, pouring her grief into the slim book that she now presented to Mary.

Mary glanced at Kateryn before being quickly drawn back to the words that had been written by the heartbroken queen. Kateryn had lost much in her life. Maybe that was how she could understand and connect with Mary so well. First two husbands, and now lovely, young Margaret, one more soul who would welcome Kateryn to heaven when her day came.

"Which of the prayers do you feel were particularly inspired by Margaret?" Mary asked, knowing that Kateryn would cry if she talked about it, but also knowing that was what she needed and wanted.

Silently, Kateryn tuned a few pages and gestured toward her own lines. Mary read them, first to herself and then aloud.

"In this my tribulation, Lord, hear me; for Thy name's sake, help me, and send me succors from Thine holy place," Mary paused, her throat choked with grief. Taking a deep breath and clearing her throat, she carried on, "Strengthen and comfort me, O Lord. Remember the self-sacrifice of Thy well-beloved Son, who prayed for me in the days of his life. For His sake, I say, be merciful unto me."

By the end of the short reading, Mary was whispering, and she closed her eyes, silently pleading for God to hear the mourning woman's prayer for comfort. "It is beautiful," she murmured, looking back to the book.

Noticing that Kateryn had signed the manuscript, 'Kateryn the Quene KP,' Mary was ashamed that there was such a need to differentiate this queen of Henry VIII from other Catherines. Or was it simply that Kateryn was independent enough to wish to cling to her former initials?

Mary softly closed the book and waited a moment before she spoke. "I must ask your forgiveness," she said at last.

Kateryn frowned. This was not what she had been expecting.

"I confess that I was jealous of the closeness between Margaret and yourself." Mary remembered that night only a few weeks earlier when Margaret had cuddled in close to Kateryn in her chair. It turned out that her illness of the previous year was returning, and this time her thin frame could not claim victory over it.

"How I have longed to feel that . . ." Mary did not know how to finish and felt foolish for beginning. She hung her head and placed her palms over her face to hide her shame.

Then she felt Kateryn's hands on her back. They slowly made their way up to her shoulders in a gentle massaging motion. "But do you not know," Kateryn asked, "that I love you the very same way?"

They fell into each other's arms then, crying - for Margaret and all the times that they had felt unloved.

After a few moments, they wiped tears from each other's faces and began to laugh in spite of themselves. "Don't we make a lovely pair?" Kateryn said, choking on tears or laughter, Mary was not sure which.

She could only nod in return, so overcome was she with what they had just shared. Mary had held doubts when her father chose Kateryn as his sixth wife, but now she thanked the Lord that he had. The moment was overflowing with healing and renewal that Mary did not believe she would have experienced with anyone else.

"What a blessing that you will be able to share your book with the world," Mary said, turning back to the manuscript.

Kateryn's lips turned up in a weak smile. "I have written it for myself more than anyone else, yet if God would use it to benefit others I would be honored."

Mary continued to finger the pages, but her smile faded just a bit when the doubt crept into her mind over what her father would think. Would he be proud of his wife or see this as her overstepping her bounds?

September 1545

A year of war on multiple fronts left the kings of England, France, and Scotland ready to sue for peace. Henry, visions of glory that had spurred him on fading, was content to take what gains he could. The sinking of the *Mary Rose* had shaken him more than he cared to admit, and he was dismayed to find war less entertaining than he remembered it being when he was a younger man.

Mary was pleased to hear him imply as much, though he would never admit his weakness in direct words. Whatever her father had done in the past, she wished him safely home. She was also elated by the proposal that sealed peace with three betrothals. Unifying England with the Holy Roman Empire, Mary would be wed to Charles V, while her sister would marry his son and Edward his daughter.

Despite years of fighting, Henry had not succeeded in creating the desired marriage alliance with Scotland. Therefore, Edward would have as his future queen a princess of Spain instead.

Above all, Mary desired to be married. She did not know if that was dishonoring the great plans that her mother had for her to reign as queen of England, but the idea of raising children who would inherit other crowns of Europe appealed to her just as much. Love, peace, and a family - they were simple wishes. And now it seemed that they might be soon fulfilled.

December 1545

"I humbly thank God for the small qualities he has seen fit to bestow upon me and pray that I have utilized them for greatest effect in giving him glory."

Mary watched as her father gave a speech to Parliament on the eve of Christmas. He had risen from the mechanical chair that was often used to move him around due to the great pain in his legs. Watching him stand tall before the gathering of the kingdom's noblemen, Mary could forget that she had recently seen him in a rage over his own physical limitations. At this moment, in his heavily embroidered velvet and cloth of gold, he appeared majestic and powerful, and his words delighted her.

"No prince in the world more favors his subjects than I do you," he paused to beam at them like a proud father. "and no subjects more love and obey their sovereign than I see you do for me."

Mary watched the faces of the men in Parliament from her private position on the outer edges. She saw love akin to worship almost without exception. That was good, for she knew not if her father would be capable of such a speech again.

"Saint Paul wrote to the Corinthians about charity," he continued in the tone of a patient tutor. "Charity is gentle. Charity is not envious. Charity is not proud." Another pause was carefully placed, and he moved his gaze slowly through the hall to ensure that he had their full attention. "Is it charitable, my lords, when one Englishman calls another a Papist? Another an Anabaptist? By no means!"

Quiet shuffling sounds and a few cleared throats were the only evidence of discomfort at the king's words. Mary stood with her head held high, hoping that each would take the words to heart.

Henry ignored the grumbling and continued, "We have now a gift from God that was not made available to our ancestors. The word of our Lord in our own tongue." He laid a large hand on the book lying in front of him just for this moment. "My purpose in giving you this gift is for the education of your children, for the edification of your own faith, and personal devotion. The word of God should not be used as a weapon, used on one countryman by another!"

As his voice rose, men seemed to shrink in their seats. Even if they had seen the sickly king pushed around in his chair, that image was forgotten as his voice boomed through the great hall.

"I would request....no, I demand," Henry amended as if he had just reconsidered his words rather than practiced them for days, "that we use scripture for its intended purpose: to grow in our love of God and each other, rather than create division."

His speech continued long enough that he was exhausted by the time he returned to his rooms. Kateryn used all of her considerable skill to calm him and relieve his pain with tonics and balms. Mary assisted as she could, but this was mostly with the mixing of herbs and ordering servants to bring items to comfort her father.

He did not allow anyone besides Kateryn to be with him at these times, so Mary occupied herself with praying for his healing. She also had great hopes that the public debates over religion would now come to an end. If her father's speech had inspired his country as much as it had his daughter, her hope would be fulfilled.

May 1546

By the following spring, Mary had to concede that her dreams of a family of her own had been just that. Her father and the Emperor had not come to any agreement on the marriage proposals. Mary, now thirty years of age and a less appealing choice of wife than ever, began to ask God for the strength to endure letting another dream die.

She would not have Reginald Pole, the husband desired for her by her mother, and it seemed neither would she have Charles of Spain. It was a match her mother would have been just as pleased with, maybe even more so, he being her nephew and the Holy Roman Emperor. It could not be helped. Mary would be content with what God chose to give her . . . or not.

As her chaplain recited the lauds mass, Mary knelt on a velvet pillow, deep scarlet and embroidered with gold. Her mind was on her own private prayers as his voice sank into the background. How she wished God would reveal his plan for her. If her brother was going to be king, she would not be queen. Was she not to be a wife either?

A deep breath filled her lungs, and she let it out slowly with the prayer that her worries were carried with it. She knew not what else she could do but wait and trust.

As the mass ended, Susan captured Mary's attention. "Chapuys awaits you," she said, gesturing toward the door. The Spanish ambassador must be in her privy chamber.

"Thank you," Mary said with a tilt of her head before she strode off quickly to see the man who was one of few constants in her life. Chapuys had been her mother's most strident supporter, and had transferred that loyalty to Mary after Queen Catherine's death. She went to him with none of the trepidation that filled her when attending to her own father, for Chapuys had always loved her more unconditionally. She knew not what she would do without him.

Pleasantries were exchanged, wine poured, and now Mary moved her mouth soundlessly, unsure what words she was attempting to get out.

"I am returning to Spain," Chapuys had said in a low, gravelly voice. "It has been a joy to serve your grace," he continued, seeming to understand Mary's struggle. "Your mother was the finest woman I have ever known, and I see much of her in you."

He patted Mary's hand and pretended that he did not see tears welling up in her eyes. "His Majesty, the Emperor, continues to wish you well and values your friendship above all others."

The woman who knew little love grasped at the words, not understanding their common usage. "Then stay, Chapuys," she begged. "You have been so good to me."

He was already shaking his head and holding up a hand to stop her. "An envoy from the Pope is already on his way," he sighed as if he were reluctant to leave. "The new peace with France, it could mean reconciliation with Rome as well. It is better if I leave. I am a remnant of different times."

Mary knew that her father would be open to discussing these sorts of things with a man other than Chapuys and that meant he should go, but how could she release him and lose another part of her life that connected her to her mother?

"I pray that you are correct," she finally agreed with a reluctant sigh. "For England to be restored to the Church is more important than my selfish desires." Mary struggled to contain her disappointment and believe her own words.

Now that he had her agreement, Chapuys was quick to offer comfort. "You are the least selfish princess that I have ever known," he said with an almost toothless smile. "If other women had half your grace," he paused shaking his head, "well, the world would be a much finer place."

He moved to stand, his work done, and Mary was dismayed by the pain evident in his slow movements. Chapuys deserved to go home, if Spain could be called his home after sixteen years in England. But how she would miss him.

~ ~ ~ ~

Within weeks, Mary was at her father's side when he admitted the Papal envoy to his presence chamber. Gurone Bertano had made a moving case for reconciliation with Rome, and Mary's eyes shone with excitement. Her father had made his point that kings must have authority in their own kingdoms. Now he could restore the church without feeling that he was crawling back like a prodigal son but rejoining as equals.

"No."

The single word carried a surprising amount of anger in the deep, rumbling voice that echoed around the chamber gone silent.

"You seem to misunderstand my intentions, Bertano," Henry continued in a slightly more civil tone. "I am the Head of the Church of England. The Bishop of Rome has no power over me and I have no need of him."

The envoys cheeks grew a purplish shade of red that almost had Mary rushing to his side before he took a deep breath and slow sip of wine. This routine appeared to calm him and his face became a healthier pink.

"You would see your people separated from God's Church?" Bertano asked, and Mary's eyes went wide that anyone would dare to press her father further seeing his current mood. "You are responsible for more than your own salvation," he insisted. "Would you damn every last Englishman?"

Mary held her breath as she slowly pivoted her eyes to her father. His piercing blue eyes narrowed at the brave envoy, and he seemed to be weighing his words rather than exploding with the fury she had expected.

"I am God's anointed," he said slowly, methodically measuring each word. "My people need not fear hell as they worship without the interference of one who does not understand their needs. This peace proves that God smiles upon the Church of England and its people."

He smiled as if mirroring that of God. Mary shivered, praying that God's smile never provided such a thin veneer to violent anger.

Bertano's dark eyebrows squeezed together as he considered Henry's words. He had been prepared for some negotiation but not for a man who thought more of himself than of God, more of his personal desires than his people's salvation.

"Perhaps, God has allowed us this time of peace as an opportunity to correct any wrongs that we may have done and be reconciled to him," Bertano countered.

Henry settled back into his cushioned chair and his grin widened. "Then Pope Paul had better correct the wrongs he has done. As for England, we are content to feel God's favor upon us."

Mary's hands had been fidgeting in her lap and snagging at the jewels on her skirts. She knew that it was not her place to speak, that she would be sent from the chamber if she did, but it broke her heart to see the opportunity to be reunited with the Holy Mother Church scoffed at. She was watching her hands, willing them to be still, and all had gone quiet.

She lifted her eyes to see Bertano's upon her. He seemed to be willing her to speak up, to convince her father of something that she knew was beyond her power. She looked at her father. He looked pleased with what he saw as a victory. Bertano's face fell when she shook her head and looked back down at her hands.

The moment was lost.

Falling to her knees at compline, she begged that God forgive her for failing to be his witness and spokesperson when given the chance. Might she have changed her father's mind? Should she have tried or should she continue to be careful with her words and remain in his favor?

After mass she sent a page to the queen. Kateryn was the one person she could be honest with about her fears, her doubts, and her feelings regarding her father.

"Mary, you need not request an audience with me," Kateryn said with her arms outstretched in welcome when Mary entered her rooms that evening. "Was it not I who was recently a member of your household?" she added with a grin.

Mary's heart warmed at the welcome as she said, "Thank you, your grace, but it was late in the day and I did not wish to disturb you if you had retired for the night."

"You could never disturb me," Kateryn insisted as she examined Mary's face. "Does something worry you?"

Mary poured her heart out to the one person she knew that it was safe with.

She had no more answers than before when she wearily walked back to her own rooms late that night, but Mary was glad she had bared her soul to Kateryn. She could do no more and must stop feeling that she must take responsibility for her father's actions.

Despite a feeling of emptiness that seemed to be becoming an almost constant companion, Mary found her bed after matins feeling refreshed and reassured. Her sleep was more restful than it had been for many nights.

July 1546

Mary enjoyed spending time with Kateryn and her ladies. She had never before been a part of a group of women who were capable of substantial discussions that covered more than needlework and potential husbands. As much as Mary appreciated stitching, talk of husbands was more often than not hurtful whether that was the intention or not.

Therefore, she adored these times spent discussing scripture as her father had commanded, for personal growth and nourishing deeper relationships with each other and their Lord. If Kateryn occasionally shocked Mary with comments that seemed to favor reformist ideas, she told herself that these points were important to discuss among trusted friends for the increasing of faith.

A comment snagged Mary's attention, and she almost pricked her finger when her needle slipped. The speaker was Catherine Willoughby, who had been left a widow when the blustery Charles Brandon had died last autumn.

"She is in the Tower. It is said that she undergoes worse torture than has ever been performed upon a woman," Catherine said in a whisper that was both horrified and excited to be the one to share shocking news.

Mary dared not ask who Catherine spoke of. She was too often the one who did not understand what was going on when others seemed to know by nature. Instead, she waited for the comments of the other women who leaned in as one.

"Have you heard her speak?" one asked.

"She has been on the rack – can no longer stand," said another.

Looking at her hands in her lap to avoid giving away her shock and confusion, Mary finally heard a name.

"Anne Askew will be burned. If you have been with her, you

should put her heresy out of your mind at once as if it had never been there."

Mary's head snapped up toward the speaker. One of the older ladies in Kateryn's retinue, she kept her tone matter-of-fact as she instructed them all as children.

"This may not end with Askew. For all the king's fine words, begging your pardon, Lady Mary, he will not abide with heretical rubbish. Your grace, you may wish to temper your tongue until this matter has passed."

Kateryn's small smile accepted the woman's words without conceding to their significance. "My husband appreciates my ability to discuss matters of faith with him. He knows that we are one in the worship of our Lord."

The matron shrugged and reverted her attention to the mending in her lap. She had seen queens come and go and had fulfilled her duty to advise this one.

Mary considered the words more carefully. Had her father given any indication that he was displeased with Kateryn? She did not think so, but the older woman likely observed more than Mary did, even if they saw the same things.

~ ~ ~ ~

"It was simply the most horrid thing I have ever seen!"

The words came to Mary's ears in a rushed whisper though she knew they were not intended for her. She lay abed, her headache once again keeping her from lauds. Her women were beginning to rise for the day and believed her to be asleep.

"To think! Torturing a woman that way . . ."

"I heard she had to be carried to the stake in a chair."

Quiet tutting and sniffling drowned out the next woman's words, and Mary squeezed her eyes shut as if that could keep her from hearing more.

"Askew kept her faith until the end though," Susan's voice was almost wistful. "She would not give up others or recant her beliefs."

"Much good it did her."

The words faded away as the women moved from the range of Mary's hearing through the summer bed curtains and sounds of preparation for the day. Askew had been a traitor. A heretic. Surely, her father had done the right thing.

Yet, she could not keep the tears from spilling from her eyes. She felt the throbbing of her heartbeat pulse through her suddenly aching head and knew that she would be missing Kateryn's company for a few days.

When Mary once again felt well enough to join the circle of Kateryn's ladies, she found the group much more subdued than before. The story of Askew's death was no longer whispered, for all knew the gory details.

Worse than that, two more women had been interrogated, and these were not outspoken evangelicals but women of court. Mary wondered if the arrest of Lady Hertford and Lady Denny was intended to send a message that heresy would not be tolerated in any circle and if they were truly guilty of that crime.

After long moments of uncomfortable silence, Kateryn rose to loosen stiff muscles and smooth her skirts.

"Mary, would you attend me? I would like to stretch my legs and walk in the garden," Kateryn said, already moving toward the door. "The rest of you may stay here."

Her words were casual enough but held an edge of concern. Mary quickly followed.

"Have you been in attendance upon your father?" Kateryn asked as soon as they were alone.

Mary quickly shook her head. The king had decreasing desire to have anyone but a trusted few in his presence. He could not tolerate people seeing him in his weakening condition. "I must apologize, your grace," Mary almost groaned, feeling useless once again. "I have not. He does not call upon me."

"There now," Kateryn said, entwining her fingers in Mary's as they strolled down a path more casually than either of them felt. "It is not your fault. It is just that I hear whispers."

Mary turned wide, innocent eyes upon her friend and stepmother. "Whispers?"

Kateryn swallowed as if to keep down words that she could not say. "Have you enjoyed our talks, Mary?"

"Of course, your grace," Mary quickly insisted, nodding to underscore her enthusiasm.

Kateryn laughed and gave her hand a squeeze. "As have I," she said before growing more serious. "I have reason to believe, however, that your father grows weary with . . . lively conversation on topics of religion."

"I see," Mary said, hoping that she did. Kateryn's quizzical gaze seemed to wonder the same thing.

"I ask nothing of you," Kateryn finally continued. "I only wish for you to know that I must humble myself before your father. He must know that I do not mean to challenge him as Head of the Church. I tell you this because you must do the same if the situation demands it."

"Alright," Mary acquiesced in little more than a whisper.

Kateryn stopped walking and pulled her hand from Mary's in order to grasp her by the shoulders. "Do not be proud. Do not choose a battle not worth fighting. If your father demands that you submit to him, do so. Belittle our conversations in any way you must. Ask him to guide you in all spiritual matters."

Kateryn gave Mary a little shake to emphasize each statement, and Mary felt the queen's fingers and rings dig into her arms. Her head began to ache. "I will do as you wish," she replied, though she did not feel that she fully understood.

Kateryn released her, though she continued to search her face.

"I understand," Mary insisted, and hoped Kateryn believed her.

"Very well," Kateryn said, the mood immediately lightening. "Let us return to our gossiping ladies."

~ ~ ~ ~

When Mary later heard of the attempt to arrest Kateryn and her father's rebuke of the order he must have signed, she ran to the chapel to thank God that he had given Kateryn the foresight to evade disaster. She could not bear to have tragedy visit the royal household again. Besides her mother, Mary had never loved one of her father's wives the way she did Kateryn. She simply could not tolerate losing her, especially not at her father's hand.

December 1546

Mary was pleased to be out of bed and feeling restored after her the illness that had plagued her upon hearing of the attempt to arrest Kateryn. She envied the queen's ability to remain active without ever displaying any evidence that the pace of court wearied her in any way. The two of them, along with their ladies, were preparing Greenwich for the Christmas season, and Mary could not remember a recent holy season that she had looked forward to more. The only element missing to make it perfect was the presence of her father.

Henry remained at Whitehall. Though he was ill, he would not leave the governing of his kingdom to celebrate the birth of the Christ Child with his wife and daughter. Mary convinced herself that he had vital issues to deal with and did not wish to display his poor health before the ladies, but in her heart of hearts she knew that he was preparing for his death.

Mary had observed her father's failing health with little fear because he still appeared to her as too powerful, too majestic to simply lie down and die like a mortal man. She wondered if others saw him that way as well. Clearly, not all men did, as at least one had attempted to take advantage of the king's decline to place his own family in a position of advantage.

The arrests of Thomas and Henry Howard just a few days earlier had attested to the king's fears for the succession and the steps that some would begin taking in the grasp for power that was inevitable upon the accession of a child king.

The earl of Surrey may have spoken accurately when he lauded the skill and royal bloodline of his father, the duke of Norfolk, but he had not been wise. Henry Howard had spoken too freely of plans to set his father up as king in place of Prince Edward when the king died. There was no way to consider this anything less than treason, but Mary prayed that her father would be lenient. Edward would need men like Thomas Howard to guide him when his father could no longer do so.

These morbid thoughts, however, for once could not dampen Mary's joy in the scent of fresh evergreen boughs that were scattered throughout the hall and the roaring fire that lent its cozy warmth. If people were concerned that their king was not present and rumored to be dying, it was not evident in the festive atmosphere of the scene before Mary.

Sipping spiced wine and tempting each other with sweetmeats, those who had joined Mary and Kateryn at Greenwich were enjoying themselves with games of checkers and cards. It was a relief to leave worries behind, if only for a little while, and spend time being thankful for the rich blessings of friends, good food, and luxurious surroundings.

One of Kateryn's small dogs bounded up to Mary, and she happily scooped it up. She snuggled it close and straightened its red velvet collar, trying to avoid the dog's rambunctious kisses. Finally, she gave it a squeeze and placed it back on the floor, its energy too much for her. Brushing loose dog hairs from her emerald colored gown, Mary stepped further into the room and was rewarded by the attention of several people turning in her direction.

Mary knew that the blend of her dark green skirts and sable kirtle suited her well. Rich amber gems studded her slim waistline and collar. Absentmindedly, she caressed the fabric of her long sleeve between her thumb and forefinger, finding comfort in the fine texture.

Kateryn made her way through the crowd to reach Mary's side and give her hand a squeeze. "I have been to the stables and seen your new gelding," Kateryn said with a smile. "It is the most beautiful grey, more of a shimmering silver when freshly groomed."

Mary's grin mirrored her stepmother's. She adored the fine horse that had been a recent gift from her father. "When next we have a fine day for riding, we shall take her out," she said.

Kateryn nodded in agreement as she led the younger woman through the room to tables heaped with food. "I've made sure that your favorites are prepared," she admitted, giving Mary an assessing look, "but you appear healthier than I had anticipated. I am glad, but you can still enjoy the nourishment and comfort that wonderful food brings."

As she was speaking, Kateryn had been loading a gold plate with choice items for Mary. Unable to fit any more upon it, she redirected her to the head table and indicated a chair.

"You care for me as if I were a child," Mary teased, though the demonstration of love filled her with warmth.

"And I will continue to do so until I am completely assured of your recovery," Kateryn said as she pointed a finger at her charge for emphasis.

Laughing, they settled into their seats and selected favorites from the heaping plate. The shocked feeling that accompanied happiness for Mary was beginning to fade, and she had Kateryn to thank. Not only did the woman demonstrate her own affection but she had melted the heart of the king toward his oldest daughter as well. Mary felt, for the first time in many long years, that she could grow accustomed to being happy.

As if sensing her complacency and needing to place her back in the center of tribulation, a page arrived at Greenwich the following day. Seeing her father's green livery, Mary had a sinking feeling that made the evening before feel like a dream. Kateryn invited her to hear the message with her, and Mary could not decide if that was a kindness or if she would rather be left with nothing worse than a sense of foreboding for a little bit longer.

The king had ordered his will brought to him for changes that he wished to make.

The man had said more, but this was the only portion of the conversation that Mary could remember once he stood to leave. Was her father truly so severely ill or was he simply attending to the work of his kingdom? He had not sent for Kateryn or herself, as he surely would if he felt his time remaining in this world was growing short.

"Would he not?"

"Of course, he would," Kateryn assured her, and Mary realized that she had spoken aloud. She smiled weakly that Kateryn had understood to what she referred.

"Let us go to the chapel and pray for your father," Kateryn added, standing with a hand out to Mary.

Mary took it and was willingly led from the room like a child. The cold stones of the chapel were forbidding to some, but Mary found comfort in their solidity. They were as unbreakable and permanent as she had always thought her father was. She fell to her knees upon the unforgiving floor and prayed fervently for the recovery of the king.

January 1547

Mary and Kateryn attempted to gain comfort from their time at prayer and tried to convince each other that the increasing days without news indicated that Henry was fine. The new lines around Kateryn's eyes and dark shadows beneath Mary's evinced their disbelief in the lies. But why did no one come?

"We shall go to Whitehall," Kateryn announced once the days had stretched into a fortnight. She tried to infuse her voice with joy, but even Mary could discern the strain and frustration behind her words.

"I will have our ladies begin packing," Mary agreed without a hint of reluctance. She had been longing to go to her father but did not dare as he had not called for them. Her years spent in the shadow of his disfavor had scarred her more than she cared to admit. However, if she were following the orders of the queen, she was confident about going.

The decision made, neither woman hesitated, and they had their retinue eager to move within days. Horses shifted impatiently and ladies huddled within carriages under layers of blankets. Heated bricks at their feet attempted to ward off the worst of the winter chill. Despite the icy air, everyone seemed to share a keenness to reach Whitehall and gain insight as to the king's condition.

Although Mary would not admit it, not even to Kateryn, she silently prayed that they would arrive in time.

~ ~ ~ ~

The snow-covered miles felt as though they flew past under the silver gelding's hooves. Mary spent some time in a litter with the queen but preferred to ride. She stayed behind one of the few knights with them for protection, allowing his bulk to keep the harshest of the winter wind from chapping her face.

The landscape was beautiful in the way that a cruel woman can intrigue one with a striking appearance. One cannot help but admire, though peril lies close beneath the surface. In this case, the same ice that sparkled like diamonds when it coated the branches of the trees provided what could be a fatal slip when it hid silently beneath the fluffy snow upon the road.

Mary was thankful that the path was well trodden and churned before her mount reached it. Those in the front of their party had the dangerous work of making a way for the rest of them. She wished that they had been able to travel by barge, but unseasonable cold had made the Thames treacherous with ice. Was the very earth preparing to mourn the death of a king?

Did Edward know what was happening? Could he hope to fill the gaping hole that their father would leave? She did not know but prayed answers would be in greater supply once they reached the palace at Whitehall.

Rooms had been prepared for them, and Mary whispered thanks to each person who helped her to get inside where she could warm herself before an enormous fire. Her face felt like the flames were reaching out to touch her as her frozen nerves were revived to life. Stepping into a warm, dry dress, Mary was planning to rush to her stepmother in hopes of an audience with her father as soon as possible.

Kateryn reached her first. As Mary's laces were being tied, the queen strode into the room, frustration painted across her features as Mary had never seen her display.

"He will not see us," Kateryn said, throwing herself to the settle with enough force that it scraped a few inches across the floor.

Mary only gazed at her in confusion. The idea that they

would not be admitted upon arrival had never occurred to her. She opened her mouth, and then clamped it shut again as no words came to her.

"I know that they are hiding something," Kateryn grumbled, "but I do not know why."

"What could there be to hide from us, of all people?" Mary asked, her voice low and raw from cold. "It must mean that my father is not as poorly as some have said." She lowered her voice even further before continuing, "If you were soon to be serving as regent, he would need to see you."

Kateryn appeared to be appraising Mary before she spoke, and Mary felt her cheeks flame from more than the lingering effects of the cold. She knew when people looked at her like that they were trying to decide how much she knew, what she really understood, and if they should try to enlighten her. Kateryn seemed to decide that she would.

"What if he has not named me as regent?" she whispered conspiratorially, leaning close enough for Mary to smell the warm mulled wine on her breath.

Mary jerked away, from the scent and the words. "But who would he choose in your stead? Edward is but nine years old and will need the guidance of a steady and devoted hand . . . if my father does not recover," she hastily added. "He named you regent before, why would he not do so again?"

Kateryn smiled in that way that Mary recognized again. How did others always seem to know more about a situation than she did?

"It is one thing for a king to leave his queen a regent when he is confident in his ability to return to his throne. It is quite another for him to leave the combination of a woman and a child to reign for years without his counsel," Kateryn said with no small amount of venom. "He is cutting me out. God help him if he has removed you and your sister from the succession again as well."

Mary's face fell. The possibility had not occurred to her. "Would he be afraid that Edward is so many years from having children that he wishes to name a male heir? But who?"

Kateryn shook her head in frustration. "I don't know." She stood and began to pace the room. The rushes were fresh and her skirts caused the scents of herbs to swirl through the air. "If only I could gain a few moments with him."

Mary was torn by the frustration she felt and her desire to focus on praying for her father's recovery. Surely, they were taking on concerns that were not meant to be lain upon their shoulders. She wondered if she should suggest that they visit the chapel before doing anything else.

Seeing Mary's despair, Kateryn put on a mask of calmness and placed an arm about Mary's waist. "I am sorry," she said, her tone affectionate. "How could I forget that it is your father we speak of. Your concerns are, quite correctly, not for the governance of the kingdom at the moment. Let us find solace in prayer and leave our concerns in God's hands, for his are much more capable than our own."

Mary smiled and her eyes shone with relief as they walked arm in arm to the chapel.

~ ~ ~ ~

The next day, Mary opened the door to Kateryn's rooms. Her presence had not yet been noticed, and she heard the ladies' chatter before silence struck announcing that she had been. The gold in Mary's eyes appeared to glitter when she looked down her nose at them. She narrowed her eyes to better focus on their faces and it only added to the haughtiness of her glare.

"Where is her grace, the queen?" she demanded.

Mary was surprised when Kateryn's voice came from the corner of the room where rumors were being shared. Her stepmother stood, drawing Mary's eyes to her where they had not found her before. She felt angry and humiliated and considered turning to leave.

"Mary and I would like some privacy," Kateryn said, not sounding flustered at all in contrast to how Mary felt.

The ladies hurried from the room and Mary kept her head down to avoid eye contact with any of them. Therefore, she did not see Kateryn approach her, but did feel her arms go around her.

"I am so sorry, Mary," she whispered.

Mary felt warm breath on her ear and it somehow added to the betrayal. She yanked herself from the embrace.

"How could you talk about my father that way?" she cried.

Kateryn raised a hand as if to reach out to her before changing her mind.

"It is not your father I speak of, but men who I believe are keeping the truth from us," she explained. "I did not share my concerns with you only to spare you more pain. You have endured more than your fair share."

Mary shook her head, angry with Kateryn for her duplicity and herself for the tears that she could not control. Now Kateryn did lay a hand upon her arm.

"Mary, I would give anything to protect you from pain."

"Then how could you say such things?" she repeated.

"Come and sit with me," Kateryn pleaded. "I will share everything with you, though it may include much that you do not wish to hear."

Mary sniffed and wiped her eyes with the back of her hand. Nodding, she allowed herself to be led.

"My dear friend," Kateryn began once they were settled. "I do believe that your beloved father has died and that men who wish to consolidate their power are keeping the truth from us."

Mary could not have been more horrified, and emotions ranging from fury to fear raced across her face.

"I do not believe that any mean us harm," Kateryn quickly reassured her, "but I do think that they may not be following the king's final commands."

"But how can you know this?" Mary asked, shaking her head in wonder, closing her eyes as it began to ache. "His meals are being delivered to his room. Men continue to come and go."

"But they are not admitted," Kateryn interrupted. "Not one has been invited in for the past two days. Not one," she repeated when she saw Mary's lingering doubt. "Only Wriothesley, Seymour, and select others actually enter the king's room."

Mary slouched into the cushions. "But that cannot be . . . How?"

Even as she questioned it, her mind was filling in the blanks. Slowly, she could see how Edward Seymour, might be arranging things for his greatest advantage before his nephew took the throne.

"Yet, he has nothing to fear. Does he?" Mary asked, her mind still working the puzzle. "Seymour was Queen Jane's brother. Edward will likely raise him even higher."

"Your brother is a boy," Kateryn said, becoming insistent as she saw realization dawning. "Seymour will want control, even more than Henry left to him. He is taking it now."

"But what can we do? I thought my father would name you as Edward's regent."

Kateryn was shaking her head before Mary finished speaking. "I told you before. Your father would not trust a woman with such a task. The question is, what were his wishes and what is being done to supplant them?"

"If he has died," Mary pointed out that the most vital question, the one that would change her life more than any other, had not been answered.

She could not believe that a man could die, a king no less, and that grief would not outweigh political scheming. Would these men, who had served Henry for decades, be capable of keeping his death a secret? Looking at Kateryn, more concerned for her place in a world that did not include Henry than the fact that he was gone, Mary realized that they probably could.

~ ~ ~ ~

The conversation with Kateryn prepared Mary for the day when Edward Seymour presented himself not long after. A chill stole through Mary's body at his calm demeanor, and she wondered if he was so tranquil because he had already had days to accept the news of the death of his king.

Mary stood as tall as she could, wishing to make the earl feel small, but he towered over her with his shallow appearance of grief. Rumors had been seeping through every crack and crevice of Whitehall, and the only time Kateryn had been called to see her husband had been days ago. Seymour did not need to say a word for Mary to see that the rumors had been true and he had been keeping her father's death a secret.

The earl of Hertford bowed before Mary and his sandy blond hair fell forward as he did so. He rose and brushed it back, reminding Mary of her brother. This man's nephew. England's new king.

"Seymour," Mary spoke in her most imperious tone. "I believe I know why you asked to see me."

He had the grace to appear guilty, like a child who knows he deserves to be scolded. "Lady Mary," he began apologetically, "it was vital that I bring the news to the king, your brother, first."

And so Mary learned of the death of her father, a man who had always seemed larger than life, indirectly. She did not cry or even move. Seymour was somewhat taken aback by her lack of reaction and his hands fidgeted with the missive he held.

He realized that she was not going to say anything and stumbled over his words for a moment before continuing. "Your beloved father, the king, was called home to God three days hence. With establishing the council that he had commanded to direct Prince Edward . . ."

"King Edward," Mary corrected, still unmoving.

"Yes, of course, King Edward," Seymour stuttered. "I apologize, but I have handled this to the best of my abilities as Lord Protector."

"Lord Protector?" A single auburn eyebrow rose in question.

"Yes, my lady," Seymour's bumbling disappeared and he smiled confidently before her. "God has blessed me with the opportunity to guide my nephew as he rules this great kingdom."

"Indeed."

Seymour's smile disappeared but his confidence did not. "Your brother will be making his way to London as soon as possible, and the council has much to do in preparation."

Mary could tell that these were his departing words to her, but she was not ready to let him go, not with that smug look upon his face when he should be submissive before her. She narrowed her eyes at him, not bothering to hide the fact that she did not trust him or his motives. He cleared his throat and looked like he was struggling to stand still.

Finally, Mary spoke, "I look forward to greeting my brother, the king, when he arrives. Please, do let me know of his arrival before several days pass. Now, I will go to say prayers for the soul of my father, may God receive him as a true prince who spent his life in the almighty's service."

Seymour bowed again, mumbling words of parting that she could not hear. Rising, he swept from the room with the air of one who has taken care of a distasteful chore and can move on to more important tasks.

Mary slowly crossed the room and fell to her knees at her prie-dieu, wondering at the dryness of her eyes. She had known that her father was gone but had still expected the confirming news to break her heart. With a jolt, she realized that part of her believed that her life might improve with her brother on the throne, and guilt washed over her at the thought.

Her father had wounded her heart many times, but he still deserved to be properly mourned. As Mary remembered moments of her childhood when her father praised her as a beautiful princess and more recent times that he had noticed her poise and asked her advice, she began to sob at last for the loss of King Henry VIII.

February 1547

Mary curtseyed low before King Edward VI. Her gown of deep azure pooled around her, glittering with interwoven threads of silver that heavily lined the hem and collar. Edward's coronation had been marked by pageantry and celebrations surpassing anything Mary had ever seen. As she waited for the small boy to raise her up, she prayed that God would bless his reign, that the pains her father had put the country through to gain a male heir would all be worth it.

"Dear sister," Edward said, taking her hand.

Mary stood, keeping her head tilted down toward him, "Your grace," she said and could not keep the smile from stretching across her face. "I have heard some are calling you the new Josiah. May God so bless your reign."

"I do pray so, Mary," Edward replied. "When Elizabeth and I received the news . . ." he trailed off, his eyes seeing the scene of Edward Seymour approaching them at Enfield once again. "I am glad you are here with me now."

Mary thought he looked like he would rather curl up on her lap than attend to the tournaments that would carry on for days in his honor. She would no longer mother him, much as her arms ached to do so. He was now the king and would have to grow up quickly.

Therefore, instead of bundling him into an embrace, Mary directed Edward's attention to the men who were preparing to joust. Though the air held a chill and the ground remained hard from winter frost, the atmosphere was warm and festive. If any continued to mourn the last king, they hid it well as they celebrated the new one.

Edward led Mary to the pavilion that was set up for his use and indicated that she should take the seat at his right side. She did so gladly, knowing that her brother would be more open to her council than their father had been. Together, they would be able to do much good.

Highly decorated men and horses created chaos around them, but they both enjoyed watching the swirls of color, displays of riches, and demonstrations of chivalry. Mary and Edward each pointed out those they admired and laughed as some clumsily warmed up for their matches.

A rosy glow lit up Edward's cheeks and his smile caused a tightness in Mary's chest. She loved this boy and would protect him from those who sought to use him for their advantage.

As if the thought had conjured him, Edward Seymour approached.

"His grace the duke of Somerset," Mary greeted him with a curtsey that was proper yet not overly respectful. Her initial suspicions had been correct, and Seymour had raised himself not just to protectorship but also awarded himself a dukedom.

"Uncle!" Edward greeted the man much more enthusiastically, and Mary felt a creeping fear of what she was up against.

"Your grace," Seymour said with a barely perceptible tip of his head. "Lady Mary."

She bristled again at his informality and knew her disdain must be evident on her face, for he smiled like one who has won a game against an opponent who has only just realized they were supposed to be playing.

"My brother intends to win the day for you, your grace," the new duke of Somerset said to his nephew, pointing out the younger Seymour upon a horse that appeared to be carved from ebony.

"Uncle Thomas has every reason to be confident," Edward

agreed with some wistfulness in his voice. Henry had never allowed the boy to participate in activities that he himself had adored as a young man. A king with one son must take precautions.

Mary let the chatter of Thomas Seymour's attributes flow over her without comprehending them until she heard a word that always caught her attention.

"Excuse me, dear brother," she apologized. "It seems that my mind has wandered."

Edward gave Somerset a look that all men shared when they were faced with female foolishness, and Mary felt her face begin to burn.

"I was just saying," the young king said in a condescending tone, "that the Baron Sudeley needs a suitable wife."

Mary did not yet think of Thomas by his newly acquired title, but mention of a marriage made her recall the moments shared between he and Kateryn before she had become Henry's sixth wife.

"You, too," Edward continued, "find yourself in need of a suitor."

Mary felt her eyes go wide as her mind searched for a reply. Somerset was looking on with amusement. He appeared certain that he would always be one step ahead of the king's sister.

Taking a deep breath, Mary composed herself as she had been trained to do from the time she was a small child. "When the Lord sends me a husband, I will love and honor him as God commands."

However, she was quite certain that Thomas Seymour was not who God had in mind for her. Baron Sudeley indeed.

Thankfully, Edward was content enough with Mary's submission, and Somerset had moved on to other topics that he felt deserved the king's attention. Mary sat quietly by, thinking that perhaps it would be better if she advised Edward from one of her own estates, where she could avoid the schemes of men.

April 1547

As Mary's retinue came to the end of its journey, the appearance of the walls of Beaulieu Palace brought relief. Weary from lingering grief, the anxiety of being at court, and the rigors of the road, Mary looked forward to a rose-scented bath and her spring coverlet.

This estate was as comfortable to her as Whitehall was unsettling. She could advise her brother through letters and avoid conflicts with those who surrounded him. Mary convinced herself this would be more effective, for she knew that her well-being depended upon it.

Her father had provided for her generously in his will, and she was thankful. For the first time, she could live confidently and without fear. As a rich heiress in her own right, she need no longer await the favor of an inconsistent king.

She may be thirty-one and without husband or children, but at least she had her freedom. After how her mother had been treated, it was not a gift she undervalued.

Mary knew that the Seymours were reformists and that they would attempt to coerce her brother to enact greater religious changes than had taken place under their father. As Head of the Church, Edward had the power to make sweeping changes where her father had been largely content to simply not answer to the pope. Mary sighed as she stiffly stepped from the carriage with these thoughts presenting themselves for her to worry over.

Her father had assigned a council to guide Edward, and she would write him often. She had to accept that there was little else she could do and trust that Edward could discern what was best on his own as he matured. Surely, no changes in the Church of England could occur until Edward was of an age to make them, and court was simply not her place.

The power plays and pushes for reform were not the only things Mary was running from. As she smiled to see her household capably unpacking and setting Beaulieu in order, she thought back to her farewell from Kateryn.

They had grown so close in the years since Lord Latimer had died, but now Mary felt as if she hardly knew her. Mary had expected Kateryn to remain with Edward. Though not named to the council as she had hoped, Kateryn would have been given a place where she could serve as mother to the young king.

However, that had not been Kateryn's plan. Apparently satisfied with the inheritance her years with Henry had earned her, Kateryn had quickly moved to her own estate even earlier than Mary had. Since Beaulieu had not been ready for Mary, she had stayed with Kateryn for several weeks. During that time, she had watched a scandalous romance rekindle between Kateryn and Thomas Seymour.

The smile faded from Mary's face as visions of the couple giggling and sneaking away together flashed through her mind. Kateryn deserved happiness and a husband of her own choosing. Mary could not take issue with that, but Kateryn had not seemed to mourn the king beyond his funeral before Thomas was accepted as a caller.

Mary realized that someone was addressing her and shook her head free of remembrances.

"Yes, Fran?" Mary turned her head to the woman she had asked to join her ladies at Beaulieu. Not only was Fran the wife of Edward Waldegrave, nephew of Mary's household controller, but she was the daughter of Edward Neville, who had been executed with Henry Pole. Mary felt it was her duty to give her loyalty to those who had always believed in her.

Fran turned a sweet, heart-shaped face to Mary. A dash of

freckles and strawberry blond ringlets made the woman appear much younger than the one she served, though, in truth, they were separated by only two years. Mary was so accustomed to the elements that weighed down upon her and ruined her looks that she did not even think to be jealous of the lovely, lighthearted woman.

"I've already ordered your bath prepared, your grace," Fran said, and a dimple appeared on her left cheek. "Manchet and wine shall be sent up, and I will send Susan to comb your hair."

Mary felt the tension begin to leave her back and shoulders already. "Thank you, Fran. You are so thoughtful."

Fran tipped her head as if to relay that she was only doing her duty, loosening a few more reckless curls. Then, in a whirl of blue skirts the color of a winter sky, she was gone to see that it was all accomplished according to her exacting standards.

"How can Fran be such a bundle of energy," Susan groaned as she made her way to Mary's side. "I feel as though I will be sore for days. There must be bruises covering every inch of my body."

Mary smiled at her friend's moaning until she heard a low masculine voice offer, "I could perform an inspection to verify that claim."

Susan giggled, but Mary's head spun around to reprimand the one who would dare speak so inappropriately to one of her ladies. Clearly the man had preempted his mistress' reaction because the only evidence of him that remained was the blush upon Susan's face. Mary considered questioning her regarding the source but knew that she would get nowhere, and she was simply too tired to care.

She ignored Susan, who had begun chattering to divert from the man's impropriety. Peering up at the springtime sun and silently pledging to take a walk in the gardens once she was rested,

Mary strode forward and entered the Palace of Beaulieu.

May 1547

The gardens at Beaulieu brought Mary great peace and helped her recover from the death of her father and the stressful months in London. It was the ideal time to enjoy the morning quiet and delicious fragrances as blooms burst forth from their buds. She had placed a small basket over one arm and carried clippers so that she could select a few flowers for her room. There was something about choosing them herself that gave her additional joy each time she looked upon them.

Mary's arrangements were eclectic. She would combine roses and posies one day, daisies with the thorny, yellow flowers her governess had favored the next. Some of her ladies tried to tell her that she did not pair them correctly, but she did not care and ignored their advice. The flowers in her private chamber were whatever caught her fancy on a given day. They made her happy.

The approach of Fran was not unusual so early in the day, but Mary was surprised to see a letter in her hand.

"A messenger already?" Mary asked as she took the offered missive.

"From the Lord Sudeley," Fran replied not even attempting to hide her curiosity or disdain.

"Why would Thomas Seymour write to me?" Mary asked as she broke the seal. "Surely, my brother, has not again mentioned the possibility that we be wed."

Mary's words had slowed and quieted as she scanned the letter's contents.

"I've a feeling it's not that at all," Fran observed.

"No," Mary whispered. "It is worse."

This seemed to impress Fran rather than disturb her. She frowned, but her eyebrows shot up in her eagerness for news. Mary crumpled the paper in her hand and shook her head as if that could change the message. They were alone, but she still scanned the garden to be sure.

"Let us respond to this right away," Mary said and began storming off.

Fran rushed in her wake. "You haven't even told me what it says," she objected breathlessly.

Mary stopped so suddenly that Fran almost tumbled into her. Their eyes met and Fran flinched at the anger she saw there.

"Thomas Seymour has married Kateryn."

They said nothing more until they were in Mary's room, where she was pacing and raging at what had occurred.

"I can believe he would do it," she said, not for the first time, "but Kateryn? How could she?"

Fran shrugged and pressed her lips into a thin line. "She should know better," Fran agreed.

"They ask for my blessing!" Mary cried, shaking the wrinkled letter at her.

"Asking for forgiveness where they knew they could not get permission, if you ask me," Fran observed.

"Well, they will not get it from me," Mary said with a stomp of her foot. "I have loved Kateryn as I have few others, but my father is not cold in the ground and they married without permission of the king. It is he they must beg forgiveness from."

Fran was enjoying the drama of the scandal, but also knew when she should attempt to soothe her mistress. "Now, your grace, as you've said, you love Lady Kateryn. The fact that she asks your blessing, though she doesn't need it, shows that she loves you too."

"Do not come to her defense with me," Mary warned, though her words were absent of venom. "And for a man like Thomas Seymour," Mary said, now sounding more hurt than angry. "He is a rake . . . will break her heart."

"Let us pray that he does not," Fran said, placing a comforting hand on Mary's arm. "Now let's decide how you are going to break this news to your ladies before they start gossiping about it, and then you can puzzle out how you're going to answer that letter."

Breathing deeply, Mary nodded. "You are right. Thank you, Fran. I must also write to Edward to guide him in this matter, though I am certain that Somerset will have his brother's back."

Mary did not know how she was going to announce the marriage of her father's widow not six months after his death, but she straightened her back, said a silent prayer, and determined to handle it like a princess.

July 1547

Following terce, Mary wandered the grounds wondering if she would ever recover from what felt like a betrayal by one of the few people she had dared to get close to. Kateryn had been more than a stepmother to her. She had not shared that sort of friendship with anyone else in her life, but Kateryn clearly had not seen anything special in it.

The cheerful sun and burst of colors in the flowerbeds escaped Mary's notice as she walked without seeing the beauty surrounding her. Thomas and Kateryn had belatedly received King Edward's blessing upon their marriage. What else was he to do when his uncle and stepmother had already consummated their relationship? Mary did not blame him for what was a good political decision, but she could not yet extend the same forgiveness herself.

Her note to the couple had been passively aggressive, claiming that she had no knowledge of wooing matters. As a maiden in mourning for her father, she knew little how to respond to the news. She was sure that the arrow had hit Kateryn's heart but that Thomas had laughed it off. She had received no further correspondence from them.

"Am I so easy to set aside?" Mary asked a rose as she plucked sunburnt leaves from its stem. The red and the white of the bloom touched but did not seem to truly blend, each color stubbornly keeping to itself. It caused Mary to contemplate the reason for the creation of the new Tudor rose, but it mattered little for all who had fought under the red and white roses were gone now.

Mary was pleased to see her chamberlain, Robert Rochester, approaching her. His long stride took him through the gardens with as little notice as Mary's slow shuffling had. His sense of purpose set her heart beating a little faster, and she welcomed anything that would take her mind off her sense of rejection and loneliness.

"Your grace," Rochester said with a respectful bow. "I meant to speak with you directly after mass but was occupied by my nephew." He smiled as he stood in clear admiration of the younger man. "I believe that you could not have a more staunch admirer than Edward Waldegrave, your grace. He was concerned about some members of the household not seen at mass. Knowing that you expect us all to keep the hours, he felt that he should point it out as direct disloyalty to you."

Mary returned his smile. "It is nice to know that he is so concerned for the spiritual health of my household." She could not say that it felt wonderful to be appreciated and defended, but the satisfied feeling spread within her just the same. "Please tell him that I am well pleased with his service. I shall also tell Fran when I see her. She should be proud of her husband."

"As I am sure she is," Rochester agreed. "Unfortunately, what I have sought you out for is decidedly less pleasant. It may be advantageous for us to discuss the most recent news from court within the study."

Already waving aside the idea, Mary moved to a garden bench and indicated that he should join her. He did so without argument. Rochester only made suggestions once and then trusted Mary to know her own mind.

"It is your brother, the king," he started, but then amended, "or rather, it is his council. A comprehensive list of reforms is being introduced, or may have already been. It is what we have feared, your grace."

"They command changes in the Church using my brother as their puppet," Mary said, seeming to physically deflate with the words. "He is not yet mature enough to have come to these decisions on his own. Perhaps I should return to his side to provide guidance and spiritual council. I am his godmother and am responsible for his growth in the faith."

Rochester almost reached out to pat her hand but pulled back before taking that improper step. "I am not certain that it would have changed anything had you been there, your grace," he soothed, "and your health would have suffered."

She awarded him with a weak smile. "You know that I have not the stomach for court scandal and manipulations, but he is my brother."

"He is king," Rochester quietly corrected. The stern look he gave her reminded her of tutors she had when she was younger. Then he relaxed and it was Mary who was the authority again. "I fear that reforms will make it impossible for us to practice our faith as we always have."

"No," Mary stood, too passionate to remain seated. "Those who pretend that my brother is the clay that they would form into their own image will never take my faith from me. Better that I give my life for God than that I live it in a false, damning religion."

She had turned and stalked toward her rooms. Just as Rochester rose to follow, she turned on him. "This will not do. I will write to my brother and the council pointing out the folly of their ways and the disrespect that it is to my father's memory to make such changes to the church he established. If any corrections are to be made, we should be reconciling with Rome, not pulling further away."

"Yes, your grace," Rochester said submissively, attempting to follow her and stop when she did to emphasize a point.

"And we shall write to my uncle," she commanded with the final pause before she made her way inside.

Charles, the Holy Roman Emperor, may not have become Mary's husband as she had once hoped, but he was her best ally in the faith. Who better to help guard her from the evils of the Reformation that were spreading like a contagion across Europe? With Mary's fervently written words, she prayed for him to come to her support before her brother's councilors caused irreparable damage.

Once it was done, she gave it over to Rochester's capable hands to see that it was sent upon its way. All earthly steps she could discern tended to, Mary went to her knees to request heavenly help.

August 1548

A lute in her hands and late summer sun streaming through the window should have put Mary in higher spirits. However, her fingers fumbled on familiar tunes and the bright rays were making her head ache. Setting the instrument aside, she pressed her fingers to her temples, though she knew it would make no difference. Once the pain began, days abed awaited her.

The loss of Kateryn to her new husband and her brother to a hovering circle of councilors had affected Mary more than she could say to the ladies who attended her at Beaulieu. She had none whom she could truly confide in, and letters to Charles simply could not fill the emptiness left by her lack of close companion.

Kateryn was now with child and spending her lying in time at Sudeley. Mary was determined to go to her. She prayed fervently for Kateryn's health and safety, for childbearing was always dangerous, even more so when the first time mother was thirty-six years of age. Her concern enabled Mary to set aside any disagreements she may have had with Kateryn and attend her during her time of need.

The painful throbbing increased in Mary's head, and she slowly rose, knowing that she must get to her bed before it became incapacitating. Her physician's orders would be strictly followed on this occasion to ensure her ability to fulfil her vow to repair her relationship with Kateryn before the babe was born.

"Susan," Mary called. Although the woman was not within her sight, she knew that she was never far away. "Please help me undress. I am unwell and wish to retire early."

"You poor thing," Susan tutted as she quickly appeared at Mary's side. "I will see you to bed and call for the physician."

"I would also hear mass," Mary insisted, knowing that the time for vespers would be upon them shortly.

"Of course," Susan soothed. She did not agree with Mary continuing to keep her household according to the old traditions when reforms were cascading across the land, but she assumed that the king's sister could get away with things that everyday Englishmen could not.

"And my writing desk," Mary added as Susan unlaced her gown and prepared her for bed. "I would write to Kateryn while I am still able. It may give her some comfort to know that I plan to come to her."

"Surely, it will," Susan agreed complacently.

"Thank you," Mary whispered as she found relief in her soft mattress. She was asleep before either priest or writing materials arrived.

When she did awake, Mary was disappointed that she felt worse rather than better. Aches pervaded her joints, and any movement was agony. Still, her chaplain was able to say mass which gave her some comfort. After all, what was her agony compared to the suffering of Christ?

She would bear it as best she could but was forced to accept that her visit to Kateryn must be delayed. During a few moments when she felt well enough to pen a few lines, Mary wrote a short missive to Kateryn with her hopes that she would join her at Sudeley soon.

Tears filled Mary's eyes as she signed her name, so deep was her disappointment. After so many months away from each other, it was these forced days that seemed unfair. She carefully swept the tears away before they could fall and stain or smear the ink. She handed the letter to Susan with strict instructions on seeing it delivered as soon as possible, and sent her silent prayers after it.

September 1548

Finally, Mary was up from her bed and regaining her strength. She hardly took note of the changing autumn landscape that she usually loved to admire. The natural show of color that easily outshone the effort of any artist passed largely unnoticed. Instead, Mary was obsessively creating a mental list of what must be done to see her on her way to Sudeley.

She had sent for Susan so that packing could commence, but the woman arrived with a forlorn look upon her features and Rochester at her elbow. Mary's gaze moved suspiciously from one to the other, wondering which would give her news that was clearly not something she wished to hear. Mary's mind automatically began scrolling through the names of her loved ones and asked God to protect them, though she knew it was too late.

"What is it?" she demanded, seeing that the two were each waiting for the other to speak. Mary's heightened anxiety gave her insufficient patience to wait.

Rochester stepped forward, "A messenger from Lord Sudeley, your grace," he said with the hesitation of one who must inflict pain that they wished they need not.

"No," Mary whispered, her hand reaching behind her for support. Susan rushed forward and guided her to a cushioned chair, murmuring words of empty comfort.

Rochester fell to his knees before her. "It is her grace, the queen dowager," he said, failing to keep the catch of emotion from his voice. His head was bowed low, in respect and to hide his tears. "You have my deepest sympathy, your grace," he continued so quietly that Mary almost asked him to speak louder. It did not matter. She knew what he was going to say. "Lady Kateryn was delivered of a girl on the last day of August, but the mother has given her life in exchange for that of the child."

Mary closed her eyes as if it could keep her from hearing the words. "The child?" she asked.

"Said to be in the best of health at the time the messenger was sent," Rochester assured her. "She is given the name Mary in honor of your grace."

On hearing this Mary could not control the sob that left her thin body. Kateryn had loved her and forgiven her obstinacy at the end. It was a gift she did not deserve, but it gave her some small comfort in her mourning.

Susan was there, shushing and offering a handkerchief. Mary allowed herself to be wrapped up in the woman's arms, feeling that there was no one else who was left to embrace her.

Mary had not recovered her health sufficiently to bear the depression that enveloped her upon hearing of Kateryn's death. Therefore, it was a cousin, Jane Grey, who served as chief mourner at the funeral. Hearing news of the service some days after it had occurred, Mary was disappointed to learn that it had been conducted in the new faith.

Thinking back on the hours of conversation that she and Kateryn had shared on the topic of faith, Mary wondered if it had been Kateryn's wishes or Thomas following the letter of the law in order to ingratiate himself with his nephew, the king.

Her brother. Mary felt that she had failed him, as a sister and a godmother. She could remember the celebrations that had taken place at his birth. He was the long awaited son and heir, entrusted from birth with future of the church their father had created. How had things turned out so wrong?

Mary remained away from court because of the reforms that flowed from Edward's council. She communicated with him by letter because she was afraid of the consequences should she personally confront the king and his circle on the rejection of the mass and other blasphemy that was falling upon the land.

Just thinking about it could send her to bed for days. She must regain her strength and find a way to return to court. Her brother needed her, before it was too late.

March 1549

Rochester held out a cheaply bound book to Mary, and she reached for it with confusion clear on her face.

"It is the proposed new prayer book," he answered her unasked question. "The king will be introducing it within months, but a working copy has been made for your perusal."

He did not meet her eyes as he said this, and Mary discerned that it would be best not to inquire as to the source of the book. A casual glimpse through it told her that it was made up of the heretical philosophy that she had been concerned about her brother falling too deeply into.

Mary cursed herself as she flipped through the pages. She had not felt well enough to attempt traveling to court all winter, and now she held the evidence of her neglect in her hands. Edward had ignored the words that she had painstakingly written to him and created a book that offered the directions for blasphemous services that would take place throughout the kingdom.

"What shall I do?" Mary whispered as her fingers traced the lines of print. She glanced up at Rochester, but he was looking to her for instructions rather than offering advice. "We will not worship according to this in my household. 'As for me and my house, we shall serve the Lord,'" she insisted.

Rochester nodded gravely. This is what he expected her to say, but what would be the consequences? "Will that be safe?" he asked.

Mary's eyes widened as if she had not considered that there might be consequences. After all, she was the king's sister. But this book was his law, she realized. What would he do to enforce it?

She thought of her father and how he had finally forced her to give in and sign away the rights that her mother had fought so hard for her to keep. "No, I will not give in to this," she stated, shoving the book away from her. "I will stand firm in the true faith and be an encouragement to others who desire to do the same."

"God give you strength, your grace," Rochester said with a shadow of a smile.

After Rochester left her, Mary reached for the book again. Her heart broke to see the changes in worship that her brother had been manipulated into making. She should have been there to guide him. It was a sin she must confess, but what could she do to remedy it now, she wondered.

She set the book aside and pulled out her writing tools. This was a concern she had to take to one of the few people remaining to her whom she trusted for advice. Her cousin Charles would tell her what she should do.

As Mary scratched the words to the Holy Roman Emperor, she wondered if she should leave England and go to his kingdom where worship in the true faith was celebrated. Her fear of her future in Edward's England intensified each time she looked at that devilish book. A messenger was immediately dispatched with the letter. Mary would not feel at ease until she received a response from Charles with advice that she was certain would be sound.

August 1549

Discontent and revolt had met Edward's religious reforms to such an extent that Mary's fears for herself proved unnecessary. There was no time to be spent on bullying the king's sister into proper religious observances when the Seymour brothers were fighting for supremacy and Norfolk was in rebellion.

Still, Mary kept from court. She debated with herself whether her duty was to shine the light of true faith where she was, leave England for the marriage her cousin suggested to Dom Luis of Portugal, or attempt to advise and sway her brother. In the end, she did nothing, frozen by indecision.

By others she was encouraged to join the growing contingent intent on removing Somerset from his pinnacle of power. He now reigned like a king, but Edward would soon be of an age to not need him at all. Many were too impatient to wait, but Mary would not get involved in these devious machinations, even if they might benefit her in the end.

Mary had even been offered the regency during her brother's remaining minority, but she had made it clear that she did not desire this. Usurping her brother's power would not win his heart or his mind, and it simply was not her place to attempt to rule over him. She only prayed that with Somerset removed, Edward would gain the maturity and independence of mind to redeem the errors that had been made in his name.

John Dudley was Mary's second reason for declining to become involved. He was the earl of Warwick and had led the coup to rid Edward of Somerset, but Mary was certain that he had less than honorable intentions. She would be no tool of a man led by ambition rather than God. He frightened her in a way that no one besides her father ever had, and she prayed her brother was equipped to handle him for she worried that she was not.

February 1550

It was not until the following spring that Mary was in good health and strengthened by the encouragement of Charles V. She finally made her way to London to visit her brother and discuss her future. Enough time had been wasted keeping to herself on her Anglian estates. For both their sakes, she ordered her household made ready for travel.

The chill was already giving way to the warm of spring, and Mary hoped that indicated a pleasant summer and bountiful harvest. England groaned under the burdens of heavy taxation and Edward's enclosure policies. Both made it increasingly difficult for the common man to support his family. Good weather could make all the difference.

Mary took a deep breath of the cool morning air as she stepped into her litter. A caravan of attendants, wagons, and guards began to wind their way out of the courtyard and onto the road toward London as a pale sun rose in the frosted sky.

The household had just heard lauds together, and now they left this one bastion of faith where it was still given. In Edward's London, worship was ruled by the book that had frightened Mary into staying away as long as she had. But no more. She would confront her brother and offer him the love and guidance he so desperately needed.

She closed the curtains of her litter and burrowed into thick blankets with a warmed stone at her feet. Nothing would be missed by veiling herself from the bleak winter landscape. Instead, she planned to spend the time in prayer and contemplation, so that she would be prepared and confident when they arrived.

Before Mary was ready, she heard the excited conversations that indicated that the city was in sight. The hours had rushed by, and soon she would see her brother. For a moment, she considered him only as her brother, rather than a young king. It would be pleasing to see how tall and strong he had grown and hear how much his voice had deepened. Mary felt forgotten love for Edward overflow in her chest, and she realized that she was glad that she had come.

Now that they had arrived, Mary did not wish to delay any longer. Leaving her gentlewomen to prepare the rooms and unpack, she went to visit her brother. The corridor was cold and the sound of Mary's footsteps echoing around her gave her an unexplainable sense of foreboding.

The feeling did not decrease when Mary was left in the outer chamber for an unusual amount of time as courtiers far beneath her own status filed in and out of the presence chamber. Mary sat with her spine stiff and head held high. She was cold, but willed herself to not shiver or appear uncomfortable. Maybe she had misjudged her brother and depended too much upon their shared past to maintain their bond.

The temperature dropped as the sun disappeared below the line of windows, and Mary could not control the fidgeting of her frozen fingers within the folds of her skirts any longer. She reached for her rosary and it felt like ice in her hands. Still, the motion soothed her and eventually generated some warmth.

She would not wait for someone like John Dudley to come out and inform her that the king did not have time for her. Before he could have that satisfaction, Mary stood, ignoring the pain that shot through her stiff joints as she moved after sitting for so long in the chilly room. Without speaking to anyone who remained, she strode out at a dignified pace, as though it were her who had decided that she need not see the king that day.

For the next two days, Mary repeated the process of going and presenting herself, only to be ignored by Edward. She did not complain or attempt to use her position to gain entrance to the presence chamber. She sat there silently each day and waited. The only thing she did differently was to take a pair of warm gloves so that her hands did not become sore with cold.

Mary was preparing to leave once more without having seen Edward when Dudley took half a step out of the connecting room and gestured for Mary to join him. Coming to her feet slowly, not as if she had been waiting for hours for this opportunity, she walked through the door as if the earl of Warwick was not there. Before he could close the door behind her, Mary had curtseyed low before her younger brother.

He did not immediately raise her up, but Mary was content to endure the minor indignity. When he did indicate that she should stand, Mary gracefully did so while keeping her head submissively tipped down.

"It gives me great joy to see you, your grace," she said, and discovered that she meant it with all her heart. "You look well, my brother," she added with a smile that he did not return.

"You have waited a long time to see me," Edward said in a voice that was still childishly high pitched though he attempted to appear manly in clothes that were smaller versions of the rich outfits their father had worn. "You must have something you wish to say besides observing that I am not sickly."

Mary could not control her shock, and she involuntarily shifted away from him.

"Indeed, we have much to talk about, your grace." Her reply was dripping with false cheer. "We have been apart for far too long and I would spend some time with my dear brother, if you can spare some time away from your duties, of course."

Edward appeared uncertain and his eyes shifted to Dudley. Before the earl could offer his advice, Mary spoke again.

"There is much that I would tell you, and I am eager to hear of your plans."

Edward considered this for a moment before he dismissed Dudley with the twitch of his finger, and Mary allowed herself a grin. When Warwick was gone, she moved closer to Edward and laid a familiar hand upon his arm.

"I apologize that I have not been able to visit you more often, my dear brother. My poor health has troubled me too much for travel, and, of course, I would never seek your company if I believed that I might carry a contagion."

"Of course," he repeated as his eyes moved from the hand that touched him to her face. His examination was unsettling, and Mary wondered what had happened to the exuberant little boy she remembered.

"It has given me great joy to receive your letters," Mary continued as if her brother were participating actively in the discussion rather than peering at her as if he were determining whether or not he could trust his own sister.

Sighing deeply, he finally said, "Unfortunately, I cannot say the same of yours." His expression of displeasure reminded her vividly of their father, and Mary's hopes sank.

"I am told that you continue to have the mass said within your chapel, despite my laws to the contrary," he said with emphasis on the 'my' that could not be missed.

"I would eagerly discuss that topic with you, my dear brother," Mary replied, her words coming too quickly in her nervousness. "As your godmother and older sister, it is surely my duty to guide you in religious matters, but it distresses me more than anything else that I have failed you in this."

She would have continued babbling in this vein, but Edward cut her off with an upheld hand and his own voice. "I am king, and it is your duty to advise me in nothing." He took in her shocked expression, and then carried on more kindly. "You perceive me to be a small child, but, as you can see, that is no longer the case. I will soon rule in my own right, and you must accept that. I have not been misled into my reforms, neither will I see them ignored."

Mary was dumbstruck. This was not going according to her plan at all, and she realized with dismay that she no longer knew her younger brother. Seeing her struggle, Edward took pity on his sister, who looked so much older than he remembered.

"As you have said, we have long been absent from one another. Let us enjoy meal together and amend that." Edward did not wait for Mary to respond. He was already ringing a bell that immediately brought a servant to see to his wishes.

By the time Mary returned to her rooms an hour later, she was sure of nothing that had brought her so confidently before the king, and he had not given her permission to continue mass at her home.

However, Mary was not willing to give up. Edward may believe that, at the ripe age of twelve, he was equipped to provide her with spiritual guidance, but she did not. She also saw that he was not open to changing his mind at the moment, for it would mean the king's word was fallible. Her strategy must be adjusted.

The next day, when she went to visit Edward again at the appointed time, Mary's words were better prepared. After a few moments of small talk, Mary plunged into the first of her two topics.

"Our good friend, the Holy Roman Emperor has presented me with a marriage offer," Mary said. She did not allow her reluctance to leave England to color her voice. No sacrifice was too much for her faith, so if leaving her home was the solution God proposed she would accept it. "He suggests Dom Luis of Portugal," she added when Edward did not speak.

The king's face was stony, and Mary waited for him to reply, clutching her hands together to keep herself from filling the silence with unnecessary words.

"The match is unacceptable," Edward stated without explanation.

Mary did not argue, partly because she did not dare, but mostly because she had a preferred solution to offer. She dipped her head to Edward in acceptance of his judgement.

"I am content to privately practice my faith then until you come of age and God has prepared you to make decisions of religion for the entire kingdom," she said.

Edward seethed. Her submissive tone had not worked to soften the message. "Yet I have already done just that," he pointed out. "Do not think that you can disobey me because you are my father's daughter. Indeed, that should ensure your steadfast loyalty."

"I am disloyal to you in no manner," Mary objected. "However, I would have it be your ruling that I obey rather than that of councilors who plot to deceive and manipulate you. When you rule in your own right, I am entirely prepared to submit to your laws."

Edward's color deepened, and Mary thought this must have been what their father looked like when he was a young boy in a rage.

"I have already ruled on this topic," he stated. "If you continue to break the law, I will not protect you from your fate."

"Edward!" Mary cried. "I am your sister."

"Familial status has not always protected traitors from just punishment," he said coldly.

Mary could only stare at him as she considered the truth of this. Her own dear governess, Lady Margaret Pole, had been executed, as had that lady's father, brother, and oldest son, regardless of, or perhaps because of, their close connections to the throne. Her mother's fate had not been much different, though she had been the anointed queen.

This was not working. She would have to escape. With this thought at the forefront of her mind, Mary curtseyed low before the boy king, mumbling her submission and farewell. Her tears were falling before she had escaped the room, but she did not bother to hide them. She rushed back to her own apartment and ordered her household to pack. It was time to leave London.

June 1550

Mary had not quickly recovered from her disappointment at the hands of her brother. Since returning to Woodham Walter, Mary had contrived plans and written to Charles, begging for his assistance in her escape.

Now, the time had come. The Holy Roman Emperor had acquiesced to her wishes, and a small fleet would soon arrive, their mission to whisk Mary away. She would live out her days at Charles' court, though she despaired at leaving Edward to his fate if he carried on his heretical ways. Still, when she remembered her mother's impoverished, lonely death, Mary assured herself that she was doing what she must.

Whispers had crept through the district that Mary was plotting to leave the kingdom. It was impossible with a household the size of hers to prepare for such a feat without some rumors spreading, but no one from the king had arrived. If news had reached Edward, he had not taken it seriously.

Mary paced the corridors of her estate. There were more productive tasks that she could be attending to, but she could bring her mind to focus on none of them. Instead, she found herself memorizing the precise color of the region's bricks and the smell of honeysuckle, for she was afraid that she would forget these small details of her daily life that would not exist in her new world.

Pain was her constant companion since leaving her brother. The headaches had been like nothing she had experienced before, even when she lost her mother. She had grown pitifully thin, because most food nauseated her. Mary would not trouble herself or others over this though. Soon, she would be relaxing in the Low Countries, at peace and snacking on fresh oranges.

The idyllic image brought a smile to her face. She deserved some peace in her life. If her brother was as independent and astute as he claimed, she need not feel that she was abandoning him.

She was not sure how many circuits of the corridors she had completed when Rochester found her. Before he uttered a word, she could see that the news had arrived and her deliverance was at hand.

"Ships have been spotted," he whispered. His handsome brow was creased with worry, and Mary felt some guilt for the stress that she put him through.

"You have served me more loyally than any other," Mary said. She had the urge to put a hand to his face to soothe the tension in his rigid expression, but it would not have been proper. Her words served to soften his clenched jaw a bit, and that would have to suffice.

"I would be willing to suffer death for my faith if that was what I felt God was calling me to do," she added, though she owed him no explanation. "England is no longer a place for me."

Rochester nodded with his lips pressed into a thin line to hold back any disagreement he might have given voice to. He had agreed to go with her, for as much as he was uncertain of the plan he would leave no one else responsible for Mary's safety.

"Let us then be about our business," he said. There was no reason for him to say more. The plot had been discussed at length. Four ladies had been chosen to accompany the princess, but they would carry little with them. Disguised as commoners, they would leave Woodham by boat and meet the Spanish ships. It was deceivingly simple.

Mary spun, her skirts stirring the rushes, and fled to her room. As soon as she entered, she dismissed all except the four she trusted to travel with her.

"Fran, our clothes," she ordered, sending the woman

scurrying without further instructions needed. "Susan, the jewelry."

They could not carry anything of great size or weight, so Mary's precious jewelry would be distributed among them. Besides the largess of Charles V, it is all they would have to live upon.

A few other frantic whispers sent the ladies to their preassigned tasks, and they were ready in less than an hour to depart. Part of Mary was thrilled by the adventure, but her guts were twisted with anxiety and uncertainty that she could not alleviate.

Rochester arrived to lead them to the water's edge. He was confronted by five pale faces with wide eyes following him from under dark wool hoods. "Are you ready?" he asked.

"Yes," Mary said with much more confidence than she felt. "God be with us."

"Amen," the four other women murmured as they left the room in a somber single file line.

Mary was thankful that her head had cleared as she followed Rochester's broad form, yet she was still plagued by a growing sense that something was wrong. The small party left the manor for the canopy of stars and darkness of night, and their path was clear. No one on watch noticed them to inquire who they were or what their business was. Through the summer foliage, they made their way to the pier that stretched out into the river.

The boat that was usually utilized for trips to the port town of Maldon was bobbing upon the low waves. Besides the fact that they were leaving in the dead of night, there would be no reason to suspect this boat when it took their intended course. Once they reached Maldon, their success was assured by the presence of Charles' warships.

Rochester stood at the side of the boat, ready to hand the

women across the span between the dock and the vessel. He had not spoken the words, but his countenance told Mary that he retained doubts. She stiffened her spine and told herself to stop second-guessing.

In a moment, she was on the boat, her ladies huddled tightly around her more to soothe their fear than to ward off chill. Mary realized that the summer night was mild and pleasant. It seemed odd that it had taken her so long to notice.

The boat was rowed by Rochester and a younger man he had chosen to assist him. No one spoke as they made their way up the dark river. Mary marveled that the water's vivid turquoise of day was replaced by an oily black at night. The murky river was more eerily threatening than the same calming scene in the warm summer sunshine.

In that darkness, Mary's imagination conjured up images of a gloomy hell that remained in shadow despite the inferno of flames. Souls in agony twisted and screamed in eternal pain that nothing could soothe. Mary closed her eyes in vain as the images continued to dance upon the back of her eyelids. Her brother's face appeared upon one of the wraithlike figures being tortured by the demons, and his eyes bored into her accusingly.

You have left me to this fate, his face seemed to say. Mary's eyes flashed open, and the vision disappeared. It was replaced once again by the disapproving countenance of Rochester and her terrified ladies. She searched the dark water for answers as their boat silently cut through its surface.

That darkness would not only swallow up her brother and his evil advisors. Mary started counting the little waves, pretending that they were Englishmen who followed her brother's heresies to their doom. Squeezing her eyes shut, her face crumpled in mental anguish.

"I cannot do it," she announced.

When no one responded, Mary wondered if she had not spoken the words aloud. She forced her eyes open, and found that her ladies were looking to her in confusion. Then her gaze met Rochester's and found understanding. He had stopped rowing, and now gave a signal to the young man to halt as well.

"I cannot leave my people to this future," Mary repeated more confidently. "Whatever I can do, I must, though it may cost my very life."

Rochester nodded his approval as the women embraced Mary with happy exclamations and the boat was turned around. Mary wondered how upset Charles would be that she had changed her mind at the last moment, with his ships there waiting to receive her, but she found that she did not care. A great peace had enveloped her when she made her decision, and she knew that God had plans for her yet in the kingdom of England.

July 1550

Mary's certainty regarding the abandoned escape waned as the days went by. Pressure came from the Spanish ambassadors for her to recommit herself to the plan before the fleet must be recalled.

"It would be impossible for me to go now," Mary insisted when Jehan Debois attempted to salvage the risky and expensive venture. He had no desire to go to his emperor and inform him that the entire escapade had been thwarted by a young woman's vacillation.

"Your grace," Debois pleaded. His power to keep his frustration from his voice was failing. "Your passage is secured as if God himself has cleared the way for you."

"But God is not leading me to take that path," Mary explained calmly. "I thank you and wish for you to extend my thanks to his grace, but I simply cannot leave the country that I was born to serve."

Debois swept the cap from his head and crushed it in his hands to vent his frustration. "You understand that several of the king's advisors are encouraging him to place you under arrest. Some even wish to pursue your execution."

Mary felt a stirring of fear. She did know, of course, and this was not the first time that Debois had reminded her, but the image of her brother lost forever to the depths of hell had scared her more.

"It shall be an honor to give my life for my faith if that is what God calls me to do," she insisted and was thankful that her voice carried strong and clear without the hesitation that she felt deep in the pit of her stomach.

Rochester stepped forward. It was possible to forget that he was in the room when he stood in the background at Mary's beck and call. She was glad for his support now.

"I believe her grace has made her decision clear," he said. There was no threat or anger in his voice, but the finality seemed to break through Debois' arguments.

"Very well," the Spanish ambassador sighed. He bowed low to Mary and left to call off the secret mission. Their princess did not want rescuing.

Mary stood and turned to Rochester. "Thank you for all that you have done for me," she whispered, "even when you did not agree."

They shared knowing smiles, and Rochester performed his own bow before following Debois from the chamber.

Mary released a deep breath as she stared unseeingly at the door they had both recently stepped through. She was afraid. That could not be denied, but she was also confident that she must serve her country until the end of her days. If that meant that they would be short under the heretical reign of her brother, God's will be done.

She moved purposefully to her prie-dieu and committed herself wholeheartedly to whatever mission it was that God had in mind for her. When the image of Spanish summer and bowls of oranges slipped into her mind, she firmly shoved it aside.

December 1550

Sweat trickled down Mary's sides despite the winter chill. She had been invited to spend Christmas with her brother, but it felt more like she had been summoned for judgement. Fervent prayer had been her constant companion since the last Spanish ship left English shores that summer.

Charles would not attempt to liberate her again after that debacle. Mary was on her own in a hostile land. It was easy to fool herself into thinking that it was not so when she was cloistered away on her own estates with her household contentedly keeping the liturgical hours and attending mass, but her arrival at court had been a harsh reminder that the rest of the kingdom had changed.

Edward had not welcomed her yet, so she waited patiently, trusting the Holy Spirit to give her the words that would lead to reconciliation with her brother. He was thirteen now, a man and a king. She must tread lightly if he was to listen to her advice. She had closed her eyes to focus on breathing deeply to calm herself when she heard a man say her name.

It was a deep voice that she did not recognize. I have been away for a long time, she reflected as she opened her eyes and struggled to focus them on the figure that was just far away enough to give her trouble, especially with the sunlight streaming in behind him. Mary blinked as the realization struck her.

"Edward?"

He was taller, though not yet broad. His deep tone had some of the strength of their father's. Edward was no longer a little boy. Though Mary had known this, the physical proof of it astounded her.

She fell into a graceful curtsey, quickly composing herself, and he promptly raised her up. Mary had to look up several inches higher than before if she were to meet his gaze. A lump formed in her throat, and she swallowed it. Her words had been planned for guiding a child, but this was an intelligent young man before her.

"I have greatly looked forward to seeing you again," Edward said, covering for her lost words. He indicated that she should regain her seat, and she thankfully did so. His frank examination of her features made her uncomfortable, and she found herself fidgeting for her rosary.

Edward's eyes fell upon it, and any remaining remnant of childhood hardened in his countenance.

"You insist upon your heresy," he observed without raising his voice. Mary remembered how that had made their father all the more frightening. It was easier to dismiss the ranting of one who had lost their temper, but the calm disappointment froze her entrails.

Edward continued when she still failed to speak. "You have been reminded that the mass is outlawed in my kingdom."

Mary could only nod. She did not drop the beads, feeling that would somehow draw even more attention to them.

"I have sent many representatives to you to request that you observe the law of the land. This grace has been extended to you out of the great love and respect that I have for you as my beloved sister."

He had grown quite wise, Mary noticed. All of the correct words carried a subtle emphasis that let Mary know just how much she had disappointed him. She struggled to clear her throat to respond, but he was not done.

"Would you force me to make an example of you?" he asked, searching her face. "Is that what you want?"

"No, your grace," she managed to whisper.

His eyes narrowed as he weighed this response. "It is not

your desire to become a martyr for your faith?"

She shook her head. "It is not my desire, but if it is God's then his will be done," Mary said, and she was glad that her voice had grown confident and assured.

Edward leaned back in his chair with the shadow of a smirk upon his lips. "Indeed," he said. After a moment, he added, "And I am God's anointed. Surely, you would agree with that."

"Yes," Mary quickly agreed. "Yet, not all who guide you are."

He tilted his head as though considering this. Mary realized that his control over anger was not as similar to their father's as she had initially believed. Edward was a deep thinker, not given to spontaneous rages, while Henry had used his simmering quietness for effect.

"That is true, of course," Edward admitted after a moment of reflection. "They are no more chosen by God than you are."

Mary's head jerked back reflexively. This was not a tactic she had anticipated.

"Therefore, you can appreciate," Edward continued, "that I have taken into consideration the advice and opinions of many people who are equally qualified – or unqualified – to advise one who is God's anointed. Yet, you continue to disobey me and hold your opinion higher than your king's."

Her lips formed a thin, tight line, as Mary considered what she should say. Edward was confusing her. What seemed so clear when she was at prayer became fuddled under his intellectual appraisal.

"God's truth is not a matter of opinion," she managed, though she sounded less certain than before.

"Hmmm..." Edward was thoughtful again. His long, slender fingers steepled under his chin as he narrowed his eyes to consider her.

Mary's confidence was given a nudge by his seeming willingness to consider other ideas. "The true faith has been practiced since the time of our Savior," she pressed. "Do you believe that men, who have only recently devised these reforms, have greater knowledge than those who walked with Christ himself? We must hold fast to the faith of our ancestors if we are to enjoy the treasures of heaven and lead our kingdom in righteousness."

Edward's face reddened, and Mary knew that she had said something wrong.

"It is MY kingdom," he stated firmly. "You are my dear sister, but you are not my queen. You will never be queen, and you reach too high if you hope to offer correction to your king."

Edward had not moved, but his entire body exuded a tension that reminded Mary of lions in the menagerie. She cursed herself for her choice of words. The rest of her argument had been lost upon Edward because of one little word.

"My deepest apologies," Mary cried, falling to her knees before her brother. "I only wish to serve you in any way that I can in bringing people closer to God."

She lowered her head and halted her words, no longer able to continue through her tears. When Edward spoke, he sounded unmoved.

"You dishonor God with these superstitions that you claim glorify him. You freely disobey me, your king, and refuse true worship. If out of nothing more than your love for me, I urge you to cease this doubly damning error."

Mary felt within the folds of her skirt for her rosary as her mind searched for a response, but Edward did not wait for one.

"I suggest that you follow my command to put an end to the

mass upon your estates. It does not bode well for a king to be disobeyed by his own family. In fact, your rank magnifies your offense. Do not make the mistake of believing that I cease to be king when I speak as your brother. I have refused those who urge me to take more decisive action against you because you are my sister, but do not test my limits."

With those words, Edward stood and stepped around the crumpled figure at his feet. A few seconds later, Mary heard the door close behind him, and her tears were unleashed.

~ ~ ~ ~

Fran had eventually found Mary on the floor and gently led her to bed. She had not risen in the several days since. In between headaches and stomach spasms that left Mary breathless, she wished that she had the manipulative powers of speech that both of her siblings seemed to possess. Mary herself was no less finely educated, but that natural ability to twist someone around to her way of thinking was absent from her character.

As she drank bitter potions to counter the pounding in her skull, Mary reflected that it did not matter. On the most important points of law, Edward was right. She owed him her allegiance as his sister and his subject. However, she would not give it, for she knew that God was still on her side, and he alone was more powerful than the king of England.

Her place was not at court. That much was clear. When her health allowed, she would return to Beaulieu, where the mass would continue to be heard by any who cared to come and listen.

March 1551

Mary had recovered slowly from the physical and mental strain that her brother's words had caused her. Now, just a few months later, she prepared once again to return to court. She would gratefully remain isolated with her own people, but the full council was called to hear the case against her.

The idea of facing a room full of men who were filled with animosity toward her, some who were in fact hoping for her execution, turned her bowels watery, but there was nothing to be done for it. Mary had pled poor health all winter, and she could ignore the summons no longer.

"Be merciful to me, O God, and hear my prayer," she whispered as she knelt before her chaplain for the last time before her retinue departed. "Give me your words and your strength to face those who would speak against you."

The prayer in her head was less eloquent than the words she spoke aloud. In her head, Mary begged God for protection and rescue. His plans seemed to, once again, differ from her own, for she was soon on the road toward Westminster, despite her deep desire to stay away.

The road was not yet dusty with the heat of summer but was also free of the dangerous snow and ice of winter. Optimal travel conditions did not improve Mary's outlook, but she forced herself to remain calm and plan the words that she would use before the council as they plodded forward.

She did not wish to be caught unprepared again, as she had been before Edward at Christmas. Mary had underestimated him and the hostility toward her. Multiple letters from the council ordering cessation of the mass at her estates were evidence that Edward meant every word he had said. He had personally rebuked her one more time before she had left court, and Mary knew that their relationship was forever altered.

She must let go of the idea that she was fighting for Edward. He was a man of his own mind. The mission Mary now took up was a greater battle, that for the true faith and the souls of every man, woman, and child in England.

When choosing those who would travel with her, Mary had been open about her undertaking. Addressing her household, she had said, "I will be taking a stand for the true faith. Any who feel led by God to do the same are welcome to travel with me." She had paused to fix her gaze on each of them in turn. "We will proudly wear our rosaries as we enter London, just as we do here." Her hand had instinctively grasped at the smooth beads that hung at her side.

In the end, all had been willing to go with her, and she had left it to Rochester to choose which would stay and which would go. Her heart had soared at the showing of support, but the greater distance that opened between her retinue and her home, the more her doubt grew.

Debois had warned that Elizabeth would be placed above her. That was fine. She cared little for her own position. Edward would be king for the rest of her life anyway, so it made little difference which of his sisters was held premier.

Dudley had threatened her with the Tower, but she was sure she had not let him see how much the idea terrified her. That had been the final destination of her beloved governess and two of her step-mothers. Mary wondered if it was her fate to spend her last days within the ancient Tower walls as well. As the outskirts of London came into view, she knew that she would find out soon.

The sun disappeared early during the spring months, so the council room was lit by wall sconces and candles when Mary was escorted there as soon as her caravan entered the city. She had been proud of her ladies as they sat upright on their palfreys with their rosary beads glittering at their sides. Even those who did not typically display them had worn them boldly at least as much to honor their mistress as their God.

Many people had crowded along the street to get a glimpse of the king's sister, especially those who were old enough to have fond memories of her as the previous king's pampered daughter. The younger ones who leaned toward religious reforms and adored their young king had taken in the scene in stony silence. It was similar to the welcome that she now received from her brother's council.

"The Lady Mary, the king's sister," she was announced. Mary bristled internally at her brother's continued insistence that his sisters were not princesses. The thought made her wonder how she imagined she could sway him on more important matters.

Dudley spoke first. "The Lady Mary has been ordered innumerable times over the past four years to recognize the king's laws on religious matters. She continues in disobedience, despite these direct commands and personal intervention by King Edward himself."

Several men grumbled at once, but Mary could not discern what any of them said. She would not speak until she was questioned. Her dignity must remain intact for her steadfastness in the true faith to be effective.

"Is this true?" one man asked above the din. "Is the mass kept within your household?"

Mary tried to attach a name to the man's face, but she could not identify his features well enough in the poorly lit room and at the distance the table placed between them. It did not matter. She stood to address them as one.

"I do observe the faith of my mother and father, and my

household is encouraged to do the same. Is it not the responsibility of each of us to see to the salvation of those placed in our care? Just as I was given the gift of faith by those who raised me, I, in turn, share it with those that God has entrusted to my care."

Dudley jumped upon her words, "That is a rather fine speech, my lady," he said with a smirk, "but did your father also teach you to undermine the authority of the king?"

Another voice added, "We know that her mother did."

This brought low, hesitant laughter all around and a blush to Mary's cheeks. Her indignation overwhelmed her planned caution.

"You would all do well to remember that I am the daughter of your late king and speak to me with respect! Not one of you would have dared to act thus when my father ruled. It is not I who dishonor my brother with our disagreement but you who do so with your flawed counsel and disrespect for the power that God has anointed him with."

She sat, no longer feeling that they deserved to have her stand in their presence. Her heart beat erratically, and her breath came in short gasps. However, her outburst had little effect. A few men had the dignity to look abashed, but Dudley shook his head dismissively.

"You sugarcoat your disobedience with fine words while you attempt to paint us as the villains before the king," he said, his volume increasing gradually as he spoke. "It is you who breaks the king's law. Continuously, and without repentance."

"That is a matter between the king and myself," Mary insisted. "It does not concern lesser men who have no right to address me as one of their rank."

The room grew silent. Though he was but an earl, few stood up to the ambitious John Dudley. While he attempted to control his features as if Mary's words did not affect him, his fuming anger was evident to all.

"I think we have heard enough from the Lady Mary," he said with a wave of his hand as if he was dismissing a servant.

The roomful of eyes shifted to Mary. Swallowing her hatred and desire to respond to Dudley's behavior, she slowly stood. She let her eyes move around the table, knowing that they would not realize that she could not make out their faces. Then she turned and strode from the room as if she walked in a royal procession.

Mary entered the rooms that had been assigned to her and found her women chatting happily as they unpacked.

"Stop," she ordered, and all motion halted in shocked silence. "We will be leaving immediately. Unpack only what is needed for a day or two, because I plan on returning to Beaulieu as soon as possible."

"Is that wise?" Susan asked.

Incredulous glances were sent Susan's way, and she shrugged as if to say that she only asked what the rest of them were thinking.

Mary closed her eyes to calm herself before responding. "I will speak to my brother on the morrow and inform him of my decision, but I will not stay here."

In the end, Edward had not prohibited her. He had issued another order for her to get her religious house in order and let her go. How this would all end, only God could tell.

August 1551

The months away from court restored Mary's spirits and her health. The summer had brought more letters from Edward and his council, but she simply ignored them and carried on providing true worship to those who were able to come and hear it. She had decided that it was enough until she felt a clear urging from God to do more.

Mary strummed absentmindedly on her lute as she enjoyed a fresh breeze that stirred through the room. The day was idyllic, warm but not too hot, with a cheerful sun and bright blue sky. It was a day when children went outdoors to explore and housewives opened up their homes to air out unsavory odors.

The feeling of contentedness was unfamiliar to Mary, and it made the day that much sweeter. She was through worrying for the future, for its troubles arrived soon enough. Edward had problems of his own and would not likely bother with her if she lived quietly as was her intention.

He had recently been betrothed to Elisabeth of France, discarding the betrothal that his father had fought to gain for him to Mary of Scots. Mary smiled at the idea of her baby brother married. With a wife and children of his own, he would have much greater concerns than his conservative sister.

Rochester's entrance drew Mary from her reverie, and she laid the lute aside, seeing that he held a letter with a thick seal. Her hand reached for it, but he shook his head. It was then that she noticed his sickly pallor and deep worry lines.

"What is it?" she asked as part of her wished to leave whatever it was until later, so that she could continue to bask in the perfect day.

Rochester stammered uncharacteristically, his hands shaking in fear and frustration. Mary stood and took the paper regardless of his wishes. Her eyes widened in disbelief as she read.

"They have summoned you?" she cried.

"And Waldegrave," he confirmed.

"What is the meaning of this?" she demanded of no one in particular. "They cannot do this."

"As it turns out," Rochester said, recovering himself, "they can."

Mary's brow was deeply furrowed as her eyes moved from him back to the missive. "No," she whispered. "This cannot be."

Now that he had Mary's fear to ease, Rochester could suppress his own. "There, your grace," he said reassuringly. "You have taken your stand, and now it is time for Ed and I to take ours."

"They call you chief instruments in causing me to hold to the old religion," she cried in disbelief as she continued reading. "It is utter rubbish!"

"As they well know," Rochester said. "They have not been given a free hand to deal with you as they see fit, so they look to those they can punish. Do not worry about us, your grace. We shall make you proud."

Mary imagined those who served her most loyally languishing in the Tower. What if they were tortured? "No," she stated. "I cannot let you go."

Rochester took the letter from her clenched fingers. "You must," he said. "Don't you see? If we disobey them on this, you are nothing but a disloyal subject. You must hold firm on the topic of religion but respect your brother in all else. We will go."

He stood taller than he had when he had arrived with his news. Mary was touched that he was willing to put himself at the council's mercy for her cause, but her heart was breaking.

"If God is for us, who can be against us?" she asked him. He smiled and tipped his head to her.

"I must discuss this with Waldegrave," Rochester explained as he moved to leave.

"I will not forget this," Mary vowed, though she had no idea what she could do about it or how she would ever be able to demonstrate her affection for these men who were willingly accepting their punishment for her sake.

Rochester seemed to understand her inner thoughts, and he appeared imbued with much greater strength as he moved to leave than when he had arrived with the devastating news.

"God go with you," Mary whispered as the door closed behind him.

She stood frozen, wondering how the day had gone from tranquil to horrific in the space of a few moments. The look on Rochester's face when he had first entered the room haunted her. He had replaced his manly mask by the time he had left, it was true, but she knew that the same fear still lied beneath.

Mary's fist curled as her indignation rose. "How could they?" she shouted to the empty room.

Her brother's council could not reach her, so they took aim at those who served her. It would all seem so petty if they did not hold the lives of good men in their hands.

The men who had been summoned left at dawn the next day. There was no point in delay, and they would not have their failure to respond reflect poorly upon their lady. Mary fought tears as they bravely rode away.

Fran joined Mary in the chapel that day. She was proud of her husband but also frightened that she might never see him again. Mary was relieved that Fran did not seem upset with her for placing them all in this situation.

As if reading her mind, Fran offered Mary assurance when

they left the chapel to take some supper.

"Thank you for allowing us to make a home with you, your grace."

Mary was surprised. Of all the things she thought Fran might be feeling toward her at that moment, gratitude was not one of them. She did not feel worthy of her kind words.

"Were it not for you," Fran continued, "where would Edward and I practice our faith? You are a light shining in the darkness, your grace. Thank you."

"Do you truly not blame me for your husband's arrest?" Mary could not keep herself from asking.

"Of course not!" Fran exclaimed as if the thought had never crossed her mind. "Our Lord demands much of us at times such as these." She took Mary's hands and squeezed them tightly. "It is good that he gives us each other to lend us the strength to endure our trials."

"Yes," Mary agreed, her tight throat keeping her from saying more, but Fran knew her well enough to know what she was thinking and said it for her.

"If God is for us, who can be against us?"

~ ~ ~ ~

King Edward, as it turned out, could be very much against them. Waldegrave and Rochester did not promptly return from London, leaving Fran and Mary desperate for news of their well-being. It was not until almost a fortnight later that they received any news, and it came in the unwelcome form of Lord Chancellor Richard Rich.

They did not exchange any words, but Mary and Fran reached for each other's hands as they watched the highly decorated retinue gather in the courtyard. Mary wondered if they had finally come to arrest her and what would happen to those in her household if they did. It was too late to reconsider whether she had done the right thing, if she should have obeyed the king or escaped to Spain. She would stand firm against the opposition now that it was before her.

Mary received Rich in the hall. She had dressed herself as elaborately as possible given the brief notice of his arrival. A light coronet graced her auburn hair, and jewels glittered at her throat and fingers. Her chair, that would be considered by most to be a throne, was on a raised dais, making it easy for her to look down her nose at the upstart baron.

He appeared to be intimidated by none of it. Richard Rich strolled in as if into his own hall and offered Mary the most casual of obeisance. He had the conceited aura of one who has pushed and shoved their way into a position rather than been born to it, as if that made him superior to his peers. His growing paunch was evidence of a lifetime of not having enough food available, leaving him without the ability to maintain self-control around it once it was plentifully supplied. His swarthy looks might have been handsome if his manner were not immediately recognizable as evil.

In a snide, arrogant tone, he informed Mary that Waldegrave and Rochester were retained in London.

"And what is it that keeps them?" Mary asked, her voice calm and regal. "I do not recall assigning them tasks that would keep them long," she added as if she had sent them herself.

Rich smiled knowingly. "They are in the Tower."

A few gasps were heard, but Mary maintained her stony control. She had been expecting this.

"Of what do they stand accused?"

"Each has disobeyed the king's orders," Rich said. When Mary only lifted an arched eyebrow in response, he continued.

"They refused to deliver messages regarding the illegal practices taking place in this household."

"Was it wise to appoint servants to take control of my household and see it ordered as you see fit?" Mary asked indignantly. "Surely, any such missive should have been directed to me and could only come from the king, as he is the only one with a rank and title greater than my own."

"I had no idea that the bastard daughter of a dead king was such an elevated status," Rich replied, and the hall went silent.

Mary knew that all eyes were upon her, and her mind raced as she attempted to lay aside her hurt and anger to respond in a way that would put Rich in his place rather than let him know that he had scored a point. She hated that her brother left her a bastard in the word of the law, but most people had the grace to not point it out.

She did her best to appear dismissive. "Your words have always been ill to me. It wearies me to fulfill the responsibilities that my controller would normally see done on my behalf. I expect Rochester and Waldegrave to be returned to me before my official protest can reach my brother's ear."

"Who do you think ordered their arrest?" Rich replied with a smirk. "Lady Mary, you have no idea what you are up against. You have no hope of winning, whatever it is you are trying to accomplish here." He included her gathered household with a sweeping gesture. "What shall you do when Edward is a man full grown, rather than an adolescent with sentimental feelings toward you? Do you think that he will hesitate to execute you for your treason any more than your ancestor Edward IV did to rid himself of the treacherous Clarence?"

Mary felt her face grow red, and the fact that her emotions were visible only exacerbated them. "You and your council will be the cause of my death," she cried. "I have been made sickly by your deeds, and whether by that or the axe should I die, it is a sin that God will hold you accountable for."

Rich feared the invisible God even less than he feared the slight, haggard woman before him. He pulled a packet from inside his doublet that Mary knew must be the orders that Rochester and Waldegrave had refused to deliver. After handing them to the closest of Mary's attendants with a flourish, he gestured to a tall, emaciated man standing at his side.

"The king has seen fit to provide you with a new controller to ease your burden and ensure that your household is run according to the king's laws."

The man offered a shallow bow but remained silent.

Through clenched teeth, Mary said, "I am the king's most humble and obedient servant in all things save those where my conscience leads me to follow God." The words, so reminiscent of her mother, helped Mary to relax. Her voice was under greater control as she continued. "When his majesty is mature enough to judge such matters, I shall gladly lay my head upon the block if he so wishes, as many saints have done before me."

Richard tipped his head quizzically. "Do you wish to be a martyr, Lady Mary?"

"I do not, but God's will be done," she said, and then thought to add, "and I will have no servant of yours within my household, nor will I endure you or them for more than an hour. You will leave and take anyone you have brought with you. Do not think to take over my house with mere servants where your betters have failed."

Her words had finally struck a chord, and Rich angrily gestured to those with him. As they began to file out into the courtyard, he directed his next words toward Mary's chaplains. "It is the king's order that the Book of Common Prayer be the only order of worship used. Stray from this command, and you will be charged with treason."

Mary's jaw was tense, and she felt the animalistic urge to bite the throat out of that wicked man who had so bloated his own importance that most people now seemed to believe that he was due greater respect than she was.

The mention of George of Clarence had given Mary's mind a pathway to the past that it now travelled to ignore the heartache of the present. He had been the father of Mary's governess, Margaret Pole. Under her tutelage, Mary had been raised as her father's heir, a beloved princess who would one day rule in her own right, at least that is what Margaret and Mary's mother had taught her.

It had not been until much later that Mary realized that this was a dream held only by these women. Her father had taken on heaven and earth to replace her with Edward. Would he have done it all over again if he could see the end result, Mary wondered. She was surprised to find that she missed her father. He had been cruel, selfish, and tyrannical, but, for the first time since his death, Mary wished that he was there to take the situation in hand.

Rich's voice, directed toward Mary, brought her mind back to the hall. He was once again pressing her to accept the man who had been appointed as a substitute for Rochester.

"I will appoint my own officers, as I have proven myself more than competent to do so," she interrupted him. "Do not dare to leave this man within my house. You are dismissed."

Emotions flickered across Rich's face as he considered his options. Apparently deciding that he had done enough for the time being, he bowed and followed his attendants from the hall.

Everyone watched his retreating back before shifting their

gaze to Mary for guidance. She sighed and took the papers that Rich had left. Flipping through them, she saw what she had expected. They were nothing new, just more threats of what would happen if she insisted upon continuing the mass.

Her automatic response was to hold them out to where Rochester should be standing, but, of course, he was not there. This was one blow too many. Mary tossed the pages containing the king's signature to the floor and stomped from the hall, leaving her household in a state of uncertainty and fear.

December 1551

Refusing an invitation to spend Christmas at court, Mary had decided to look to others who may be in positions to offer the support that was not forthcoming from her brother. While they had a reputation as reformers, the Grey family was also closely related to Mary and had invited her to share the season with them at Tilty.

Frances Grey had been a close companion of Mary's as the oldest daughter of the late duke of Suffolk. They were first cousins, and Frances' daughters followed Elizabeth in King Henry's Act of Succession. While no one expected the Grey children, or Mary or Elizabeth for that matter, to ever hold the crown, it gave the women a common bond.

Mary was joyfully embraced by a woman who could have been her sister as soon as she arrived. The cousins were only months apart in age and shared the auburn hair that identified them as members of the royal family. Frances, with her adoring husband and three daughters, had experienced greater joy in her life than had Mary, and it was evident in her fuller figure and more gently lined face compared to Mary's thin and weary form.

Frances was ever the perfect hostess, and her only comment on Mary's appearance was, "Well, we shall have to fatten you up a bit shan't we?" as she squeezed her fiercely and led her into a hall that was bustling with festivity.

A warm feeling filled Mary at the informal affection that Frances so freely offered. It was a bittersweet reminder of Kateryn, who had been a dear friend to both of them. Mary happily allowed herself to be led and presented before being handed a plate piled heavily with tempting dishes. To think, that some people always lived like this, Mary thought, comparing the joviality of the Greys with her own solemn household.

With pride evident in her posture and countenance, Frances presented her three daughters to Mary. The youngest, their visitor's namesake, was tiny for her five years, though she did her best to curtsey respectfully before the lady her mother introduced as the Princess Mary.

Mary moved toward the child and gently stroked her soft, red-gold hair. "We have been introduced before, little one, but you likely do not remember me."

The younger Mary gazed thoughtfully up at the princess but did not reply. She already had the reputation for one who thinks much and speaks little.

"God bless you," Mary said before gliding over to the next girl.

This daughter shared the features of her sisters while putting them together in a more visually appealing way. It put Mary in mind of her own younger sister, who was the more beautiful though she and Mary were immediately recognizable as siblings. She glanced at the next daughter, Jane, and wondered if she had similar thoughts regarding the lovely Catherine.

Only eleven but already strikingly beautiful, Catherine Grey dimpled and gracefully curtseyed and said, "We welcome you, Princess Mary, and are honored by your presence."

Mary smiled. No, this girl was not like her own sister, she mentally amended. She was one who was beautiful yet still difficult to feel envious of, for she was too kind and open with her affection to cause jealousy.

"Thank you, Lady Catherine, and God's blessing of peace to you," Mary replied before moving to the Grey daughter with whom she was most anxious to converse.

"Jane, of course, requires no introduction," Frances said, giving her eldest daughter a rather indelicate shove forward.

Although three years older than Catherine, Jane demonstrated an awkwardness where her sister had been graceful. She was not rude, but had the aura of one who is more comfortable with her books than with guests.

"Princess Mary," Jane said. "It is my greatest pleasure to welcome you to Tilty. I hope that we will have the opportunity to become reacquainted during your visit."

She had said the words as if they were what was expected of her, but Mary wholeheartedly agreed, "I would love to speak with you when we can steal a few quiet moments together."

Jane's eyebrows rose slightly when she did not receive a casual response and formal blessing, but she recovered herself quickly.

"Indeed, your grace. Please join me in my rooms whenever it is convenient for you."

Frances smiled boldly as the girls filed away, their duty successfully completed. Mary's grin was almost as wide, as she too watched her young cousins' postures relax increasingly the further they moved from their mother.

"I must thank you again for inviting me to share Christmas with you, Frances," Mary gushed. "It has been too long since I have enjoyed the simple pleasures of friends and family."

Guiding her to a relatively private alcove, Frances murmured a polite response. Once they were seated, her face became filled with purposeful determination.

"I wished to speak of you regarding a possible marriage for Jane."

Mary nodded and considered the serious young lady. "She will make a good wife," she said noncommittally. "Who have you in mind?"

Grasping Mary's hands, Frances blurted her reply as one

who has been holding it back too long, "Your brother."

Furrowing her brow, Mary considered aloud, "This is not the first time such a possibility has been put forth." She looked at Frances' hopeful face, and felt that she should warn her. "You must know that my brother will not be guided by me in any way. In fact, you may be better off if you do not appear to have my backing, though I think the match would be a good one."

"It is as bad as that?" Frances asked, her face falling at the thought. "Could you not repair the fissure between you?"

Feeling slightly annoyed but not wishing to damage this cherished relationship, Mary shrugged. "Edward is becoming a man of his own mind. The chasm between us grows greater, if anything, as he grows into his rule."

Frances released a sharp, disappointed breath. "Still," she said, brightening slightly, "It is, as you have said, an idea that has been on the mind of the king for quite some time."

"I do not wish for you to be disappointed," Mary said, "but I feel that I should point out that my brother is betrothed to Elisabeth of France."

Frances was already waving away the inconvenient truth. "A tool of the moment, nothing more. He has no intention of carrying out that treaty."

Mary could only shrug again. "Then it appears that you have greater insight into the king's intentions and desires than I do. I am sorry that I cannot be of greater help."

"It is no matter," Frances assured her, patting her hands. "Now, let us enjoy ourselves."

She rose and held her hands out to Mary as an invitation to dance. Mary tried to remember the last time she had danced, laughed, and enjoyed herself. Deciding that it had been far too long indeed, she took her cousin's outstretched hands.

When Mary woke the next morning, she was surprised to see bright light streaming into the cozy room that had been appointed to her. "I have missed lauds," she whispered to herself before remembering that the liturgical hours would not be kept here.

Not wishing to incriminate the Greys, she had not brought her own chaplain to say mass while she was their guest. Her remaining chaplain had remained at Copped Hall, while any that had received the order to cease the mass by Richard Rich had been dismissed. Mary would not have them punished for treason for serving her household, so she had let them go with a heavy heart.

She rose, content to say her own private prayers as long as she was in residence at Tilty. Once her morning devotions were complete, she set out to find Jane.

It was not difficult to locate her. The hall, where the constantly burning yule log kept the temperature warm and inviting, was where the family naturally gathered. Jane sat close to the hearth, hunched over a book that was tilted to catch the firelight.

A pang in Mary's chest caught her unaware. Her old anger toward her father was suddenly inflamed as she realized that she should have her own studious daughters reading before the fire and a husband who doted over their children. Frances enjoyed the life that Mary's father had refused her, and her brother would do no different as long as she disobeyed him.

Jane seemed to sense that she was being observed, because she turned her head and reluctantly closed the book in her lap. Seeing who it was, she rose from the chair and lowered into a curtsey in one fluid motion.

Mary rushed to her side. "Please," she said, raising her up. "Do not hold to formalities during this visit. I only wish to enjoy time with family, though you honor me greatly."

"Very well," Jane said without emotion as she retook her seat and gestured to another, which Mary settled into.

Now that she was here alone with the girl, Mary felt oddly intimidated. Jane was so self-assured and their time together with Kateryn felt rather far away. She searched her mind for small talk that could lead to their shared memories, but everything felt awkward.

"Did you wish to hear of Kateryn?" Jane asked.

Mary's eyes widened. "How did you know?"

Jane gave her a questioning look. "Whatever else would you wish to ask of me?"

Mary had not thought about it quite that way, and she felt guilty that her selfish motives were that obvious. She was stammering over an apology when Jane interjected.

"I beg you to accept my apology," Jane pleaded in a softer tone. "My mother often chides me for my lack of tact."

Offering a weak smile, Mary reached into the purse at her girdle. "I do wish to speak to you of my step-mother, but I also have a gift for you."

Interest lit Jane's eyes as she followed Mary's hand. A string of shimmering pearls and rubies that sparkled like new ice was drawn from the pouch. The glittering light was reflected in Jane's eyes as Mary presented her offering.

"Your grace," Jane said in a hushed voice. "You are too kind."

When Jane took the necklace, Mary realized that the piece appeared gaudy in the younger woman's hand. She had failed to take into account Jane's greater youth and simplicity. The necklace that so beautifully complemented many of Mary's dresses, would look out of place in Jane's wardrobe.

Jane either did not notice or was a good actress, for she thanked Mary profusely as she examined the gems, holding them up to catch the light. Mary smiled, deciding that maybe the young woman would like the piece and just had not had the opportunity to dress more opulently.

When Jane had tucked the gift away, she delved directly into the topic that she knew Mary longed to hear of.

"I was with Queen Kateryn at Sudeley," she began, her eyes searching the fire for images of her memories. "She was like a second mother to me, caring for me even after you and your sister had gone."

Mary noted Jane's failure to keep the venom from her words at the mention of Elizabeth but remained silent.

"I was so pleased to attend to Kateryn at her happiest moment," Jane whispered. "But it was God's will that it be quickly followed by her last."

Tears began to fill Mary's eyes, and she was once again overwhelmed with regret that she had not been there. Demonstrating her eerie prescience, Jane continued.

"She understood why you were not there and loved you dearly until the end. That is why she named the baby for you."

"If only her daughter had lived," Mary whispered. She would have loved to raise the little girl as her own, but the guardianship had been given to Jane's grandmother. Unfortunately, the babe had fallen victim to an early illness, the way so many did.

"Is it odd for me to say that I was proud to be chief mourner at her funeral?" Jane asked candidly. Her face crinkled in thought, and she described the black swathed chapel and carved coats of arms to Mary. "There was one for each of her husbands," she said. "Including your father's."

Mary nodded as she wiped away an escaping tear.

"She enjoyed those last months at Sudeley. The setting and weather was idyllic. She and Thomas had smoothed over their disagreements for the sake of the unborn babe." After a pause, Jane asked, "Do you think it is better that God takes us during a happy time, though the grieving for those left behind is made more poignant? If he takes one during the valleys of life, does it not leave us with only sadness to look back upon?"

Frowning, Mary thought on this. Was there a better time to lose a loved one? "It always hurts," she said, thinking of her mother, who was abandoned and destitute when she died, "but I think you may be right. It gives me comfort to imagine Kateryn smiling as she strolled through fragrant gardens with her hand resting upon her swollen belly."

Jane smiled. "Yes, and perhaps it should be a comfort then that she was quickly reunited with her daughter."

Mary examined Jane and reminded herself that she was but fourteen. "You are a very wise young woman," she said. "It is difficult for even the most devout to focus on the eternal, yet you, for all your youth, seem to have a strong grasp upon it."

Most girls would have lowered their head in self-deprecation and blushed at such praise, but Jane received it in silence with a hint of a smile and gentle tilt of her head.

"I am eager to see what future God has planned for you," Mary said before they settled into companionable silence before the cozy fire.

March 1552

After returning to her own household after Epiphany, Mary was struck more than ever before by the quietness. She missed the girls' laughter, lively conversation, and music. Mary was hesitant to hire musicians since anyone under her roof could become a victim of the same unfair justice that had put Rochester and Waldegrave in the Tower. However, she and her ladies had polished off rusty skills and dusted off instruments to provide their own entertainment.

It could not compare to the revelry of Tilty, but the improved atmosphere went far to cheer Mary. She also found that her health improved. The soothing music and decreased stress caused her headaches to fade away, and she was able to enjoy eating and put on some weight. Susan smiled victoriously when Mary had admitted that she needed some dresses let out a bit.

They continued to hear mass, and Mary was certain that her brother had too many concerns of kingship to worry about how his sister was worshiping. It would have been a peaceful and relatively happy household if it were not for the empty places where Waldegrave and Rochester should have been.

Mary wrote to her brother and members of his council frequently on the men's behalf. Her pride in their refusal to deliver the king's orders to her was overshadowed by the guilt that they had felt the need to do so. She could bear it only because Fran never accused her of wrongdoing though it was her husband who suffered.

As if the thought of her had conjured her bodily, Fran appeared before Mary. Tears were streaming down her face incongruously with her broad smile. Her mouth moved, but words did not form.

"What is it?" Mary cried, jumping to her feet and rushing to her.

"Oh, your grace!" Fran sobbed. She could say no more and simply indicated the window.

Mary hurried to it and cursed her poor vision once more. She could see figures on horseback, but had no idea who had arrived. She shook her head in an unproductive attempt to clear the blurry image.

"What is it?" she repeated.

Fran realized her error and regained her voice at once. "It is my Edward!" She was at Mary's side pointing, and Mary understood that the other figure must be faithful Robert Rochester.

"God be praised," Mary whispered. Her arm encircled Fran's waist, and she squeezed. "We must go to greet them."

"Oh, your grace!" Fran exclaimed again as she flew from the room and into the eager waiting arms of her husband.

Later, when the household had settled from the unexpected arrival of two of its own, Mary sat with Rochester over glasses of wine.

"I am extraordinarily grateful," Mary said, "but why were you released?"

Rochester savored a slow sip of wine in the way that one does when they have not tasted it in far too long. After he swallowed and licked his lips, he shrugged.

"I honestly cannot say, your grace. It seems that your brother wished to show you some small mercy."

"God bless him then," Mary said, smiling. "I will not question the goodness of God or who he chooses to work through. There may be hope for our king yet."

"Nothing is impossible with God," Rochester agreed as he closed his eyes to focus his full attention on his next sip.

February 1553

It had been months since Mary had seen Edward, and there had been a time when she had wondered if she could ever enter his presence again without risking imprisonment. However, the attacks on her household had ceased when Rochester and Waldegrave were released. She believed that it was safe to visit the king.

In the autumn, Edward would turn sixteen, the age at which it had been determined he should rule in his own right. To a great extent, he already did, and Mary wondered if the reduced dependence upon councilors had led to her kinder treatment.

The one man who was reluctant to let go of control was John Dudley. He had been raised from earl of Warwick to duke of Northumberland, a position that Mary felt was far too high for such a man, but he saw fit to reach higher. Mary wondered what would happen when Edward asserted himself beyond Dudley's control.

Either way, it was not likely to affect her much. As she led her procession down Fleet Street to the joyful cheering and jubilation of the Londoners, Mary shoved Dudley's political scheming from her mind. She would continue to live quietly, except for infrequent moments like this when she was reminded of the love her brother's subjects bore for her.

Arriving at the gates of Whitehall, Mary was surprised and pleased by the respectful welcome that she received from Edward's council. Those who had disdained her for years now treated her like a princess, and she wondered at the change. It could only be her brother's doing. Was he ready to heal the rift between them?

With this in mind, Mary was shocked once again, when she was informed that she could not see Edward right away.

"I apologize," Dudley said with false sincerity, "but the king is rather poorly with a feverish cold."

Mary was disappointed, but Dudley continued. "Your cousin, Lady Suffolk, also awaits an audience with the king," he said. "Perhaps you would like to visit with her grace while you wait."

She had not seen Frances Grey since Christmas over a year earlier, so this was a pleasing suggestion. Frances could fill Mary in on what she had missed at court and would be a good person to pass the time with.

"Is Jane yet betrothed to my brother?" Mary asked half-jokingly after initial pleasantries were exchanged.

"Not quite," Frances admitted in a tone that made Mary lift an eyebrow. "He has named her as his heir," she sighed, "but I do not know that he will ever marry her."

Mary felt her insides squirm, but she forced herself to remain calm. "What do you mean?" she asked.

At this point, Frances seemed to recall that it was Mary who had been Edward's heir should he die without having children. She had the dignity to appear ashamed of her thoughtless words.

"I thought you would know," she lied. "Edward has named my Jane as his heir should he die before they can marry and have children."

Struggling to process the news, Mary turned her face away from her cousin. Why would Edward include this in his will now if he planned to wed Jane anyway? Why had her treatment improved as he was in the process of disinheriting her? "Is he dying?" she blurted.

"No, no, of course not," Frances insisted, shaking her head unconvincingly. "You tend toward illness yourself," she pointed out. "Surely, this is no more serious than your own frequent bouts."

Mary wondered, but did not bother to ask Frances any additional questions. As fond as they were of one another, their interests did not lie along the same path in this matter. Mary was glad when Northumberland returned to inform her that she could see Edward.

She took her leave of Frances with a few hurriedly said words, and allowed herself to be escorted to a room that was too warm and filled with the stench of rotten flesh. The pomanders hung throughout Edward's chamber fought in vain to sweeten the air. Their effort was joined by the herbs that were stirred in the rushes as Mary flew to her brother's side.

"Dear Edward," she cried, taking up his hand. It again looked like that of a small boy rather than that of a man. "I would not have stayed so long from your side if I had known how great was your need of me."

Edward coughed and was offered a sip of water before he formed his reply. "Just a cold," he insisted, but his eyes told her that he was grateful for her presence.

She wanted to say that she would pray for him, but she did not wish to bring up their differences of religion. So, she squeezed his hand and rubbed his arm, wishing that she could take his pain upon herself.

A doctor approached, poured a vile looking cordial down Edward's throat, and examined his eyes and throat.

"Is he improving?" Mary asked. She could not ask if he would recover. The illness of a king was a tricky subject, and too much discussion of it could land one in prison, especially if one were heir to the throne as Mary was. At least, she thought she was.

The doctor mumbled his assurances with only a passing glance in Mary's direction. She wished to force him to tell her the truth, wished that she could talk to Edward, but she saw that it caused him too much pain. She would have to do what she always did and turn it over to God.

It felt like no time had passed when Northumberland told her that it was time to let Edward rest. Mary considered fighting him, but Edward had fallen asleep and had only uttered a few words to her when awake. She would come back when he was feeling better. Suddenly, it seemed important that they reconcile, but it would have to wait. Mary would not delay so long before planning her next trip to London and left instructions to be informed as soon as her brother's condition improved.

"God's blessings on you, little brother," she whispered as she traced the sign of the cross upon the king's sweaty brow. When the heavy door to his chamber closed firmly behind her, Mary attempted to ignore the feeling of foreboding that washed over her.

May 1553

Mary felt sure that there were plots afoot that she did not understand. At the same time she received word that her brother's health was greatly improved, she was also informed that her cousin, Lady Jane Grey, was marrying Guildford Dudley. Why, if Jane could marry Edward and be queen, would she settle for the youngest son of the duke of Northumberland?

Letters had been dispatched to Edward, Frances Grey, and even her sister Elizabeth, but answers had not been forthcoming. One communication that she did receive only succeeded to trouble her further. Northumberland, who had fought to keep Edward under his control and to bully Mary into obedience, had sent Mary her coat of arms.

It had been almost exactly twenty years since Mary's father had broken up her household and disallowed the use of the coat of arms that had been hers as princess. What message was Dudley sending to her now by reviving its use?

Edward's will, in which he attempted to replace Mary as his heir had turned out to be more than a hope of Frances Grey. He had publicized his intentions, despite Jane's match with Guildford, but had yet to finalize them by act of Parliament. Mary knew that it was only a matter of time and did not believe that it mattered much. Her much greater age meant that she was unlikely to outlive him anyway.

She was missing something, she was sure. But what was it?

July 1553

Mary's face was lined with concern as she examined the letter that had arrived from the duke of Northumberland. On its surface, it increased her worry for Edward. He had been feeling poorly when she had last seen him, but she had no reason to believe that the strong young man would not recover, as she herself had many times.

But it was something deeper, something she was missing between the lines of Northumberland's summons that bothered her. He desired that Mary and Elizabeth visit Edward as it might cheer him during his illness. However, Mary knew that it had been years since her presence was a comforting one to her little brother.

Her intuition told her that she should not obey, but she needed to consult one with greater ability to discern the hidden motives of others before she decided. For one of the few times in her life, she wished that Elizabeth was with her. One advantage to having a manipulative streak was recognizing the same trait in others.

Mary sighed, and then quickly was cheered by the entrance of Rochester. Without hesitation, she turned the letter over to him. The lines in his face deepened as he read it. Before he reached the end, he was shaking his head and causing dark hair to fall into his face.

"I cannot advise you to put yourself at the mercy of Northumberland. His concern is neither for you nor the king."

"I agree," Mary said. She eagerly looked to him for more advice.

He took a deep breath as he shoved the hair from his forehead. "Yet, it may be to your advantage to appear to be submitting until we learn more."

"More?" Mary asked. Clearly Rochester saw something that

she had been unsuccessfully searching for in the note.

He looked into her eyes and pressed his lips tightly together as one does when they are deciding how much they should reveal to another. Finally, he seemed to come to a decision. "I am afraid that the king may be dying," Rochester said. His voice was full of sympathy, and he did something that he never did. He reached out and laid a comforting hand on her arm.

Collapsing into the nearest chair, Mary let devastation crash over her. Her brother had made her life difficult, just as her father had, but he was so young, and she loved him in spite of it all. With sudden realization, pieces fell into place, and Mary saw the scheme that she had been missing as when a curtain falls away from a new painting.

"They plan to bypass me," she whispered.

Rochester nodded sadly. "I fear that is their intention, your grace."

"Jane," Mary whispered again, her mind conjuring up an image of the studious young woman seated before the fire at Tilty. "How could...." Her voice trailed off. She knew how they could. It was the same thing that had been happening since the beginning of time. The love that Frances, and to a lesser extent Jane, held for her would not be enough to keep them from usurping her throne if they were given the opportunity.

"No," Mary stated firmly. "I simply will not abide this." She looked at Rochester to see if he would council her otherwise, but he held his tongue. "I was content to see my brother rule, as was his right though the kingdom is no better for it. None besides myself holds the right if God has chosen to take him."

"Let me be the first to pledge my loyalty to you, your majesty," Rochester knelt as he said the words that made Mary's confidence soar.

"Stand, dear Rochester," she said, her voice thick. "We may have a battle ahead of us, but I feel able to face it with you by my side."

Her hand on his arm gently urged him upward. "Locate Waldegrave and we shall meet in the study. I believe it is best if we move the household to a more secure location."

He nodded his agreement and was gone. Mary took one moment to herself to wonder if she were doing the right thing. The last woman to attempt to claim the crown of England had thrown the country into a savage civil war. But Maude had been fighting a man. Jane Grey, much as Mary loved her as a cousin, would not take her place as queen.

Mary had scarcely believed Frances when she had gloated that Jane had been made Edward's heir. Sadness that she may never have the opportunity to reconcile with her brother was overshadowed by her anger that he had attempted to disinherit her. Her feelings were a jumbled mass within her.

It took only a few minutes for Mary to be joined by her chamberlain and his nephew. Both knelt before her as they entered the room.

"That is not necessary," Mary insisted, but her cheeks glowed with pleasure. "We must determine the most prudent path to substantiate my claim while limiting bloodshed. I would not have my countrymen believe that I place my own power above their well-being."

Rochester surprised her by speaking urgently, "I believe that we should remove you to safety before we take the time to plan further."

Mary's eyes widened at the inference of danger that was greater than she imagined. One glance at Waldegrave told her that he agreed.

"What would you advise?"

Taking a step closer to her, Rochester continued, "We could get you to Sawston Hall. Tonight."

Seeing that Mary was taken aback, Waldegrave offered his support for the idea. "With a small party, we can ride quickly through the night. We can leave instructions for the household to join us at Kenninghall."

A deep breath filled Mary's lungs, and she allowed them to slowly deflate. This was the moment her future pivoted on. Did she believe her brother was dying? Could she be bold and courageous?

"If God is for us, who can be against us?" she asked them with a smile. "See my mare saddled, and select two women to attend me who are accomplished riders."

Both men's faces lit up with grins as if they were small boys awarded a prize at the fair. With hasty bows to the woman they were sure would be their queen, they went to work.

Within the hour, their party of seven was cantering away from Hunsdon, leaving the past behind. With none of the weariness or aches that would typically have plagued her travel, Mary made her way determinedly toward her first stop on the path to Westminster.

The dark did not frighten Mary as it sometimes did. Despite traveling with such a small retinue, she was not afraid as the blanket of night thickened upon them. Instead, she imagined that her ancestors were shining down on her along with the stars and blessing her journey.

She was surprised how quickly they came upon Sawston Hall. One of the young men chosen to accompany them had ridden ahead, and Sir John Huddleston welcomed them as though it were the middle of the day. Only the absence of candles reminded Mary that they must move in secret.

Settled in the hall with bread, cheese, and wine, Mary asked Huddleston what news he had from London.

"Your grace, I believe you will be quickly discovered," he said bluntly. "It is my advice that you prepare to move on at first light." Waving over his steward, he continued, "I will provide you with any food, horses, and supplies that you need. Do not take my words as a desire to see you gone, but a great wish to see you enthroned."

Mary's heart swelled as he directed his next words to the steward, ensuring that Mary would have all she needed. Her decision was quickly made.

"Then we will do as you have counselled," she said, rising from her seat she directed her next words to the entire party. "We shall ride on after lauds," she paused to see if any would object, but they did not. "Good Sir Huddleston shall be remembered for granting his assistance at this vital time. And now we must be to bed."

The room buzzed with lingering excitement over their mission as people prepared to be led to their rooms, which had been hastily prepared as they ate. Mary wondered how much sleep any of them would be able to get, but she soon fell into the content sleep of the weary.

Mass was said and prayers for success raised before the party set out again with the rising sun.

The next two days flew by in a whirlwind and the constant staccato of hooves. Resting only for a few hours at a time, Mary's party rushed toward Kenninghall in Norfolk where they had decided she should be proclaimed.

Only one event remained fixed in Mary's mind after this series of chaotic days had passed. It was the moment that a messenger arrived with confirmation of her brother's death. The letter she had received, had, in fact, been an attempt to neutralize her and enable a smooth transition of power to her brother's chosen heir. She could scarcely mourn his death, but had to quickly decide what to do.

She received new orders from the council to show herself at court and recognize her cousin, Jane, as queen. No longer was Edward's death kept a secret, but they trusted that the docile Lady Mary would do as she was bid. She mourned for the young king, taken to heaven too soon, but at the same time her frustration with him had never been greater.

Mary no longer had any doubts and did not consider obeying the council for a moment. Her choice had been made the moment her small party had fled from Hunsdon. The bulk of her household was joining her at Kenninghall, and her quest was just beginning. It was those who had long and loyally served her that she would address first. The people of her household had stood by her through much political turmoil.

As she prepared to go to them, she spared a moment for those who were no longer there but had been instrumental in shaping her destiny. Her mother. Margaret Pole and her son, Lord Montague. Kateryn. That they would pray for her as part of the great cloud of witnesses was her greatest hope.

Chosen for its central location in East Anglia, Kenninghall would be a convenient place for Mary's supporters to gather, or at least she hoped they would. What if none came?

"I can do all through Christ who gives me strength," she whispered to herself as she nodded to her page to open the heavy, wooden door.

She stepped out and her fears evaporated.

Knowing the pace that she had kept to arrive, Mary could

not fathom how so many others had already taken up the call. Those of her household gazed at her with unadulterated admiration, and some that she did not recognize had joined them. Murmuring faded to silence as she came into their presence.

First, she announced her grief over the death of her brother. Her voice remained strong, though she had not been given opportunity to mourn for him in the days since his death. Before she could carry on, a cheer was raised.

"Long live the Queen! Long live our Queen Mary!"

Others quickly joined the chant until the sound reverberated through Mary's bones. She felt blessed as she had at few times in her life when she looked at the love and joy on their faces. Unsure how long they would continue, Mary raised a hand to gently bring order.

"The right to the crown of England has descended to me by divine right and human law," she began and was forced to pause and allow the cheering to lapse. "In London, there is a plot to usurp the throne, but, with your help, I will claim it as my own."

The cheering continued long after Mary had turned and reentered the palace.

Wishing only to bask in the glow of the love she had been shown, Mary forced herself to summon Rochester and Waldegrave to the study that had been appointed for her use.

The light dimmed as the three strategized through the hour for nones mass, which, of course, they were not supposed to be keeping anyhow. Mary did not realize how the poor light was straining her eyes until Waldegrave lit a candle and placed it on the table between them. She had to close her eyes and wait for the glowing images to disappear from the back of her eyelids. This gave her time to realize how weary she had become, yet she was surprised to not feel the familiar pain in her head.

She gave the men a smile as she rose. The peace, confidence, and candlelight gave Mary a beauty that made both men look upon her as if they were witnessing God's blessing upon her and their plans.

"Let us be to bed now," Mary said through a poorly concealed yawn. "We will see on the morrow how many have responded to my call. We will send our messenger to the council and determine how long is prudent to wait before moving to Framlingham." Seeing the men nod in approval, she continued, "Now join me at matins before we take rest."

The next morning, the household was in chaos before the sun rose. The earliest ray of light found Mary at her prie-dieu, her rosary beads slipping naturally through her hands. Only with God's blessing could she become the Queen of England, as her mother always said she would.

When she entered the courtyard, she heard none of the grumbling and arguing that typically accompanied the settling of a household at a new location. Excitement was in the air, and even those who had served her to her highest satisfaction before, now managed to infuse their words and actions with an even greater level of respect.

They believed in her. She could almost convince herself that they even loved her.

As the sun rose in the sky, carts arrived heaped with supplies and men arrived to pledge loyalty to their queen. Mary felt an optimism she had rarely experienced. The absence of illness with the pace she had been keeping was further evidence of God's blessing upon her goal.

The day was spent cloistered with Rochester, Waldegrave, and a scribe. Letters were sent to the council, rejecting Jane's claim, and to the noblemen of the land, calling them to her cause.

Gentlemen of East Anglia began arriving almost immediately. When Huddleston arrived and informed her that Sawston Manor had been burned to the ground as consequence of his service to her, she vowed to see him rewarded for his loyalty once she wore her crown. If any were disappointed that no dukes joined their number, none expressed that concern to Mary.

By midmonth, they prepared to move the burgeoning force to Framlingham. That castle was built for defense, unlike Kenninghall. A moat and stone wall would offer protection while the deer park provided the sustenance required by their ever-growing numbers. The council was not accepting Mary's excuses for not coming to court and accepting Jane's reign. They were coming for her, and she must get to Framlingham first.

The circular that was crushed in Mary's hand had convinced her that her stand would not be swept away as a woman's fancy. Northumberland had called upon justices of the peace throughout the country, demanding that they capture the bastard daughter of the late king before she could cause unrest in the land.

"How dare he?" Mary asked no one in particular, but Rochester was the one who was near.

He took the circular from her hand and tossed it into the fire. "He aims only to hold on to power for himself, cares nothing for you or Jane . . . or the wishes of your brother for that matter."

Mary just shook her head, but she did not feel doubt as she might have once, only anger that men and their lies stood in her way.

"Do you remember, your grace, when the Pope refused to recognize Edward as king?" Rochester asked.

Mary closed her eyes, wearily wondering why he brought this up now, as frantic packing went on around them. They would soon be at Framlingham and then she could rest for the first time since her brother's death. She still had not had the time to properly mourn him, poor boy taken just at the cusp of adulthood.

"Your grace?" Rochester interrupted her thoughts. "The Pope said that you were your father's true heir," he reminded her. "Your father may have made himself head of the church and made laws to reflect his desires, but not even Henry VIII could change the Word of God." He dared to place a hand on her shoulder. "You are the true queen. We will not fail you."

With a weary smile Mary replied, "Then I shall do my best to not fail you."

~ ~ ~ ~

The strong stone walls of Framlingham appeared more welcoming than intimidating to those who looked to it for refuge. As their carts slowly rumbled under the raised portcullis, Mary gazed up to see the family crest of the Howard family carved into the stone. The fortress had reverted to the crown about the time of her father's death due to the earl of Surrey's plotting. He had lost his head, but his father, the old duke of Norfolk, remained in the Tower.

Mary eagerly anticipated getting her first true rest since her quest had begun. The eight foot thick walls surrounding Framlingham offered security that made Mary feel safe enough to sleep soundly this night.

All thoughts of sleep left her for the moment as she made her way into the inner courtyard. Hundreds of people, some who had come with her and others who had arrived to join them, milled about with an almost festive atmosphere. She grinned at Rochester, who had not left her side. He smiled back but indicated that she should follow him.

Curious, she shrugged and allowed him to lead the way,

despite her reluctance to leave the setting where she felt such overwhelming support.

She was surprised that he made his way to one of the thirteen towers rising above the castle wall. Not wanting to appear weak, she conjured up the strength to climb the worn stone stairs. She wanted to call out to him and ask what their mission was, but she was out of breath and a stitch pierced her side.

As she ascended the top, a chill breeze struck her face, taking away what remaining breath she had. The sun filled her vision until her eyes could adjust. When they did, she saw Rochester standing at the edge, beckoning her forward with a look of triumph upon his face. She furrowed her brow but trustingly stepped forward. What she saw was a vision that would remain a treasured memory for the rest of her life.

Below the castle was the deer park that was needed to keep her followers fed. She now saw that it was offering her more than she could have imagined. At her approach, thousands of people who had gathered there called out, "Long live our good Queen Mary! Love live the Queen!"

Pure joy brightened Mary's face as she stood in wonder that these people, her people, were willing to sacrifice all they had, their very lives if necessary, to see her crowned. God had blessed her indeed. Tears filled her eyes, and she blinked them away. She would not have this moment remembered with a blurry image. She could not make out individual faces from where she stood, but if she squinted she could make out a sea of color. The sun shone on hair that was glossy black, cornsilk white, and every hue in between. Among the milling crowd, she noted many doublets of brown but also a variety of shades of blue and green. They were all there for her, the bastard princess who had so often felt unloved.

As Mary settled into her bed late after matins, it was that

moment that she focused on to ensure that her dreams would be sweet.

It was her priority the next day to review the troops in person. This was the first time that she had allowed herself to think of them as troops rather than just a gathering of faithful followers, but with Northumberland's forces approaching, she must recognize them for what they were and give them her encouragement.

Following terce, Mary had her palfrey saddled. The particular animal was chosen for its snowy coat that shimmered beautifully under the summer sun. She had learned the importance of a good impression from her father, even if she had not always been skilled at following it. The horse was beautiful draped with fabric proudly displaying Mary's coat of arms. Her riding dress was not as elaborate as she may have worn to court, but she knew that it would impress those she went to meet with its fine embroidery and vivid blend of colors.

She already felt like a queen as she rode down to the deer park where men stood in loose ranks that were not quite complete disarray. As soon as they saw her approach, their cry rose into the air, "Long live Queen Mary!" and she beamed at them, looking beautiful with the sun turning her hair to molten copper and joy radiating from her countenance.

A few enthusiastic men fired arquebuses into the sky to welcome their queen, and the palfrey sidestepped in fright. Mary whispered into a white silky ear, but another shot sent the animal rearing and Mary grasping for her seat.

Rochester was immediately at her side, pulling the palfrey's reins so tightly that it had little choice but to obey. Mary swallowed her fear, refusing to let a scared mount ruin this moment.

"Waldegrave," she called. "If you would assist me in

dismounting, I would review my troops on foot."

He was quickly at her side and the horse taken away. Rochester looked as though he was not sure about Mary, whose head came almost to his shoulder, wandering through the crowd of hardened men, but he would not publicly question her. When he reflected upon it later, he was glad he had not.

By walking the mile through the makeshift camp, Mary demonstrated her love and loyalty to her troops that only increased theirs. This lovely woman who had endured so much heartache in her life, made a vital connection with men as the thanked them for their goodwill and service. Her gratitude shone on her face as her dress collected mud and dung that could never be removed.

Men, who had arrived at Framlingham out of duty or because they enjoyed a good fight, were caught by the heartstrings and would fight for this petite woman to their dying breath because she had cared enough to walk through the muck for them.

At the evening meal, Rochester admitted his feelings to Mary, "I will not doubt your judgement again, your grace. The people love you. Jane's queenship will not last the fortnight."

"She is not queen at all," Mary corrected him but without malice. "My poor cousin has been manipulated into this position. It is not with her that I have a quarrel."

Rochester tilted his head to her in agreement as he wondered just how innocent the precocious Jane Grey truly was. However, he held his peace. Mary was, after all, his queen.

The next day, all thoughts of the sixteen-year-old claiming Mary's throne were set aside as Mary was invited into the hall to receive new supporters, some of whom brought heartening news.

The fleet that had been sent to Great Yarmouth to prevent Mary's escape had mutinied in her favor. Although Mary had no intentions of leaving England, she was awed that she could now add ships to her growing reserve of military to be used against Northumberland. When the man who had brought news of this stepped back, his story complete, another moved forward and knelt before her.

She did not recognize the man who was introduced as Sir Edmund Peckham, but she greeted him with a smile as he stood. "You are welcome, Sir Peckham, and I thank you with all my heart for your loyalty," she said.

Peckham was clearly nervous, fidgeting as though bugs crawled beneath his clothes, and his voice shook as he replied, "I could do nothing less than support my God-given queen." With a bit more confidence he added, "With the Lord's help I was able to bring more than my poor skills."

With these words, he signaled his page who struggled under the weight of a great chest. Mary frowned toward Rochester in curiosity, but he grinned reassuringly. His burden set at Mary's feet, the page backed away. Sir Peckham opened it with a flourish, and coins glittered in the weak streams of sunlight that fought their way into the hall through high windows.

Mary gasped and lifted her eyes to reevaluate the giver of this generous gift.

"Sir Peckham," Rochester stepped in to clarify, "served your late brother in the royal treasury." There was almost a hint of laughter in his voice.

Her mouth still slightly agape, Mary shifted her eyes between the two men and the treasure between them. People across the countryside had given generously of their livestock, harvest, and even themselves, but Mary knew that soon she would need the cold, hard coin that Peckham had provided.

"You have me at a loss for words, Sir Peckham," Mary whispered as though in a dream. "You have taken great risk for me, and I will do my best to prove that your trust was not misplaced."

He bowed before her, and then surprised her by speaking again. "I have seen tracts throughout London proclaiming your right to the position that has been usurped. With Northumberland leading troops to capture your grace, the council has fallen apart. More abandon Lady Jane's side each day."

"Your insight as one who has been in the city is remarkably valuable. I would ask that you confer with Rochester and Waldegrave to ensure all are as educated as possible on the current situation."

"I would be honored, your grace," Sir Peckham said with another bow. Before he could straighten, another voice boomed through the hall.

"Pray that I could be included in that conversation, your grace, the better to serve you and direct my troops in your name."

Those in the hall turned as one to see John de Vere, the earl of Oxford, stride in as one who knows exactly the impression he is making. Mary controlled her features. Oxford was invaluable to her cause, and of course the man knew it. She would pretend to forget that the man led a lifestyle that Mary could not abide and accept his strong sword arm.

"I believe it is time to announce our intentions," Mary said. As she stood, all around her knelt, heads bowed low. Her proclamation released that very day was signed, "Mary the Queen."

August 1553

The early August day was hot and dry, but not a single word of complaint was heard. As Mary's retinue made its progress toward London's Aldgate, she could only think that her path had been predestined. Her opponents had fallen before her with unexpected ease. Some, such as Robert Dudley, one of Northumberland's many sons, had turned coat and pledged his allegiance to her when he was supposed to be attacking her forces.

Mary accepted any who declared for her. After all, if she imprisoned all who had been lured to support Jane, there would be nary a nobleman left free in England. She would need them, little as she felt she could trust them, and now she had them owing their life to her.

Paget, Pembroke, Arundel, and almost all of Jane's council had recognized Mary's claim by the time the procession was welcomed to London where Mary would be lodged in the Tower of London, not under arrest as she had frequently feared, but to await her coronation. One particular supplicant had tugged at Mary's heart. Her cousin, Frances Grey, had pleaded to see her, though it had been the middle of the night, that she might beg for the life of her daughter.

As they neared London, Mary recalled the nocturnal visit and her proud cousin on her knees before her during a stop at Beaulieu. She blamed it all on Northumberland, of course, and Mary was content to ignore the fact that Frances had happily married her daughter to the man's son.

They had been victims of the duke's scheming, Frances had claimed. Mary could have believed that of Henry Grey, for he had never been strong-willed or a leader of men. Frances had gambled and lost, as had many others who now received Mary's forgiveness.

Mary's vengeance had never been targeted at Jane though.

It was Northumberland, who had surrendered at Cambridge amid news that all had abandoned him, who would bear the brunt of Mary's wrath.

Frances had even claimed that Northumberland had attempted to poison her husband. This had surprised Mary and she demanded proof. It gave them both an outlet to place the blame for the sins of the past fortnight on John Dudley, and he alone.

Almost before the city was in sight, church bells could be heard proclaiming the new Tudor queen. The interview with Frances was forgotten as Mary's ears became tuned to their music. The ringing grew louder with each step, and to that sound was added shouts and singing. Smoke of bonfires could be seen rising above the rooftops, despite the unseasonable heat.

Mary had mixed feelings as she heard one anonymous voice yell, "Lady Mary is proclaimed queen!" Praise be to God that she would never have to endure being called Lady Mary again. It still struck her with surprising pain when she was reminded that her father had cruelly stripped her of the title Princess, but the name of Queen would be a satisfying balm.

The Lord Mayor of London stood proudly at the gate to greet his new queen. Kneeling before her upon fabric carpeting the ground to protect the men's fine clothing from the muck of the London streets, he held the city's mace toward her. "This is but a token of the loyalty we swear to you as our well-beloved queen," he said in a clear, authoritative voice.

Mary motioned to be helped from her horse that she may thank them more personally. Raising the Mayor and his entourage up with a gently laid hand, she looked up to each of them with gratitude shining in her eyes. "It is I who should honor you for your steadfastness in the face of adversity," she said, subconsciously arranging her purple velvet gown carefully around her. "You men have stood for me when other, lesser men, would have abandoned me. A queen can do little without the love and devotion of her followers, and, therefore, I thank you for yours." She paused to gaze into each person's face. They deserved that moment of attention from their queen, and they would remember it always. "I would be grateful if you would join my procession and escort me to the Tower."

Cheers rang out anew, and a few men wiped tears from their eyes. As Rochester watched the scene before him, he was certain that the men present would follow Mary anywhere. It seemed that she had learned a few lessons from her father.

Restored to her saddle with skirts of velvet blanketing her mount's flanks, Mary ensured that her gold embroidered sleeves hung just so and held her head high before nodding that the party should carry on. Her auburn hair reflected the sun as if a crown had already been set upon it.

Close behind Mary, rode her sister, Elizabeth, and her remaining stepmother, Anne of Cleves. Anne was a respected friend of Mary's, but her relationship with her sister had grown strained as the two matured into rather different women. While Mary rode on, a blissful smile upon her face as she tried to acknowledge as many in the crowd as she could, Elizabeth waved quietly. Mary took no notice, but Rochester watched with a creeping feeling that the younger Tudor sister had machinations running in her mind that she was careful to keep secret.

Dressed in virginal white, Elizabeth was radiant with youth and beauty that, despite love held for Mary, one could see the older sister did not possess. The fourth wife of Henry VIII was pleasant and matronly, one who was as easily dismissed by the crowd as she had been by her husband. Behind them, came the duchess of

Norfolk and marchioness of Exeter, having joined Mary's retinue in time to appear that they had leant their support from the beginning.

Before Mary, the earl of Arundel carried the sword of state. He had abandoned the usurper Jane as soon as Northumberland had left London, and was rewarded now for his loyalty, as belated as it might have been.

The city seemed to sway with the movement of the impressive procession and the thousands more who cheered and pushed for views along each street. In contrast with the stories that had reached Mary's camp regarding Jane's entry to the city, the people enthusiastically welcomed their rightful queen.

The Tower of London came into view, and Mary had none of the mixed feelings that sometimes accompanied this sight. She would not think of those who had endured imprisonment, torture, or death. On this day, she would only think of those who had resided here before her to prepare, as she would, for the crown to be placed upon her head.

Her determination to do so was aided by the crowd of children that stood ready to perform. Their high, sweet voices raised in an oration left Mary speechless. Much as she wished to thank them, she could only tip her head to them with a hand clutching at her heart. How she prayed that she would have her own children soon.

The thunder of cannon startled her from her reverie, and many of the children, who had stood properly and followed their orders admirably, squealed and covered their ears. The very earth beneath their feet seemed to quake with the ongoing barrage, but, after the initial shock, Mary felt no fear. This was her fortress, welcoming its queen.

More people waited for her upon the Tower Green. Three

men and one woman, each thinner and more scruffily dressed than the last time Mary remembered seeing them, bent low before her. Again, Mary dismounted before speaking, making it even more difficult for those not immediately before her to see her petite form. However, for those that she presently raised up with her own hand, the moment would never be forgotten.

The supplicants did not lift their eyes to her until she spoke. "These are my prisoners, and I would see them set free," she commanded. A sob was heard, but she could not discern which of them had released it. Mary moved to each of them in turn.

"Good bishop," she whispered as she embraced Stephen Gardiner, who had been imprisoned by her brother for refusing to abide by his heretical reforms. "I will have great need of you once you have had the time to recover properly."

"I am honored, your grace," he replied with uncharacteristic humility. "Praise to God for our Queen Mary."

He had said it quietly, but to Mary it was as loud as the cacophony that could still be heard from outside the Tower walls.

Next, she moved to the duke of Norfolk, who had been imprisoned for his son's ambition since shortly before the death of Mary's father. His eighty years caused him to rise more slowly than Gardiner, but plenty of life still gleamed in his mischievous eyes.

"It was God's hand that saved you," she said in reference to her father's failure to sign Norfolk's death warrant before his own demise. "Therefore, I am assured that he still has good work for you to accomplish."

"Your grace," Norfolk replied gruffly, making Mary wonder if it had not been the old man's sob she had heard.

"Dear Anne," Mary gushed, embracing the duchess of Somerset. Whatever the woman's role in her husband's schemes to control King Edward, all could now be forgiven. "My good gossip, Anne," Mary said with a laugh, "we must share fine wine and conversation as soon as you are able."

"I believe it will be you who has the busier schedule, your grace," Anne replied with trademark dryness.

Mary simply squeezed her arm and moved on to the final prisoner freed by her ascendency. He was the first to preempt her right to speak.

"Your grace, my cousin," Edward Courtenay said without rising from his knees. "God be praised for your beauty is only surpassed by your intellect."

Edward was dashing and handsome, as were most who counted King Edward IV as an ancestor. Mary felt herself blush in spite of herself. She grasped her right hand with her left to keep it from brushing the hair from his face. Somehow, his blond locks appeared soft and clean in the August sun, regardless of his fourteen years of imprisonment.

"Edward, do rise," she said without touching him. She wanted to, and that was just the reason she did not. His lopsided smile informed her that he had taken notice. "Your family was not treated with compassion," she continued with words that she knew would remove his smile, "but I will see that set aright today. Your mother is here to embrace you."

With that, Mary stepped aside so that Gertrude Courtenay, marchioness of Exeter, could embarrass her grown son with her hugs and kisses. Gertrude had been the wife of Henry Courtenay, who had been executed alongside Henry Pole. The connection caused Mary to feel especially joyful to reunite the mother and son. Mary had also offered Gertrude a place as one of her ladies.

The party, including those who had just gained their freedom, then made their way to the royal apartments of the White

Tower. As Mary gazed up at the immense structure, she felt as if the monarchs who had walked through these doors before her were there beside her, offering their support.

Within days, the men of the council who had sought to arrest Mary and crown her cousin in her place were bent before her in submission. A storm of emotion raged within Mary's breast, but she understood the need for reconciliation. With that in mind, she breathed deeply and formed her words with care.

"You have thought to usurp the crown of England," she began and saw fear flash in the eyes of several before her. "You have followed what was wrong when you should have stood up for what was right and true." She paused and looked down imperiously at them before lightening her tone. "But I understand your challenges and forgive you as our Lord in heaven has forgiven me. I would see you each serve your queen that you can give glory to God in your words and deeds."

Men cleared their throats and sniffed as emotion reduced even the most stalwart of men to tears at their queen's compassion. Mary prayed that she was doing the right thing by pardoning men who had wronged her so grievously, but she could not escape the fact that she would have need of them. Surely, once she was their God-anointed queen, they would serve her loyally.

The only person she had refused to receive had been the duchess of Northumberland. Mary did not have her arrested, but neither would she listen to her plea of mercy for her treacherous husband. Even Henry Grey had been released from the Tower and returned to Frances and their younger daughters.

Northumberland's fate was never in doubt, but how would Mary solve the problem of her young usurper?

Mary's uncertainty regarding how to handle Jane was only increased by the letter that she received from the girl just days after her own arrival at the Tower to prepare for her coronation.

"I am at your majesty's mercy," Jane had written. "I can have no hope of forgiveness. Although I could place the blame upon those who have attempted to give to me that which was yours, I am ashamed that it was my own hand that accepted the burden they offered. I deserve heavy punishment, yet hold onto the hope of your great clemency that may follow my sincere confession."

Her heart had been squeezed painfully as Mary read the words. Others had confirmed that Jane had taken the crown reluctantly and given it up willingly days later, but that did not change the fact that she had worn it, and all expected her to suffer for it.

September 1553

Within the royal apartment of the White Tower, Mary prepared for her coronation. She practiced kneeling and walking in each change of clothes, as well as taking note of how each gown shifted with different movements of her arms. Each moment must be perfect, and she knew each fold of fabric and how it would fall with her motions.

She was aware that many were reluctant to accept a woman as their ruler and that questions of who she would marry were foremost in the people's minds. That made it especially vital that her coronation be free of missteps of any kind. It must appear to be as blessed by God as she knew it to be.

Mary's mind was also not able to set aside the problem of a husband for very long before it was bringing it back up for her consideration. She thought of poor Jane, imprisoned within the same castle complex where Mary's preparations were carried out. She had been given no choice in marrying Guildford Dudley and little more option when she was thrust onto the throne. Shaking her head, Mary vowed to herself that her own husband would be her choice.

Gardiner, in his new role as Lord Chancellor, had been quick to encourage her to consider her cousin, Edward Courtenay, with whom he had long been imprisoned. Mary had the impression that he thought of the younger man as a son. She could not deny that the handsome Courtenay stirred something within her and would create an important bond between Tudor blood and the remnant of the previous dynasty, but he was so young and had spent so much time closed off from the events of the world.

The boy's mother, too, offered glowing reports of him. The fact that Mary thought of him as just that, a boy, was all evidence she required to counter Gertrude's hopes for her son. Mary prayed that the woman would count her blessings that Edward was free and not press his marital suit too enthusiastically.

Charles V had been one of Mary's father's choices for her once upon a time, and Mary looked to him as one that she could trust above all others. Yet, he had not offered his hand to her, and, if he did, she was not sure she should accept it. Would marriage to him make England a part of the Holy Roman Empire? Mary had to think about what was best for her kingdom above her own desires.

She remembered the dream of her mother and governess, that their children would be united. Reginald Pole was a cardinal of the Catholic Church, but had never taken orders. He could be an ideal candidate to assist her in healing the damage caused by her brother's reforms. However, she wondered if he would be better placed to do that as her husband or an archbishop.

Mary sighed, no closer to an answer than she had been before, and gestured for her ladies to assist her out of the heavy coronation robes she had been practicing in. For the first time since her brother's death had sent her on an unexpected adventure to gain the throne, she felt the onset of a headache.

~ ~ ~ ~

Her time spent abed had given Mary time for reflection when pain was not lancing through her too much for thought. Upon rising, she knew that she would have to take further steps toward reconciliation, and that she would indeed require a husband. She simply could not depend upon her own frail body to carry out the duties that would be demanded of her.

Thankfully, she also had a solution to that dilemma. Charles had written to her, not with his own proposal of marriage, but to offer his son, Philip. The peace that had come over Mary with the arrival of that letter reassured her that this was the path God had chosen for her. She would not veer from it.

Neither would she remain proud before her council. Those who could not be forgiven had been removed, and the rest she would be fully reconciled with. Determined to have them see her sincerity, she had knelt before them, humbling herself and expressing her desire that they work together for the glory of God and the good of the kingdom. Some men wondered how they had ever seen fit to betray her.

As the date chosen for her coronation approached, Mary felt that she had successfully quelled the attempted usurpation and gained the love of her people. Most importantly, the mass had been restored and had been said regularly in the royal chapel since she had arrived in London.

Gertrude Courtenay had demonstrated that she wished desperately to be the queen's confidant since joining Mary's household. Mary was pleased to welcome her as one, except for the woman's insistence that the queen must marry her son. She gestured to Gertrude now for assistance with her dressing. Once complete, Mary also requested that she join her at mass.

"I am so grateful to see your grace's health restored," Gertrude said, though her voice was more stern than gracious. "Now you can hear Cranmer's statement as he attempts to defend his treason and heresy."

Mary gave Gertrude a warning look. The woman took liberties that the other women in Mary's household did not. "I shall," was Mary's only comment on Cranmer. She would see him punished, for his support of Dudley and for crimes that went back much further. "Soon my cousin will be here to cope with the heresy that has been planted and encouraged to grow in the kingdom since the death of my father. We will see true worship again in our land."

Seeing the look upon Gertrude's face, Mary knew that she had said the wrong thing and given the duchess the privileged information she longed for. "When should we be prepared to welcome the cardinal?" she asked innocently.

"That has not yet been decided," Mary snapped, angrier with herself than Gertrude. God help her quickly learn the rules of politics.

Gertrude was not giving up easily. "Perhaps, Cardinal Pole will be present for your wedding," she stated with a lilt of question in the statement.

Mary stared at her, trying to decide if the woman had heard rumors of Mary's plan to marry Philip of Spain, a secret that had been shared with very few. There was also the possibility that she believed Mary hoped to wed Reginald. Gertrude's face revealed nothing, frozen as it was in innocent curiosity. It seemed a good strategy, so Mary said nothing, as if she had not heard the question, and led her ladies to mass.

As the familiar words of the priest resounded through the chapel, Mary's thoughts returned to the execution of John Dudley the previous month. Northumberland had seemed to be her true enemy as she had made her way toward London, but his recantation of the heretic faith had raised doubts within her. Had he been misled by man or his own ambition? She wondered if he had truly repented. Mary had taken the advice of men who insisted that she must follow through with his punishment, and now she prayed that it had been the right thing to do.

"Forgive me for any wrong I may have done," she prayed, "even for sins I was not aware that I was committing. Heavenly Father, surround me with good councilors who will aid me in doing your will."

She had to let go of the guilt that she felt over Dudley's death. If his conversion had been authentic, he now enjoyed the peace of heaven. If not, he had deserved his death as a traitor and heretic.

Mary had found her advisors surprisingly willing to offer mercy toward the duke of Suffolk. As Jane's father, one might have wondered if he were guiltier than Northumberland, but no one who knew the two men accused Henry Grey of being the mastermind behind the plot. It had given Mary joy to release the man to her cousin Frances, his wife.

Feeling her mind wandering too far from the words of the mass, Mary shoved the thoughts aside and focused on her worship of the God whose help she knew she would be sorely in need of in the coming months.

More evidence of that need was set before her within moments of returning to her chamber. The Spanish ambassador, Simon Renard entered the room with all the familiarity of a close relative. Mary noticed the knowing looks that were exchanged by her ladies, but she did not care. As representative of her uncle Charles, Renard was given the respect that Mary would have given the Holy Roman Emperor had he been there.

Without being told, the ladies cleared away. Mary had already established a habit of speaking to him privately, and many wondered how much control Spain would have of England, regardless of whom Mary chose to wed. The queen ignored such talk. She could trust Renard more than most of her English councilors.

"Your grace," Renard said in accented English as he gracefully knelt before her. He was handsome in a dark, seductive way, but it was a form of attractiveness that had always repelled Mary more than appealed to her.

He rose without waiting for her to speak and poured himself a goblet of wine at her sideboard. "You must do something about that sister of yours," he said in a teasing tone as the red liquid filled his cup.

Mary raised an eyebrow, and nodded toward another goblet, which he quickly filled for her. He continued as he handed it to her, "Elizabeth is allowing the Courtenay boy to court her. He is smart enough to know that he will not be given the hand of the queen but dimwitted enough to grasp at the sister without permission."

Finally breaking her silence, Mary asked, "And what makes you believe that my sister is welcoming Edward's advances?"

Renard made himself comfortable in the plush cushions of the chair nearest the queen before he responded, "Ever since you restored him to the earldom of Devon, he has been acting as though you handed him a crown." He leaned closer to her and lowered his voice despite the fact that they were alone, "Many pay court to him as though they too believe that he may become king. However," he leaned back and casually continued, "seeing that your interest in him is rather nonexistent, his eyes have settled upon your heir."

"Little good it shall do him," Mary countered. "It will be my own son who will be heir soon enough."

"Of course," Renard agreed noncommittedly. "God's will shall be done in that matter, I have no doubt. Yet, you may wish to ensure that your sister does not have other plans." Seeing Mary hesitate, he added, "She is a clever one, and not to be trusted."

Mary sighed and sipped her wine. In her heart, she knew that Renard was right. He was not the only one to make such remarks about Elizabeth, but how she wished that they could be close and supportive sisters rather than adversaries. On the matter of Edward Courtenay, she would have to speak with his mother and leave the responsibility of dealing with him to Gertrude.

"As for the cardinal," Renard switched subjects, assuming that Mary would do as she had been told when it came to the first, "you should delay his arrival. The people are pleased to see the church restored, but you must ease them into their old traditions. You must remember that young people of this day have never known the Church of Rome."

Mary sat upright and alert, but Renard cut her off before she could speak.

"I know what you would say, that it is precisely the reason to move forward. Your devotion is unquestioned, but you must also learn to be politically savvy."

Mary released her breath without uttering a word of the defense she had been preparing to sling at him. His words echoed her earlier thoughts, so she indicated for him to carry on.

"Your subjects have endured the early death of their king, God rest his soul, a usurpation attempt, and are about to hold a coronation for the first queen regnant of England. They do so with joy, but you must also give them time to breathe before you ask more of them."

Mary nodded slowly as she gazed into the wine in her goblet. She gently moved it in small circles causing the liquid to swirl and catch glimmers of light.

"I value your counsel," she admitted slowly, still forming her words and not wanting to give him too much cause to feel he had gained a victory. "I will give the matter of my sister more thought and pray upon a solution. The other matters you have raised will also be given greater consideration, though you must remember that my cousin is eager to return to his homeland and set about the work God has set before him."

She felt that she had remained in control, but Renard still had the look of a satisfied cat. What she would not do to have one person to guide her who was not motivated by self-interest and ambition! Mary rose from her seat, and Renard seemed surprised, quickly rising from his seat and setting the goblet aside.

"I believe I will retire," Mary said. "I have much to think about. Please send Susan and Gertrude in to attend me on your way out," she commanded, already turning her back on the arrogant Spanish ambassador.

He was soon replaced by Mary's women, who wordlessly took up their tasks to prepare the queen for bed. Mary considered Gertrude's profile for a moment as the older woman worked before addressing her.

"How is Edward enjoying his newfound freedom?" she asked and then realized that the question could sound sinister to one who had less than pure intentions.

Gertrude only smiled and gushed, "He daily gives thanks to God for his merciful queen."

Mary furrowed her brow. To whom did she give the greater trust, the Spanish ambassador or the marchioness of Exeter? Did the son carry on behind his mother's back? He would not be the first. She decided not to press the matter for the moment.

Once she was in bed, Mary reflected upon her sister. Mary pictured her younger sister's profile as she had seen it when they attended mass together. Had she been genuine? It was so difficult to tell with that young woman who kept her true thoughts so carefully cloaked.

Mary rolled over and sighed. She must release her worries and find rest. A headache teased at the edges of her mind, but she could not allow illness to encroach.

The day of her coronation was quickly approaching.

October 1553

The blast of trumpets joined the ringing of bells as Mary walked toward Westminster Abbey. She had been determined to wear crimson velvet robes as her father and brother had and not be carried in a litter as she had been in the previous day's procession. Her coronation must include the traditions of those who had gone before her, with the vital exception that she was not male.

As she stepped onto the azure fabric that was spread across the floor of the abbey, she smiled at the brilliant contrast it made with the vibrant hue of her coronation robes. Sunlight danced upon the rich fabrics and Mary's loose red-gold hair, creating a spectacular vision of majesty. She took a deep breath and entered, her form dwarfed by the soaring pillars and high ceiling of the abbey.

Followed closely by Elizabeth, who wore a stunning combination of snow white and bright scarlet, Mary approached the altar where Bishop Gardiner stood ready to crown England's first queen. The coronation chair was high atop a platform, and Mary felt her heart flutter at the thought of alighting those steps and sitting where kings of England since Edward I had sat as the crown was placed upon their heads.

She prayed that the crown would be lighter than the one she had borne yesterday. During the parade from the Tower to St. Paul's and finally to Whitehall, Mary had been tempted to rest her heavy head in her hands, her neck aching from the weight of the elaborate piece.

Before she could ascend the steps to the seat of highest honor, she prostrated herself before the altar. Given the comfort of a soft velvet cushion, Mary remained facedown as prayers were said above and around her. She felt as though she were enveloped within the cloud of witnesses that God assured her in his word surrounded her.

When it was time for her to kneel and pledge herself to her kingdom, she was confident, promising to uphold the just laws of the land before the song of the choir filled the air and drifted to those left standing outside.

As they sang, Mary stepped into a curtained area to change for her anointing. Despite her hours of practice, this was the part that unnerved her. Susan, Fran, and Gertrude moved quickly with deft movements that calmed Mary's nerves. The heavy robes were removed and a feminine violet petticoat replaced them.

Mary looked and felt vulnerable as she returned to the altar free of the masculine robes that had protected her throughout the service up to this point. She felt herself shiver without their heavy warmth. Her eyes found Gardiner's, and his fatherly smile encouraged her. Kneeling before him, Mary closed her eyes as the bishop anointed her shoulders, chest, and forehead with the precious oil from Flanders. As his warm fingers reached her temples, she peered at him and took strength from the utter confidence he exuded.

Gardiner was certain that he did God's will in making Mary God's representative upon the throne of England. She could only move forward in that same confidence and obedience to God's plan for her.

A mantle of deepest crimson affixed about her shoulders, Mary climbed to Saint Edward's Chair as the Te Deum rang through the church. The crown, designed just for her, was placed upon her head, and she looked out at the hundreds gathered, imagining even greater numbers waiting for a glimpse of her outside. A grin spread wide across her face.

She was Queen of England.

~ ~ ~ ~

After the passage of only a few days, Queen Mary prepared to open her first Parliament. She had dressed carefully, choosing the brilliant blue dress that she had worn for her procession from the Tower to Whitehall the day before her coronation with a cloth of gold mantle. Each were reminders of her majesty and the love of the people that had enabled her to restore her crown from the usurper's head without fighting a battle.

It had bothered Mary to be crowned while the laws of the land still named her a bastard daughter of a late king. Therefore, that was one of the first changes she had instructed Gardiner to make.

He opened Parliament with a statement regarding the poor state of the kingdom due to heresy and unjust laws before proposing that the marriage of King Henry VIII and Catherine of Aragon be declared valid once and for all.

Mary had not yet spoken from her perch upon her throne, but she watched the men carefully for any sign that they would dispute her legitimacy.

None did.

The moment passed almost as if it had been inconsequential. As Gardiner began speaking on the next topic, Mary realized that her mother's battle had finally been laid to rest. Without fanfare or even a moment of reflection on anyone's part but her own, Mary was a true daughter of the king and queen of England, the legitimate heir, and no longer a bastard.

She closed her eyes, letting Gardiner's words fade into the background, as she silently thanked God and wondered if her mother was celebrating this victory in heaven. As much as she desired to bask in the moment, she forced her attention back to the task at hand: repealing the religious laws that had been passed by men who had taken advantage of her brother's youth and immaturity. Although he had insisted that the laws were his own and had been upon the verge of manhood when he died, Mary could not believe that Edward had been the one at fault for the ruination of the Church of England.

"As the Supreme Head of the Church of England," Gardiner's voice was booming, "our good Queen Mary has discerned errors in recent acts concerning the practice of our faith. With the salvation of each of her subjects heavy upon her heart, her grace proposes the following changes."

Mary despised being referred to as the Supreme Head of the Church almost as much as she had abhorred being called Lady Mary. The head of the church was rightfully the pope, but she and Gardiner had agreed, much to Cardinal Pole's dissatisfaction, that changes must be made gradually to avoid confusion and misunderstanding among the people.

Gardiner was listing the laws that would be repealed, "the mass is reinstated as of this day, and criticism of it is forbidden. The offense of the marrying of priests shall be ended. Finally, the newly created Book of Common Prayer, which is filled with heresies and text that has the power to lead people to damnation, shall be removed from every church in the land."

Unlike the lack of reaction that had met her Act of Restitution, the list of religious annulments created a quiet stir in the room. None seemed willing to speak out, but Mary could see known Protestants squirming in their seats while those of the old faith sat up a little bit straighter with satisfied grins upon their faces.

Mary frowned, creating a deep crease between her eyebrows. They should be rejoicing that true worship is restored, not looking as though they have won an earthly victory. This was not about politics; it was about salvation. She lifted a hand to indicate that she would speak.

"These matters discussed here today are those closest to my heart," Mary began. She knew that she should smile and attempt to win them over, but she was not good at putting on an act and her heartbeat was beginning to pulse too loudly in her head. "There has been some resistance," she continued, thinking of the poor dead dog that had been thrown through the window of her presence chamber. It had been shaved to resemble a tonsured priest or monk with a rope tied tightly around its poor scrawny neck. "However, I pray that we can work together for the good of our kingdom and the glory of God."

She paused and considered sitting, hesitant to say too much. The memory of her father urged her to carry on. "I would see justice and peace restored in my beloved kingdom, in addition to the practice of true faith that is pleasing to our Lord. In contrast to mercy, justice rewards the obedient and punishes those who are deserving of it. I have been merciful where such mercy has been prudent," she let these words swirl around the chamber for a moment, letting each man present consider the difference in the treatment of John Dudley compared to their own. "I would not wish to be moved toward a sterner form of justice that makes these acts of mercy impossible."

The whispering and shuffling that had been a quiet but constant noise within the hall was replaced by an eerie silence, and Mary finally was able to force her lips to part in a smile. "Let us do this good work together," she finished and nodded for Gardiner to continue.

If any man in attendance took issue with the queen's words or proposed legal changes, none dared to speak of it openly in her presence. Mary felt that she had successfully completed her first day of Parliament without allowing any to look down on her for being a woman, but the headache that accompanied her to bed was her poor reward for the stress of the day.

She spent the next day in bed, rising only to hear mass. Gertrude brought Mary her letters, and helped her prop up with pillows to read through them. As queen, she simply had too many responsibilities to allow her poor health to keep her from getting work accomplished.

Mary perused correspondence from Cardinal Pole, tracing the letters with her fingers and wishing she could be as bold as he called upon her to be. She sighed, closing her eyes and leaning back into the pillows. Had her efforts at Parliament been enough? Pole urged her toward complete reunion with Rome, which was in truth her wish as well, but her councilors had encouraged caution.

The people were thankful for the restoration of the mass, but other areas were less clear. When Mary's father had dissolved the monasteries, he had done more than forever change religious life. Much of that land and riches was now held by men who were afraid to lose it, regardless of their religious beliefs.

Flipping through the pages written in Reginald's fine hand, Mary wondered how she would ever balance it all. When she read his advice, she was eager to follow it. When Paget explained that it would be too much, too soon, he made sense as well. It was only when Renard, as the voice of the Emperor, had also urged caution, that she had been willing to listen.

As if the thought of him had conjured his person, Renard's voice was heard in the next room. Susan soon entered the bed chamber with his request to see the queen. Mary toyed with the idea of sending him away, but only for a moment. She was a queen and must act like it.

"Give me another sip of that tonic and help me dress," she

wearily ordered Susan.

Mary cringed before the sour liquid even hit her tongue in anticipation of its well-known horrible taste. Slowly chewing a mint leaf as Susan laced her dress, she felt some small relief before she entered the connecting room where Renard casually flirted with Mary's ladies. They quickly scurried away when they saw their queen.

"Reports are that you performed very well for your first Parliament," he said hardly rising from his seat and bowing before reclaiming it.

"Thank you," Mary said, quickly taking the seat next to him. The nausea that she so dreaded was joining her headache in its attack. She shook her head fervently against the wine Renard offered, then regretted the movement as new pains shot through her skull.

He pretended not to notice and carried on with his task. "You will soon bring my liege's proposal to their attention?" he asked.

"As far as I am aware," Mary countered, "I have received no official proposal." She clutched her hands together to keep them from rubbing her temples in Renard's presence. He already knew too many of her weaknesses.

"Ah," he interjected as if she had reminded him of something. "You will be most interested in this letter."

Mary's eyebrows rose as Renard reached into a pocket and revealed a paper clearly bearing the seal of Charles V. She grasped it from him, causing him to smile as he watched her read.

She squinted at the print, which was so fine that it must be that of a scribe, and swallowed as her heart rose into her throat. "The Emperor offers a greater match than I deserve," she whispered.

"Prince Philip is indeed admirable and virtuous," Renard agreed, "but no more so than his intended bride."

Mary gave him a doubtful sideways glance. Her heart had been set upon Philip since the idea was first proposed, but now that it was becoming a reality, doubts assailed her.

"He is but twenty-six," she pointed out. "A man so much younger is likely to be disposed to amorous desires that I have never welcomed or taken a fancy to."

She fought to control the blush that rose up her neck to her face, but she had heard too many stories of Edward Courtenay's escapades since his release from the Tower to have any curiosity about what Philip's expectations would be. Renard was already waving away her words.

"Prince Philip is so stable and settled in his character that many mistake him for a man of greater years. He has already been married once and is more than capable of quelling any doubts you have of him as a husband. As your king, he brings his experience as ruler of the Low Countries and Spain. It is an ideal match," Renard assured her.

Not wishing to give away too much, Mary replied, "You present a good case, but I have many councilors who would rather see me take an Englishman, such as the earl of Devon, as a husband."

Renard smirked. Mary had spoken too often and too vocally against Courtenay for him to take this challenge seriously. "Has Courtenay decided which sister he prefers, then?" he asked with false innocence.

Mary pressed her lips tightly together, feeling her cheeks heat up. "He has no interest in the Lady Elizabeth. Her faith is in doubt and she is too proud . . . too much her mother's child," Mary retorted, mentally chiding herself for letting Renard get under her skin.

"Yet, you would have him who your sister rejects as a suitor?" Renard pressed further.

Mary's head throbbed when she shook it. She had let him get the best of her, so she may as well admit it. "No," she quietly confessed. "I have no interest in marrying Courtenay."

"Of course, you do not," Renard soothed. "He is not worthy of you or your kingdom. Prince Philip will relieve you of the pain of the men's work that you are forced to undertake and bring you joy that our Lord gives only through matrimony."

Mary smiled weakly, thankful that Renard had eased in his attack and seeing the wisdom of his words. "That is well," she said, not wishing to commit herself with her stomach churning and her head pulsing. "I would invite Prince Philip to visit England to decide if the land and proposed bride suit him."

Immediately, she knew that she had made a mistake. Renard flinched away and stumbled uncharacteristically over his reply, pulling at his doublet as though he might find the answer in a secret pocket.

"That would be impossible, your grace," he said. "I am sure you can understand that Prince Philip is as busy as yourself with the demands of his realm. It would not be fit for him to be paraded like a horse at market to determine his worth."

Mary knew that he was right but also would not allow him to pressure her into saying too much. She rose slowly, feeling her stomach wish to rise faster than the rest of her. Renard also stood.

"I have much to consider," she said. "Your proposal is a fine one, yet I would spend time in prayer and contemplation before I respond."

"Of course," Renard said, tipping his head to her and trying to hide the disappointment in his voice.

The next day, Mary summoned Rochester to assist her with the day's work. He understood her moods and ailments, and she could be herself before him as one who had offered her loyalty long before most others.

"Next is the plea of Henry Stafford," Rochester said as he set aside one paper and took up the next. "He requests financial assistance."

Mary's brow furrowed in concern. "He is married to Ursula Pole," Mary said reaching for the letter. "They have endured much," she whispered as she narrowed her eyes to bring the words into focus.

"Indeed," Rochester agreed, leaning back and rubbing his own tired eyes. "Raised with the expectation of the dukedom of Buckingham, his reality since the execution of his father and Ursula's mother is debt and disappointment."

Mary felt grief wash over her as if the death of Margaret Pole was not more than ten years in the past. "He writes that I am a 'merciful mistress, who daily restores rightful heirs,'" she whispered.

Rochester laughed, but cleared his throat to cover it when Mary's eyes flashed at him. "He does know how to form an appeal," he agreed with chagrin.

"I wish to grant him the office of chamberlain of the exchequer," Mary announced, passing the letter back to Rochester.

He simply nodded, made a note, and said, "I will see it done."

"Good," she said with finality. "Are we through?" She was in need of a walk outdoors to replenish her spirit and energy and was surprised when Rochester cleared his throat once more to speak. Mary had already begun rising from her seat but settled back into it.

"I would speak to you of your marriage plans, if I may be so bold."

She gazed into his eyes, wondering who had put him up to this. "I believe you have earned that privilege," she replied.

He tipped his head to her in thanks before speaking. "I would request that you give greater consideration to the earl of Devon."

Mary snorted. "Courtenay? Has Gardiner spoken to you?"

Rochester ignored her question and pressed on. "This country that we both love has been through so much turmoil. I fear that the rule of a foreign prince is more than it can take."

She saw that he was sincere, but her anger flamed at his words. "I am the queen," she corrected him. She saw that he would reply and spoke first. "Whomever I marry will be my comfort and guide as any husband must be to his wife, but I am the ruler of England. How could you, who helped me get to this place, doubt me?"

Mary watched the emotions play across his face. It was not in his nature to argue with her, so he must feel strongly about the Courtenay marriage. She felt just as strongly against it.

"Do you think that I would make any decision were it not for the good of my kingdom?" she asked him. As he shook his head in denial, she continued, "Yet my husband must also be one of my own choosing. He must be one that I can bear an heir with and trust to give me good counsel. I cannot stand the thought of Courtenay in that position."

Rochester took a deep breath and rolled his head from side to side, causing popping sounds to come from his neck. "Very well, your grace," he conceded, as she had known he would.

"I appreciate having your support," Mary said. She knew that she did not have to, that it was his duty to do her will, but he deserved her gratitude after staying by her side through so much.

His smile was fleeting and he shrugged. "I will not be the only one who attempts to convince you otherwise," he warned her. "Many are concerned about what it means for England's future to be ruled by the future Holy Roman Emperor. We have no wish to become a part of Philip's empire."

"I do not wish it either," Mary insisted. "I will continue to rule England in my own right, and Philip's power will not extend beyond my lifetime, when my child will reign."

Rochester nodded as if this is what he had expected her to say and remained less than fully convinced.

"Say you will speak for me," she demanded.

He stood and smoothed his clothing before answering. "You can depend upon me, as always, your grace," he said before bowing low and leaving her alone with her doubts.

Rochester was correct. Within days of the presentation of Prince Philip's proposal, Sir John Pollard, speaker for the Commons, met with her to express the concerns that he assured her were shared by many of his peers and those he represented.

With Rochester at her side, Mary admitted the lawyer and his small entourage. Pollard's roles as speaker of the house and judge were evident in the way he presented his case to his queen. Carefully outlining each argument that had ever been voiced against her marriage to Philip, he was wearing quickly on Mary's thinning patience.

"Your grace," he appealed to her with his finely manicured hands in a position of prayer, "we, your subjects, wish only happiness and a long and glorious reign for you, our beloved queen. Yet, we cannot help but give thought to our own plight, should tragedy occur and we are left to the guardianship of a Spanish king." Mary opened her mouth to speak, but Pollard continued as if he had not noticed. "It is our greatest desire to see God bless your grace with an heir to carry on your noble line, but what if they are burdened by the crown before their age of majority? Should they be guided by one who has self-interests beyond our shores? Even for yourself, your grace. Will not a foreign husband make demands upon you that will force you to choose between he and your kingdom?"

He carried on, saying nothing that Mary had not already endured from others who felt they knew her heart better than she did herself. Pollard seemed not to notice her sighs and the fact that she took a seat rather than continuing to hear him out while standing. She began examining the embroidery on her skirts, wondering if he would ever complete his rhetoric. Her head snapped up at Pollard's next words.

"What if he were to remove you from the kingdom altogether, as would be his right as your husband?"

"That is enough!" Mary shouted, jumping to her feet and glaring at the men gathered before her. She had intended on allowing Rochester to speak for her, but the man's impertinence had gone too far. "Must I remind you that I am your sovereign? I thank you for your counsel but find it strange and unsuitable that you would take such liberty as I am certain has never been taken with a king of England."

Rochester stood next to her and looked as if he would speak, as was his duty, but she held up a hand to him.

"I shall marry, for the sake of my kingdom more than for myself, for it is contrary to my own inclination," she said, controlling her emotion with great effort and looking each of Pollard's followers in the eye for a moment as she spoke. "It is not right that you would question me in this, for the welfare of my subjects is my foremost concern. To doubt my motives is disrespectful at best and offensive at worst. I will not marry one of my subjects, and you must dissolve your hopes that my decision in this matter may be altered."

Pollard stood as if frozen, speechless by the queen's dismissal of his sensibly formed argument. Before he could think of a response, Rochester was leading him with his men from the chamber, murmuring words of dismissal.

Returning to Mary's side, Rochester found her shaking with anger as she paced the floor. He filled two glasses of wine before he approached her, holding out a glass with one hand as he gestured her back to her seat with the other.

She gratefully accepted the wine and took a sip before taking the proffered chair. Was she too high-tempered in her response? Would it be demonstrating further weakness to ask? She longed for Philip's arrival, so that she would have one who was truly her equal whom she could bare herself before, all of her doubts and fears, and not risk belittling herself.

"You managed that rather well, your grace," Rochester said as if he could read her mind. "Your father would be proud."

Remembering her father's rages that had never failed to put men firmly back in their place, Mary finally smiled as she brought her glass to her lips.

November 1553

The incident with Pollard may have been counted by Mary as a victory, but it had triggered her headaches and sent her to bed for several days to recuperate. The tutting and sidelong glances that she received from Gertrude Courtenay as she ministered to her mistress told Mary all she needed to know about where she stood. If only Mary would stop being stubborn and marry her son, much of her stress would be relieved. The woman was perceptive enough, however, not to give voice to her thoughts.

Mary did what business she could through Rochester and was eager to meet with her council regarding her betrothal as soon as she was well enough. She cursed her feeble body as her head laid heavily upon the pillow, wondering what schemes sparked like wildfire while she was unable to attend to her duties.

After several days of following her physician's recommendations to the letter, Mary felt well enough to force herself to face her responsibilities. Instead of whispering rumors and speculation, her council would hear from her directly and the matter of her betrothal could be put to rest. Fran attended Mary, and the queen was thankful for this quiet, loyal attendant on this day when Susan's bright chatter or Gertrude's digging for information would have instigated the piercing pain that Mary hoped to avoid for a few hours.

Seeming to understand Mary's needs, Fran hummed quietly as she tied laces, affixed jewels, and arranged hair. Mary's thanks was clear in her eyes, and Fran simply nodded her receipt of it before leaving the chamber.

Before Mary left her private sanctuary, she closed her eyes for a moment as her rosary beads slipped through her fingers. She prayed for strength and wisdom to face her hostile council. Pollard's angry face came uninvited into her mind, and she wondered how many of her council would share his beliefs.

Prince Philip was an ideal match, and it infuriated her that so many dared to speak out in opposition to their queen. Had she been a king, marriage to a princess of Philip's standing would have been lauded as an ideal arrangement. Did she not deserve the same respect?

The increase in volume of noise from the next room alerted Mary that her escort was ready. Pulling in a slow deep breath and then releasing it, she cleared her mind of everything except the words she had prepared for her council and the confidence that her God stood firmly beside her.

Her pomander swung as she moved down the corridors at a quick stride. The scent of rosemary and lavender filled her nostrils and calmed her nerves as well as held her headache at bay. Fran again, she was sure. How wonderful it was to have one who served her out of pure love and devotion rather than ambition. She found that she was able to hold her head higher due to this small measure of encouragement.

She entered the hall where her council had gathered feeling reassured, only to shrink into herself upon seeing their faces. Mary examined the men gathered around the long, dark table and found no support there. Before she had even spoken, she knew that hers was a lone voice, so she spontaneously decided to attend to another topic before addressing her marriage plans.

A murmur of surprise moved like a wave through the room when Mary, instead of announcing her betrothal, wanted to discuss the fate of her young cousin.

"I wish to begin with a discussion of the validity of the marriage between Frances Brandon and Henry Grey," she announced.

Eyes widened and the immediate hush was replaced by

frantic whispering. Nothing had led them to expect this. Mary continued as if nothing was amiss.

"Henry Grey was betrothed to the daughter of the earl of Arundel before he married my cousin," Mary said, tilting her head toward the earl to indicate that he could add to this if he would like. He simply nodded back to her, so she continued. "This precontract makes the children of Frances Brandon illegitimate and not eligible for the line of succession."

Mary forced her hands to be still and attempted to keep the flush from her cheeks. Guilt assailed her though she made this move only to protect the couple's daughter. If Jane were not seen as a potential threat, Mary hoped that calls for her execution would cease.

"Would anyone else speak on this?" she asked.

No one seemed eager to be the first to comment, especially since it would be difficult to disagree with Mary's argument. The betrothal had been well-known at the time, even if the Grey's marriage had never been brought into question because of it.

"The usurper must still stand trial," one of the men called out, and Mary wondered which it was who was so reluctant to offer the sort of mercy that he had so gratefully received from his queen.

"Very well," she gave in. The murmurs of agreement had convinced her that she must carry out this expected next step. Jane could be brought to trial, but she would never pass judgement on her. She prayed that giving them this victory would make them open to her next topic.

Her fingers instinctively gathered her rosary and fumbled at the beads until she saw Gardiner watching her hands. Clutching her fingers together, she announced what one and all already knew.

"God, who has performed so many miracles in my favor,"

she said as she pinned each man to their seat with her gaze, "has blessed me once again with his choice of a husband. I have given my solemn promise to marry Prince Philip of Spain and shall love him perfectly as God commands."

A few managed to appear shocked, though Mary knew that none were surprised by her news. Gardiner's face was reddening and he fidgeted with his robes as if to keep himself from speaking. Others averted their eyes or shuffled documents. None even made a show of rejoicing with her as they should.

Mary decided to continue, "This partnership will benefit my beloved kingdom as well, for nothing I do is considered without knowing that it is the best for my people above my own wishes. I am, first and foremost, England's queen and strive to do all for the good of my subjects."

She took her seat, unsure what else to say in the face of such a dire reception. Mary controlled her face but her heart beat erratically in her chest, and pain crept up her stiffening neck ready to encapsulate her skull.

Suddenly, the silence was broken by a dozen men all speaking at once, and not one voice was raised in her support. Mary allowed herself only seconds to close her eyes and let her nostrils search for the calming scent of herbs before she tuned into the words swirling angrily about the room.

"Your grace," Gardiner made himself heard over the others and they bowed to his authority. "Let me advise you as one that has your best interests at heart as well as an understanding of your people's fears."

His chest puffed out as he spoke in an inadvertent physical manifestation of his arrogance. Even now, he expected the queen to concede that he knew what was best for her in this, and all other, matters.

"A foreign match will simply not be abided by your people," he said with a shrug. "They cannot understand why their queen would place them under the rule of a Spanish prince, subject to his demands which may require that they support or participate in wars not of our own making." He waved a hand about the room to indicate all those who agreed with him before concluding, "Your majesty can find conjugal happiness and peace for your realm by selecting one of your own subjects as consort."

Many murmured their agreement, even if they had not joined Gardiner in putting forward Courtenay in the past. He was preferred by far to the Spanish prince.

Mary watched them bobbing their heads in assent, as they had not done for her and felt her anger rising and heat rushing to her face. Pain lanced through her temples and her heart struggled at an irregular beat. She stood, and all fell quiet.

"I have made my vow before the Holy Sacrament. I will marry Philip, and, as much as I had prayed for your approval, I expect nothing less than obedience in this matter. Ambassador Renard has prepared a draft of the marriage treaty for your perusal. We shall meet again once you have each had an opportunity to read it and consider its terms. It is only regarding the specifics of this contract that I require your advisement. The marriage itself is not up for debate, so I hope that I have made myself understood."

Without taking a moment to perceive the effect of her words, Mary strode from the chamber with her guards scurrying to take their places around her. Hot tears filled her eyes, only succeeding to exacerbate her anger. Her feet, so eager to carry her back to her room, tripped on her heavy skirts, and she would have stumbled were it not for the quick grasp of the guard closest to her.

She did not even look up to see who it was, too embarrassed by her council and her own reaction to reveal her tear-streaked face to him. Resentment filled her as she remembered Paget assuring her that Edward had known his own mind when it came to religious reforms. They trusted her adolescent brother with salvation, but not her with deciding whom she should marry!

Mary did not remember arriving in her rooms or slamming the door in the face of her women, but she suddenly found herself prostrated upon her bed wishing never to rise from it.

When she did eventually draw herself from the soft, welcoming bedding, Mary had determined her next step. If the people, her own privy council, would not rally to her, she would call upon one who undoubtedly would. Her cousin had been writing to her, desiring nothing more than to return to his homeland and aid her in the restoration of the church. Mary had cautioned him to wait due to the restlessness and uncertainty that had reigned upon the death of her brother, but she would welcome him now.

It was time for Cardinal Reginald Pole to come home.

December 1553

Mary clutched the portrait of Philip close to her heart. Since she had received it, she had slowly fallen in love with her betrothed, or at least the idea of him. He was her knight in shining armor who would rescue her from those who would oppose her. Philip would love her and give her a child to carry on the Tudor name. How could she do anything but love him?

Her love for Philip was the only thing keeping her from utter devastation. The evils that were spoken against her betrothal took her breath away. How could the same people who had welcomed her to London as their queen and abandoned the usurper turn on her so viciously?

The crackling fire and scent of evergreen that permeated Richmond Palace did little to lift her spirits. She normally loved the masques, music, and other entertainments, but they failed to restore her humor this year. Being cozy inside as snow blanketed the palace usually gave Mary a feeling of security, but now she struggled to stay warm and wondered if messengers from Philip and Reginald would be able to reach her.

She had pinned her hopes on the two men. One would help her save the church. The other would bring her the happiness that had eluded her throughout her thirty-seven years of life. Both would give her the support she needed to rule. Yet, she knew not when either of them would arrive, and it was this disconcerting thought that kept her from enjoying a season that she usually adored.

Instead of filling her with joy, this time set aside for giving thanks for Christ's birth served as a reminder of those who were no longer there to celebrate with her. Her father, mother, and brother, all gone to God, along with Kateryn and Margaret. All those she had been closest to, except one.

Elizabeth was holding her own quiet Christmas at Ashridge. Mary had not the time nor patience to deal with her younger sister, so she had simply given her permission to go away. It was one more topic to drive her into depression. Elizabeth had always created a diverse blend of emotions within Mary, but she began to wonder if they would ever be close.

Mary had first despised the infant who had displaced her in her father's affections. When forced away from her beloved governess, Margaret Pole, and into the household dedicated to Elizabeth's care, Mary had sworn that she would never love the girl, never do more than was required. However, that had been too difficult for a woman drawn naturally to children and constantly searching for one to give her love to.

As a child, Elizabeth's precociousness and shared blood had captured Mary's heart more than she cared to admit. With the girl's mother gone, Mary could afford to be forgiving, even loving, but somehow she could tell that it was Elizabeth who had held back.

It was not something against Mary personally, at least she did not believe so. Elizabeth seemed to hold her love and a part of herself back from everyone. Mary had never seen her give unguarded affection to anyone, and, unlike Mary, she seemed not to miss having that connection with another person.

Mary had put forth some small effort since her brother's death to welcome her sister into her confidences, but it always felt like Elizabeth was putting on an act, laughter at her older sister twinkling in her dark eyes.

Already, several had warned Mary of Elizabeth's ambition for her throne and those she might marry to assist her in that goal. It was wearying. More than that, it saddened Mary that Elizabeth did not seem to share Mary's wish to be with her or to join her at mass. It had been easier to let her leave when she requested permission to do so.

Mary moved closer to the fire to escape the bitter cold that fought to seep through every crack and crevice. She could not remember a December so frigid but found it suitable to her mood.

Memories of the Christmas spent at Tilty with her Grey cousins invaded Mary's mind, giving her no comfort. Jane had stood trial. They had made a tragic quartet: Jane, Guildford, and his two brothers. How was she the only one in the kingdom not eager to send these young people to their deaths? The outcome of the trial had been no surprise, yet Mary still hoped to free Jane. Eventually. Somehow.

They had all pled guilty and thrown themselves on the queen's mercy. Mary was in no better position than before, and had not even bought herself much time with the suggestion of the trial. The men had been sentenced to be hanged, drawn, and quartered. Mary shivered at the thought. However, Jane's sentence to be burned or have her head cut off 'as it will please the Queen' also made her queasy.

What must the duchess of Northumberland be thinking with her husband dead and her sons imprisoned? Mulling it all over again had not brought Mary any closer to a tenable solution.

At least Henry Grey had repented of his sins and embraced the true faith. If he could lead his family, especially his oldest daughter, to do the same, it would be one more reason to offer Jane a pardon.

Gardiner had warned Mary that it was an inconvenient time for her to leave court while many remained dissatisfied, but she had insisted. She needed time away for the good of her health. He was left with the task of preaching in favor of the marriage he had attempted to talk her out of while she was away.

A rebellion was stirring, Gardiner had asserted, by way of attempting to make her stay. He had advised against letting Elizabeth leave and claimed that she was at the heart of the movement along with Mary's discarded suitor, Edward Courtenay. Mary was not sure if she did not believe him or did not care, but she had gone and given her sister leave to do the same.

Whatever she felt regarding Elizabeth, she did not believe that her own sister would rebel against her. Would she?

January 1554

Mary enjoyed giving generous Twelfth Night gifts, and it raised her spirits to do so for the first time as queen. Each of her ladies was presented with jewels that had been selected specifically for them. Fran was beaming at the pearls that were elegant and simple as Susan admired the sparkle of her diamonds. Mary realized that she was genuinely happy for the first time in weeks as she observed them holding out their gifts for each other to examine.

"Your grace."

Mary looked up to see Rochester, and the expression on his face made her own fall. The moment of peace evaporated as quickly as springtime dew. She rose and went into the adjoining room with him.

"What is it?" she asked, snapping at him more than she intended.

"I apologize for disturbing your grace," Rochester said with a humble bow. "It is the rebels. Rioting has begun," he said without raising his head.

"Where?" Mary asked, shocked that her people were truly this angry about her proposed marriage. Maybe it was in the north, where she was not well known.

Rochester looked up then, his eyes full of pity. "Right here in London, your grace. The Spanish ambassadors have been attacked, but none were hurt," he quickly added. "Thankfully, the rioters' weapon of choice was snowballs." One side of his mouth quirked at the idea. "They were more of a nuisance than danger, but it is feared that this will lead to something more serious."

He moved her further from any potentially listening ears with a hand on her elbow and lowered his voice. "Traitorous tracts have been found throughout the city, and there are whispers of uprising in Kent."

"There are always whispers of uprising in Kent," Mary countered, attempting to brush off the melodrama of the moment. She began moving back toward her ladies, but Rochester stopped her with a hand on her arm. Mary looked down at it and let her eyes follow his arm up to his face, which was searching hers for understanding, begging her to take him seriously. "You're serious?" she asked incredulously.

"Quite, your grace," he insisted. "The Spanish embassy arrives tomorrow, and I fear the consequences if we do not take special care to quell rebellious words that can too easily turn into actions."

She studied his face, knowing that he had only ever advised her toward her greater good. "Very well," she acquiesced. "Send what men you feel are necessary to neutralize this problem."

"I will do so immediately, your grace," Rochester said gratefully. He awkwardly attempted to bow to Mary as he was already moving toward the door. "Thank you, your grace."

His hasty retreat gave Mary a queer feeling in her gut. A true threat must exist for him to demonstrate such concern. Instead of returning to her ladies, Mary made her way to the chapel where she prayed for the safety of the ambassadors and begged God for peace within her realm.

The feeling of dread only increased and followed her to her bed that night.

The next day dawned cold, both in temperature and the reception that Londoners offered the Spanish retinue. Mary had hoped that this would be a day of rejoicing and that her betrothed would be anxious to join her in the kingdom that they would rule together. However, the dismay clear upon all but Spanish faces and uncertainty about when Philip would be able to make his way to

England dampened her spirits once more.

She was somewhat uplifted by the gifts that were sent by Charles and Philip. A handsome ambassador bowed low over Mary's hand as he presented a huge diamond to her and said in thickly accented English, "The Emperor wishes for you to have this jewel, which is everlasting and has no equal. It shall be a sign of the undying love between our countries. He values your friendship and wishes you to know that, already, he considers you a daughter."

The smile that split Mary's face almost hurt, so unfamiliar was the feeling. That she should finally receive the love and respect that she had hoped for from her own people from this Spanish ambassador whom she did not know quickly soured the moment for her.

"Thank you," she said, taking the jewel and admiring the reflections of light and rainbows that it cast about the room. "I, too, value the longstanding relationship with the Emperor. It has been almost half a century since our houses were tied together by the marriage of my mother and father. It is a blessing that Philip and I shall further strengthen this bond."

Tipping his head to her again, the ambassador appeared pleased with his reception. After all, if the queen was happy, what did it matter how the rest of the Englishmen felt? The luster of the diamond glittered in the queen's eyes, and everyone present knew that it was love for her promised husband shining there. Few, besides the Spanish ambassador who had presented it, believed it to be a good omen.

Mary kept the diamond with her portrait of Philip. Gazing upon them and touching them served as a reminder that she was not alone in this hostile world. She was embarrassed to be found fondling her treasures when Susan breathlessly burst into her bedchamber.

"Your majesty," she called from the door. "I beg you, come at once!"

The tokens were dropped into a lined box for safe keeping, and Mary rushed to Susan's side. "What is it?" she demanded, waiting impatiently for the older woman to catch her breath.

"It is rebellion," Susan whispered. Whether she was still breathless or she dared not utter such bad news too loudly, Mary was not sure. "In Kent."

Mary's breath was taken away as thoroughly as if a horse had kicked her. It was happening just as Gardiner and Rochester had warned, and just as Courtenay had claimed. Just days earlier, the earl of Devon had been arrested. His name had been too often linked with the rumors flying about the kingdom. Gardiner had been sent to question Courtenay in the hope that their time spent together in the Tower would encourage the young man to reveal more than he might to someone else.

"Carew had escaped across the channel," Susan continued to speak, her eyes drifting to where Gertrude attempted to fade into the background, though Mary could not quite take it all in as she thought back about how she might have managed events differently. "It is Sir Thomas Wyatt who leads the rebels in Kent."

Susan had the satisfied look upon her face of one who knows they have just shared the juiciest morsel of gossip, but Mary could only stare at her. This was not a case of one of her ladies exchanging love notes with a courtier. This was a revolt.

"Bring me Rochester," Mary ordered. She turned from Susan assuming it would be done and moved toward the dress that was laid out for her. "But first send in Fran to help me dress," she added, seeing that Susan was still standing in the doorway waiting for Mary to ask her to reveal what she knew. "Now," Mary ordered, and Susan jolted into action.

Fran soon entered and closed the door that Susan had left swinging open. With mild words of welcome, she attended to Mary's appearance just in time for her to receive Rochester.

"See that Gertrude is not allowed to leave," Mary murmured to Fran before striding away to him.

Mary's chamberlain looked as if he had not slept in days, and a flicker of doubt floated through Mary's mind. Maybe she was not doing the right thing in signing the treaty with the Spanish. It was too late, but she wished to feel as certain as she once had instead of being plagued by protests from all sides.

She stopped him with an impatient gesture before he could kneel. "Just tell me what is happening," she demanded.

Rochester nodded wearily and obliged. "Sir Carew ignored the summons and has fled." Mary was waving this aside, so he moved on. "We have Courtenay, and he has revealed the three-pronged attack that was planned to force the abandonment of the Spanish marriage. If I may, your grace, my belief is that the plot may have been more nefarious than confessed. There is a possibility that Courtenay hoped to depose your grace and marry your sister."

"Elizabeth!" Mary grasped for a chair. "My own sister plots against me?"

Renard had been attempting to convince her of this from the beginning, but she had refused to believe it. Could the girl not be content with being the heir apparent until the birth of Mary's first child? Must she scheme to wear a crown as her concubine of a mother had done? Mary's features hardened as she considered the sister she had tried so hard to please, to love.

"Arrest her."

Rochester had not expected this and his eyes widened at the

fury he had unleashed. "Your grace?"

Mary's eyes flashed. "You would recommend anything less for a suspected traitor?"

"No, your grace," he said, lowering his head and not meeting her eyes. "I will see that it is done."

Mary had never felt anger burn through her veins as it did as she watched Rochester scurry from the room. Her hands shook for something to throttle in place of her sister's slender neck. Finding nothing suitable, she took up a cushion and threw it ineffectively at the closed door and screamed in frustration.

Then she remembered Gertrude and called her into the room. When the older woman curtseyed low and reverently before her, Mary knew that she was aware of what was happening.

"I only ask if you have been a part of your son's scheming," Mary said.

"I assure you that I have not, your grace," Gertrude insisted, sounding more like a groveling courtier than a marchioness. "I beg you to understand, my Edward was not quite prepared for the world that he was suddenly released into by the mercy of your majesty." She kept her head bowed and her hands tightly clasped.

Mary examined her for a long moment before responding. Gertrude may not have actively planned with her son, but she had long been a schemer and was prone to self-preservation. Had not her husband died and her son endured long imprisonment while she retained her freedom?

"You are excused from my household," Mary stated, her voice void of emotion.

Gertrude started to object, but the words were lost before she could form them. Realizing that she had no defense to offer, she curtseyed again and said, "As you wish, your grace."

She silently left the room to pack her belongings, leaving

Mary alone.

Collapsing into the chair, Mary held her head in her hands and wondered how it had come to open rebellion when people had joyously received her as their queen just months earlier. Were affections so fickle? How could subjects so lightly abandon their anointed queen?

Mary had not heard the door open, but Fran appeared at her side. She handed Mary a goblet of wine and began smoothing tendrils of hair that had loosened from her pins without saying a word.

Tension left Mary's neck and shoulders under Fran's ministrations, and she sighed, "You are too good to me, Fran."

"Nonsense, your grace," Fran replied with a quiet laugh. "How could anyone be too good for a queen." Fran moved in front of Mary and crouched down to peer into her eyes. "You are the woman who has so often reminded me that God is with us, therefore it matters not who is against us. You are my liege, and I may even dare to call you a beloved friend. I have every faith in you and will do whatever small thing I can to aid you in the trials our Lord sets before you."

Mary had to blink away tears and take a moment to compose herself before she could respond. When she did, she took up Fran's hands and said, "Thank God for you, Fran. He has sent you to bless me when my own strength has failed."

Fran smiled, patted Mary's hands, and stood. "The good Lord knows what he is doing, your grace. With his help, you shall overcome those who would claim the kingdom for their selfish purposes. You are the one he has chosen."

Mary's face was furrowed with sorrow, but it began to be replaced with determination. "I must thank you again, Fran," she said, "for reminding me of truths that I should know by heart."

Mary stood and took a deep breath. "And now I believe I will spend some time at prayer before my council convenes."

~ ~ ~ ~

"Wyatt has to be our focus," Gardiner argued, emphasizing each word with a fist to the tabletop. "Suffolk's fight was over before he could begin."

Mary's heart fluttered and her head ached. What had Suffolk been thinking in joining the rebels? His daughter, Jane, was still held in the Tower, though many had encouraged Mary to have her executed. She had refused, not willing to sign the warrant that would send her sixteen-year-old cousin to death. Had her father not realized what a challenge that had been, that all would be lost now that he had fought in her name once more?

The men, however, were not concerned about that. Their voices rose as they argued about what to do about Wyatt, who many said rode toward London at the head of at least 4000 men. As they discussed the placement of the fleet that was intended to keep the rebels from crossing Rochester Bridge and what could be done to ensure the safety of Londoners, Mary raised her voice above the tumult.

"What has been done to secure my sister?"

Gardiner cleared his throat in the silence that had suddenly overtaken the room. "The Lady Elizabeth has been summoned with a request that she come to us in all haste," he said, and added, "for her own safety, of course."

Mary's eyes narrowed at him. "I do not care for her safety or if she is offended by harsh words. Her presence is not requested. It is demanded."

"I understand," Gardiner replied in a tone Mary imagined he used with small children. "Lady Elizabeth is suffering from illness and will attend to your grace as soon as she is capable."

Mary stood and forced herself to keep her voice low, remembering how much more frightening her father was when he did not yell. "I do not wish for her to attend me, and I do not care for her stories of poor health. I would have her questioned regarding her own part in this conspiracy not coddled as if she were an innocent bystander."

She surveyed the room and was astounded by how many refused to meet her eyes. Why did they fight her on this, of all things? Only Gardiner, Paget, and Rochester returned her gaze. Something in the arrogance of one and pity of another made the pieces fall together in her mind.

They hesitated to move against Elizabeth because they were certain that she would be their queen. Maybe not as a result of this rebellion, but they were afraid to move against her nonetheless. Mary would only be obeyed as far as it did not endanger the council's future with Elizabeth.

Mary controlled her anger and did not allow a flicker of knowledge to appear on her face. She would not react impetuously as she had in the past. Some time must be spent considering what she would do with the knowledge that her subjects were already looking to their next queen. She sat and saw those in the room relax as one.

Instead of carrying on herself, she nodded to Rochester to speak for her.

"We have clear evidence of the Lady Elizabeth's involvement in this plot," he said. Papers were placed upon the table as the physical manifestation of Elizabeth's guilt. "These letters were found with the French ambassador."

A few men cringed at the proof of guilt that could not be ignored, but most fought to appear neutral. Mary wished to watch no more of the pathetic display. She stood to leave, but gave one parting command.

"Send Norfolk to Kent. He has great experience with quelling rebellion." Mary ignored the whispers that Norfolk, at eighty, was hardly the best choice. "Also, see that Elizabeth's portrait is removed from the gallery and her person placed within the Tower."

February 1554

"He demands my surrender?" Mary repeated incredulously.

Rochester seemed permanently bowed, and part of Mary felt guilty for forcing him to bear the brunt of her anger, for he was never the cause of it but indirectly.

"Your grace," Rochester pleaded, "no one would expect you to take his proclamation seriously, but I felt that you should have knowledge of it just the same."

He no longer met her eyes, and Mary missed the times that they had spoken more as equals. She missed the advice that he grew increasingly wary of giving.

"What course do you believe I should take?" she asked in a much calmer tone.

He straightened slightly, clearing his throat. Suddenly, he looked so old and grey. "Rally the people," he finally offered. "Wyatt calls upon the common men to join him in supposed protection of the realm. Remind them with your presence of their love for you. If the people of London stand firm for you, there is little to fear."

Mary considered this and pictured herself upon her palfrey, riding through the city and handing out coins as she had done not many months previously. "Yes," she agreed, "I will do as you say. People have remarkably short memories, so we shall stir them up by demonstrating my own love for each of my subjects."

Rochester smiled and some of the weariness of the past weeks melted away. "I shall begin making arrangements, your grace."

"I am thankful that all I entrust to your worthy hands is well done," Mary said, hoping that he knew that she spoke of more than the task at hand.

They exchanged a glance of mutual respect, and then he was

gone to call for heralds, guards, and musicians to accompany his queen through the buzzing crowds. While he arranged the practical matters, Mary turned her thoughts to what she should say. She was no practiced orator like her father, but she knew that her words had meant a great deal to those who had chosen to follow her against the usurper.

After traveling through the streets carrying her scepter and swathed in cloth of gold, she entered the Guildhall and called her people to her once more.

"I come to you in person to address the traitors assembling at our gates," she began, thankful to hear no tremor in her voice. "These rebels wish you to believe that they fight on your behalf, that they would ask your aid in resisting my upcoming marriage. My loving subjects, do not be drawn in by the manipulations of men who would wrest power from your anointed queen to have it for themselves."

She paused to scan the crowd as best she could. Squinting, she still had trouble making out the expressions on any faces, but neither did she hear grumbling.

"You have vowed to me your allegiance, and I pledge mine to you. I love you as a mother loves her children and know that you love me in return. Therefore, let us cast off these traitorous ideas and overthrow those who would disturb the peace of our realm."

The roar of the Londoners cheering was almost deafening, and Mary had to struggle to keep her smile from splitting into a victorious grin. She knew she had truly won when she heard one voice somehow proclaim above the others.

"God save Queen Mary and the Prince of Spain!"

~ ~ ~ ~

Two days later, Wyatt and his army, which had swelled to an estimated 5000, reached London Bridge. Surprised to find it raised to them, cannon were brought up and siege plans laid. Only upon learning that forces were pursuing him from all sides, did Wyatt determine a new course.

Mary prayed that the city would hold for her. She had done all that she could in daring to appear before the people not knowing if their loyalty was to be counted upon. Norfolk, Abergaveny, and Pembroke pursued the rebels as they abandoned their plan to cross London Bridge and instead moved to Kingston to obtain the opposite shore of the Thames.

It was Ash Wednesday, and Mary had risen before dawn in order to attend lauds. At this hour of her greatest need, God would not find her wanting for lack of devotion. The rosary beads in her hand gave her comfort as she prayed.

Her brother had banned the usage of ceremonial ashes. Therefore, it gave Mary added pleasure to feel them placed upon her forehead. She closed her eyes and imagined that it was the hand of God, rather than the priest, that made the sign of the cross to seal her as his own.

When she left the chapel to meet with her council, she was strengthened and encouraged by the knowledge that one who ruled above all others stood firmly by her side.

Mary entered the large chamber and breathed deeply of the scent of incense that clung to her clothing as her fingers automatically caressed her prayer beads. She would not be intimidated by these men, many of whom she could scarcely trust, not when she remembered who was her greatest supporter.

"Your grace," Paget was already vying for her attention before she reached her seat. "We must compel you to leave the city. A boat is being prepared as we speak. Would you send one of your ladies to see to packing a few necessities?"

Mary tilted her head back and peered down her nose at him, managing to make him feel as though he were the smaller of them. "Perhaps you were not present when my subjects reaffirmed their loyalty to me," she said, dismissing his fears with a smirk. "I shall not be driven from my capital city, and I will hear no more talk of it."

By this time, she had gained her throne and sat upon it, giving finality to her word. "What of our forces at Charing Cross?"

"Wyatt is not more than six miles from Westminster," Paget said. "The Tower guns may prove effective against them."

"No," Mary stated firmly. "Cannon will not be used in any circumstance where those who have pledged themselves to me may become inadvertent victims."

"Your majesty," Paget explained as though to a novice, "it is an unfortunate truth of war that some innocents get caught in the crossfire."

"Then it is fortunate that this is not war, but an uprising that can and will be put down without such drastic steps," Mary stated.

Paget shook his head but did not argue with his queen.

The sound of chaos and raised voices could be heard even within their safe room at Whitehall, and Rochester leaned closer to Mary to inquire if she would not please consider taking herself from harm's way. Instead of responding to him, she addressed the entire council.

"Many of you would have me leave my city and my people, leave them to the careless destruction of selfish men. I will not leave. I may not be a man who can lead my troops into battle, but neither will I abandon my subjects to a fate that I am not willing to share. Let us dispose of the matter and focus our efforts on ending this."

Gardiner seemed willing to do just that. "When the rebel leaders are brought in, as I have no doubt they will be," he said. "I would advise your majesty to bring justice where mercy has been liberally applied before. Although I admire that your grace is a generous queen who wishes to save all from a cruel fate, it may be advantageous to also demonstrate that treason will not be forgiven."

Mary narrowed her eyes at him, wondering if he had more in mind than what his words revealed. He had pressed her to execute Jane as soon as the crown was taken from her head, but Mary was adamant that her cousin could be held but not mistreated. She would give him no blanket assurance regarding the punishment of rebels.

"I shall take your words to heart and prayerfully consider what best serves my kingdom once this uprising is ended," she replied. It would have to be enough.

Gardiner nodded, and Mary had a feeling that he was confident that he would get his way this time.

The question consumed Mary in the days following. Who would receive the ultimate justice and who would receive mercy? How could she retain the love of her people while also discouraging any from rising up against her? Scripture revealed to her that even her loving God had at times found it necessary to bring about death, but it was a heavy burden to discern who would live and who would die.

Henry Grey would receive his justice. Mary had pardoned the duke of Suffolk, defending him against her entire council after he had attempted to make his daughter queen. He had even claimed to have laid aside his heresy. Yet, when Mary had summoned him to lead her forces, he had fled to the rebels instead. There was no question of his reward.

But what of Jane? The girl's solemn face appeared in Mary's mind as clearly as if she stood in front of her. It had taken every justification Mary could offer to save Jane's life upon her accession. She did not know if she could do it again.

Mary thought of her cousin, Frances, and wondered how she could consider robbing her of both husband and her daughter. No, she could not send Jane to the block. The girl had done nothing, had probably not even known that the plot was brewing.

What of Elizabeth? What had her own sister known about Wyatt and his hope to depose the queen? Mary felt her heartrate increase at the thought of her sister, who still evaded her with excuses of illness and claims of loyalty. Could she order the execution of her own sibling as her great-grandfather, Edward IV, had? That was a question that she could not answer until the investigation revealed just how much Elizabeth had aided the rebels.

As for the common soldiers, those who had been seduced by the manipulative words of Wyatt and others, Mary had already made up her mind to show mercy. These were the ones who needed her most, who had been led astray but could be brought back into the fold, and whose loyalty would be increased due to the forgiveness they had received.

Justice proved most severe to more than one hundred rebel leaders. Trials were held with wondrous efficiency, so that corpses swung from the gallows within days of Wyatt's arrest. Mary ensured that this vengeance was balanced by a great act of mercy on her behalf.

Wives and mothers of rebels had begun seeking their queen as soon as their men failed to depose her. Mary had patiently listened to hundreds of pleas and selected four hundred men to be paraded through Whitehall's courtyard with their nooses of condemnation worn around their necks.

The whimpers of women were heard at first as a whisper but they became wails of despair by the time the men were brought to a halt in front of their queen. The evidence that their pleas had fallen on deaf ears wrenched grief from the gathered women that they would not normally expose in public. Some of the men, too, allowed tears to stream down their faces as they stood to await their final judgement.

Mary watched the reactions, saw women reach for their men only to be held back by friends or warned away by guards. She witnessed looks of love exchanged by couples who made no other move toward each other, knowing it was hopeless. A few men glared at her defiantly, as though daring her to take their lives.

She moved to speak, and all fell silent.

"You men are here today because you have committed treason against your sovereign queen." She ignored the low grumbling and continued, "Each of you has been found guilty of following the traitor Thomas Wyatt, standing opposed to the forces of God's anointed."

Mary paused, letting their guilt and its consequences sink in.

"Your wives have demonstrated greater loyalty than your own by coming before me and begging for mercy." At these words, silence reigned as the crowd collectively held its breath for Mary's decision. "I am compelled to give unto you the forgiveness that each of us has first received from God."

Cheers and cries arose, and Mary suppressed a smile at their unbridled emotion as she waited for the noise to fade enough to continue. "You are pardoned and free to live out your days as my beloved subjects. All I ask in return is that, in the future, you defend rather than threaten the peace of our kingdom." She raised her hands as if to bless them as a whole, "Now go forth to your homes and, in all you do, give glory to God."

Shouts once again arose, but Mary turned and left. Her part had been performed, and she had no place in the celebrations that her mercy had produced.

She was no sooner retuned to the royal apartments than Gardiner was before her, demanding action regarding Jane Grey.

"I have sent Feckenham to her," Mary wearily reminded him. "It is my intent to pardon my cousin, once I have an heir in the cradle and she has converted to the true faith."

Gardiner sighed in impatience. "Your grace, the mercy you wish to demonstrate is admirable, but the Spanish will not abide this threat to your crown if Philip is to come."

Mary had not considered that she would be forced to sacrifice Jane for the sake of her marriage. She remembered the guilt her mother had felt over the death of Edward of Warwick, which had been the result of her parent's negotiations of Catherine's marriage. "No," she insisted. "I will not perpetrate murder behind the veil of legality. I am not my father."

"Your grace," Gardiner pressed, "the girl has committed higher treason than most of the men recently hanged for it. You are allowing your tender emotions to rule when it is the law that must prevail."

Mary pressed her temples and felt her erratic heartbeat just under the surface of her skin. She could not think of this just now. She needed time to think of how Jane could be saved.

"Let us see what Feckenham recommends," she suggested, buying time and hoping that she would find an ally in the kindly priest.

"I shall have him sent to you straight away," Gardiner

agreed, taking his leave before she could naysay him.

Feckenham was indeed brought before Mary within the hour, but his testimony did not bring her hope.

"I apologize, your grace," he said, never fully standing from his respectful bow, "but the Lady Jane will not repent of her heresy. On the contrary, she seems most ambitious to turn me to her faith."

"Jane has always been a bright and virtuous girl," Mary countered. "Surely, she will embrace the faith of her ancestors once it has been adequately explained to her."

The priest stumbled over his next words, hearing the accusation in his queen's. "Your grace, I regret that I must contradict you – not in the lady's precociousness, in that you are quite correct. However, she displays no sign that she does not understand our faith, yet insists that she does not and will not share it."

Mary felt deflated. How was she to save the girl when she did not seem compelled to save herself? She dismissed Feckenham with a gesture, and with another sent a servant scurrying for wine.

This issue of heresy, legalized by her brother for so many years, may be deeper entrenched than she believed. While many embraced the return to traditions and the mass, Mary was surprised that some, especially those of an age with Jane, had not welcomed the change.

It would be more challenging than Mary had anticipated to restore the religious practices that would ensure the salvation of her people. She only wished that Cardinal Pole would return soon to aid her in accomplishing the work. He would know what to do and how to turn the lost back toward God.

She did not notice that Gardiner had reentered the room upon Feckenham's departure. He cleared his throat and startled her to attention.

"You see, your grace, that there is no hope for the girl," he said with false disappointment. Then, as though reading her mind, "I know it is your greatest hope that Philip come to fulfil the marriage treaty and Cardinal Pole to serve the Church of England." Shaking his head, "It shall only come to pass if you clear the way for them by ridding your realm of proven traitors."

Mary clamped her eyes shut as she struggled to take deep breaths, wishing that her head would cease its throbbing that seemed to increase with the faster beating of her heart. Gardiner was right. She needed Philip and Reginald here. Jane had made her choices.

Mary opened her eyes to see that Gardiner had silently placed the warrant for Jane's execution in front of her. She bit her lip, remembering her intention to pardon the girl rather than ever take this step.

"God forgive me," she whispered as she hastily signed her name.

July 1554

Mary had not witnessed the execution of Jane Grey or her husband Guildford Dudley, yet she experienced nightmares of them with no less frequency due to the fact that she had not been able to bear watching. She prayed daily that she was forgiven for her judgement against the young woman she had wished so desperately to free. Mary knew that Jane was guilty of treason but still would have been content to keep the girl under close guard if it had not been for her family's continued treason and the demands of the Spanish.

The months since then had been filled with preparation for Mary's wedding. And waiting.

Philip's arrival would make it all worth it. The nightmares would stop, and Mary would have the partner she desired. Her heart beat faster each time she imagined their first meeting, the wedding day, and what would follow.

She had to push aside the vision of Jane's lifeless body that had made it finally possible. The girl had gone to her death almost as if she embraced it, bringing to Mary's mind their conversation about what made a good time to die. Jane and Guildford had died on the same day, but their stubborn clinging to heresy would make their reunion anything but joyful. Mary could no longer think on it.

Thankfully, the remains of rebels that had been rotting throughout London since Wyatt's arrest had been removed as the city was cleaned in preparation for welcoming Philip's entourage and the wedding celebrations. The streets may still smell of fish, unwashed bodies, and things that were much worse, but gone was the stench of rotting flesh.

Prisoners Elizabeth and Courtenay had been released from the Tower to house arrest. Despite the efforts of those most loyal to Mary, insufficient evidence had been uncovered to charge the potential royal couple with conspiring with Wyatt. At least there had not been enough to convince Mary. Those who were less disposed to mercy had counseled in favor of Elizabeth's execution, just as they had Jane's, but Mary would need undeniable evidence to take such an unretractable step against her sister.

However, none of that mattered today, as Mary prepared to meet her husband for the first time. She was anxious, her nerves highly strung by delays and difficulties that had postponed Philip's arrival. But the waiting was almost over. News had arrived that Philip's ship had landed in Southampton.

Mary gazed at his portrait while several ladies attended to her hair and dress. Rouge was applied to brighten her pale cheeks, and costly fragrance applied to the hollow of her neck. There, they hung the brilliant diamond that Philip had sent to Mary as a gift.

The gardens of Winchester were in their full summer glory, and a bright moon cast a romantic glow across the paths. Nooks and shadows created hideaways for lovers eager to steal away from prying eyes. Mary smiled at the thought. For the first time in her life, she would be one of those lovers instead of one gazing longingly from the outside.

Her chamber opened to the garden where Philip would be brought to be presented to her. Chairs had been carefully arranged to give the couple privacy for conversation while remaining surrounded by councilors and ladies. On the morrow, they would be married.

The sounds of excited whispers and scurrying informed Mary that Philip had arrived. She examined herself in the mirror. The candlelight made her hair glow as if with its own flame. Her black velvet gown could not tame the sparkle of her silver underskirt that was heavily crusted with jewels. Even her countenance shone with a radiance that could only be described as love for the man she was about to meet.

Gardiner was there to guide her to the garden, and she smiled joyfully up at him. They had not always agreed on how to get to this point, but here they were.

Torches lit the garden in a festive manner that almost made it appear as if a pagan ritual were about to take place. Mary had only a moment to take in the splendor of her surroundings when her breath caught in her throat. Philip stepped forward and, taking her hand, gently touched his lips to hers.

Mary was certain that her body would float from the seat that Philip guided her to. He looked every inch the king in cloth of gold and the gems that Mary had sent to him. He was handsome and not much taller than Mary. His hair was thick and dark, though not as black and glossy as Renard's for which Mary was glad. Philip's skin appeared untouched by age, and she felt a pang at the reminder of his youth compared to her own years. She prayed that her appearance was pleasing to him.

As they sat, Mary searched her memory for the carefully selected lines she had planned to say. Knowing that they would be expected to sit and talk for some time, Mary had prepared a few topics of conversation to avoid awkward silence. However, it was Philip who spoke first.

"Your grace, I am pleased to see that you wear the diamond," he said, gesturing with one hand as he held onto Mary's with the other. His voice was pleasantly deep and soothing.

Mary felt her skin burn with the attention, and her free hand flew to her neck as though needing further evidence that the jewel in fact hung there.

"It was a most generous and beautiful gift," she managed in just more than a whisper. She responded in Latin to his Spanish, for her mind was in too much turmoil to form the language that was more difficult for her.

"Yet it is less than you deserve," he insisted, and Mary was forced to look away. If Philip was surprised at Mary's inexperience with courtly love, he did not allow it to show. "You will have to teach me how to say good night," he continued. "I would end the evening by addressing your lords in their own language."

Mary brightened at having a task at hand to distract her from Philip's closeness and the idea of how much closer they would be the next night. She taught him a few words of English, and they laughed together when he struggled with some of the unfamiliar sounds.

"You will win everyone's heart," Mary said once he had mastered the line.

"Ah, but I need only win yours," he said, his dark eyes full of promise.

Mary felt a stirring deep within her that she could not explain and had never before felt. "It is already yours, your grace," she said. They were so close that she was sure she could feel his breath on her cheek and smell the mint he must have chewed before greeting her. "I have long ago vowed to love and cherish you as is my duty to God and to you."

She had held his gaze for as long as she could, but shielded her eyes with cast down lashes after this revealing of her heart.

Philip's hand on her chin caused her to look at him anew. "I pray, my love, that it shall be so pleasant a duty that you will most willingly oblige me."

"Of course, your grace," Mary agreed, once again averting her gaze and falling silent as emotion closed her throat. It went unnoticed because Philip chose that moment to rise.

"This day God has granted that I am in the presence of the

one he has chosen for me. Thank you all for such a joyful reception, and now good night, my lords," he recited just as Mary had instructed.

Mary's eyes followed him as he kissed her ladies each in turn. This man, who caused the ladies to blush and giggle after he turned away, was to be her husband. Praise be to God.

Mary arose the next morning before the sun. Although she knew the day would be long, sleep had eluded her and she wished to begin her day at mass. The bells of Winchester Abbey rang for lauds, echoing through the morning mist that clung to the colorful banners hung throughout the church.

Fran accompanied Mary, and they dressed plainly to avoid attention. The women wished to be in prayer for Mary's coming union without distractions of courtiers or councilors. Prayer beads slid through their fingers as if they were an extension of their bodies, and the chaos of preparations for the ceremony faded into the background as the women were attentive to their prayers.

As soon as they returned to Mary's rooms, they noticed a change in the atmosphere. They had left behind sleeping and drowsy women and returned to a scene filled with energy. Each was giddy to wear their own finery, but none would outshine the queen.

Mary spent the next hours bathing in rose water and having her hair dried, brushed, and curled until it seemed to glow with a light of its own. Her purple satin gown boasted elegant embroidery while her snow white kirtle glittered with jewels. The finest jewelry that she wore were the two diamonds Mary had received from Philip and his father, Charles. These diamonds rested at Mary's breast and reflected light with an almost blinding effect.

"It is time, your grace," Fran murmured as she made last minute, unnecessary adjustments to Mary's hair.

Mary looked at her ladies, and each of them smiled at her in return. Whatever feelings they had about the Spanish alliance, all were prepared to make the best of this day, which was to be celebrated with greater ceremony than any of them had ever witnessed. Expecting nervousness, Mary was pleased to feel only happiness and the sensation that this day was blessed.

Several members of her council were waiting to escort her to the church. They seemed surprised by Mary's beauty, and she felt her confidence soar. Her husband would be pleased with her, she was sure.

The procession made its way through extravagant decorations, stepping on carpets that had been strewn to protect the fine shoes and trailing dresses of the ladies. Tapestries proudly displayed Philip's regalia and streamers fluttered in the mild breeze. The raised platform upon which the ceremony would take place came into Mary's view.

And she saw Philip.

He, too, was dressed in white satin. The doublet and hose had been a gift from Mary, and she noticed that they suited him quite well. His shoulders were broad, testifying to the soldiering drills that he had spent a lifetime perfecting. His newly acquired Order of the Garter ribbon drew attention to his fine, muscular legs. He was beautiful, and he was hers.

She approached him without hesitation, ready to give herself to the man God had chosen for her without reservation. Mary was beaming as together they turned toward Bishop Gardiner.

"It is the wish of the Holy Roman Emperor that I precede today's ceremony with an announcement," he began in a voice that effortlessly filled the large space. "It was thought that her grace, our Queen Mary, would today wed a prince, but the benevolent

Charles V has bestowed upon his son the kingdom of Naples that she may marry a king."

Exclamations of shock and approval filled the air, and Gardiner patiently waited for them to fade before he continued. After reading the banns in Latin, he asked if any man knew of a reason that the marriage should not be performed.

Mary felt her first lance of nervousness as silence fell over the congregation. Would one of those who had spoken against the Spanish treaty use this moment to make a last stand?

Before she could even finish the thought, Gardiner had carried on, stating that the marriage had no impediments.

The wedding mass was an event that made Mary feel closer to God than ever before. When it was time for her to say her vows, she did so in a voice choked with emotion.

"This gold and silver I give to you, along with myself, mind and body," she said, gazing adoringly up into her husband's eyes. "I pledge to you my love and obedience."

Philip placed the simple gold band first upon Mary's thumb as he recited, "With this ring, I wed thee, in the name of the Father, and of the Son, and of the Holy Spirit." With each member of the Trinity, he slipped the ring onto the next finger, so that it came to rest upon the third.

He returned her smile, and if his was not filled with joy the way hers was, she did not notice. They turned, holding hands, to follow the sword of state from the cathedral. Trumpets announced that the deed was done, and cheers rose up from the crowd outside as the newly wed couple led the way to the feast that was to follow.

Mary took her seat at the head of the banquet eager for the festivities to begin. She ate from plates of gold, while Philip ate sparingly from silver. He leaned over and whispered to her that he wished not to feel heavy in the gut for the events of the day. After a pause, he added with a wink, "and the night."

She tried to hide her flush behind her wine glass, but the drink only served to make her cheeks feel even hotter. Philip gave her a lop-sided smile, seeming to enjoy the effect he had upon her.

The candlelight and blush had been kind to Mary the evening before. In the harsh light of day, Philip could see the lines and looseness of skin that attested to his bride's greater age. Still, he was a man who knew his duty. His father had made sure of that. Regardless of his personal preference for the mistress left behind in Spain, he would do his best to please the queen of England.

If nothing else, she would prove a devoted bride, as evinced by the tender gazes that she constantly sent his way. She was merry enough, a willing participant in the dancing and singing that went on throughout the evening. During the entertainments, she held his hand and squeezed it at moments of suspense or excitement.

Soon, it was time for the couple to depart for the event that Mary had been both anticipating and dreading since Philip's proposal had been first received.

Suddenly, it was Mary who seemed the younger and Philip the experienced. Her ladies had prepared her for bed, brushing her hair until it looked like heated bronze and scattering rose petals throughout the room. She had pulled Susan aside and dared to ask, "What shall I do, Susan? What will he expect of me?"

Susan had simply laughed and patted Mary on the hand, "Just submit to his wishes, your grace, as you have vowed to do, and you shall be pleasing enough to him," she said, dismissing Mary's fears with an incredulous shake of her head.

Mary dared not inquire of anyone else, and prayed that her husband would indeed be satisfied with her. Should she soon bear him a son, she would be certain that she had delighted both Philip and God.

The men arrived, and Mary gulped in breath, terrified that she would fail somehow. "God help me," she whispered, automatically reaching for the rosary that did not hang from her robe.

In contrast to Mary's tense fear, Philip was at ease. Until Gardiner hushed them all to give the blessing, he spoke lightly to his gentlemen about the activities of the following day. Once the bishop had prayed that, "God bless the union with a son, that their joy would be complete," Mary and Philip were left alone.

Snug in the luxurious bed, Mary could not bring herself to meet her husband's eyes, so she closed them and concentrated on the feel of his hands as he reached for her. She realized that she was tense and forced her body to soften at his touch. His laugh startled her.

"You truly are untouched, aren't you?" he asked in surprise.

Against her will, Mary's eyes opened. She was not sure what to say. "Of course, I am, your grace," she admitted. Did he think that she would not come to her marriage bed a virgin?

He laughed again and rolled away to reach for wine. Expertly turning back to her without spilling a drop, he handed it to her.

"Here. This will help, my innocent bride."

Mary took it and was thankful for the warm feeling that grew in the pit of her stomach. She gave him what was a rather uncertain smile, and he replaced the goblet on the table. He then took up a handful of her soft, loose hair.

"Your hair is quite beautiful," he said, stroking its length.

Mary thought his tone held a hint of surprise, and she wondered why. As his lips found hers, the question was forgotten.

~ ~ ~ ~

Mary woke slowly the next morning, not wishing to let go of the sweet sensation of Philip's closeness. Her body felt swollen and sensitive, but she reveled in the feeling because it was evidence that the night before had truly happened, had not just been a dream.

Her hands slid to her soft abdomen, and she wondered if it would soon grow with new life. Feeling Philip begin to stir, she moved her hands to his body. Where hers was soft, his was firm with muscle and she wondered at how exquisite it was to be free to explore his sleek body.

Philip did not share her desire to linger. He left the covers and Mary's outstretched arms without a backward glance. She was disappointed but could not deny that she had needs to attend to as well. Sighing, Mary crawled from the bed to begin her first day as a married woman.

Philip had soon left to attend mass, but Mary was content to remain closeted with her ladies, storing away the memories of the past twenty-four hours as treasures to retrieve for future admiration. After a quiet morning in prayer and devotion, the ladies enjoyed some singing and dancing before leaving Mary alone once more to enjoy supper and the evening with her husband.

Mary listened as Philip narrated the activities of his day with great animation. At one point, she was afraid that he would spill his wine with his enthusiastic hand movements that emphasized each important point. She did not mind that he did not ask her about her day. After all, she had not much to tell and enjoyed listening to him speak.

On this night, they were each prepared for bed by their attendants with less ceremony than the previous night, but Mary's nerves were in no less of a tangle. She did not know if she had been pleasing to him or if he was there out of duty. Mary was not a young bride, so conception of a son was paramount.

Philip was just as gentle and playful as he had been with her on their wedding night, and Mary was overjoyed. She was certain that he must be as happy with their union as she, right until the moment he left her bed. Instead of staying with her, he made mumbled excuses about needing sleep to refresh himself and a busy calendar the next day. Then he was gone.

Mary sat up in bed, still warm from Philip's body, and wondered if she should take him at his word or be concerned that he did not long to be with her. She pulled the covers up under her chin and blinked rapidly as her eyes searched the room for clues. A nagging feeling haunted her that she was nothing more than a commitment that he attempted to make more palatable with his courtly manners.

Before her tears could do more than begin their familiar burn in the back of her eyes, Mary shook her head free of negative thoughts. Philip was her husband. He had vowed to love her just as she had to love him. And how she did love him, utterly and completely.

The next morning, Mary decided not to move from her bed, and, instead, called Susan to her.

With an expertly performed curtsey, Susan asked, "What may I do for you, your grace?"

"I would hear mass said in my own chamber this morning," Mary said, rubbing her temples and finding a headache there. "Also, have my physician brought. He will likely see that I require bleeding, so have some broth sent up. That always seems to help."

"Certainly, your grace," Susan replied, never one to counter Mary's word even if she doubted the usefulness of the physician's ministrations. "Shall I have Fran come in with her lute?"

"No!" Mary insisted almost before Susan had spoken the

words. Now that she was aware of it, the pain in her head seemed unbearable. "Just see that I am left alone."

"Yes, your grace," Susan said quietly as she left the room without a sound.

It took Mary several days to feel well enough to rise from her bed. During that time, Philip had not visited. Mary herself had insisted that this be the case, since she would not have him sicken if she were suffering from a contagion. However, she had missed him greatly and wished that he had thought to write or send her some small token that he thought of her.

When she had dared to whisper of this to Fran, she had simply laughed and given Mary a squeeze, saying, "That is husbands for you, your grace. Whether king or plowman, they struggle to have a thought for anyone but themselves."

Mary had joined in her laughter, not greatly comforted but at least feeling a common union with women of the world.

Knowing that she would not feel fully well until she had visited her husband, she made her way to his rooms. Though weak, she felt optimistic and light-hearted. Even more than being a queen did she treasure being a wife. And when she became a mother? She could not imagine her joy!

Philip's men were bantering amongst themselves, so Mary slowed her approach, unsure how to make her presence known. She felt awkward, though she knew it should not be so, she being the queen in search of her own husband. Then she heard her own name spoken.

"The queen could make herself a bit more appealing to our poor Philip if she were to dress a bit less like an old maid," one said to the amusement of his listeners.

Another agreed, "How he manages in bed . . ."

"He is likely imagining his sweet Marguerite."

"Ah, I do miss Spanish women."

Their conversation continued, but Mary backed away, tears streaming down her face. She could not bear to hear more, so she rushed back to her own chamber and ordered Fran to help her undress.

"It seems that I have had a relapse," she said in anguish, "and will need to return to my bed."

"Your grace," Fran cried. "You look as though you have had a blow!"

"And so I have," Mary agreed distractedly as she struggled to pull the hateful dress from her body.

Fran's fingers gently pressed hers into stillness, and she said, "Let me, your grace." Allowing silence to calm her mistress for a moment, she asked, "Would you like to tell me what has happened?"

The question was asked casually as she continued preparing Mary for bed, not with the titillation that Gertrude would have scarcely contained had she been witness to the scene. Mary took a deep breath and released it slowly as she tried to decide how much she should share with Fran.

"I inadvertently overheard some of Philip's men . . . they were discussing women," she admitted.

"Ah," Fran knowingly sighed. "The ribald talk of men is not proper for ears such as yours."

"No," Mary stated firmly. She wished she could bring herself to say more.

Her task complete, Fran gave Mary's arms a reassuring squeeze. "Don't you worry yourself over whatever it was they said. I have no doubt that your husband would be rather cross with them if he knew they had upset you in this way."

Mary shook her head. The fact that Fran had not pestered

for details made her more anxious to share them. "They said that Philip must imagine another in order to . . ." She could not bring herself to complete the thought.

"Oh, sweet Mary," Fran whispered, pulling her queen into a motherly embrace. "That is nothing but the tasteless jokes of men. Do not take it to heart."

Allowing herself to be comforted by the warmth and true affection in Fran's touch, Mary began to relax. Could she believe it though? Who was Marguerite?

With her habit of preconceiving just what Mary's worries were, Fran held her at arm's length and insisted, "Your husband loves you. Has he ever given you reason to doubt it?"

Closing her eyes, Mary considered this. She did not know exactly how a husband should behave, had only the example of her own father. Philip seemed to care for her with much greater steadfastness than she had ever witnessed demonstrated by him.

"Maybe you are right," Mary admitted, her voice filled with doubt.

"Of course, I am," Fran stated firmly. "You have simply risen from bed too soon and received a shock. You will see. All shall be well for you and your handsome prince." With this last Fran gave Mary a wink that would have brought a blush to her queen's cheeks coming from anyone else.

She tucked Mary into bed as though she were a small child, and Mary decided it might be best to forget the incident as though it had never happened.

September 1554

Mary sat within the small privy closet smiling to herself. She was almost certain that she carried Philip's child. Although she no longer told herself that he loved her with the same passion that she had for him, he had given her what her heart desired most and what her kingdom desperately needed.

She had been checking almost obsessively for bleeding, but none had come since their wedding two months earlier. Irregularity had been a problem for Mary since her courses began, but her instincts told her that this was different. She would have a son, and he would carry on her legacy.

"Are you quite alright, your grace?" Susan's voice came through the door.

"Oh yes," Mary assured her as she stood and smoothed her skirts.

She would not tell anyone, not even Susan. Not yet.

Mary stepped from the privy to come under the curious stare of her lady-in-waiting. Susan seemed to suspect that there was something she did not know, and that was a feeling she did not like one bit. However, she also understood when she should, or should not, approach her queen with questions or teasing because she now remained silent.

The queen swept past her and moved toward the looking glass. "Please, attend me, Susan," Mary requested as if she had not noticed any inquiry in the woman's gaze. "Philip will be visiting in a moment, and I would look my best for him."

She may not believe that her husband returned the depth of her love, but she was sure that one day he would. Pinching her cheeks, she remembered one of Philip's gentlemen commenting on her sickly, pale complexion. He would find her rosy with health today.

Mary had been heartbroken and confined to her bed when she had first come to the realization that Philip did not fully return her feelings. Time, as it often does, helped her to see that she could not wallow in her rejection forever. Philip had proven that he was willing to play the part of a devoted husband. She would make it her mission to see that love grew from that dedication.

When he arrived, Mary was sitting on one side of a small table that was heavy with bread and cheeses. An empty seat on the other side waited for Philip. She did not rise when he entered. Susan had warned her of the dangers of appearing too submissive, especially with Mary being a queen. As much as Philip's love, she needed his respect.

He did not seem bothered that she remained seated, nor did he comment on her appearance. Philip sat, took a few morsels from the tray and contemplated them for a few moments before speaking.

When he did, Mary could not disguise her shock.

"The French have laid siege to Rentry," he said with incongruous nonchalance. "I do not know how long I will be able to remain in England."

Mary's mouth fell open though it was empty of words.

Philip pretended he failed to notice, popping a bite into his mouth and swallowing it whole before continuing, "I may require English support in this and have already sent some of my own men to begin assessing the situation." He took another bite, keeping his eyes on the food before him rather than his wife.

"But, Philip . . ." Mary was not sure what to say. Should she tell him that she believed herself to be with child?

"Do not worry," he said before she had a chance to complete her thought. "My father has ordered that I remain here while others see to Rentry."

She was not skilled at reading the underlying emotions of others, but she sensed the bitterness in his tone now. He wished to leave, to be a soldier, but his father demanded that he see to his new wife. Should she be grateful to Charles or angry that it was not Philip's desire? Mary did not know, so she said nothing.

"I have brought too many with me anyway," Philip said, not bothering to assess his wife's feelings. "The duke of Alba actually complained to me that he has nothing to do!" Philip laughed at the irony of men stuck in a cold, rainy kingdom while there was much to do in their more appealing homeland.

"Your grace should do with your Spanish retinue as you see fit," Mary agreed. Many people, even Renard the Spanish ambassador, had been shocked to see how large a party Philip had brought with him. It left his household, already stocked with English attendants, over staffed by far and increased the fears of those who believed the Spanish were taking over English lands.

He glanced up as though surprised to see that she was there. "Yes," he agreed. "Your English are a nervous bunch, are they not? The heretics are fleeing to join their damned brethren on the Continent." He laughed again at the futility of that gesture.

Mary frowned. The exodus of Protestants did not amuse her the way it did Philip. She wished to restore her people to God, and she could not do that if they left before she had the chance. Now that they were married, she looked forward to the return of Cardinal Pole and full restoration with Rome, but Philip did not seem to share her passion for that undertaking. Reginald had been postponed several times, and Philip was alert to news from his lands more so than the events in England.

"We should also see to my coronation," Philip said as if he were suggesting nothing more of note than an afternoon hunt.

"My council has advised against it," Mary blurted without

thinking. This was not where she had wanted the conversation to go.

Philip paused with his next bite hovering in the air. Slowly setting it down, he examined her countenance for the first time since entering the room.

"I am sorry, my beloved," he apologized, pulling his chair around the table to be closer to hers. "I had so much on my mind that I gave little thought to your concerns."

He took her hands in his and gently caressed them. Mary looked down at their intertwined fingers and smiled. She had waited too long for moments like this. As she watched, one of his hands untangled from hers to rise to her cheek. Mary closed her eyes and leaned her head into his warm palm until light pressure from him turned her face up to meet his.

He kissed her softly, but not too quickly, before speaking again. "You must forgive me, my dear wife, for thinking too much like a bachelor when I am responsible for the happiness of a queen."

Mary laughed lightly, feeling the heat rush into her cheeks. It embarrassed her that he still had that effect on her, and she wondered if he always would.

"Let me reassure you," Philip said. "I have no plans to leave. I have utter trust in those I am sending, but you surely can understand my concern for the events taking place in my own lands, just as you must dedicate yourself to the needs of England."

"Of course," Mary agreed, wondering how it seemed so reasonable all of a sudden. "I am sorry too, my love," she said, gazing into his eyes to forge this moment in her memory. "It is just that I may be a bit emotional myself." She took a deep breath. "I believe that I am with child."

Mary could discern the precise moment that the words were

processed by Philip's quick mind. His entire face lit up, and she felt encouraged that he was indeed beginning to feel deepened devotion to her.

"My love," he cried, standing as though the news could not be taken sitting down. "That is wonderful!" He paced the room with his hands moving up as in thanks to God, before spinning back toward her. "When will our child arrive?" he asked as he knelt before her.

Mary was startled by the question, for she had not yet considered it herself. It had been enough that a child was on its way. "In the spring, I think," Mary guessed, squinting as she struggled with the calculation under Philip's impatient gaze. "Yes, April or May," she settled on with a satisfied smile.

"Seven more months," Philip mumbled, turning his face away from her.

"Yes," Mary agreed. "We should not announce it just yet," her smile faded slightly, "just in case. But I could not keep this joyous news from you, my beloved husband."

He brightened again and turned a charming smile on her. "I am ever so glad that you have, sweet Mary." He leaned over her in a possessive manner and kissed her again. "I shall immediately see myself to the chapel and give thanks to God who has provided us with the heir we have both begged him for."

Mary began to rise, thinking that she would accompany him, but his hand on her shoulder kept her in her chair. "Dear Mary!" he exclaimed. "Your highest duty now is to our child. Please, stay here in comfort, and I shall have a chaplain sent to you."

"That is very thoughtful of you," Mary thanked him, but she wondered if he heard for he was already on his way out the door.

As nice as it sounded to take her ease for the coming

months until the babe's arrival, Mary knew that she had important business to attend to. Cardinal Pole's return to England had been delayed far too many months, and she felt that he would be key to the successful reuniting of England and Rome. Her council would also have a ledger of other concerns and issues for her to consider.

With that in mind, she rose and called Fran to assist her in preparing for meeting with her council. Her hand rested upon the soft, yet still relatively flat, flesh of her abdomen. The future king of England would go along with her.

Rochester went before her as they entered the council room. Mary could hear the men already debating issues, but their voices went quiet when they noticed her presence.

Since she had learned that it was necessary to immediately bring up any issue she wished to be considered, Mary addressed the council as soon as she was seated. "I will be writing to Cardinal Pole today to invite him home. He will be an invaluable resource in our work to restore our kingdom to the true faith."

She would not reveal to them that she had been in communication with Pole since her brother's death. Mary had learned a few lessons, one of which was determining what this circle of men would have shared with them and where she would keep her own counsel.

"Your majesty," Paget was the brave one, never afraid to counter Mary's wishes. "You will remember that Cardinal Pole remains accused of treason."

Mary's eyes narrowed at the councilman who had been quick to switch loyalties to Jane and back again, but always seemed to be a thorn in her side. "Please, see that you deal with that problem," she demanded, turning his objection into more paperwork for his desk. "Are there any other points to discuss on this matter?" she asked.

Arundel spoke but not with the same confidence that Paget had. "Your grace, I know that your subjects are as eager to embrace the faith of our ancestors as I am, but there remain the concerns over land and buildings that have been redistributed in the years since your father, God rest his soul, had so many of our monasteries dissolved."

Mary could see by the nodding of heads and thankful looks turned Arundel's way that he addressed the concerns of many in that room. How many of them had become rich from the bounty of church lands that had been gifted or purchased for a fraction of their value? Yet, her duty was divided between the church and her subjects, so she could not dismiss their complaint.

"Cardinal Pole has been made aware of this as well as some of the other challenges that we face. The sooner he is here, the more promptly we can begin the process of overcoming them. It is not my intention that any of my subjects should find their estates diminished on my order."

It was almost as if her council released a collective breath. She pressed her lips firmly together to avoid smirking at their greedy behavior. Could they not have grander vision?

"The Lady Elizabeth has, once again, requested an audience," Paget spoke up again.

Mary almost rolled her eyes. "My sister should be content that she is not in the Tower and enjoys relative freedom at Woodstock. She is not mistreated, and I cannot spare time for her dramatic speeches." She was pleased to impart the news that would make them all less concerned with Elizabeth's complaints. "It pleases me to announce to you good gentleman that I am with child." The pleasure of triumphing over her sister and these councilmen's secret schemes even kept the blush from her face as she spoke on such a private matter.

The room exploded in exclamations, well wishes, and praises to both God and queen. For once, everything was working out in Mary's favor.

November 1554

Mary was aglow. She and Philip had dressed to open Parliament in matching ermine trimmed crimson robes. He was majestic, and she felt that all eyes could perceive the slight swelling of her abdomen. The dress she had been fitted for months ago had been let out to accommodate her growing child.

The open litter placed her in full view of those who had gathered as the royal couple made their way to Westminster, and their cheers, waving, and small gifts made Mary feel especially loved. She had been faithful, and God was giving her generous rewards.

In response to those signs of favor, Gardiner began the session with a bill to disinherit the Lady Elizabeth. She remained a bastard, after all, and the birth of Mary's child would make it unnecessary to give Elizabeth the hope of inheritance that fed her willingness to scheme and conspire with rebels. However, Paget voiced another side of the argument.

"It seems to me, your grace," Paget began as if he was performing a distasteful duty, "that this bill is unnecessary. With the birth of a prince, the queen's sister stands far from the throne. The only result of this bill would be displeasure among the reformers who hold the Lady Elizabeth in high regard." Paget held his arms out, hands open in willingness to hear any response to his reasonable stance. "Bishop Gardiner, if we are to welcome these lost sheep back into the fold, surely we can avoid antagonistic and needless moves such as this one."

Mary felt anger brewing within her, but she forced it down. Did Paget have a point? She did not wish to move against anyone out of vengeance or jealousy. If Elizabeth had participated in treason, that would be proven and the bill was pointless. If she had not, the birth of Mary's son would weaken her claim and douse the enthusiasm of her followers. Mary surprised Paget by agreeing with him.

"Thank you," Mary said, tilting her head toward him. "You have enlightened me to the wastefulness of this bill. Let us move on with more pressing matters."

Paget's mouth dropped open at the ease with which he had convinced his queen of his argument. Truth was that he would have ignored any such proposal if he were in Mary's position. But he shook his head and managed to reply, "You honor me, your grace."

Philip had his own ideas about how to neutralize Mary's sister. "We should consider a husband for the Lady Elizabeth that she may focus her considerable talents upon a family rather than rebellion," Philip said with a condescending smirk. The men in attendance rumbled with laughter. Each of them shared Philip's discomfort with women participating in the political power game.

"Who would you recommend?" Paget was the first to ask.

Not one of the men dared to mention Courtenay, though he was certainly the first to come to each of their minds. Instead, it was Philip who spoke again.

"I believe that we should consider a match with the duke of Savoy. He is one of my most trusted generals and has more than enough stamina to handle a strong-minded woman."

More appreciative laughter met his comments, but not too loudly in respect of their queen who looked on.

"It pleases me that my suggestion meets your approval," Philip said, though none had actually agreed to it. "Savoy will arrive in England within the fortnight. The two can meet and determine if the match is acceptable."

Quiet blanketed the room. Sharing quips on the need to manage troublesome women was alright, but they were not as comfortable with Philip behaving like a king.

To make matters worse, the next item brought to the table was the Regency Act, which would give Philip power to rule in his son's name if Mary were to die in childbirth. Seeing no alternative, the men reluctantly approved the bill as they prayed for Mary's good health and safe delivery.

Mary allowed herself to smile broadly as the attainder against Reginald Pole was repealed. None expressed any argument opposed to it, so it was almost anti-climactic when Parliament approved the homecoming of the first papal legate in England since before Edward's reign.

Within the fold of her robes, Mary caressed her rosary and gave silent but greatly heartfelt thanks to the God who had made it all possible. If her mother was allowed a view of her daughter, Mary hoped that she was proud.

The remainder of the Parliament session was consumed by too much discussion of less important matters. Mary found herself tiring and her mind wandering. She would see to it that the Cardinal was welcomed with grand ceremony. The people would understand and appreciate that this was more than the return of one man. It was the first step in returning England to the true faith and reunion with Rome. God had entrusted Mary with a great responsibility, and she would do her best not to fail him.

She was grateful when the session closed for the day, and Philip offered his arm to lead her to her rooms. A supper had been prepared for them, and they shared their meal in comfortable silence, both too weary of hearing voices to speak now.

It was not until Mary felt an unfamiliar fluttering in her abdomen that she broke the silence. At first it frightened her, and her hand flew to the slight bulge where her baby lay. She felt the blood drain from her face, and saw that Philip noticed.

He was moving toward her when Mary felt the sensation again, but this time she smiled as realization struck. This was not an evil omen, but the movement of her child now grown large enough to be felt. She beamed at her husband.

"It is the babe, Philip! I feel it."

Mary looked down as if she believed she would also be able to see the faint movement, so she did not see the wave of relief cross Philip's face as he eased back into his chair.

"It is your son, making his presence known," Mary happily cried, lifting her eyes to her husband.

"Thanks be to God," Philip said, sounding drained of emotion.

"You are weary," Mary observed as she took his hand. "Let us give thanks for this sign of growth and good health at mass and then be to bed."

Philip agreed with a nod, and they walked to the chapel hand in hand.

The next day, Mary's thoughts turned from the rose in her belly to the thorn in her side. A letter arrived from Sir Henry Bedingfeld, the man who was responsible for the care and keeping of the Lady Elizabeth.

Susan and Fran could tell by the way Mary's fingers tightened and her lips clamped together until they disappeared as she read that the news was not what Mary wished to hear. They shared an understanding look, shook their heads, and cast their attention back to their sewing. It never was news to cheer their mistress where her younger sister was involved.

"She requests a royal physician, disdaining the help of local doctors," Mary complained to anyone who cared to listen. "Her constant pleading to be moved to one of her own estates is driving poor Bedingfeld to the edge of even his considerable patience."

Mary continued reading and none of her ladies responded to her exclamations.

"He asks if he should grant Elizabeth the English Bible that she has requested," Mary cried incredulously. "Is she being purposely provocative? Why can she not be content that I have released her from the Tower and not insisted that charges be pressed against her?"

Fran could see that Susan was amused by her queen's frustration, so she went to Mary herself. "Your grace," Fran said in a soothing tone, taking the letter from her clutched hands and setting it aside. "Your sister has always been one to push the limits of propriety and speak in instigating words, but you are the queen. Do not let her upset you so."

Mary sniffed and looked away.

"Think of the child," Fran insisted, knowing that any mention of the baby brightened Mary's mood. It did so now.

Mary smiled and turned her head back to Fran. "You understand people so well, much better than I do," Mary admitted. "I will think of my child. Please see that a message is sent to the Lady Elizabeth that a royal physician is not available at present and that we pray that she will be more grateful for Sir Bedingfeld's thoughtful care."

"I will tell Rochester such is your will, your grace," Fran agreed with a tip of her head. She was thankful that, while Mary could become inflamed with emotion at the hint of a spark, she was also quick to come down from her ledges.

~ ~ ~ ~

The day had arrived. Mary did not well remember her distant cousin, Reginald, but she had heard about him all her life. Whether her mother proposed his qualities as an ideal prospective husband, or her governess held him up as a great example of an Englishmen standing firmly by the true faith, Mary had intently listened. Her image of the man about to arrive was one of a living saint, and she had no concerns that he may not be able to fulfill that vision.

With the leadership of Cardinal Pole, the church would be restored in her kingdom and the salvation of her subjects ensured. She felt as anxious for his arrival as she had been for Philip's four months earlier. Caressing her growing belly, she felt satisfaction that her husband's work had been successful. Mary had no doubt that God would be even more eager to bless Reginald's.

The late November afternoon was overcast, but neither clouds nor the chill in the air could dampen Mary's spirit. She waited impatiently for Reginald's arrival at Whitehall. Philip would receive him first and then bring him to the queen.

Her clothes, jewels, attendants, and the Long Gallery had been carefully prepared for the welcome of Cardinal Pole. Only weak sun filtered through the high windows, so torches and candles had been lit. Mary preferred this arrangement, for she knew that the soft firelight better suited her features and made her gems glitter more impressively than a bright sun. Silks and cloth of gold swathed the chamber, and Mary prayed that it matched the magnificence of what Reginald would have observed during his many years in Rome.

Although she had been waiting, Mary felt unprepared when the men arrived. Her throat closed with emotion when she saw the tall, elegant man with her husband who could only be Cardinal Pole. He had dark auburn hair just like his mother's, and the reminder deepened the emotions that were already paralyzing Mary. The crucifix displayed on Reginald's chest was of fine workmanship even if it was free of the jewels that Mary so loved.

When she looked upon it, she felt her babe flutter within her womb.

Overcome, Mary fell to her knees as Reginald spoke, "Ave Maria, gratia plena, Dominus tecum, benedicta tu in mulieribus."

Mary translated the Latin in her mind as Reginald raised her up and in turn knelt before her. "Surely, it was indeed the will of God that we were forced to wait for this moment. His timing is perfect," she agreed. "My child has leapt at your arrival as Saint John did when his mother looked upon the Virgin Mother."

The smile that lit Reginald's face reminded Mary of his older brother, Henry, executed twenty years earlier by her own father. Her heart broke at the thought, and her resolve grew to make right the wrongs of the past.

He replied with the words of Elizabeth, the mother of John the Baptist, "Blessed art thou among women, and blessed be the fruit of thy womb."

Mary beamed, but the rest of her carefully prepared words seemed lost to her. Therefore, she was thankful when Philip held out an arm and gestured that he would lead them.

"I am sure that the Cardinal is weary from his travels, your grace," Philip said. Then to Reginald, "We have prepared Lambeth Palace for your use. Please make us aware if there is anything that you are deprived of there."

Reginald nodded his acceptance of the arrangement, not voicing any concern that his needs would not be met. Philip continued to make small talk as they left the gallery, but Mary only heard half of what was said, so complete was her joy that she could only gaze up at the Cardinal in wonder.

As they walked, they could hear church bells ringing and choirs singing Te Deum to welcome the Cardinal to England.

Mary was no less star-struck when she observed Reginald as

he addressed Parliament just a few days later. He once again skillfully mirrored the words of scripture in his speech.

"I come not to destroy or condemn, but to build. Let us forget actions of the past as if they have been cast into the sea, and be reconciled in faith." His voice was that of an orator, filling the space without sounding like he made any effort to do so. "In recognition of this great commission, I ask you, the lords of Parliament and leaders of this great kingdom, to repeal the legislation that is not in accordance with our goals. With these obstacles removed, we may rejoice in our reconciliation as a family that is reunited in love."

Mary grinned at her husband as Reginald's words were received with great rejoicing. For once, Philip seemed as happy as she, their passion for the church more equal than their passion for each other. He took her hand and squeezed it before raising it to his lips. Mary blushed at the public display though it thrilled her to her core.

She would not say so, but she missed Philip in her bed. Not that Mary would ever suggest that they should endanger the health of their babe, but she would have loved to feel his arms around her. While she missed his presence, Philip seemed content to see Mary only as needed now that he was not required in her bed.

These concerns could not dim Mary's hope for the future on this day. As Parliament repealed the Act of Supremacy that had been created by her father, Mary overflowed with a sense of purpose and fulfillment. The schism created between her kingdom and the kingdom of heaven would be mended, and she was the one to see that it was done.

With the act revoked and Parliament's official apology presented to the Cardinal, the entire audience knelt before him as the representative of the Pope and also of Christ. Reginald stood, held his hands out to them as if he would embrace each one, and said, "I welcome the return of the lost sheep of England and grant you absolution for the sins of the past. Be received into your Mother Church."

"Amen! Amen!" shouted the multitude as Queen Mary wept in exultation.

January 1555

In the weeks since Reginald had arrived, Mary had become as comfortable around him as she had been with the rest of his family. She still looked to him as her greatest helpmate in restoring the true faith to her kingdom, but she also felt that he was a friend rather than one of untouchable greatness. Sitting together on this icy January morning, they were both thankful for the roaring fire and warmed wine.

"The kingdom has been aroused from sleep, as Gardiner preached a fortnight ago," Mary mused. "The crowd that gathered to hear him is eager for God's Word."

Reginald nodded his agreement. "Their piety must be sincere to kneel upon that frozen ground." He shivered and Mary realized that he must no longer be accustomed to the climate of his homeland.

"We cannot turn back the clock," Mary said with regret. "We cannot fully restore the monasteries or all of the traditions that my father and brother eliminated."

Reginald sat forward with the enthusiasm that he brought to every conversation. His slender hands moved as he spoke. "And neither should we," he assured her. "It is right and good to clear our hearts and our sanctuaries of idolatry while not replacing it with heresy." Seeing Mary's widened eyes, he held up a hand and continued. "The problem was that your father had the wrong motivations. He wished to reform the church to satiate his own desires, not for the good of people's souls. Your motives, being pure, will see things set to right – not back the way they were – but the way they should be."

Mary paused to reflect. She had never considered that her work was not simply to return the Church of England to its former self. It was difficult to contemplate, for at the center of the church she envisioned sat her mother and the faith that had enabled her to give up everything and stand up for what she believed. Was the path she trod leading to a less familiar place?

Reginald saw her uncertainty and sought to assure her, "God does not change, he being perfect. But people, those of us who make up his church on earth, are imperfect and must sometimes change when we become aware of where we fall short."

Mary slowly nodded, though she was still not sure that she fully understood or agreed. However, her trust in Reginald was as complete as her trust in God. "How would you have us proceed?" she asked.

He was ready with his answer. "Your decision to renew the statutes for punishing heresies was the right one, and I readily supported you in it. Now we must discern how best to apply it that the least need be punished and the most saved."

This, Mary could agree with wholeheartedly, and her head bobbed in enthusiastic approval. "I have been accused of showing mercy when I should have brought chastisement. I look to you and my lord husband to advise me."

"That is only right. God has created woman to be nurturing and merciful and man to rule, with strength when necessary. Together, the people will benefit from the gifts that God gives to both."

Reginald's wisdom and perceptiveness comforted Mary. This was the support that she had hoped to receive from Philip, but he seemed ever more anxious to return to his own lands. Much to Mary's dismay, he had begun expressing increasing desire to leave England with the assurance that hers were more than capable hands. Those hands now rested upon the mound of her belly, and she wondered what this prince would think of his parents.

"Now that the punishments for heresy have been reinstated,

it will be vital to apply them with great care," Reginald continued.

Mary felt her stomach turn in a way that had nothing to do with the baby. He was talking about burning. There was hesitation to say it in so many words, but Reginald was telling Mary that she would need to send some heretics to burn if she was to save the rest.

"If the proper punishments are meted out, it will deter others from the crime that damns their soul," he reassured her.

Closing her eyes, Mary swallowed hard and nodded. The picture that formed in her mind was one of a man screaming in pain as flames licked at his skin, so she opened her eyes again to instead take in Reginald's compassionate features.

He seemed to understand what she was thinking. "It may not be necessary to burn those living," he said. Seeing her face crinkle in confusion, he added, "Have you considered disinterring heretics who have already gone to their punishment and burning their remains? Those still living will reconsider their stance and we will not lose any who are not already lost to death."

Mary slowly shook her head, her brow deeply furrowed. "I am not sure that will be sufficient to turn those who have had their blood heated by heresies of the past years. And what of those who continue to preach dangerous lies?"

Reginald sat back in his chair, holding his slender hands as if at prayer. He was not afraid to let silence stretch for the purpose of ensuring that he said the right thing. After a few moments, he hesitatingly agreed. "The flames are but a foretaste of hell that we must do our best to save your subjects from. Those who burn may have a change of heart, not wishing to endure such pain for eternity, and those who witness will turn to the true faith."

Mary could not bear to think of what it would be like to die in such a horrific way, let alone suffer that punishment forever.

"Yes, it is my duty to see to my people's salvation as much as it is to ensure their safety and well-being here on earth," she concurred.

"It will take only a few instances of the most extreme measures for people to open their eyes to the error of their ways," he assured her, and himself. "Most will repent and be saved, and they will thank their beloved Queen Mary for shepherding them in truth and love."

Finally, the image of torture faded from Mary's mind and she smiled at the new picture of cheerful Englishmen worshiping together and praising their queen for her good works. "We shall punish only those who have most horrifically broken the laws of God, those who have led others astray and put their eternal souls in danger."

Reginald nodded, better able to disconnect his emotions from the business that needed to be done than Mary was, though he had not desired to take this step. They both looked forward to this part of their work being over and moving on with the more rewarding work of fully reuniting with Rome.

"I must apologize," Mary said as she pushed herself up from the chair with pain etched across her countenance, "but I am in need of rest."

"By all means, your grace," Reginald said, quickly rising to assist her. He gestured to Mary's attendants who were seated far enough away to give them privacy, and Fran was almost immediately at Mary's side. "Please see that her majesty is tended to with great care," he ordered.

Fran had learned since the Cardinal's arrival that he did not intend to sound demanding, yet he was one who was accustomed to having others do as they were told. His heart was in the right place, and Fran could tell that he did love Mary. Therefore, instead of bristling at his command, he dipped her head and said, "It would be my pleasure, your grace. And should I have some food sent to you as well?"

A frown crossed his face as if Reginald had not yet considered if he was hungry. Deciding he was, the corners of his mouth turned upward. "Yes, Lady Waldegrave," he said. "That is most thoughtful of you."

Fran simply smiled and led Mary away. Once they were out of the Cardinal's sight, Mary leaned heavily upon Fran and groaned in pain.

"Your grace, should I send for a physician?" Fran asked in alarm. Her simple nod toward the queen's chamber sent Susan hurrying ahead to make sure that Mary's bed and nightclothes were ready for her.

"No," Mary moaned. "I do not believe I could endure his ministrations at the moment. Let me rest first."

"If that is your wish," Fran demurred, leading Mary into the room. She was pleased to see that the fire had been lit earlier, as evinced by the brightly glowing embers. The room was warm and cozy for Mary, who suddenly appeared strikingly ill.

"Just bed," Mary repeated, sensing Fran's continuing desire to summon a doctor.

"Yes, your grace," Fran acquiesced.

She and Susan removed Mary's layers of fine clothes and dressed her in the simple nightshirt that she found most comfortable. The queen's eyes seemed to be closed throughout the process, and Fran met Susan's gaze as she sent up a silent prayer for Mary's health.

The next morning, Mary knew that she would not rise from her bed before she opened her eyes. Her head felt crushed and a lance of pain pierced her womb. Her fervent silent prayers began before she was fully awake. She prayed not for herself but for the life of her child. Hers could willingly be traded for it, she offered.

She came fully awake when she heard Philip's voice outside her bedchamber. The struggle to make out his words was too much to bear with the blood pulsing so loudly through her ears, so she attempted to wait patiently for one of her ladies to come to her.

Finally, Susan did. She tiptoed across the room and peered inside Mary's bed curtains. Sensing her presence, Mary forced an eye open.

"It is your lord husband," Susan whispered. "Shall I send him away?"

Mary moaned and wondered what a sight she must be to her younger husband, but she could not bring herself to send him away. She was struggling to push herself up when Susan reached to help her.

"Wait, your grace, let me," she scolded. Susan took charge, plumping pillows and smoothing Mary's hair. "I will give him no more than a few moments," Susan said sternly as if it were up to her. She read the thanks in Mary's eyes before she turned back to welcome the king.

"Your grace," Susan said with a low curtsey. "The queen is feeling poorly, but I am sure that it will do her much good to see you."

Philip only nodded and stepped quickly around Susan, who rose and left, closing the door behind her.

"I am sorry to speak to you about these matters while you are ill, but I cannot wait any longer," Philip began hurriedly. His eyes moved furtively about the room, making clear his lack of desire to be there. When she did not immediately speak, his focus fell on Mary.

"My dear," he continued in a tone absent of affection. "I simply must return to the Low Countries. As much as it grieves me to leave while you are with child, I have little to do here and much being neglected there."

His words had come in a rush, and he appeared relieved once they were released. Mary could only stare at him as the pain that wracked her body now found its way to her heart. Her eyes filled with tears and she was certain that Philip must be able to hear the pounding in her head so severe did it grow.

"I see that this is too much for you at the moment, and your concern must be for the babe. We shall talk when you are feeling well," Philip said. Then he strode from the room. It was not until the door closed that Mary realized he had not allowed her to speak a single word.

The blend of illness and melancholy kept Mary abed for several days. Only Susan and Fran attended her, and she gave orders that no one besides her chaplain was to be given entrance that she may hear mass. King or not, Philip was not welcome. If he could not talk to her, he could not speak of leaving.

On Mary's first day up and dressed, she considered Philip's words, and, more than that, his manner when he had last visited. Her hands protectively massaged her belly, and she wondered how he could possibly wish to travel at a time that ensured he would miss the birth of his son.

A sigh escaped her. She had to admit to herself that for every show of affection that she received from Philip, she endured twice as much evidence of his indifference. That would change when she presented him with his son and heir. Their love would blossom into something beautiful, the way God intended. All she could do was continue to give herself to him, heart, body, and soul.

Susan had been sent to invite the king to dine with his wife privately in her room. Mary was not yet well enough for a meal in the hall, but she knew that she could put conversation with her husband off no longer. At that thought, she heard the tread that she recognized as his and rose from her window seat.

"My love," he gushed with enthusiasm that even Mary could perceive was false. He knelt before her and kissed her hands.

A shiver raced through her and warmth began to grow deep within her, but she reminded herself that he was playing a part to get what he wanted. This time it was Mary who would get what she wanted.

"Philip," she said. "I must thank you for visiting me during my illness and apologize for not being able to properly receive you." She had led him to a table and chairs and gestured for him to sit but did not give him a chance to respond. "Now that I have had time to consider your concerns, I must insist that you remain at my side until the birth of our child. Once we know that our prince is safely delivered and in good health, we can revisit the possibility of your tending to your other responsibilities."

Philip's eyes widened in surprise and his lips parted in awe of the assertiveness demonstrated by his submissive wife. Then he caught himself and replaced the mask of loving husband.

"Of course, it is my desire to be with you always," he said, reaching across the table and taking her small, pale hand in his own. "It is not that I wish to leave, but my kingdoms have increasing need of me."

"Of course," was Mary's only response, and her face did not soften in any way at his appeal.

"Let us enjoy this fine meal," Philip said, changing tactics and opening his hands to indicate the dinner that was far too elaborate for the two of them.

At this, Mary smiled sweetly, and agreed. "I have ordered your favorites to be prepared. How I have missed you."

She seemed to revert into the adoring wife he had been

expecting, and Philip wondered if Mary was not more skilled at playing court games than he had believed. Or maybe she was learning from him.

Mary ate little while Philip happily enjoyed the bounty that she had set before him. It was not like him to indulge in rich foods, so it made her wonder if he was frustrated or eating to lessen the expectation of conversation. She did not care as long as he was staying.

Philip left Mary's rooms with more light statements of love that were not supported with his actions, and she was left nibbling on the leftovers. Mary had to admit to herself that she had not been prepared for married life. She had believed that if she loved her husband and did her duty to him that she would be loved in return. The truth was so much more complicated, and it made her head begin to pound again.

Before she could dwell too long upon her troublesome romance, Mary was distracted by the arrival of Bishop Gardiner. Mary jumped from her seat, glad for something else to think about, until she realized the purpose of his visit.

"I have completed the first trial involving five heretics," Gardiner informed her. His face was stony, but Mary could understand that. She, too, hoped to soon be done with this horrid business. "The Bishop of Gloucester, John Hooper, is notable among them," Gardiner continued. "As you commanded, those with the greatest ability to lead the innocent to hell are those investigated."

Mary went cold as the reality struck her that a man was going to be sent to his death on her orders. Not just any man, but one who proclaimed to be a man of God, and not just any death, but one that would be excruciating and publicly performed. She clutched her rosary and reminded herself that it was for the glory of God and salvation of her subjects that she must bravely stand firm. "Tell me," she commanded.

"He has been arrested before for seditious preaching, and it does not seem to have been effective in causing him to consider his blasphemy and turn from his heretical ways. As Bishop of Gloucester, he, of course, is in a powerful position to draw others into the depths of hell."

Mary nodded and Gardiner reached for some of the cheese remaining on the table as if he needed strength to continue.

"He has been condemned along with John Rodgers, and both have been examined thoroughly by the council. Rodgers, as you well know, has preached loudly and boldly against the reconciliation with Rome. Since he himself has defended burning as a punishment for heresy, it is appropriate that he suffer that consequence for his own."

"Because they are so outspoken with their heresy, the message will be equally loud when they experience hell's flames," Mary said confidently.

Gardiner leaned forward, his piercing eyes not allowing her to look away. "Your grace, you are well known for your mercy, even when others have advised against it. Is it your intention to offer pardon at the moment of last hope to these men?"

Is that what Gardiner hoped, Mary wondered. She examined his face but could not discern if he prayed that she would apply her trademark grace to the situation or if he was urging her to stand by the sentencing. She thought of her duty and what the consequences would be if she forgave men for the most heinous of crimes, that of leading men away from God.

"No," she said firmly before she realized that she had opened her mouth to speak. "In this, I cannot waver. The only way to end the heresy in this land that I love is to stamp it out firmly and completely. It would not be mercy to allow more people to suffer hell that a few men might enjoy a longer earthly life."

"It is my hope that those men also see the error of their ways and repent that they may see heaven," Gardiner said.

Mary nodded once. Their faces were painted with the same grim determination to see the work done, as little taste as anyone had for it.

February 1555

Mary sat alone in her room. The cold February sky was gloomy and without color outside her window, but she was not really seeing it. She imagined that she could perceive smoke billowing up and smell burnt flesh, though that was not possible. Moving from the window seat to her prie-dieu, she prayed fervently that souls would be received into heaven should the sinners truly repent. Even more, she begged God to use these punishments to change the hearts of those who witnessed them.

"Let this work for your glory," she whispered as she silently begged God to remove the images of flames from her mind and replace them with visions of the glory of heaven, the glory that so many more would enjoy once her work was complete.

A soft knock came at the door, but Mary remained on her knees, naming each of the five men who went to their death that day and pleading on their behalf with the only one who could save them. The hinges of the door creaked quietly and footsteps approached, but Mary could not bring herself to raise her eyes until she felt a large hand upon her shoulder.

Mary looked up to find Reginald standing over her, love and understanding carved into the lines of his own sorrow upon his face.

"Bless you, Mary," he said in a low voice. "It is done."

Mary closed her eyes again and lowered her head into her hands. She did not feel victorious or even content. "God has called me to the most difficult of tasks," she cried.

"Yes, he has," Reginald agreed, "and he always equips those he has called to extraordinary work."

"Truly?" she asked, feeling low enough to expose her weaknesses to him. If she could not speak thus before the Cardinal, who could she pour out her heart to?

"He does," Reginald insisted, helping her up and directing her to a cushioned seat.

She noticed that his eyes moved to her stomach and that a look of concern briefly crossed his face. It was gone so quickly that she was not sure of what she had seen.

"Your grace," he said once she was settled with a glass of watered wine. "Do you recall that Moses complained to God that he did not have the skill to speak for him or that David was just a boy when he defeated Goliath?"

Mary nodded. Of course, she did.

"Those men did not have the talents required to do God's work, but they allowed him to work through them, just as you do now."

Reginald's elegant hands moved as she spoke, and Mary found herself mesmerized by them as much as by his words. Was he really comparing her to the great patriarchs of their faith? She may be queen of England, but the honor the Cardinal bestowed upon her felt like one she was unworthy of.

"You have inherited the title of Head of the Church of England, and you will be the first to hold it who leads people to God rather than away from him."

Mary's head shot up at that. She had never liked that part of the titles that she had inherited from her brother. It was not her place, but the Pope's, to be the head of the church. It surprised her to hear Reginald felt differently, and she said so.

"You believe God intended me to bear that title? I do not believe that I am worthy."

He smiled. "And that is just what qualifies you."

~ ~ ~ ~

If only Mary could have held onto the feeling she had that

day. She wished to keep it bottled up that she might take a sip of it whenever her courage failed. Reginald had assured her that she was doing the right thing, that her hand was guided by God, but clearly not everyone agreed upon that.

Protestants had come out in crowds, not to turn from their devilish ways, but to cry out against the cruelty of their queen. Mary had been astounded and hurt. This was not the way things were supposed to unfold. The hardening of the heretics' resolve broke her heart for she knew that it meant more punishments would be necessary.

She was the Head of the Church of England and could not let her country or her God down.

Instead of seeing the flames as a sampling of hell to be avoided, the Protestants were proclaiming that those who went bravely to such a horrible death demonstrated that theirs was a faith worth dying for. The terrible lies could not be allowed to spread, so Mary was forced to order that arrests increase.

Illness crept up upon Mary again as her councilors argued over how best to move forward. To her surprise, Gardiner proposed an end to the burnings while Paget was her unlikely ally. He and Pole insisted that there could be no veering from the chosen path if they were to successfully stamp out heresy. Gardiner's health failed along with the queen's as the public outcry was often against him, the people not understanding who they should focus their anger upon and he being the easiest target.

However, the betrayal that hurt Mary the most was Philip's. In order to distance himself from the controversy, the king had insisted that his confessor preach against the burnings. God had chosen him to be Mary's helpmate in bringing the true faith back to England, and he had let them both down.

The damage to her relationship with Philip bothered Mary

even more than the continued plotting in favor of her sister. Rumors continued that Elizabeth would marry Courtenay and that the couple would depose the queen. Mary was finally brought to bed once again when the news reached her of another hurtful rumor. People were claiming that she was not even pregnant.

March 1555

Philip was making the best of his gilded captivity in England. While Mary was increasingly kept in her bed due to illness and difficulty with her pregnancy, he planned tournaments and entertainments to amuse himself until he could make a better case for leaving. Both prayed fervently for a son if not for precisely the same reasons.

If Philip no longer put as much effort into pretending that he had feelings for Mary that did not truly exist, he also never completely neglected his duties as husband and king. He carefully planned to meet her between the liturgical hours for she was adamant about hearing mass at each time, certain that this would ensure the health of their babe.

On this day, he entered her chamber with the same nonchalance that he always did. It was that lack of deep feeling that worried Mary. Regardless of how much time went by or the extent to which she showered love upon him, he simply was creating no attachments to her or her kingdom. Always, just below the surface, she could tell he was itching to be gone.

"Husband," she chirped, determined to continue trying, "it pleases me to see you looking so well. You bring with you the scents of the outdoors. How refreshing!"

A lazy smile crossed his face, and he said, "Yes. It is cold as the Alps, but I cannot bear sitting inside all day."

Mary ignored the jab at her habit of keeping indoors through the cold months. Could he not see that she dared not risk the baby even if she did enjoy freezing her fingers and toes to participate in winter activities?

"I have come to speak to you on a matter that continues to plague you and your councilors," he said, this time insinuating that she was inept as well as lazy.

Mary pressed her lips together and nodded for him to continue.

"Since the rumors of Elizabeth and Courtenay persist, and at least one of them is undoubtedly giving people reason for their whispers, why do you not send them abroad? I can place them in appropriate situations where they need not concern you."

Tilting her head, Mary considered the offer. Elizabeth had stoutly denounced marriage to the man of Philip's choice, the duke of Savoy, and Mary had not had it in her to force the girl. Perhaps time at the court of Charles V or some other suitable appointment would be more appealing to Mary's sister.

Mary shook her head. Why did she still care if Elizabeth wanted to go? The girl was trying to steal her crown! The movement made the familiar pulses begin behind her eyes, and Mary closed them and prayed for it to go away rather than grow worse.

"I am sorry, Philip," she said, "but I believe I will have to consider Elizabeth's situation after my confinement. Your wise advice is much appreciated. That may be just the way to remove them from tempting situations and those eager to plot in their names."

Philip accepted this without complaint and without inquiring into his wife's health. She was always complaining about aches and pains of some sort, so he did not think he needed to ask.

He stood, and Mary's eyes widened in surprise. "Must you take leave so soon?" she asked and could not help the pleading that shone in her eyes.

Philip frowned but retook his seat. He knew his role, but he was growing weary of playing it.

April 1555

By the time Mary was prepared to enter her confinement rooms, Elizabeth and Courtenay had been dealt with as effectively as possible. Not surprisingly, Elizabeth had balked at the idea of leaving England, but the earl of Devon had not been given the option.

Edward Courtenay was sent to Brussels on a diplomatic mission for Philip, while Elizabeth was brought to court. No one could speak the words aloud, but all understood that if Mary died in childbirth it would be vital to have Elizabeth under control. If the baby died as well, Elizabeth would be queen.

The fact that Mary could not justify disinheriting her sister altogether irritated her like a wound that refused to fully heal, but her best alternative was to name her cousin, Mary Stuart, her preferred heir. This younger Mary was of the true faith, while Elizabeth's salvation was in question, but she was also in the pocket of the French. Therefore, the English council would never give their approval to her claim.

Mary held fast to her faith that God knew what he was doing and would see her son safely born, eliminating the need to choose between two unpalatable options.

Philip and Mary moved their household to Hampton Court. Mary had mixed feelings about this as a location for her child to be born, for the palace was filled with memories of Elizabeth's mother, the woman who had caused Mary so much personal heartache. Mary also placed blame upon Anne Boleyn for the kingdom's fall from true worship. However, it was a place of security and free of illness, which made it a better choice for their child than Mary's preferred Windsor.

She would do anything to see her child safely born. Although she dared not give voice to her concerns, Mary worried that she had not had to let out her dresses much after the first few months. The flutter of movement never became the strong kicks and nauseating rolls that she heard other women describe. When she undressed, her belly was larger, but still flabby rather than stretched out tightly by the growing child. She spent increasing amounts of time on her knees, praying that nothing would go wrong.

Mary saw her attendants give her sideways glances and perceived the question in their eyes. Fran assured her that she had simply miscalculated. The babe was likely due a month later than they had been planning for. Mary felt that giving voice to her doubt would give life to her fears, so she bit her lips and blinked back her tears.

The queen's chambers at Hampton Court were prepared for her confinement as if none had any doubts. Upon the cradle that would hold her child, words were skillfully carved into the dark wood.

The child which Thou to Mary, O Lord of might, has send, To England's joy, in health preserve, keep and defend!

The fingers of Mary's right hand lightly traced these letters as her left hand cupped beneath her womb. Clothes atop a nearby table were ready to wrap the baby in as soon as he was born, and midwives were ready to attend her at her first cry of labor pain. She moved to the window, unable to withstand the torment and doubt that the baby's things caused.

Outside, the beauty of spring was marred by the guards standing at intervals around the castle. Burnings had continued, despite the protests that met the first one, and some of the heretics grew violent in their response. It saddened Mary that she now required protection from the subjects that had happily made her queen in the place of the usurper, Jane.

"Lord, open their eyes to your truth," Mary prayed without moving her eyes from the contingent of guards.

The sound of her ladies talking in low, conspiratorial voices broke her reverie, and Mary moved toward the door. Guilt brought a flush to her cheeks, but she stopped to listen before moving into the next room.

"Philip will marry her no doubt."

"Hush. It is not right to speak of."

"Lady Elizabeth arrives any day. Do you think that is by accident?" the first voice challenged.

Mary recognized her defender as Fran but could not quite place the other. Fran had not deigned to reply to the lady's question, so she continued.

"Between you and me," her voice lowered and Mary strained to hear the rest, "I don't believe that her grace is with child at all. She is as likely to die of a tumor as she is in childbirth."

Mary gasped and stepped away from the door as if it had burned her. She heard Fran's command, "That is quite enough. It is cruel, not to mention treasonous, and I shall have no choice but to report it if I hear you make such statements again."

The rebuttal did nothing to salve Mary's wounds. People believed she would die. Believed it and did not care, were simply waiting for it to happen. But why? Why did no one seem to care for her the way she cared for them?

Mary returned to the cradle, lowered herself heavily onto the stool next to it, and sobbed with her head resting against the empty baby bed.

~ ~ ~ ~

"Your grace, I have someone here that I would like to present to you if you feel up to it," Fran said, peeking her head into Mary's private sitting room.

Mary glanced up from her Book of Hours and took in the excitement that was clear on Fran's face. It almost made her smile, but not quite. It had been some time since happiness had lit her face, and the permanent lines in her face gave testimony of it. She set aside the prayer book and moved to join Fran in the next room.

Opening the door wider, Fran said, "Your grace, Lisbet use to work in the laundry here until her pregnancy made it impossible." The woman was just coming into Mary's view when Fran added, "As you can see, she has had her hands too full to come back to work since giving birth."

Mary's breath caught in her throat at the sight of three perfect infants peeking from matching ivory colored wool blankets. The woman who had to be Lisbet held one in each arm, and a girl of about twelve held the other. This girl tried to hide her face behind the babe in the presence of the queen.

"Oh! Praise be to God!" Mary cried rushing toward the precious children. "Three at once? I have never seen such a phenomenon." She looked at each perfect little snub nose and their matching milky blue eyes in turn. "How marvelous!"

No one said anything as Mary cooed over the babies and held her arms out to hold one of them. Fran was pleased to see the first genuine smile on Mary's face since they had entered her confinement rooms.

After a few moments, Mary said, "Fran, please."

Fran walked to a chest at the side of the room, understanding Mary's wish. She returned with a pouch of silver pennies, and Mary gestured for the gift to be given directly to Lisbet. The woman's eyes widened in wonder as she turned over one of the babes to the older child in order to receive the gift.

"Thank you, your merciful majesty!" she exclaimed. It was

the first words she had spoken, but they seemed to open a floodgate. From that moment, she babbled about the babies and how she went about caring for three at a time as Mary listened enraptured.

It was not until Fran took the babe from Mary's arms, saying, "Your grace, it is time that you rested," that Lisbet halted her speech with reddened cheeks.

"Thank you for sharing your children with me," Mary said, reluctantly giving up the tiny child in her arms. "This is a moment that I will remember always."

Lisbet's blush faded and she grinned widely at the idea that she, a mere laundress, had so pleased the queen of England.

Mary was still filled with the euphoria of the children's visit when she looked for Fran later that evening. She wished for Fran to help her prepare for bed and to thank her again for bringing Lisbet to her. Surprised that Fran did not seem to be in her rooms, Mary peeked into the corridor. Fran was there being confronted by Philip.

"I don't know quite what you mean, your grace," Fran was insisting as she took a step away from the king.

Philip moved and closed the space as soon as Fran had opened it. "Yes, you do, Lady Waldegrave. You know exactly what it is that I ask of you."

Mary felt fury grow within her. She was beyond being disappointed that Philip did not love her. Was he going to flaunt the fact with one of her closest attendants?

"Your grace, we are outside your wife's confinement rooms," Fran objected. "I believe that should be sufficient to answer your question."

Philip rolled his eyes and persisted, "But is she truly with child?"

Mary gasped and backed away from the door certain that they must have heard her. She rushed into her bed chamber, so that they might convince themselves that someone else had left the door ajar and been eavesdropping on their conversation. Philip was not suggesting that Fran become his mistress as Mary had first believed. He thought that Mary was lying about being pregnant.

She sat at her vanity and fingered the lined up objects without looking at what she picked up only to immediately set it back down. Why would he think that she would lie? She would not cause him to be sent from her rooms, giving her no opportunity to become pregnant, if she were not with child already.

Fran walked in, and Mary could tell by the pity on her face that she knew. Mary cursed the tears that filled her eyes. She wanted to be angry. She wanted to yell not cry, but Fran, who had defended her to her doubting husband, did not deserve that.

"Oh, sweet Mary," Fran cried as she ran across the room and embraced the woman who, at this moment, was simply a hurting friend rather than the queen.

Mary let her tears fall without saying a word until she regained control of herself. When she could speak, she had to ask, "Fran, do you believe that I am with child?"

Her bloodshot eyes sought Fran's concerned ones.

"Why, your grace, the doctors have confirmed it, and you suffer many of the symptoms."

Mary closed her eyes and shook her head. "But do you believe it?" she insisted.

"Yes, your grace," Fran said. "Of course, I do."

But they both knew that she was lying.

May 1555

Elizabeth curtseyed low before her sister, so that Mary saw only the top of her head, covered with gloriously bright red hair. Mary's face was drawn and haggard, giving Elizabeth the impression that the weeks in confinement were anything but relaxing. It took no more than a glimpse at Mary's waistline to see that she did not have the healthy rounded look of one about to give birth.

Mary examined her sister's face as Elizabeth rose. She could not help but have a begrudging respect for the control the younger woman had over her features. Looking at her now, none would guess that Elizabeth had been railing against her sister, the queen, for months and begging for an audience just as long. She appeared pleased to be presented but without an iota of the submissiveness that Mary believed she was owed.

That was the first pin in Mary's reserve of patience. The second was the way Elizabeth shared many of Mary's features while managing to arrange the same sharp nose, pale skin, and russet hair in a much more pleasing manner. Mary had not been as beautiful, even at Elizabeth's age, and now the queen knew that she wore the countenance of a weary, old woman.

Yet, it was she who was queen. Mary stiffened her spine and gestured Elizabeth to a seat so that she would not be forced to look up to her. A shadow of a smirk told Mary that Elizabeth recognized Mary's reasons and counted it as one more minor point scored.

The glances that Elizabeth kept unsubtly directing at Mary's abdomen made Mary's mind race back to the midwife's visit just days earlier. Susan had insisted upon bringing the woman to Mary, dissatisfied as she was with the doctor's ongoing insistence that Mary must have simply miscalculated her due date.

The midwife had examined Mary thoroughly, much to her

humiliation and displeasure. She could not bring herself to speak to the woman once the torture had concluded. Therefore, it was Susan who had received the diagnosis that the queen was not pregnant and the doctors who told her differently were just afraid to say otherwise. Mary was still attempting to decide what to do with the conflicting information, but her sister was the last person she would discuss it with.

How pleased Elizabeth would be to learn that her golden red head was once again only a small step away from England's crown.

Instead, Mary placed a delicate hand upon her womb just as though she firmly believed a baby thrived there and glared at her sister. Prayers had been said by the queen and her ladies in preparation for this moment, but now that it had arrived Mary felt only sinful hatred toward the younger sister who longed to take her place on the throne, just as she had taken Mary's place in their father's heart.

Elizabeth seemed to sense the tension in the air, and moved to reposition herself more favorably by throwing herself down at her sister's feet.

On her knees, Elizabeth conjured up crocodile tears and begged, "God preserve your majesty! I beg that you find me as true a subject as can be found in your kingdom, whatever others might say or do."

"Oh, do get up," Mary commanded, looking away from Elizabeth's attempt at humbling herself. "God alone knows the truth of your confession, and it is he who will judge you."

Mary could not find one drop of the compassion and love that drove her to pardon others to spare for her manipulative sister. Elizabeth seemed to see that she had misplayed her hand and slid back into the proffered seat.

"Do you really believe yourself wrongly punished?" Mary asked, though she knew Elizabeth would only speak in riddles of the type not used by the genuinely innocent.

"I am your true subject," Elizabeth repeated, as if Mary would fail to notice that she did not answer her question.

Mary's frown deepened as a dull throb began behind her eyes. "You shall remain here until the prince is born." Mary paused and the women stared at each other, each daring the other to voice aloud that neither of them was sure a prince, or any babe for that matter, was going to come from Mary's swollen womb.

"If it pleases your grace," Elizabeth said with a lowering of her head.

"My husband believes that you should be at your full liberty."

Elizabeth's head snapped up, her eyes full of eager anticipation that Mary was delighted to disappoint.

"I will decide whether or not I think this a prudent path forward," Mary continued with the slightest of smirks, "after the child is born."

Elizabeth did not let her face fall, but even she could not keep the light in her eyes from dimming at the prospect of waiting for an unlikely event to gain her freedom. The jab seemed to free her tongue.

"Your grace, I am yours to command. Were you aware that the bells rang in London a fortnight ago when rumors arrived that you had already been brought to your childbed? All rejoiced at the arrival of a new prince for England. I do hope that they will not have to wait long to renew their celebrations."

Heat rushed to Mary's face, but she could not look away from Elizabeth's cruel, teasing eyes. "You may go now," she said, turning away before Elizabeth could say any more. Mary forced herself to look out the window without seeing any of the scenery until she heard the door open and close behind her. Mary was hurt, but she was too angry for tears.

"Dear God," she cried, clutching her rosary and eyes squeezed shut, "what shall I do if the midwife and my spiteful sister are right?"

At that very moment, a pain like none Mary had ever felt shot through her womb. She gasped and dropped her rosary to feel her abdomen for signs of change. Could she be in labor?

"Fran!" she yelled, not concerned for propriety and scared for her life. "Fran, I need you!"

In seconds, Fran was there, her face white as fresh washed linen and her wide eyes quickly taking in the scene before her. She did not speak, but her eyes asked the same question that Mary was asking herself. Was she going to give birth?

"Let us get you to bed, your grace," Fran decided. "Tell me about your pains."

"It was just one, but fierce," Mary explained as she allowed Fran to lead her to bed. "It seems to be fading somewhat now."

"And what did it feel like?" Fran asked, her voice now calm and soothing as she took control of the situation.

Mary did not hesitate with her answer. "It felt like the pain I've always imagined men must feel when they are run through with a sword."

Fran furrowed her brow, supposing it was possible to describe labor pains that way. Most women described a fearsome tightening of muscles beyond their control that worsened as time went on, the early pains hardly more uncomfortable than monthly cramps. By the time Mary was tucked under the covers and looking to Fran for encouragement, her face was arranged to offer it.

"Any more pains yet, your grace?"

Mary shook her head. "No, it is thankfully much more bearable now."

"Right, then," Fran replied, fluffing pillows and arranging covers, but not looking into Mary's eyes. "I am going to bring some spiced wine and food. If it is your child coming, you will need your strength."

Mary watched Fran leave the room with purpose in her stride. As soon as she was out the door, Susan entered.

"I have been sent to sit with you, your grace," she said with a smile. "I do pray that the baby is on his way."

Susan was the first person to seem sincere when they mentioned the baby, and that helped Mary relax and forget for a moment that the child might not exist. The pain had scared her. She had grown up hearing of the trials that women faced in birthing, but nothing had prepared her for that feeling. She could not bring herself to hope that it would return, even if it had to in order to bear her child.

Susan had started babbling away about inane topics, so Mary laid her head back and dozed off to the sound of cheerful chattering.

"Your grace . . . Mary," a voice was calling her out of her dreams, but Mary did not wish to wake. The voice reminded her of her mother, but that could not be right. Her mother had been dead for almost twenty years.

"I hate to wake you, your grace, but I've brought the doctor."

It was Fran, not Catherine, who had long ago gone to her heavenly home, Mary realized. She did not want to wake, certainly not to be poked and prodded once again by arrogant physicians who would only repeat what they had been saying for months.

Mary groaned. "Send him away." The piercing pain had not

returned, but she felt a dull ache in her womb that was mirrored by the pounding of her head. Her heart fluttered and struggled to beat evenly in her chest, and she simply could not bear the ministrations of a doctor right now.

Fran was pleading gently for Mary to allow the examination, but Mary shouted at her for the first time either of them could remember.

"No! Get him out of here and leave me be!"

The volume of her own voice made it feel as though her head would explode, and Mary retreated under the covers, hoping that they would all leave before she had to resurface for fresh air. Her own stale breath filled the space beneath the covers as she waited for the sound of scurrying feet to fade.

Slowly drawing the cover back, Mary allowed her eyes to open just a slit to confirm that she was alone. Her body was wracked with pain, but she would be birthing no child that day.

It was full dark when Mary next woke. The time that had passed since she had gone to bed was unclear in her mind. Had it been just a few hours or had most of the night passed? She was not sure, but she lay fully awake considering her situation with greater clarity than she had in many weeks.

God was punishing her. There would be no child. Mary would be publicly humiliated, but, worse than that, she would be forced to recognize her sister as heir. Despite their personal differences, Mary would be able to accept this path if it were not for the fact that she had lingering suspicions that Elizabeth was a heretic.

Elizabeth carefully put on just enough of a show of piety to make it difficult to question her devotion, but Mary had known her all her life and recognized when Elizabeth was sincere. Those times seemed to grow fewer and further between as she matured.

Mary was not adept at the manipulative games that her sister played, but one truth was becoming clear to her. The only reason that God would force Mary to leave her kingdom to a heretic heir was because she had not been completely devoted to eradicating heresy from her kingdom. As little as Mary liked the idea of increasing punishments for any of her subjects, their salvation depended upon her ability to crush the devil's followers in her realm.

An image of doctors who must perform painful surgeries in order to save the life of their patient came to mind. Better to lose an arm than a life. At that moment, Mary made a solemn vow. When she exited her confinement chamber, with or without a child, she would set aside her weak tendency toward misguided mercy and see her land healed and returned to God.

July 1555

What Mary had privately confessed to herself over a month earlier, she continued to struggle with publicizing. She remained in confinement, though Hampton Court was becoming unfit for habitation. The weeks passed and refuse piled up, raising concerns for sickness as the air throughout the estate held the stench of a household long past the time when it needed refreshing.

A letter had been secretly posted to Reginald informing him of Mary's concern that God's judgement would be brought down upon the queen and her kingdom if heresy were not more ambitiously dealt with. The Cardinal, for his part, offered up for judgement a canon of St Paul's.

John Rodgers was led to the stake for preaching heresy, but was offered a pardon if he would recant on the spot. Much to his gaoler's surprise, he refused, choosing the flames over repentance. His wife looked on weeping as Rodgers held his hands out to the flame as if he would wash them of sin.

When Reginald wrote to Mary of the event, he expressed his concern that the burnings might sometimes work to spread the fervency of martyrdom among the heretics rather than increasing their fear of hell. But if the flames of hell did not turn them, what would?

Mary's tears fell in earnest when she read this. Her hands rested on her shrunken womb, and she begged God to guide her. "What can I do?" she cried to the empty chamber, but only her own anguished words returned to her.

Other letters came from Philip. He was more eager than ever to leave due to the death of his grandmother, Queen Joanna. Charles continued to postpone the interment of her earthly remains as Philip sent repeated assurances that he would soon arrive. His letters never accused Mary of pretending to be with child, but neither did he inquire as to the progress of her pregnancy.

These missives concerned Mary just as much as those from Reginald. She had begged Philip to stay until the birth of their child, but if she was not pregnant it was even more vital that he remain. She was an almost forty-year-old queen with no child, and therefore with great need of her husband.

Finally, at the end of the month, Mary's courses began as though they had never stopped. No evidence of a child was present. It was as if the past ten months had been nothing but a figment of her imagination.

August 1555

In the end, Mary decided to simply leave Hampton Court. The rumormongers could spread whatever stories they would regarding her long stay in confinement that had not resulted with a child. Neither Mary nor her doctors could explain why she had demonstrated all the signs of pregnancy for months only to have them slowly fade away, so she would make no attempt to do so.

The procession had slowly left Hampton Court behind, moving toward the fresher air of Oatlands. Mary had not looked back at the red brick façade. She hoped that she would never see it again.

Her only encouragement had come from the fact that Philip had ridden at her side. The late summer sun had shone upon his fine features, making Mary smile. She was so grateful that he had not left her, even when pressures to do so had been severe. They would share the intimacy that Mary had been missing during her long weeks of confinement, and with God's blessing she would get with child this time.

After staying at Oatlands just long enough for rest and the sending of messengers to go ahead of them, they had carried on. The autumn air rejuvenated Mary more than most of the vile potions that doctors insisted would restore her health. Or maybe it was the presence of her husband.

Philip seemed to sense her gaze and turned toward her. His smile was hesitant, and Mary perceived that his thoughts were not in line with her own. It did not matter. They were together now, and she would be thankful for it.

Mary had been disappointed to learn that Philip's desire to leave England had not been dampened. He had agreed to travel with her as the retinue returned to London, and then he would take his leave. She would not think of his departure until she had to. The time with him was too precious.

He had not come to her chamber during their nights at Oatlands, but she would demand it if she had to once they reached Greenwich. She felt her cheeks heat up at the thought but pressed her lips together in determination. If he was going to insist on leaving, she would insist that he leave her with child.

As they reached the outskirts of the city, a crowd began to gather along their route. She may not have given them a prince, but the people still longed for a glimpse of their Queen Mary. That she, Philip, and Cardinal Pole rode together made the opportunity too rare to pass up for people who would likely never lay eyes on any of the three of them again in their lifetime.

Mary smiled and waved to her subjects as if she were happily rejoining them, as if her heart were not breaking at the absence of the child that should have been with her, as if her husband was anxious to share her bed rather than escape her kingdom. She was somewhat encouraged by the loyal display and exuberant salutations, but they failed to lift her completely from her pit.

The sight of Greenwich did bring her some cheer. It was a place filled with many happy memories, and the grounds were as beautiful as they had been when she was a child strolling the paths with her governess, Reginald's mother. As her retinue clattered into the courtyard, Mary imagined her own children spending their formative years here. This succeeded in bringing a smile to her face as she turned to her husband.

"I am glad to see that it pleases you to be here, my love," Philip observed. In a lower voice he added, "It would also please me to visit your rooms later if you are feeling well enough."

Mary's grin widened as she felt the secret parts of her enflame at his words. Maybe things would turn around for her after all, she thought.

"I have greatly missed your company," she admitted with downcast eyes.

She did not therefore see that Philip took a deep, bracing breath before continuing, "Then I shall look forward to it, dear wife."

By the time Mary could bring herself to lift her eyes, he had ridden away. Yet she cherished the promise of his visit and left Susan to manage the unpacking so that she could prepare herself.

Amidst the chaos of the household resettling, Mary ordered a bath. Fran was pulled away from her duties to attend upon the queen. Skin must be scrubbed, hair must be arranged, and the bed must be made inviting. Fran performed these tasks with cheer that may have seemed false to some but was an encouragement to Mary.

Food had been sent up, but Mary took only a few bites. Her stomach was twisted as it had been on her wedding day. It had been almost a year since she had shared a bed with her husband, and her fears of not being capable of pleasing him returned in full force. Accompanying those concerns was the fact that she had little time to become pregnant. Philip planned to cross the Channel within a fortnight.

"Just relax," Fran soothed as if she could read Mary's thoughts. "He will be in as much anticipation as your grace," she lied. Mary happily accepted the exaggeration without comment.

After a few more unnecessary adjustments and murmured assurances, Fran left Mary alone to wait for her husband.

He arrived earlier than he usually retired to bed, and Mary wondered if she had not misjudged him. Maybe he really did desire her. Philip strode in casually. He had clearly not taken any of the pains that she had to appeal to him. The scent of horses and autumn air still clung to him, but it did not matter. He took her breath away.

Fran had left Mary in bed with her hair loose and fanned around her. Philip began removing his clothing as soon as he had closed the door, and Mary felt an excitement that she had never experienced. He wanted her.

After snuffing the candles, Philip's work was done quickly and expertly. Mary was left breathless and astounded. She had misjudged Philip and, in the depths of her depression, believed that he did not love her and was anxious to abandon her. She snuggled up against him and thanked God that she had been wrong.

Mary was almost asleep, warmed by Philip's body and her own contentedness, when he stirred. Her grip on him tightened, but he grasped her wrists to free himself as he slid from under the covers.

"Philip?" She said, groggily wondering where he was going.

"Forgive me, love," he whispered. "I thought you were asleep. I have tasks that I must attend to if I am to leave as scheduled."

Mary was stunned awake but had not thought of what to say before she heard the door closing behind him.

~ ~ ~ ~

He had come to her each night, performing his duty as it was just that, a duty. Mary had welcomed him and tried to pretend that he was driven by desire for her rather than the need to leave her with a child that would keep her from begging him to return. How foolish she had been to think he had developed feelings for her.

She was glad that he extinguished the candles before joining her in bed, so that he could not see her shame or the desire that she felt for him despite it. Did he pretend that she was someone else, perhaps the mysterious Marguerite, she wondered after he was gone.

Her feelings churned within her, each surfacing in their turn. One moment she would be thankful that he was there, at least playing the role of a loving husband. The next, she would hate herself for settling for a farce of affection. Yet, she would wait eagerly for his next visit.

Mary had no one to confide in. None of her attendants were a close enough friend for her to speak of feelings and troubles that were so intimate. She had only God to go to, and to him she poured out her heart and begged for healing in her marriage.

Until the day Philip came to Mary to say goodbye, she had convinced herself that something would make him stay. However, when he stood before her with greater joy on his face at the prospect of leaving than he had ever exhibited to be with her, she realized the depth of his dissatisfaction and just how much he had been pretending.

If they had created a child during Philip's roleplaying, would the future ruler be scarred by the deception and lack of love that had gone into his formation? It was too soon for Mary to know if she was pregnant, but one of her hands rested hopefully upon her abdomen nonetheless. If Philip noticed, he made no comment upon it.

He fidgeted, restless to be on his way and tired of Mary's weeping. For this reason, he had convinced her to share their farewell here at Greenwich, though she would have been happy to follow him to the coast and stay by his side for as long as she could. This was better for them both, he had insisted.

Greenwich's great staircase sprawled away from them, and Philip looked as though it took all his willpower to keep his feet from racing down it.

"I will return to open Parliament with you in October," he reassured her, squeezing her hands and wiping tears from her eyes.

Mary nodded, unable to speak through the lump formed in her throat. It was difficult enough to let him go, heartbreaking to see the happiness he did not trouble himself to mask. He had begun to turn away from her when she found her voice.

"May God go with you, my beloved husband. May he bless you and keep you until you can return to me."

Philip bowed to her and then was gone.

Each of Philip's attendants took their own leave of the queen, respectfully kissing her hand. She murmured a few words to each, wishing that they would hasten. Once the last of them filed past, she rushed to a window that offered her a view of Philip's ship.

Alone in the window seat, Mary narrowed her eyes in an effort to capture one more glimpse of her husband. All was a blur and she cursed her poor vision. One man appeared to be Philip's build and wearing similar clothing, so Mary fixated on him and imagined that she was sure it was him.

Her hand pressed against the window as if to touch him one more time and great sobs wracked her body. She wondered if she would ever see him again, and then realized her mistake. Another person on the ship was waving his hat to her. Philip had noticed his grieving wife, and it cost him little to offer her one more token of his false affection.

Mary attempted to smile, but her face was contorted by sorrow. She remained in what she imagined was relative privacy of the alcove until Philip's ship had sailed from her sight. Only when she finally stood to leave her spot did she realize that eyes that had witnessed her display of sorrow averted when she turned back to the room.

At that moment, she did not care. Now that he was gone, Mary had to do what she could to ensure that Philip returned. His assurances had not appeased her, and she suffered a deep sense of foreboding. Back in her rooms, she took up her writing desk and wrote the first of a series of letters that would greet Philip at each stop along his journey.

September 1555

A fortnight had passed since Philip's departure, but Mary could not lift herself from the gloom that weighed down upon her. Keeping to her private rooms, she spent hours writing him letters to which he did not frequently respond. And she wept, for countless hours her hot tears fell in mourning for the hopes that she had held for her marriage.

Since she was not currently at the task of writing, Mary sat in the dark letting her rosary beads slip through her fingers. A soft knock at the door caused her to jump and drop them. It was Susan's head that peeked around the door frame.

"Your grace, the Cardinal is here to see you," she whispered.

Mary blinked. She did not wish to speak to anyone. Then she remembered her conviction when she left Hampton Court without a babe in her arms. God was displeased with her, and she must make it right, with or without Philip.

Susan had almost closed the door when Mary spoke. "Please, Susan, make me presentable for his grace. I would speak to my wise cousin and seek his guidance."

Susan's face brightened. The miserable queen sent so many away when they might have done her good. Susan was animated as she tended to Mary's hair and dress. When she moved to apply cosmetics, Mary waved her away.

"Surely, such things are not necessary before God's representative."

"Of course, your grace," Susan said with a curtsey before she left to fetch Cardinal Pole.

He entered wearing dark robes that could have been cut from the same cloth as Mary's dress. She could see that his eyes took in every detail of the room in the time it took for him to cross the floor to her and offer her a blessing. Reginald noticed, therefore, the untouched tray from the kitchen, discarded drafts of letters to Philip, and the unfreshened linens. Mary silently chided herself and made a mental note to have her room tended to after he left. She had not realized just how long she had closed herself in.

Reginald broke her reverie and drew her attention back to him. He had a voice that demanded attention without loud harshness but the captivating tone of a natural teacher.

"I am concerned about you of late," he admitted to her. "You spend much of your time consumed by business. What time is not spent with your councilors is expended here." His open hands indicated the unkempt room.

"Am I not to be about the business of my realm?" she asked, pretending that she did not deny food and sleep in her ambition to drive all emotion from her day until she allowed herself to wallow in it completely, as she had been doing when he arrived.

He nodded as if he had been expecting this reply. "And who will do so if you strain yourself with labors to the extent that you sicken?" he asked reasonably.

Mary delayed her need to respond by gesturing that they should sit. Her nerves were almost permanently on edge and she found it difficult to think clearly. She looked to Reginald.

His slender fingers were woven together and rested comfortably in his lap. Mary stared at them and wondered if she could ever be as calm and at peace as he was. Moving her eyes to his face, she saw his gentle green eyes patiently waiting for her to respond. His eyebrows were slightly raised in inquiry.

Mary sighed and looked away. "I feel like a lost sheep."

"Then it is good that the Lord has sent you a shepherd," he said with a smile. "I have written to your husband and made him aware of my observations. His return would likely cure much, but you must see to yourself regardless of Philip's actions. God has given you great responsibilities."

"Yes," Mary agreed. She was energized by having Reginald on her side. With his support, she could bear Philip's absence and what she knew she must accomplish. "I believe that God desires greater conviction from me. I have been weak when he required strength. It is for this reason that my child was taken from me. If I am to bear an heir, I must perform the difficult task that he has set before me."

Reginald lifted one hand toward to her, indicating that she should carry on.

"The people are tightening their grip on heresies behind the mask of patriotism. We must not allow it to continue. It is not true mercy to allow heresy to thrive which draws men closer to hell."

Mary's weariness and depression were momentarily forgotten. She would do what she must to save her people.

"I would give anything, even my very life, if God so requires it," she said with fervor. "Let him take all if it secures my subjects their places in heaven."

Nodding in appreciation of her words, Reginald said, "It is for this reason that God has placed you here. Just as he used Queen Esther to save her people, he shall use you to save yours. That you have made yourself a willing vessel for his work is the vital first step. Your father refused to put God's desires above his own, but you shall make propitiation for his sins."

"Yes!" Mary's face was radiant with purpose. She would not let her kingdom crumble under false teaching because she did not have her husband at her side. She had her God. And she had Reginald Pole.

October 1555

Cardinal Pole performed mass before a congregation that included two strikingly similar women who were also irreconcilably different. The Tudor sisters knelt devoutly, their bronze and copper heads close together, but all knew that rather different thoughts ran through those clever minds. Though their postures were identical, somehow the observer could discern that there was greater sincerity in the older sister's worship.

Mary received the eucharist, all the while silently praying that the body of Jesus would strengthen her own and that his blood would join hers to give her his will. When the mass was over and they rose to file out of the chapel, she glanced at her sister and wondered what she was thinking. Had Elizabeth felt the same oneness with God that Mary had, or was it all for show?

Between her playacting husband and insincere sister, Mary wondered if anyone in the world was genuine. Glancing back toward the altar, she released a sigh of relief. Yes. Reginald was as he appeared and dedicated his life to their shared hope, to see England restored to the true faith. The reminder encouraged her as much as the service had.

Her steps quickened as she also remembered that Reginald would be making his way to her chamber as soon as he had completed his duties. She imagined him reverently placing the bread and wine in the tabernacle and removing his vestments in the sacristy before he came to her. She smiled and ignored her sister's sidelong look.

It was wonderful to be of one mind with someone who was also one of her few peers. Her relationships with Philip and Elizabeth were simply too shallow, while others such as Susan and Fran were too far beneath her to be true confidants. Reginald shared her royal blood and had almost become pope. She could be close to him like she could be with no one else.

Mary murmured an absent-minded farewell when Elizabeth left her side to return to her own rooms. She no longer concerned herself much with what Elizabeth did. She endured her presence because Philip had encouraged her to do so for appearances sake. That was all. The girl could not be trusted to be included beyond that. At that moment, Mary decided to give Elizabeth permission to leave court for Hatfield. They would both be happier for it.

Upon entering her own rooms, Mary was pleased to see that Susan had already prepared a space for her meeting with Reginald. A light meal was set out, along with Mary's favorite wine and a few sweetmeats. Sun dappled the room and gave it a warm, cozy atmosphere that was further established by the vases of lavender, rosemary, and carnations that Susan had scattered about the room.

Mary breathed deeply of the sweet, spicy scents that filled the air. Her heart was full and content for the first time since Philip had left her for Brussels. There would be no more tears for him. She had work to do.

Within minutes, she was seated at the small table with Reginald. "I have great confidence that you have the ability to overcome the damage that has been done, that your good preaching shall bring those who have been misled back into the fold," she said.

He bowed his head to her in humble acceptance of the praise, but did not speak until he had taken several sips of his wine and considered his thoughts.

"Your grace is most kind in your assessment of my skills. We must determine the best way to act in the Cranmer case." He saw Mary's features darken and held up a calming hand. "I understand your animosity toward the archbishop. That is why I wish to advise you where he is concerned. You must do what best serves God and your kingdom rather than what satiates any desire for vengeance."

Mary's eyes widened, and she begged, "Cardinal, forgive me for my sin. You have convicted me where I was blind to it."

She moved to kneel, but she stopped her with a light touch.

"Dear Mary," he soothed. "The line between righteous punishment and revenge can be a fine one. You would not be the first to consider crossing it. Cranmer does deserve punishment, and I have every confidence that you will let go of your personal anger in favor of what is best for your subjects."

Mary nodded enthusiastically, once again filled with gratitude for this person who was more than a spiritual leader and advisor. For the first time in many years, she felt that she had a true friend.

Reginald continued, "You have been patient and prudent where Cranmer is concerned. Despite the fact that it was he who gave your father the power to cast out your mother, you have waited until the right time to bring him to trial. That is evidence of your great faith and fitness to rule."

He returned the smile that she beamed at him.

"But now what?" he ended abruptly.

Mary frowned. She had expected him to deliver the answer, and she found herself spinning her feelings for Cranmer through her mind. With her thoughts turned inward to retrieve her memories, she spoke quietly.

"I remember your mother telling me that my father had secured his divorce. I cannot recall if she said then that it was Cranmer who had granted it, but it was not news that could be kept from me." Mary sighed and plucked a sprig of rosemary from the closest vase. As she reviewed her memories, she rolled it between her fingers, releasing its savory fragrance. "It was he who married my father to his concubine, though he also had a part in her downfall. Even if I could set aside his past sins, I cannot excuse his preaching against the mass and eucharist that he has done since I became queen."

"And you should not," Reginald quickly assured her. "His punishment is due. My only concern is that your subjects understand that he suffers for his heresy and is not a victim of personal vengeance. His fate has the power to affect many. We must proceed carefully and be guided by God."

"I agree, but," Mary could not stop the anger from building within her as the mental calculation of Cranmer's sins increased. "Bringing him low is what my subjects need to see. He must be broken."

Her features had grown as hard as her heart was toward this one person for whom she had no mercy. The Cardinal examined Mary's countenance until she softened under his gaze.

"You allowed him to officiate your brother's funeral," he stated. It was not a question, but it was clear that he awaited Mary's explanation.

She looked down at her hands. "I confess that it was not my wish." The silence grew, and she realized that he would wait for her to finish. Reginald was not one made uncomfortable by silences and did not feel the need to fill them. "They had tried to replace me with a heretic queen. God forgive me if my brother suffers in hell because of my decision, but I was advised to allow the funeral to be carried out according to his wishes."

"If your brother is separated from God, it is because of the decisions that he made while he was alive not those that you made after he was dead."

The bluntness of this statement brought Mary up short. Reginald had not taken his habitual time to consider but had blurted out the judgement as if it was something he had long desired to say. Mary tilted her head, studying him from a new angle.

"This is why it is vital that we stamp out every spark of heresy in your kingdom," he asserted. "How many have already been lost for eternity?"

"Cranmer has written that the pope is the antichrist. He denies the body and blood of Christ in the eucharist. What can we do besides send him to the flames?" she asked.

Now it was Reginald's turn to grow stern. "Latimer and Ridley also await their just punishment. Send them first. Let Cranmer watch."

~ ~ ~ ~

The Protestant trinity of Latimer, Ridley, and Cranmer would only be silenced by death. They had preached against the mass and against their queen. Whether heresy or treason was the charge, their punishment was certain. The leaders of Henry VIII's reformed church had never anticipated that they would come under the power of his Catholic daughter.

Being forced to watch his comrades burn had a deep effect upon Cranmer. Mary received letter after letter from him, but had turned the affair over to the capable hands of her cousin. Reginald had, in turn, advised Cranmer to recant the faith he had worked for decades to establish. A public repentance by the man who had formed the Church of England with his own hands would be a priceless arrow in the quiver of the counter-reformation.

Now, Mary could scarcely believe the message written on the paper in her hands. She shook with emotion as she read the words again, as she already had countless times.

Though unworthy either to speak or write unto your
highness, yet having no person that I know to be mediator
for me and knowing your pitiful ears being ready to hear
all pitiful complaints, and seeing so many before to have
felt your abundant clemency in like cause . . . .

It took considerable concentration for Mary to restrain her hands from forming into fists and crumpling the letter within her grasp. Thomas Cranmer, of all people, was begging her for mercy. He who was least deserving of all men. How dare he?

She had summoned Cardinal Pole, and the letter was burning in her hand to be released to him. Mary did not even trust herself to respond to the man in writing. As soon as Reginald entered the room, the paper was thrust into his hands.

"I will endure this man no longer," Mary cried. "Obtain his recantation and see him put to death."

Reginald did not share her hysteria. He took the time to carefully read Cranmer's plea for mercy and insistence that he had taken no part in the attempt to enthrone Lady Jane in Mary's place. No emotion transformed Reginald's countenance when he finished reading, and that helped Mary to calm her own.

"He is a desperate man," Reginald said, handing the missive back to Mary. "His sisters also write him, one to encourage steadfastness and the other to beg his return to God's teaching. Heretics look to him alone now that Latimer and Ridley are dead, and he is not equipped to lead them."

"That is as it should be. I want his signed statement that he rejects the falsehoods that he has plagued this nation with," Mary demanded.

Reginald bowed low. "It shall be yours, your grace."

December 1555

"I have a letter that you will be pleased to see, your grace," Reginald said as he joined her before the fire in Greenwich's great hall.

Mary was not participating in the Christmas festivities, so those that did go on were low-key with a somewhat dreary atmosphere. Unspoken concerns filled the space where joyful music and the sound of laughter should have been. Poor harvests caused by never-ending rain left every household touched by hunger. Even the royal table was not as heavy as it would normally be for the annual celebration of Christ's birth.

Although she looked up at Reginald's announcement, Mary did not appear eager to hear his news. Then she remembered the demand for Cranmer's confession and recantation and her countenance brightened.

"Have you done it?" she asked with the light from the Yule log dancing in her eyes.

Reginald examined her quizzically for a moment before he realized her misunderstanding. He shook his head, though he seemed no less optimistic.

"It is from Rome," he said, holding out the thick paper. "Cranmer is officially stripped of his archbishopric, and the pope gives you leave to punish him as you see fit."

Some of the excitement that had drained from Mary's face upon hearing that the paper was not Cranmer's statement relit with the news that his case could finally be ended. Neither she nor the Cardinal had dared to move forward against the man while he was still Archbishop of Canterbury according to Rome.

"Finally, you will be able to take your rightful place as England's premier archbishop," Mary happily cried.

However, Reginald waved that away. "I would not campaign

to become pope five years ago, and neither will I seek position now. The work God has given me is the same regardless of what title men give me."

"Still, I am gladdened to be able to impart the well deserved honor upon you," Mary insisted, though with somewhat less enthusiasm. She had felt herself rather pious until she began comparing herself to her cousin.

"And honored I am," he replied with a look of gratitude that was a balm to Mary's minor hurt. "First though, let us consider the fate of Thomas Cranmer."

He sounded pleased to say the name with no honorific, and Mary was relieved that even the Cardinal drew some satisfaction from the man's worldly fall.

Mary's attention was suddenly grabbed by the light fare upon her table and the thinness of her servants. This famine, this judgement from God, she finally recognized it for what it was.

"We must see to his punishment immediately, now that it is sanctioned by God's representative. I must also refrain from granting mercy to other heretics that I could not extend to Cranmer," Mary said. She looked to Reginald to gauge his feelings, but, of course, she could not. "This," her hands indicated the entire room, "is because I have not served God faithfully."

"And how have you not done that?" Reginald calmly inquired.

"He has demanded the removal of heresy and I have given pardons. Those who have recanted their beliefs and claimed a return to the true faith have been given a second chance, as I believed I should have given them based upon the teaching of our Lord. However, this plague of hunger currently upon us has opened my eyes to the error of my thinking."

Reginald was intently listening but looking at the fire as it warmed the room. Was he thinking about how curious it was that they needed this fire for warmth but those punished by it begged to be relieved of its heat, Mary wondered.

"You would refuse those who repent?" he asked.

There was no inflection to his voice to guide her in her response, and Mary felt less sure of herself than she had just a few moments earlier. She knew that not all who recanted at the last minute were spared their punishment and had heard that a few sheriffs took far too much joy from their duties. However, she also knew that heretics infamously lied to escape their punishment and then returned to their devil's work.

"If they truly repent, they shall be given strength by God and quickly received by him," she said. "If they lie, the flames may lead to their true repentance that they may avoid the eternal fires of hell."

The Cardinal nodded slowly. "And the people who observe?"

Was he asking her or himself? Mary was not certain, but she answered nonetheless. "They will see that they must examine their faith before they are brought to justice. We will see repentance rather than protest and rebellion."

"Your reasoning is sound," Reginald admitted with a hesitancy in his tone. "I beg your majesty to give me leave to think on this and pray for guidance."

Mary lowered her head to him as he rose. "I would have it no other way, your grace."

She watched him stride purposefully from the hall, and did not realize that her gaze had remained upon the empty doorway long after his passage until Fran tapped lightly upon her shoulder. Mary jumped and laughed nervously at herself.

Fran curtseyed with her eyes downcast for she knew it would

embarrass Mary to have her awkwardness observed.

"You sent for me, your grace."

"Yes," Mary exclaimed, "I have a task that I would have you assist me in."

Fran stood and waited for her instructions without comment. Mary was grasping at a pouch within the folds of her skirts. Retrieving it, she held it out to Fran with a wide grin.

"I would have you see this delivered to Jane Wyatt."

Fran stood still for a moment before reaching out and accepting the purse. "Jane Wyatt?"

Mary nodded, feeling pleased that she had thought of the woman and her need. If she could not show mercy to the repentant heretics, she could demonstrate it in other ways.

"It was not poor Jane's fault that her husband chose rebellion, yet I am certain that she suffers greatly for it," Mary explained. "I would not have the woman and her children starve due to the sins of their father."

"That is rather thoughtful of you, your grace," Fran said with a smile. "I am sure that most are afraid to show her favor, but seeing that she receives assistance from the queen herself will help change that."

Mary frowned slightly and said, "I do not wish to make a show of the gift."

"Of course, not," Fran reassured her, "yet enough people will know to make a difference."

"Yes, Fran," Mary agreed. The gift would be given quietly, but people would still talk. "That would be ideal. Thank you."

Fran curtseyed and was already turning away in a swirl of skirts as she stood, eager to be off to perform her good works.

March 1556

"He has requested additional time to consider his sins and pray," Reginald said with greater disdain than Mary had thought him capable of.

The person of Thomas Cranmer seemed to be getting under his skin in the same way that he had always irritated Mary's. The man had collapsed a few weeks ago, postponing his judgement, but justice would wait no longer. The list of sins that he wished to contemplate was shockingly long, but he had already been granted months to repent of them.

"You will, however, be pleased to see this," Reginald added as he held out a sheet of parchment to her. "I believe this is something that I promised to obtain for you."

Confusion creased Mary's face as she reached for the document, but it was replaced with elation when she spotted the shaky signature at the bottom. Her widened eyes sought the Cardinal's.

"He has recanted?" she asked in a shocked whisper. "Truly?"

Reginald simply nodded to the evidence which required no explanation.

She held it close to her face in order to make out the heretic's scrawl. Mary had never thought to hold such a document in her hand. The man who had ruined her mother's life and enabled her father's adultery had turned his back on the church he had created.

Mary searched her mind and body for the sensations of elation that she had expected to feel should such a feat actually be accomplished, but she felt nothing. Words upon paper could not erase the pains of the past or bring back those who had died damned by Cranmer's unfaithful teaching. She found that she was disappointed and, therefore, unprepared for Reginald's next words.

"He begs you to forgive him in your great mercy."

Confusion returned to Mary's features before the truth dawned on her. "He believes that he might be pardoned?" she cried, her voice dripping with incredulity. "He dares to inquire whether this single sheet of parchment might fully cover his lengthy list of bloody sins?"

Reginald shrugged. "You need not respond. Cranmer knows that the council has ruled against further clemency to convicted heretics. You have no need to be involved any further in his case."

Mary allowed her gaze to wander over her surroundings, as if the contents of Reginald's study could offer her some answer or support. He owned more books than anyone she had ever known and had written a good number of them as well. The Cardinal seemed capable of keeping his emotions in check because he poured them out onto paper. She wondered if he had ever, possibly in his youth, let any strong emotion carry him away.

"Your grace," he said, pulling her back to the present. He looked at her inquiringly, but said no more.

"I wish for him to read this statement aloud before his fire is set," she commanded as her face hardened in determination. In any other situation, Mary would feel compelled toward mercy. Cranmer may have been the sole person in the world toward whom she felt no such compunction.

She was used to enduring Reginald's stare while he considered his words and any hidden meaning there might have been intended by her own. It was no longer as unsettling as it had once been. Instead, she found that she appreciated his thoughtfulness and utter lack of impetuosity. It was one of the many reasons she trusted him wholeheartedly.

"Very well," he decided. "I shall see that all in attendance understand that the good archbishop dies a member of the fold."

The document was restored to his slender fingers, and he set it aside as an issue dealt with and no longer of importance.

"Then we must discuss your installation as archbishop," Mary exclaimed, clapping her hands together like a little girl. "Now that the pope has formally removed Cranmer from the post, I would have you as Archbishop of Canterbury without delay."

Reginald lowered his head slightly to receive the praise with humility. "It shall be difficult to make the time to travel to Canterbury at this time," he pointed out with a gesture toward Cranmer's confession.

"Then we will perform the ceremony here," Mary insisted. "I would not have you go another moment without the honor you deserve."

"It shall be as you wish, your grace."

Within days, it was. Mary beamed as she watched Cardinal Pole ordained as the Archbishop of Canterbury. It was a position that he should have held years ago, so it pleased her to see this correction made on the very day that Cranmer was scheduled to go to his death after reading his confession to the gathered crowd.

Mary was ashamed that her mind wandered. Regardless of how much she had awaited this moment, she could not help but wonder what the heretics thought of their leader denouncing their faith so that he could go to his death as a true believer. How many would turn away from their erroneous ways when they heard his speech?

A rustling was heard toward the back of the hall. Since they could not make the trip to Canterbury Cathedral, the ceremony was taking place at Greenwich, but Mary had not expected to see Paget here. Though he had made a small disturbance, he had the sense to wait for the conclusion of the service before approaching the queen.

His countenance put Mary on her guard immediately. She almost glided past him and refused to allow him to speak. Whatever it was could surely wait until the morrow. Let her have this moment to revel in her cousin's rise and the knowledge that her greatest enemy was no more.

Begrudgingly, she accepted that she could not surround herself with ladies and insulate herself from Paget's words. Mary was a queen and she would face her duties, no matter how bitter a taste they left in her mouth. Indicating to him that he should follow, Mary led Paget to a private room.

As soon as he pulled the door closed, she turned on him. "What is it?" she demanded.

"Cranmer," he said as if that one word would open her mind to the disaster that had occurred.

"He is alive?"

Paget shook his head and pulled at his gloves, irritating Mary with his hesitancy when he had interrupted a solemn mass to attract her attention. Noticing her eyes narrowed at him, he softly spoke, "He began reading the recantation, but did not limit his speech to the words upon the page. Very cleverly done it was, too," Paget admitted with a hint of reluctantly given respect. "I believe it took most a moment to perceive what he was doing."

Mary glared at him, and he recovered himself. Clearing his throat, Paget continued in the deeper tone of a displeased tutor, "He disavowed his confession and blamed his breakdown upon the degradation he had endured. Claimed that the thing had been written contrary to the truth with great fear in his heart."

Paget gave a small shrug as he took in Mary's features which were becoming distorted with rage and continued, "Of course, he was quickly pulled away, ranting about false doctrine all the way to the stake."

He paused, and Mary could see that there were details that he was reluctant to share with her.

"Tell me," she ordered.

Paget seemed surprised at her perceptiveness and raised his eyebrows as if he suddenly realized that he had underestimated her, but tell her he did.

"When the fire was lit, Cranmer held out his hand like he would burn first the part of him that had led him into the sin of his recantation. He begged the Lord to receive his spirit and did not long linger."

Mary sighed and plopped into the closest chair. Had it only been moments ago that she had felt the glory of God surround her as Reginald was ordained?

"How was this allowed to happen?" she asked before realizing that she had voiced the question aloud. "He should have been silenced immediately. His hands should have been bound. Imagine the confusion of the witnesses," she cried. "This was meant to assure them of the steadfastness of the true faith, but what they have seen will leave them more lost than ever."

Paget bowed and humbly promised, "I will look into the matter personally, your grace."

"You may go," Mary replied, waving him away like a pesky insect. The investigation would not matter. The damage had been done. Cranmer had managed to grasp one more victory in his death, but hell was his reward.

April 1556

The fiercely unseasonable cold did not reach the opulent great hall at Greenwich. Mary entered with Reginald at her side and her ladies lined up behind her. He wore his scarlet Cardinal robes while her dress was a vivid purple velvet. She held her arms out slightly to the sides to display her long trailing sleeves with the finest effect. Behind her, each of her ladies wore crisp linen aprons and carried a towel and silver ewer.

Cardinal Pole stood before those gathered and reverently described what Christ had done when he washed the feet of his disciples, making the one who ruled above all a servant to those he loved. This Maundy Thursday, Mary would mirror his actions for the forty-one poor women who had been chosen to be brought before her.

The women, one for each year of the queen's life, were haggard and worn beyond their years by the harshness of their lives. Mary took in their faces, which carried a wide variety of expressions. There was awe at being in the presence of their queen. She also saw fear, love, and sadness etched into the premature lines.

Two rows of benches were provided for the women to sit on with their feet upon simple stools. As Mary knelt before the first of them, she momentarily wondered how God determined which women would spend their lives struggling and hungry and which would be queens. Then her mind was absorbed by her task.

Gently, she took up the woman's right foot in her hand. She felt the tough calluses and saw chapping caused by the frigid weather. Taking the dampened towel from the woman assisting her, Mary washed the stranger's foot with as much care as she would have employed for the bathing of a newborn.

A warm towel was handed to her for drying the woman's

foot. Then, Mary gave the woman a blessing, marking her foot with the sign of a cross. "In the name of the Father, the Son, and the Holy Ghost," she whispered before bending low to kiss it.

Mary solemnly moved on to the next woman and completed the same reverent ceremony for each of the forty-one women. Her lower back was shot through with pain, but as she stood and took in the grateful faces of the women she had served, Mary was thankful that God had used her to demonstrate his love to them. The vision blurred as joyful tears threatened to spill until she was once again distracted by duty.

Reginald held out a large carved wooden plate to her. It was heaped with morsels of bread and salted fish. Just as Christ had shared such meals with his disciples, Mary would disburse food to the chosen women. She could see many of their faces light up at the prospect, despite their efforts to remain properly solemn. They forced themselves to eat slowly when Mary handed them each their portion.

Mary's hand brushed against several of theirs as the food was given, and she wondered at their swollen knuckles and work roughened skin. She may have the cares of a kingdom upon her slender shoulders, but Mary would never endure the physical strain that these women underwent on a daily basis.

"God give them strength," she whispered as she handed back the empty platter and took up sweet wine to give each woman a sip. That accomplished, Mary was pleased to have a more lasting gift to give.

Forty-one lengths of cloth were laid out looking fresh and smooth upon the table. In one hand, Mary took up a leather pouch while Susan spread one length of cloth across her other arm. These gifts were presented first to one woman, then the next, until each had their purse of forty-one pennies and a measure of the finest cloth any of them had ever owned.

Susan grinned widely as she gave Mary each bit of fabric. This was the gift that she was sure the women would appreciate and remember the most, so it thrilled her to be a part of distributing it. Mary's eyes crinkled at the corners, but she felt it irreverent to smile too broadly.

After this rich gift, the women received somewhat more practical items. Mary's ladies pulled off the aprons that they had donned for the feet washing ceremony and picked up the towels that were now dry. Each of them stepped up to a woman and turned their gifts over to them.

Mary watched rough hands lovingly stroke the soft towels in wonder that such fine things would be used within their own home. Of course, some of them would never use them again, instructing their families that such a gift from the queen herself could never be soiled in any way.

At this point, Mary left the hall with Fran and Susan close behind her. She had one more gift to bestow.

Susan and Fran giggled quietly, fighting to remain serious as their joy overflowed at seeing the poor women's happiness. Tugging and manipulating Mary's limbs as if she were a doll, they changed her out of the gorgeous purple velvet and dressed her in a gown of deepest ebony. Draping the purple dress over their arms, they followed Mary back to the hall.

Mary had been uncertain how to fulfill this portion of her duties. As Susan and Fran stood in the middle of the benches, Mary slowly moved among the women and examined their faces. She was to decide which of them was to receive the purple velvet that was undoubtedly worth more money than any of them could ever hope to obtain otherwise.

Should she give it to the woman with watery blue eyes and

stringy blonde hair? Another had grey hair, but it was impossible to tell if she were truly older than the others. So many had bones visibly protruding through their thin clothes, and each looked hungrily at the rich velvet.

Except one.

This woman stood proudly and met Mary's eye instead of trying to peer around her at the offered gift. Her hair might have been reddish blonde once, but it had grown dull and thin. The blend of brown and green in her eyes was bold and unique, such as Mary could only remember seeing once before in her life.

She gestured for the gown to be given to this woman who so reminded Mary of her long departed but still much loved mother.

Back in her private apartment, Mary's ladies were chattering contentedly among themselves, but she chose to pass her afternoon more quietly. Images of the ceremony replayed continuously in her mind, and she was determined to remember the faces of each of the women she had served. These memories were stored up in her heart as precious treasures.

The next morning dawned a chill and bleak Good Friday. Instead of remaining in her oratory throughout mass, Mary descended to prostrate herself before the cross. As she did so, she thought of the journey that God had used to bring her here. In no more than a few seconds, she remembered walking through the gardens at Greenwich with Lady Pole, her mother's breathtaking embraces, being forced to serve her infant sister, her coronation, sharing a bed with her husband. She had endured more than her share of heartbreak, but God had used it all for good.

Mary rose and kissed the wood of the cross adoringly. How could she even consider her own sacrifices when looking upon it?

When she turned from the cross, Cardinal Pole was there

holding out the basket of cramp rings. Together they prayed and recited psalms in blessing over the small, simple bands. A few rings at a time, Mary passed them through her hands, feeling the coolness of the metal in contrast to the warmth of her skin.

Moving to a private enclosure, she knelt and confessed her sins to Cardinal Pole. He knew them already, of course. Her anger toward Philip and selfish desire to have him returned to her. Her envy of her sister's youth, beauty, and ability to manipulate others without them even realizing it. Oh yes, Reginald already knew all too well the darkest secrets in Mary's heart.

"Receive forgiveness," he said as he sealed her absolution with the sign of the cross.

Mary felt the power of God's forgiveness course through her veins. Now that she was made righteous, she could perform the next act of mercy with God's protection. Still on her knees, she retrieved the basket of rings, and the first afflicted woman was brought before her.

It was impossible to discern the age of the sufferer with the open sores distorting her features. The sight of her caused a physical ache in Mary's chest, and she reached out, free of fear, and pressed the tips of her fingers gently to one of the oozing sores. Gently, she made the sign of the cross upon the wound and pressed a blessed ring into the woman's palm.

After also receiving a gold coin on a ribbon around her neck, the first woman thanked the queen and moved to make room for the next obviously afflicted woman. In turn, four received the queen's blessing, a ring, and gold coin to aide them in being cured of their disease. No cure was known but the royal touch.

Mary washed her hands because it was part of the sacred ritual rather than due to any fear of contagion. Her certainty was not only that she would not be struck by the sores, but that the women she had blessed would be healed by the power of God.

Returning to her seat in the oratory, she listened in rapt attention as Cardinal Pole carried out the remainder of the Good Friday mass. As she observed the faithful gathered to remember the sacrifice of their savior, Mary was struck by the realization that this was a defining moment in her life. This was why God had made her queen. Her eyes locked with Reginald's, and she knew by the barely perceptible smile on his serious face that he was thinking the same thing.

July 1556

The darkness surrounding her seemed to penetrate deep into Mary's thoughts. She widened her eyes to test whether she could force them to make out vague shapes in the room, but all remained as black as pitch. Her efforts made no difference.

The soft bedding should have felt luxurious, and she knew that it was a lack of gratitude that left her filled with bleak thoughts instead of being comforted by the blessings she had received. Sleep would not come. She did not even beckon it, for she took a perverse pleasure in the company of her demons.

Philip would not return. He had left her with empty promises, but he had slowly called his household to him while sending her excuses of responsibilities and illnesses. Anything, to stay away.

Mary's hand slid to cover her empty womb, and she wondered what God meant by this. How was she to bear an heir if her husband would not come home? Time after time, he had made promises, and each time he had broken them. She did not believe him anymore.

It was not just the state of her marriage that distressed her. The faithlessness of her subjects broke her heart. Not only were there those who continued to denounce the true faith, but another conspiracy against the crown had been uncovered. Would no one return the love that she was so eager to give?

During her inner battle, the sun had begun to rise, and Mary noticed grey forms taking shape before her eyes. She rose, making a feeble attempt to pretend that she was just waking, and shuffled to her prie-dieu. Yet when she knelt there, her mind was empty of prayers. She had said so many that had gone unanswered.

"What do you desire from me, Lord?" she finally whispered.

Mechanically running her rosary beads through her fingers,

Mary thought of Reginald. He had finally been able to go to Canterbury. Instead of the words she had been taught to pray as her fingers moved over the beads, Mary pictured Reginald's understanding eyes and heard his soothing voice. By the time she stood, she had decided that it was time for her to undertake a pilgrimage.

As soon as lauds had been heard, Mary ordered Fran to see to packing. "I would like as small a party as possible to accompany me to Canterbury," she ordered, knowing that Susan would be the one to speak to Rochester, who would have to negotiate with the council to ensure that her small party was not converted into a royal progress. For once, she left them to their duties, unconcerned that she had added to their burden.

Now that she had determined to go, Mary was aching to be at her destination and each delay sent her into an irrational rage. Fran endured the undeserved wrath with patience, but many of Mary's other attendants flashed her ornery glares when they thought she could not see them.

"I have brought you a plate, your grace," Susan said cheerily. She was blessed by being little affected by the moods of others. "I do not believe you have broken your fast," she observed.

Mary would have sworn that she could feel the physical sensation of Susan's eyes taking in her haggard skin, deep blue crescents below her eyes, and increasingly thin form. Not wishing to admit to her poor health, Mary had not ordered any dresses taken in, so they hung loosely and gave her the appearance of a pauper in a queen's stolen gown.

"I am not hungry," she snapped. "The thought of food nauseates me."

Unperturbed, Susan gestured to where the food waited. "Maybe a bit later then? I shall leave it here for you, your majesty."

Without waiting for a reply, Susan gracefully glided away and inserted herself into the intricate system of workers preparing Mary's household for travel.

It appeared to be chaos to Mary, but she knew that each person knew their place and understood their duties. When they arrived in Canterbury, she need not worry that any minor item she needed would not have been accounted for. Therefore, she left them to their work and returned to the chapel for terce.

After one more sleepless night, Mary's retinue was leaving the London stench behind for the fresh air of the countryside. Although she had made the decision to travel with only Reginald in mind, Mary was pleasantly surprised by how refreshing it was to be away from crowds and the city.

She closed her eyes to soak up the warmth of the sun and the scent of summer roses. Upon opening them, Mary smiled at the idyllic rolling hills and quaint cottages that they passed along the way. For a few hours, the bright sunshine forced her demons to hide in darker corners and Mary was freed of the weight of them. She breathed deeply, her spine straightening from its hunched posture as she did so. Yes, this was just what she needed.

As they topped a rise in the road, Mary's heart leapt in her chest. It was not the worrisome palpitations that often plagued her, but a joyous dance in response to the spires of Canterbury Cathedral piercing the sky in the distance. This breathtaking structure had been welcoming pilgrims for centuries, and it seemed to be inviting her in. Mary somehow knew that she would be able to feel the cloud of witnesses surround her when she knelt before Canterbury's altar.

The entire party's energy revived at their first glance of their destination. Even the horses seemed to sense that their rest was close at hand. At their quickened pace, they would arrive within the hour.

Mary felt butterflies in her stomach that were completely unrelated to the nausea that washed over her whenever Susan or Fran suggested she partake in a meal. The sensation had only ever been felt in the presence of her husband, but now she realized that it was caused by the anticipation of seeing Reginald. Heat rushed to her face and she was thankful for the sun which would be blamed for the flush of color across her pale features.

Surely, she was being ridiculous. It was natural that she was pleased to visit the one person with whom she could share more than with any other. Reginald was a connection to family, the past, and her God. For good reason her mother had wished for Mary to be wed to him. It would have been an ideal match.

This time she had to shake her head free of the path her mind was taking. God had chosen Philip for her husband. Reginald was the Archbishop of Canterbury before he was anything else. That was why she was here. Of course, it was.

Mary examined the faces of those around her, looking for any evidence that they had read her thoughts. No, her guilt was her own, she decided, seeing that their eyes were all turned toward the cathedral rather than their queen. It was good that they were here, for Mary was desperately in need of spiritual guidance.

Soon, all would be set aright.

It was difficult to think of anything else with the cathedral looming ever larger before their eyes. Even Mary, who had always lived in palatial estates, was awed by the soaring towers and fine craftsmanship that was evident in each perfectly carved stone. How many weary pilgrims had taken in this sight and felt God's presence? She added herself to their number.

Mary left her caravan to stop at the cathedral with Susan and Fran. The hour for mass was fast approaching and Mary would experience it within this beautiful, ancient setting performed by her dearest cousin.

The ceiling within the cathedral appeared impossibly high. Graceful lines met at peaks that were far enough away for Mary to be forced to squint at the blur where they came together. The air was cooler inside the cavernous stone structure, providing a welcome relief from the sun they had endured throughout the day.

Susan and Fran were murmuring to each other, but Mary did not speak until echoing footsteps alerted her to the presence of the Archbishop.

"Cardinal Pole!" she cried in greeting. She wished that she could run and embrace him, but he continued to approach at his dignified pace.

"Your grace," he replied with a low bow once he had reached her. "It gives me great pleasure to welcome you to Canterbury."

Words tumbled around in Mary's head in such confusion that she stood speechless. There had been so much she wanted to say, but none of it came to her now that she was here. She could not meet his eye, and for once he misinterpreted her signals.

Spreading his arms as if to embrace the church, he said, "Many are struck dumb by the awe-inspiring cathedral."

He continued to examine her countenance and she was afraid of what he might find, so she blurted the first sentence to properly form in her mind. "I have greatly missed you."

If he was shocked by the confession, Reginald did not allow it to show. A pleasant smile and assurance that he was happy to be in service to her grace was his only response.

Mary found herself irrationally angry that he did not seem more affected. Had he missed her? She realized that he was dismissing himself to prepare for mass and mumbled an appropriate response.

Throughout the service, she prayed for God to clear her mind and give her his will. Mixed emotions and uncertainties confounded her when she needed to prove herself capable of ruling a united England. Mary was the head of the kingdom and of the church. She simply could not afford to lose herself in personal concerns.

Feeling somewhat restored and strengthened by the mass, she went to her lodgings after leaving a messenger to inform Reginald that she would meet with him on the following day. In the meantime, she would dispatch another letter to Philip. If only he would answer one of them.

She dreamed of Philip that night more vividly than she had since his departure. How she missed his touch, even if it had not meant to him what it meant to her. Though she had written him the evening before, Mary set to write again so full were her thoughts of him. She begged him to return, promised to do all that she could to see his desires met if he did so.

Philip had made no secret of the fact that he wished to be crowned as England's king in an official coronation ceremony. While this had been traditionally done for queen consorts, Mary's council worried that doing the same for Philip would stir up discontent for no purpose. She had agreed, but Philip's letters often dropped less than subtle hints that this is something he could be tempted to return for.

So, tempt him she did. If a crown was what he wanted, Mary would do her best to obtain it for him. The letter was folded and sealed without reading over what she had written. She knew that her words were despairing, pathetic even, but she no longer cared. She was desperate for his return.

That afternoon, she met with Reginald as planned, but with

Rochester attending her as well. Some of the thoughts that had brought her to Canterbury left her frightened and uncertain of herself. However, when she had spoken the words, "lead me not into temptation," during the Lord's prayer, she had realized that he was not. She was heading toward it all on her own.

If she had been anything but queen, all would have wondered why she would pack up and leave so quickly after arriving in Canterbury. But Mary was queen, so her orders were followed without question, and she headed back to London without delay.

December 1556

Mary had been forced to reevaluate herself and her objectives upon her return from Canterbury. With the winter chill making all memories of summer sun seem like a distant dream, she was able to push away her confusion over Reginald and desperation for Philip.

Back at Westminster, she had ordered Philip's portrait removed from the council chamber. She cringed when she remembered her pleas and promises. In return, he had sent a few members of his household back to England, but now she recognized his game. She would believe he was returning when she laid her own eyes upon him.

Her duty was to her subjects, and in that regard she redoubled her efforts. Poor harvest once again left too many hungry before the hardship of winter even got underway. Unable to bring herself to eat more than the population she was responsible for, Mary grew increasingly thin as she ordered her council to do more to feed the hungry.

She had also determined to give her sister another chance. Mary was forced to face the fact that if Philip would not come to her, Elizabeth was her heir. For the sake of the kingdom, she invited her sister to attend her at court.

No one had been able to prove whether or not Elizabeth had known about or taken part in any of the minor rebellions that had taken place since Mary took the throne. At this point, she therefore felt that she had little alternative but to give Elizabeth the benefit of the doubt. Since Edward Courtenay had died in Padua two months previously, Mary felt that it was safer to extend an olive branch to her sister now.

Illness had prevented Mary from attending the Feast of the Reconciliation with Cardinal Pole, so she almost looked forward to the company of her sister. The past and any plotting that Elizabeth may or may not have participated in could be forgiven now that Courtenay was dead. Mary also had plans to further neutralize the threat her sister posed. After a few moments of excruciating small talk, Mary set forth her proposal.

"I know that you expressed displeasure at the idea of marrying the duke of Savoy in the past, but I feel that his proposal is one worth reconsidering," Mary said. She had tried to keep her tone casual and make the statement almost as an aside as she took up her glass of wine, but she saw Elizabeth stiffen at the suggestion.

"It is my greatest wish to please my queen," Elizabeth said with a wide-eyed look of false innocence, "but I would rather die than marry that man."

Mary almost rolled her eyes. "That is a bit dramatic."

"The circumstances of my life have eliminated any desire I may have had for a husband," Elizabeth continued with no less melodrama. "I have considered my options and believe it would be best if I remained single."

"A convent then?" Mary suggested, primarily to see how well her sister could control her features when presented with the idea. She knew that Elizabeth was power hungry and mainly pretended at being a good Catholic the way Philip played the role of a loving husband. A nunnery was the last place Elizabeth wished to be.

Yet, her face would have one believe that she was seriously considering this path. "I will have to pray on this that I may better discern what God's desire is for my life," she stated, knowing that this was a decision that Mary could scarcely argue with.

"I shall pray for you as well, my sister," Mary assured her. She did not need to say that Elizabeth's future would be settled, and soon, one way or another. "I do believe that the duke of Savoy would be a great help to you in steering clear of the plots and schemes that have landed you in the Tower. I would hate for you to find yourself there once again."

A red-gold eyebrow lifted, and Elizabeth considered her older sister with a newfound respect. "You have been most generous in seeing to my recent freedoms," she said.

"I will be discussing your situation with my council when next we meet," Mary informed her as she stood to indicate that the discussion was at its end.

Again, Elizabeth seemed slightly taken aback at her sister's increased political acumen, but she would not allow herself to be physically shaken, even if she was aware that at least some of the queen's councilors continued to encourage Mary to put her sister to death, and others merely pressed for her to be disinherited.

Elizabeth performed the perfect curtsey before leaving her sister's presence, but Mary stood staring at the space she had been occupying long after she was gone.

February 1557

Rochester stood and spoke for Mary before the council. It had never occurred to her to consider his age, but as she watched him grow short of breath and grip the edge of the table for support she realized that she should allow him to retire. Few had served her as long or as loyally as Robert Rochester, and she had failed to notice that it was growing difficult for him.

She made up her mind to rectify that mistake as soon as possible just as he finished speaking, so she turned her attention to the councilors' responses.

"Our finances simply make it impossible to consider sending English troops to his majesty."

Paget, of course, was the first to speak against Mary's wishes.

"Several years of poor harvest have left the royal coffers in need of replenishment while the common man struggles to feed his children," he continued while less bold men muttered their agreement.

Rochester opened his mouth to counter them, but Mary stood upon her dais to indicate that she would speak. "This famine is God's judgement for the continued heresy that is allowed to spread within our kingdom. With false teaching stamped out, we will find ourselves free of rebellion and discontent, but, more importantly, we will be welcomed back into the blessings of our Heavenly Father."

"The punishments are not working," a voice said, but Mary could not identify it, and the men all became preoccupied by their hands, documents, or goblets. None would meet her eye.

"It breaks my heart to say this," Mary admitted, "but if the heretics have hardened their hearts, we must strengthen our efforts. More of those practicing the false doctrine must be brought to trial that the rest may be saved."

None dared speak against her, but no one rallied to support her either. She sat down, trying not to appear dejected, and nodded to Rochester to continue.

They argued over what support was owed Philip in his foreign wars, what to do about the ever obstinate Elizabeth who might one day be their queen, and how to restore those who were suffering due to famine. The conversation seemed to be the same one each time, and Mary eventually excused herself because of the unendurable pain piercing her head.

Once in her chamber, she called Fran to help her to bed and sent Susan to fetch the physician. "I do believe that I will feel better once they have relieved me of the bad humors and given me a tonic," she said wearily as the women set about their tasks.

Mary felt her heart beating erratically by the time Fran was tucking her into bed as if she were the queen's mother. When was the last time her mother had done so, Mary wondered. Had she ever?

Mary did remember her governess, Margaret Pole, sitting at her bedside and sharing rare intimate moments with her. As Mary dozed off to sleep, she could almost feel Margaret's hands smoothing her hair and hear her voice whisper a prayer. It was Margaret's green eyes that she saw with striking clarity behind her closed lids. As she drifted into sleep, they slowly transformed into the softer, calmer eyes of her son.

March 1557

Mary had not allowed herself to put too much hope in his promise. Not until she heard the guns firing in salute over Greenwich Palace did she dare permit her heart to fill with joy and her soul to soar with happiness. His ship had arrived, and he would soon be in her arms.

The thought of embracing Philip once more sent shivers through Mary's body. She ached for his touch and was increasingly aware of her need to bear a child. If she did not, Elizabeth would surely wear her crown, and she could not allow that to happen. She was not even certain that Elizabeth was really her sister.

This doubt had occurred to Mary the last time she met with the frustrating young woman. Mary had peered closely at the daughter of the concubine. They had both caused her so much heartache. Suddenly, the features that Mary had always believed they shared seemed twisted and unfamiliar. Maybe Elizabeth truly was the daughter of Mark Smeaton. It was a concern she planned to bring before the council, and to Philip, who was on his way to her now.

Concerns for Elizabeth were shoved aside. This moment would not be shared with her. Mary waited in the great hall to greet Philip formally, but her mind was already on their private moments. Once the festivities and feasts had taken their share of the king's time, he would be hers. Those moments were a treasure, and she would not lose a second of them in favor of continuing her protest over his lengthy absence.

She could not afford to. Mary needed his child.

When he stepped into the hall, she realized that there would be no need to look beyond her anger. It evaporated like morning dew as soon as their eyes met. Mary felt only love and desire as her husband approached her, and she struggled to control her emotions for the sake of their public greeting. Later, she could reveal her heart to him and pray that he would treat it kindly.

Philip had crossed the floor and now took up her hand. She closed her eyes to center her attention only upon his touch. When his lips pressed gently to her skin, she felt that she would faint. Before she could become dizzy, she looked at him and hoped that she saw her own love mirrored in his face.

"I have missed you fiercely, my beloved," she said in a low voice that she hoped was seductive. "Praise God for your safe return to me."

He stood closely, and she could smell the cloves on his breath. His hands were rougher than she remembered, but she did not mind. She began to imagine what they would feel like on her body. Later, he would be free to do more than hold her hands, but she had to stop her imagination for she was certain that those gathered about them could see the visions in her mind.

As people moved forward to greet the king or members of his household, Mary felt her first twinge of doubt. Philip had a surprisingly small number of gentlemen with him. Not wanting to know his answer, she had never asked how long he intended to stay, but this was a telling sign that his plans were not in line with her desires.

It did not matter, she reminded herself as she tightened her grip on his hand. She would just have to change his mind.

~ ~ ~ ~

A few days later, another entourage arrived to join Philip's retinue, much to Mary's dismay.

Margaret, duchess of Parma, was Philip's half-sister. She had brought along with her a cousin, Christina of Denmark. They had come to assist Philip with convincing Elizabeth to accept the suit of the duke of Savoy. Seeing their youth and beauty, Mary was convinced that was not the only reason Philip had extended the invitation.

Rumors had reached her during Philip's long absence that he had begun an affair with the sharp-witted Christina. It was much easier to ignore these tales when Mary was not a witness to the covert glances and private jokes that the two shared. They both knew their place too well to do anything that would prove their infidelity or publicly shame the queen, but their affection for each other was clear nonetheless.

Philip visited Mary each night, but she could not help but wonder if he left her to tip-toe his way down to the ground floor apartments she had assigned to the duchess. As long as Mary became pregnant, it did not matter. At least that is what she tried to convince herself.

Yet, she did not gain as much joy from their coupling as she had believed she would. The physical sensation was the same, but Mary felt that she was becoming as emotionally neutral to it as Philip was. One could only love someone for so long when that love was not returned.

April 1557

Philip had an accidental ally in bringing about England's declaration of war on the French. In the end, it was not his lobbying but the actions of the French themselves that convinced Mary and her council. Were it not for their consistent support of English traitors, it might have been avoided.

It was Reginald who brought Mary the news that was as much a blow to himself as he knew it would be to his queen. Afterward, Mary had the hindsight to be thankful that it had been him, for she could have born the news from none other.

Mary was aware of Reginald's discomfort for the first time, gone was his habitual calmness and ability to remove his personal emotions and preferences from the situation. As he held out the report to her, she thought she perceived a quake in his hand.

"It is a revolt," he bluntly stated, but she could see that it was more than that.

Surely, they had dealt with worse and he had not seemed affected. Mary chose not to spare a glance to the paper.

"Tell me," she quietly demanded.

Reginald sighed and stroked his beard before speaking. "It is led by Thomas Stafford."

Mary's jaw dropped as understanding dawned. Thomas was the son of Henry Stafford, whom Mary had made chamberlain of the exchequer upon her accession. She had been moved to do so because Henry was the husband of Ursula Pole, Reginald's sister.

"Reginald," she could only whisper his name for a moment before continuing. "I am so sorry."

He raised a hand to stop her, as if the connection was of no account, yet she had seen how shaken he was.

"My concerns are only for you, your grace," he insisted. He seemed to regain control of himself as he related the facts.

"Outfitted with a French warship, my nephew has landed in the north and managed to take Scarborough Castle."

"But why?" Mary asked, realizing that she sounded like a bewildered young child. "His parents have avoided politics since the execution of his father and her mother. Your mother," she amended.

He nodded sadly in agreement before continuing, "He is petitioning for your removal, claiming that you are more Spanish than English and do not have our country's interests at heart."

"How dare he?" Mary exclaimed, twirling away from him in an effort to hide her dismay. Her nervous energy and anger now drove her to pacing. "I have cared for your family, his family, like none other."

"You have been most generous, your grace," Reginald soothed. "I am certain that my sister must be humiliated by his actions."

"Do you not see, Reginald," Mary cried, as she turned to face him. "It is treason! I shall be forced to execute a member of your family, just as my father, grandfather, and great-grandfather did."

Her heart fluttered as her mind raced for a solution. She ran into all the same barriers as when she sought to save Jane, except that Thomas held one of her castles. There could be no argument.

"Yes," Reginald finally agreed. His face sagged, but not a tear shone in his eyes. "You must."

Mary did not know Thomas Stafford, could not remember if she had lain eyes upon him since he was a small child. Henry and Ursula carefully kept from court and found comfort in their little family. How would they bear it? How could she?

Falling into a seat as her energy deflated, Mary sobbed,

"No, I cannot! I am not my father."

"That is well-known by all," Reginald comforted with a light touch to her arm. "My mother did not deserve her death, but my nephew does."

She looked at him in wonder. How could he so precisely divide his professional duty and personal sorrow?

"The siege at Scarborough will not last long," Reginald stated with certainty, "and then Thomas must die for his treason."

Mary sniffled, taking strength from Reginald's resolve. However, she could not stop herself from asking one last question.

"How will Ursula ever forgive me?"

July 1557

Mary did not break down as she once had at the prospect of Philip leaving. He had informed her that he was needed in the war against France, and she was not surprised or even incredibly disappointed. He had done his duty, and he could leave.

Their last night together had been spent in an argument, their first. Free of the unconditional adoration that had blinded her to his shortcomings, Mary had raged at him for his plundering of England's resources for Spain's wars, his obvious adultery, and his ongoing support of her alleged sister.

"Can you not see that she resembles the lute player?" she had cried.

Philip had only shook his head at her with a doubtful expression that he made no attempt to disguise.

"She is not my sister," Mary insisted. "We share no features whatsoever, and she looks nothing like my beloved father."

Philip's doubt deepened until he appeared to be concerned for her sanity. Mary did not care. She could not take the chance that Philip would support Elizabeth as her heir were she to die in childbirth.

For that was Mary's happy news that kept her from falling apart as her husband departed once more. She was with child.

There would be no repeat of her tearful, embarrassing display that had occurred the first time he left her. She had accepted it and understood that this was likely her last chance to bear a son, though she had shared her news with no one. After her last experience, she was waiting until she was absolutely certain as she prayed fervently that God would guard over the tiny babe.

August 1557

Robert Rochester had stood by Mary's side through the fiercest battles and greatest victories of her life. The only time he had disagreed with her was over her choice of marriage, and, looking back, Mary wondered if she would not be better off had she heeded his advice.

She could not imagine a world without him in it. Yet, as she had been forced to do so many times in her life, Mary was now forced to carry on without someone she loved.

While he was alive, she never would have applied the word 'love' to her controller. Certainly, she had depended upon him like no other, but it was only after he was gone that she realized that she had looked to him almost as a father, one more loving than the one she had been born to.

Mary smiled through her tears at the words of Rochester's will. Besides the Carthusian order of which his brother had been a martyred member, he had left a single gift. To her. Loyal to the end, Rochester had left her what was a generous gift for one of his station: £100.

How many times over she would have paid it back in return for having the dear man at her side once again.

January 1558

Mary had given Philip the troops he had asked for, much to her council's chagrin. Few were happy to see English soldiers under the command of a Spaniard. The boldest of them angrily pointed out that this was exactly why they had warned her against marrying a Spaniard. Yet, she had sent them because it was what Philip wanted. This was her reward.

People no longer bothered to whisper that a woman was not capable of ruling. They did not hesitate to connect Mary's marital failures with their perceived pitfalls of the Catholic Church. None bothered to hide from her that they did not believe that she was pregnant.

The English empire had once spread from the most northern point in Britain to the south of France. Mary's fierce ancestor Henry II had held this vast Angevin territory against all odds, but his son, John, had lost most of it piece by piece.

Mary was responsible for the loss of the final English domain in France. When she had declared war on France at Philip's behest, she had trusted him to succeed, and succeed he had throughout the previous autumn. However, he had underestimated the French reprisals.

Calais had fallen.

Many had fought valiantly. She could not reproach them on that account, but they had not been able to hold out. Philip had not sent the help they required, and the last remnant of the Angevin empire was gone. It was only fitting that Mary was plagued by guilt and shame at the reminders of what her Plantagenet forefathers had accomplished where she had failed, because the man whom many considered the last of their princes had just joined her.

Reginald did not speak for several moments. She could see

that he was reading her thoughts more adroitly than many could even if they listened to the words she spoke. He could tell by her hand on her swollen belly, the lines around her eyes, and tearstains on her cheeks. Her misery was plain to see for any who cared to look. He was simply the only one who did.

Mary did not bother attempting to hide any of it. She deserved to be completely honest around this one person who would love her regardless of her failings. He understood that she had given the best of herself to her kingdom, but it had not been enough.

"You would take the entire world upon your shoulders," he said.

She was uncertain if this was an accusation or a question. "I am the queen," she said. "Where else would I lay it?"

Reginald then did something that he had never done before. He reached out and laid his slim fingers on top of hers. Mary looked down and examined the neatly trimmed nails and smooth cuticles. They were a scholar's hands with none of the tough callouses that most men earned wielding the tools of war. Only one finger bulged slightly at the smallest knuckle and was slightly stained with ink from Reginald's weapon of choice.

He slid his hand away, and she followed the movement until their eyes met. "Why has God abandoned me?" she whispered.

Sympathy shone in his eyes, but it was not the condescending pity that she noted in her ladies' eyes when she referred to her unborn child. It was something purer, and Mary knew in that moment that if Reginald could have shifted the world for her he would have.

"Our Father in Heaven would never abandon you," he said with uncharacteristic passion. "He may see the larger tapestry where we see only a few knots, but he works out everything for the good of those who love him, and I have known few others in my life who are as dedicated to him as you have been, your grace."

"I am afraid," she admitted. Mary did not need to expand upon her fears. He knew that she was afraid that she would not bear a living child, as her mother had failed to do so many times. She was afraid that she would die in the process of trying. She was terrified that her faithless sister would take her crown. And, more than anything else, she feared that she had failed, leaving thousands of her subjects doomed for all eternity.

Reginald relaxed back in his cushioned chair before responding to all the worries that he knew were behind Mary's simple statement. "Do you know what command we find in scripture more than any other?" he asked.

Mary frowned in confusion and slightly shook her head.

"Do not be afraid."

As he said the words, Mary was sure she could hear the voice of God echoing them, and a calming peace came over her.

"God says it," Reginald expounded. "Angels said it. The assurance is given in Jesus' final words. I do believe it is a hope you may put your trust in."

Mary could not speak as she struggled to control the floodgate of tears that threatened to spill as they had all too often in recent months. She bit her lips and turned her face away.

"Let me pray for you," he said.

Without waiting for a response, he stood and went to her small prie-dieu and knelt. Mary could not take her eyes from his strong back bent in supplication for her needs, could not believe that she was looking at a cardinal and archbishop, a man who had almost become pope, pleading with God on her behalf.

The floodgates were released.

Reginald almost certainly heard her sobs and sniffles, but he remained on his knees, feeling that the best way to comfort her was to beg God to do so. Mary could not have said how long they remained that way, she in tears and he at prayer, but finally he stood. Her tears stopped as if it had been an agreed upon signal. She was surprised to realize that she did feel somewhat better. Nothing in her world had changed, except that she had shared it with a person who cared. It was enough.

When he resumed his seat next to her, a new peace settled over them. Mary was content to silently enjoy this newfound calm and was surprised when Reginald broached a new subject.

"I have written Philip to inform him that you are with child."

Taken aback, Mary was uncertain how to respond. "Why?" was all she managed.

His emerald eyes pierced her. "He is your husband, Mary. He has the right to know."

She hung her head, knowing that he was right. Even before Philip's departure, Mary had suspected that she was pregnant, but she had not been able to bring herself to tell him, or anyone, for a long while. Not after her humiliation the first time she believed England would have its prince.

"I do not wish to convict you of anything, but thought that I should confess that I had taken the responsibility to inform our king of your condition," Reginald continued diplomatically.

"Of course, you are right," Mary whispered. She hoped that he was. If she had it her way, her pregnancy would be kept secret until the moment she held the babe in her arms.

March 1558

Winter chill clung to the air, refusing to release its grip that spring could arrive, but Mary chose to walk in the gardens anyway. She wrapped a thick cloak around her with ermine fur that irritated her neck but added its warmth. Despite the cold and barren atmosphere of the paths, she felt the need to be there.

Fran had been sent to ask Reginald if he would join her. She was the only one Mary felt would not question her actions and motives. Fran had stood by her steadfastly. For how much longer, Mary wondered as she heard footsteps approaching.

She turned toward the sound with her hand automatically going to her stomach. It was not swelled as it should have been but also not as flat as in her youth. This time, she recognized what was happening. Her courses had not returned, but she also would not be going into confinement. Something grew in her womb, but it was not a child.

Reginald greeted Mary with a smile as he fell in step with her without speaking. His presence brought her the comfort and peace that she had longed for much of her life. It would feel so natural to intertwine her fingers with his, but, of course, she could not.

"I wish to speak with you about the writing of my will," she said. Mary did not look at Reginald when he did not respond right away. She was used to his slow, thoughtful responses. They continued strolling, side-by-side, through the desolate garden.

"That is an advisable step for a queen preparing for the childbed," he observed neutrally.

She smiled at his falsehood and realized that she had never heard him lie before.

"I cannot name Elizabeth as my heir. She will ruin all that we have worked so hard to accomplish."

"Your sister is not as powerful as you give her credit for being," he replied. "God has had more impressive foes than Elizabeth Tudor, and he always has his way in the end."

Mary considered this. Reginald was not implying that Elizabeth would carry on the restoration of the church. They both knew that was not true, but God could raise up another faithful monarch, one who would succeed where Mary had failed. She had to be content with that.

"I have striven to do all that he asked of me," she said, her voice thick with sorrow.

Reginald stopped walking and turned toward her. "I know that you have."

Mary looked into his eyes and saw tears that had not been present through any of their trials and defeats. She had to swallow hard as her throat tightened.

"I feel as though I have searched for love all my life," Mary confessed as a bitter breeze scattered remnants of last autumn's dead leaves. "First, I hungered for the approval and affection of my father, only to have it given when it served his purposes. Then, my longing for a husband and children replaced that appetite which had never been sated."

She squeezed her rosary beads beneath her cloak so tightly that she imagined she might crush them. Her gaze did not leave Reginald's eyes. They were so much like his mother's that Mary found the strength to continue. If she did not bare all now, she knew that her feelings would forever go unspoken.

"My heart and soul were given to Philip with abandon," she said, averting her eyes as tears began their burn, "but he did not desire either one."

Unable to stop herself, she let her rosary fall to her side and her hands grasped Reginald's. She would forego prayer at this moment for the touch of one who loved her, and he did. Didn't he?

"No one in my life has ever loved me fully, with passion," she cried, caressing his hands and allowing her fingers to slide to the soft skin on the inside of his wrist. "I want someone to hunger for me."

Mary dared to lock eyes with him and search for the reciprocation of her deep yearning and affection. Her desire for his love was written so plainly upon her face that he almost gave into it. She was sure she could see it in his eyes, that he wanted to. But he would not, for he placed his love of God above his love of her.

For a moment she allowed herself to imagine that he, unlike everyone else in her life, had chosen to place her above all else. She tilted her head back with her lips soft and slightly parted. Closing her eyes, she pretended that she felt his lips meet hers. Her fingers would slide from his hands up to weave into his hair and hold him there as long as she was able. She would feel his beard, rough against her delicate skin.

Instead, Reginald freed one of his hands from hers and she felt it touch her forehead, starting at her hairline and tracing down to the bridge of her nose.

"Receive forgiveness in the name of the Father, and of the Son" he recited, and Mary could hear the emotion in his voice that he would not allow himself to act upon. His finger moved to complete her absolution. "And of the Holy Spirit," he finished, and Mary wondered if she imagined that his hand lingered there for just a moment longer than it should have.

She opened her eyes and pressed her lips tightly together. Reginald bowed low before her and slowly walked away. She knew that she should be thankful that he had been strong enough to keep them both from sin, but instead she found that familiar feeling of bitter disappointment filling her as it never had before.

October 1558

As Mary slowly flipped the pages of the book of sermons that Reginald had presented her with, she was taken back to the day she had done the same with Kateryn's book of prayers. How much had happened through the intervening years! Now, Kateryn was gone but Mary was certain that she would soon be reunited with her.

Rumors of Mary's pregnancy had simply faded away this time, as if no one had really believed it in the first place. Still, she could not stop her subconscious habit of resting her hand on her distended abdomen, though it was swollen not with a babe but a sinister growth.

She would not think of that now. Mary allowed her fingers to lightly brush Reginald's perfect script. How she loved him, not with the passion that had made her cling to Philip but with something much stronger. They were partners in faith.

The sermons had been painstakingly written out to guide priests throughout the kingdom in restoring the faith. Mary hoped that they would find an audience once she was no longer there to see it done. She should be reading the words and drawing Reginald's attention to particular sections that impressed her, yet she could not stop simply admiring his fine letters and thinking about the hands that had made them.

"It is beautiful," she whispered.

"It was not created to be beautiful but instructional," Reginald reminded her.

This brought a faint smile to her face. He was so much better at separating emotions from a task, and good that he was, she thought, remembering that cold day in the garden. Neither of them had spoken of it again, but strangely their bond seemed strengthened by it rather than weakened or made awkward.

"And are you pleased with your efforts?" she asked, knowing that his own satisfaction with the work meant more to him than her praise.

He nodded thoughtfully, "Yes, I believe I am."

"With God's help, your words will reach every man in England."

"And woman," he added.

Her smile grew. "Of course." After turning a few more pages, she said, "I shall have to name her my heir." There was no need to specify who she meant.

"Yes, I believe you must," he agreed. "Especially now that Mary of Scots has wed the prince of France."

Sighing, Mary closed the book. "I shall have to read later, when my mind is not distracted."

He tilted his head to her, acceding to her wishes. "You need not fear," he said.

"So you have told me," she groaned, "yet, I do. I fear that the people will never hear these sermons, that my sister will lead the people into even greater heresy than my brother did."

"God has a plan," he reassured her, "even if it will no longer include us."

Neither spoke for a moment. They did not often dwell on their mutually failing health, for what good would it do? Mary prayed that Reginald would long outlive her and carry on their good work. After all, he would be Archbishop of Canterbury whether she was queen or not. The sickness tearing through England left all men's future in doubt, so she gave it up to God.

"Did you receive the news?" she asked.

Reginald's lips pressed together. It was the only emotion he would show. "Charles?"

"Yes," she quietly whispered. Charles V, Philip's father had died the previous month. Throughout Mary's life, he had been one she had always felt she could depend upon. She looked forward to seeing him soon.

Philip now ruled vast territories on the continent, and Mary doubted that he would have any time for England. She was ashamed to remember the letters she had sent him, pouring her heart out and begging him to return. That hope had been relinquished like so many others in her life. She knew she would never see him again.

November 1558

A cocoon of soft warmth surrounded Mary, and the orange of a bright fire was visible through her closed lids. Still between sleep and waking, her lips turned up slightly at the loving care Fran gave her. She knew that it would have been Fran who had tucked the thick bedcovers tightly around her and kept the room cozy. No one else would have thought of these little comforts for a dying queen.

Sensing that she must be nearby, Mary spoke in a weak voice, "Has Philip come yet?"

The sound of quick footfalls, then the touch of a hand, and Fran's soothing voice, "Not yet, your grace."

Mary was not as disappointed by this news as she once might have been. Philip had been informed that Mary was severely ill. She had written to him herself when she was still able, but he would not come. From his point of view, there was no practical reason to do so, and he did not care enough for her to feel drawn to say goodbye.

"Please, assure him that my devotion to him never ceased," Mary requested with no regret or accusation in her tone.

Fran squeezed Mary's hand and did not attempt to reassure her with comforting lies. "I will do so, my friend. Is there anything you need, some hippocras perhaps?"

A slight turning away of her head was Mary's only response. The thought of any food or drink brought on waves of nausea that were soon followed by the knives to her head and fierce beating of her heart. She just wished to lie here, warm and comfortable.

"I would hear mass," Mary said. "Can Reginald come?"

Mary could not see the heartbreak on Fran's face as she referred to the Cardinal so informally, unaware that he too was abed with many concerned that he would never rise. Soon the two would see each other, but not here on earth.

"I shall call in your chaplain," Fran offered instead. "He is just in the next room."

Mary wanted to protest. She did not just want to hear mass. She wanted Reginald. But Fran was already gone.

Sleep must have claimed her again, for Mary could tell that time had passed without having any memory of the mass she had requested. She forced her eyes open despite the pain she knew the light would send through her head. Fran was there, as she always was.

"I've had the most beautiful dream," Mary told her.

Fran squeezed her hand and offered an encouraging smile.

"A score of small children were playing and laughing with the appearance of happy, little angels," Mary said, her voice soft and whimsical. She paused for breath and continued. "They sang the most pleasing notes and surrounded me to offer their sweet comfort."

Fran looked away, but she need not have worried. Mary's eyes would not have been able to focus on her tightly clamped lips or the tears upon her cheeks. She cleared her throat to say, "That does sound like a heavenly vision, your grace."

"Yes," Mary agreed. "God sends me his Spirit in my time of need, as he always has."

"People fail, but God never does," Fran said as she attempted to work some warmth into Mary's icy fingers.

Mary's chaplain entered the room, and Fran waved him closer.

"Her grace is awake?" he asked, looking for evidence of alertness in Mary's countenance.

"I am," Mary answered for herself. She forced her eyes open again, but this time it did not cause her pain. Her vision was immediately drawn to the eucharist in his hands, and she knew that it would be her final opportunity to partake of it.

She felt something that tasted like paper put into her mouth.

"This is the body of Christ, given for you."

A drop of wine.

"The blood of Christ, shed for you."

"Amen," Mary whispered.

She did not pray this time that her will and body be strengthened with that of God. The time for that had passed, and he now gave her the hope that she needed to look to the next life. Her regrets were gone, though she wondered vaguely why Reginald was not there. Why was it not his voice praying over her right now?

Sleep beckoned. Queen Mary heard no more.

Epilogue – November 17, 1558

When Fran next checked upon her royal mistress, she realized that the queen had peacefully gone to God. Mary's face appeared younger than her forty-two years with the cares and concerns of this world gone from it. Fran called in the physician and chaplain, for her own work was done for now.

In his own bed, just across the river, Reginald Pole soon received the news that his queen had died. He reacted with his trademark silence, contemplating his grief without giving it reign over his words.

None had learned how to read his stoic features to determine what emotions flooded his weary body. They assumed that he mourned the accession of the Protestant queen Elizabeth as much as the passing of her sister, but his regrets ran so much deeper.

Within twelve hours, Reginald and Mary were reunited.

Afterword

Queen Elizabeth I was declared within hours of Mary's death. She refused many of her sister's last wishes. The first had been to be given a tomb with her mother, Queen Catherine. Instead, when Elizabeth died in 1603, it was she who shared Mary's tomb. I believe both sisters would be unhappy with this arrangement, but their successor has forced upon them in death the unity that they never shared in life.

Mary had also requested for a soldiers' hospital to be established in London in her name and for her debts to be paid. Elizabeth did neither of these. Instead, she set about blackening her sister's name in order that she herself might appear more glorious. Elizabeth did not even leave her sister her motto. "Truth is the daughter of time," had been chosen by Mary upon her accession to the throne. In 1558, Elizabeth took it for herself.

November 17 became known as "Elizabeth's Accession Day" to be celebrated, rather than a day to remember the passing of England's first queen. Elizabeth successfully painted herself as the queen who saved her kingdom from war and intolerance while bringing about peace.

Those closest to Mary would surely turn up an eyebrow at this image of Elizabeth. The Waldegraves, Edward and Frances (whom I have called Fran to distinguish her from Frances Grey), who had so loyally served their queen, were imprisoned for attending mass after Mary's death. Edward died in the Tower. Others fled across the Channel, just as Protestants had done at the beginning of Mary's reign. Susan Clarencieux and the daughters of Frances Waldegrave were among them.

The burning of heretics is a phenomenon that was widely accepted and believed necessary in the 16th century, but it is extraordinarily difficult to wrap the modern mind around. We

377

certainly judge Mary for this much more harshly than her contemporaries did. Some readers may be surprised to learn that fewer people were executed under Mary than any other Tudor monarch.

Elizabeth put an end to the burnings and the counter-reformation in England. She also brought about an end of the Tudor dynasty. She staunchly refused a plethora of marriage proposals and died without an heir in 1603.

The joint tomb of Mary and Elizabeth is topped by a monument raised by King James I, the first Stuart king. After a lengthy memorial to Queen Elizabeth, Mary receives mention at the base:

Partners in throne and grave, here we sleep
Elizabeth and Mary, sisters in hope of the Resurrection.

Additional Reading

For those interested in reading more about the historical figures featured in this novel, I recommend the following sources:

The First Queen of England by Linda Porter

Mary Tudor: Princess, Bastard, Queen by Anna Whitelock

Reginald Pole: Prince and Prophet by Thomas Mayer

Katherine the Queen: The Remarkable Life of Katherine Parr by Linda Porter

Fires of Faith: Catholic England under Mary Tudor by Eamon Duffy

Crown of Blood: The Deadly Inheritance of Lady Jane Grey by Nicola Tallis

Edward VI: The Lost King of England by Chris Skidmore

The Children of Henry VIII by Alison Weir

Author's Note

I had no intention of writing about Mary Tudor, or any Tudor for that matter, for Elizabeth of York and Margaret Pole were purely Plantagenet in my own mind. It was not until a friend, upon finishing an early copy of *Faithful Traitor*, asked, "How often do we see a book from Mary's point of view?" that the idea began to take root.

My initial reaction was to dismiss the idea. Surely, the Tudors have been done. Overdone. Yet a quick search for novels featuring Mary came up surprisingly short, and sympathetic portrayals of her were almost nonexistent. The wheels were turning, and I set aside the research I had begun on earlier Plantagenets.

Queen Mary would be appalled to know that she is better remembered as Bloody Mary. For a gentle woman who believed she was working to restore England to the Church and reconcile her people to God, to be thought of as cruel and bitter would likely cause her great pain.

Not that she had not already known pain. Torn from her mother and her governess, forced to wait upon a half-sister that she believed was a bastard, Mary's adult life began much more harshly than most. With her victory to become queen, she had every reason to believe that heartache was finally behind her. She was wrong.

Instead of remembering Mary for the burnings that took place during her reign, I think of her trials, her striving for peace, love, and happiness that she never achieved this side of heaven.

While I am sure that readers of historical fiction understand the need to create personalities and motivations for historical figures, I feel that it is necessary to point out where I have taken particular license. The most notable example of this is the romantic feelings between Reginald and Mary. It is true that their mothers at one point hoped to see them married and that Mary trusted Reginald above all others once she was queen. Given that Mary had been disappointed in all forms of love in her life, I could envision her reaching out in hope of receiving it from her closest cousin. That the good Cardinal would be firm in his faith, whether he returned those feelings or not, was beyond doubt.

Reginald Pole is a captivating person as well. While evading the wrath of Henry VIII, Reginald became one of the most learned men in Europe. Had he been worldly enough to lobby on his own behalf in 1550, he would have almost certainly become pope. However, he was interested in truth much more than power, a position that would have both Protestants and Catholics at various times questioning what it was he truly believed. Reginald's search for God's truth, wherever it might be found, took him beyond the comfort zones of most of his contemporaries, leading one to say, "He has been very unfortunate . . . being considered a Lutheran in Rome, in Germany a papist."

The publication of *Queen of Martyrs* is celebrated with the release of updated editions of the previous installments in the Plantagenet Embers Trilogy. Return to the birth of Tudor England in *Plantagenet Princess, Tudor Queen: The Story of Elizabeth of York*, and witness the struggle of the York remnant under Tudor kings in *Faithful Traitor: The Story of Margaret Pole*. I also plan to add a few novellas to the Plantagenet Embers series to shine a light on some of my favorite secondary characters, such as Margaret Beaufort and Elizabeth Woodville.

Thank you for reading my novels! A special note of appreciation to those who have served as my beta readers. I would especially like to thank Troy Rodgers and Blair Hodgkinson for their irreplaceable feedback, wonderful reviews, and ongoing assistance with every aspect of my writing. Editing and reading my own work takes me only so far. It is due to the generous help of these early readers that my novels become a polished finished work. I also appreciate each person who takes the time to write a review. As an independent author, I simply cannot do it without each of you.

Connect with Samantha
at SamanthaWilcoxson.blogspot.com
or on Twitter @Carpe_Librum.

Made in the USA
Columbia, SC
04 November 2017